NIGHT THOUGHTS

She was tired, but she didn't want to go to bed.

She got up and crossed to Robbie's side of the fireplace, where Sir Frederick had sat while she read the report, and lifted the three Tolkien volumes out of Robbie's bookshelf.

Then she went back to her own side and sat down again, and started reading at random, flipping from place to place, picking out the names from the past of her original reading.

Wizards and trolls and elves with bright eyes and sharp swords, and rings of power . . .

She knew she wasn't really concentrating. Rather, she was wondering how it was she already knew that Colonel Butler hadn't murdered his wife on the morning of November 11, 1969.

TOMORROW'S GHOST

ALSO BY ANTHONY PRICE

The Labyrinth Makers*
The Alamut Ambush*
Colonel Butler's Wolf*
October Men*
Other Paths to Glory*
War Game*
The '44 Vintage*
The Hour of the Donkey

Soldier No More**
The Old *Vengeful***
Gunner Kelly**
Sion Crossing*
Here Be Monsters*
For the Good of the State*
A New Kind of War*

*Published by THE MYSTERIOUS PRESS
**Forthcoming from THE MYSTERIOUS PRESS

TOMORROW'S GHOST

a novel by

ANTHONY PRICE

THE MYSTERIOUS PRESS

New York • London • Tokyo

MYSTERIOUS PRESS EDITION

Copyright © 1979 by Anthony Price

This Mysterious Press Edition is published by arrangement with
the author.

Mysterious Press books are published in association with
Warner Books, Inc.
666 Fifth Avenue
New York, N.Y. 10103

W A Warner Communications Company

Printed in the United States of America

First Mysterious Press Printing: December, 1988

10 9 8 7 6 5 4 3 2 1

For Irene and Peter Sykes

I

AFTER ONLY A week of exposure to her, Gary the Messenger Boy was ready to die for Marilyn the Temporary Secretary, Frances judged. So it was his good fortune that the scenario did not envisage his role as being self-sacrificial.

"Any urgent letters, Miss?" he inquired, leaning hopefully over her desk as far as he dared. He had invented several extra collections a day since her arrival, and this was the first of them. The secretaries had never had better service.

"Thank you, Gary." Frances smiled at him and threw out Marilyn's chest for his entertainment as she sealed the first of Mr Cavendish's morning letters into their envelopes. The gratification of Gary's adolescent daydreams was not the worst thing she had ever done, if hardly the most admirable: it was simply the best and quickest way of doing what had to be done.

"Thank you, Gary." She offered him another smile with the sealed letters, leaning forward slightly as she did so. Although she lacked the measurements for a really spectacular view, the top three buttons had been carefully left undone to offer what there was.

"Thank you, Miss." Gary wiped his sweaty paw on the seat of his jeans before accepting the gift. But then, instead of turning to Mrs Simmonds at the next desk, he lingered in front of her, rocking on his three-inch heels until she began to wonder if the lungful of over-applied April Violets which he had inhaled was about to knock him out.

"Yes, Gary?"

He summoned up his courage. "Got another story for you, Miss—true story."

Mrs Simmonds sniffed disapprovingly, though whether it was at Gary or the April Violets, Frances wasn't sure.

"Yes, Gary? A true story?"

"The letters, Gary!" snapped Mrs Simmonds.

Frances ran the tip of her tongue deliberately over Marilyn's Glory Rose lipstick and gazed expectantly at Gary. Mrs Simmonds rated nowhere, compared with Gary; she was just a secretary, and (which was more to the point) she didn't gossip round the office like Gary.

"I read it in this book," began Gary breathlessly. "There was this Indian uprising, see—"

It had been an Indian uprising last time. Gary's reading was either limited or highly specialised.

"Comanches, they were. In Texas—"

Perhaps Gary's mother had fancied the hero of *High Noon* so much that she had imprinted him with an obsession to go with his name.

"And there was this girl they took prisoner—a blonde like you, Miss—" His eyes feasted on the dyed curls "—and they started to take . . . to take her clothes off, Miss—"

"Gary!" Mrs Simmonds fired his name like a warning shot.

"But she was wearing this—this thing—" he floundered "—it's all laced up, with bones in it—?" He blinked desperately at Marilyn.

"Whalebone," said Frances. "A corset?"

"That's it, Miss—a corset!"

"Charming!" murmured Mrs Simmonds, her back now as rigid as if it was also whaleboned and laced-up, but interested in the Texan maiden's fate against her better judgement.

"And they couldn't get it off, see—the Comanches couldn't. So when they got her down they couldn't—"

"That's enough!" snapped Mrs Simmonds. "Quite enough."

Gary shook his head at her. "But it's true, Mrs Simmonds—honestly it is. I can show it to you in this book."

"I believe you," said Marilyn encouragingly.

"But that isn't the end of it, Miss—" the words rushed out "—they shot arrows at her, only the arrows stuck in the—the—in the bones—an' she was saved by the Texas Rangers."

Before Mrs Simmonds could draw a bead on him he snatched the letters from her hand and scuttled out of the door.

Mrs Simmonds traversed her sights on to Marilyn. "*Miss* Francis . . . I know you're only a temp . . . *and* you won't be here with us very long . . . *But* you really should know better—"

The door swung half open and Gary's grinning face appeared in the gap. "If they'd caught you, Miss—the Comanches—you wouldn't 'uv stood a chance!" he delivered his punch-line.

"Don't be cheeky!" Mrs Simmonds' anger bounced off the closing door. She turned back to Marilyn. "There! That's exactly what I mean. If you give the dirty little beast a chance—but you positively encourage him!"

Marilyn examined her Glory Rose nail polish critically. That was also exactly true, thought Frances, making a mental note to uproot any roses in her garden at home which might ever remind her of this particular shade of red. And (looking down past her nails to what Gary had tried to see) Marilyn certainly wouldn't have stood a chance with the Comanches either, that was also true.

Marilyn shrugged. "He's harmless."

"Nothing in trousers is harmless." Mrs Simmonds caught her tongue as she stared at Marilyn, and Frances knew what she was thinking: that anything in trousers was as much Target for Tonight to Marilyn Francis as Marilyn Francis was for anything in trousers.

Well, that was the trick—since there was no time for a more unobtrusive approach, in order not to be seen she had to be obvious. And there was nothing more unimaginably obvious than the pink, red, blonde, brazen and bra-less Marilyn, with her eyes on all men from sixteen to sixty.

"It's all very well for you—" Mrs Simmonds began bitterly, and then brightened "—you won't be here very long . . ."

"Oh, I don't know about that . . ." Frances toyed with the idea of touching up Marilyn's lipstick. The trouble was, it would mean looking at her face, and that was not something she particularly enjoyed. ". . . I quite like it here."

Mrs Simmonds bristled. "Mr Cavendish's *proper* secretary—" there was a heavy emphasis on the adjective "—will be back from hospital in a fortnight."

"There are other jobs that come up. Girls are always leaving, as I should know. . . . I'm a bit cheesed off with this temping—I think it's time to dig in somewhere comfy, like here." The time was just about right to plant the shape of things to come, anyway. "I hear there's a secretary leaving in Research and Development—" she winked at Mrs Simmonds "—where all those groovy scientists are."

Mrs Simmonds regarded her incredulously. "You're joking—?"

Marilyn gazed into space. "Some of them are quite young. There's one that's got a smashing sports car—I've seen him in the canteen. And he's seen *me*, too—"

That was true. She'd made sure of that. And groovy Dr Garfield also worked right alongside ungroovy Dr Harrison, who just might be selling out British-American's research and development to the Other Side, what was more.

"Hmm . . ." Mrs Simmonds' lips were compressed so tightly that she found it hard to speak. "Well . . . you may not find that so easy. They don't take just anyone in R and D, you know. You have to have a security clearance, for a start."

Marilyn giggled. "No problem, dearie. I'm absolutely secure."

And that was also true. With the Security Officer already primed by the Special Branch, Marilyn's translation to the rich pastures of R and D was a *fait accompli*, whatever the opposition.

"*No* problem." But that wasn't the reason which Gary would put into circulation. "With my qualifications I can push 'em over any time—*no* problem." Marilyn fluttered her false eyelashes and decided to examine her lipstick.

"Hmm . . ." What drove Mrs Simmonds beyond words was the knowledge that Marilyn's shorthand and typing speeds, not to mention her actual secretarial qualifications and efficiency, were as far above reproach as her morals were beneath it. And it was nettling her more than somewhat, thought Frances, that she also suspected the unspeakable Marilyn was relying on her almost-see-through blouse and three undone buttons as much as 140 words a minute.

"Hmm . . ." Mrs Simmonds drew a shuddering breath. "Well, if that's what you want, you won't help yourself by making up to young Gary, I can tell you. He's a proper little chatterbox, that one—and what he says doesn't lose in the telling, either. You know he's already going round, telling everyone that you are—" Mrs Simmonds clenched her jaws "—'hot stuff'—do you know that?"

When it was all over, decided Frances, she would pad her expenses and buy Gary a copy of Jack Schaefer's *The Canyon*, and maybe Howard Fast's *The Last Frontier* too. Not even the KGB's disinformation experts could have done better.

"He can say what he likes, I don't care." She rummaged in her bag for the tawdry compact and the Glory Rose lipstick.

"Well, you ought to." The phone buzzed at Mrs Simmonds' elbow. "He fancies you. And you can't possibly fancy him."

"That'll be the day! He should be so lucky . . ." Marilyn opened the compact, and Frances examined the ghastly little painted doll's face. There was no accounting for male taste, as she knew by bitter experience. She could only hope that the thing wouldn't drag on so long that Marilyn took over completely, because then she would only let her down in bed, as always.

The phone was still buzzing, unanswered. Which only went to prove that the prospect of a temporary Marilyn converted into a permanent one was as unnerving for Mrs Simmonds as it was for her. Because it wasn't like Mrs Simmonds to ignore the phone.

"Hadn't you better see who it is?" said Frances without turning from Marilyn's reflection. The eerie fact about that little face was that it no longer belonged to a stranger, it was her face now. A week ago it had been an awful might-have-been; now it was a real face, on the way to becoming a should-have-been.

"The way he looks at you—and not just him, either. I think you're asking for trouble, young lady."

"I can look after myself." It's looking *at* myself that frightens me, thought Frances.

"I've heard that before." Mrs Simmonds reached for the phone. "All right, *all right!*" She lifted the receiver. "British-American Computers—" she began with uncharacteristic abruptness, then caught her breath and shifted into her secretarial purr "—Mr Henderson's personal assistant, can-I-help-you?"

Frances put the compact back into her bag and picked up her desk diary.

"No—" said Mrs Simmonds in her severest voice, dropping the 'sir', "—no, it *isn't*. I'm afraid you've been put through to the wrong extension."

Miss Francis relaxed. It was her contact, deliberately asking for Mrs Simmonds' number in order to establish himself as one of the string of Marilyn Francis's boyfriends.

"Is this a business call?" Mrs Simmonds' voice was like a carving knife.

Frances concentrated on the schedule. Cavendish was actually interviewing two R & D men at 10.30, presumably to brief himself on the sales pitch for the Saudi Arabians at 11.15 tomorrow. It would be advisable to double-check the booking at the Royal County Hotel, and the menu there too—

Pink, red, blonde, brazen, bra-less, but also efficient.

The opportunity for demonstrating the last in front of the R & D men was not to be missed. Perhaps she might even purchase some real coffee out of the petty cash for that 11.15 meeting: the Saudis would not know much about advanced guidance systems, but they would certainly know their coffee. . . . And after that it would be an easy day, with consequent opportunities for further voyages of discovery and Marilyn-flaunting within the British-American labyrinth.

Contact was taking rather a long time, but judging from the grave and serious expression on Mrs Simmonds' face he wasn't actually being offensive.

"Oh . . ." Mrs Simmonds gave her a strange look. "Yes, of course I will . . . It's for you, dear—that switchboard is hopeless. . . . Yes, of course I will, don't worry. I'm putting you through now." She punched the extension numbers and then turned again to Marilyn, still wearing the serious expression. "It's your father, dear."

"My *father*?" Miss Francis did not have to simulate surprise. It was contact's job to handle all routine communications up to and including Alerts. 'Father' himself would never intervene except in cases of emergency.

Emergency.

Frances grabbed her phone. "Dad? Is that you?"

"Marilyn love?"

"It's me, Dad. What's the matter?"

"Marilyn love—"

The recognition sign was repetition.

"It's me, Dad. What's the matter? Are you all right?" For once the recognition jargon rang absolutely true.

Emergency.

"It's your mother, love—she's been taken very bad. You must come home at once."

"What!" Frances piled shock on surprise.

"I'm sorry, love—springing this on you when you've just started your new job . . . But she needs you, your mother does. We both need you. You must come home to look after her."

Sod it! *Sod it*—

"Home—?" Frances caught her anger just in time and transformed it into concern. "Right now?"

"Yes, love. Right this minute. The doctor's coming again this afternoon, and you must be there for him."

Frances looked at the clock. *Home—right this minute* was a categorical order which left no room for argument: after all the time and careful planning that had gone into Marilyn Francis, and just when things were shaping up nicely, they were pulling her out and aborting the operation.

"Yes, Dad—of course. I'll leave this minute."

"There's a good girl. I knew you wouldn't let your old dad down."

Sod it! thought Frances again. Something had gone wrong somewhere, but it couldn't be anything she'd done, or not done, because at this stage she'd done nothing except be Miss Marilyn Francis, and Miss Francis as yet hadn't gone anywhere near Research and Development.

"I'll get the bus to Morden, Dad. I can get a tube from there."

"No need to, love. A friend of Tommy's is coming down to collect you—young Mitch. You've met him, when he was in the army. He'll pick you up at that cafe where Tommy came that time, in about half an hour, say. Okay?"

"Okay, Dad. Don't worry. I'll be there."

"Goodbye then, love."

"Goodbye, Dad."

She replaced the receiver automatically and sat staring at it for a moment. She had wasted a fortnight of her life as Marilyn, but now it was over and done with, and Marilyn was fading away, a gaudy little flower who had blushed unseen and wasted her April Violets and Fabergé Babe on Gary's nose. It was enough to make her weep.

"Are you all right, dear?" asked Mrs Simmonds solicitously.

But there was no time for tears: Marilyn Francis could not die just yet. Or rather, she must die as she had lived.

"Yes . . . I'm okay."

Mrs Simmonds reached across and patted her arm. "Of course you are, dear."

So Control had already planted the information.

"But my Mum's very ill, my Dad says."

"Yes, I know. Your father told me." Mrs Simmonds nodded. "But you mustn't worry. There are these drugs they've got now . . . and they're finding new ones all the time, you know."

Plainly, he had gone even further: in order to remove the daughter convincingly and quickly he had made the illness terminal. Nothing less than such a confidence could have turned Mrs Simmonds' anger into sympathy.

But that was the last thing Marilyn Francis would have noticed at this moment, with a sick mum and an inadequate dad on her hands, and young Mitch to meet in half an hour.

She turned to Mrs Simmonds. "I've got to go and look after her—my Mum. My Dad's dead useless."

Mrs Simmonds winced at the adjective, but managed to keep the Awful Truth secret. "Yes, dear—naturally."

"I mean, I've got to go right now." Miss Francis reached for her typewriter cover. "The doctor's coming to see her this afternoon. So

I haven't time to see Mr Cavendish. Will you tell him?"

"Of course I will. Don't you worry about that." Mrs Simmonds frowned suddenly. "Are you all right for money . . . to tide you over, I mean?"

"Money?" Frances realised suddenly that tomorrow was pay day.

Go directly home. Do not pass Go. Do not collect £58.55.

Mrs Simmonds reached for her bag. "I could let you have five pounds, dear."

In the circumstances that was true sisterly generosity.

"And I'll phone up the Agency and tell them what's happened," said Mrs Simmonds. "So don't you worry about that either."

It wasn't sisterly generosity at all; the old bitch had decided that the instant departure of Marilyn was cheap at £5, especially when the chance of ordering a better class of girl from the Agency was included in the price.

Frances wondered whether Sir Frederick Clinton had a better class of female operative to hand on his books, complete with 140 words a minute Pitman's.

But that was his problem now. More to the point, she wondered whether little Miss Marilyn Francis, painted and dyed, would have enough cash to tide her over at this stage of the week, and what she would do if she hadn't, and her mum was very ill and she was having to throw up her job.

Poor little Marilyn!

Marilyn burst into tears.

II

IN FACT, POOR little Marilyn revenged herself twice over on Mrs Frances Fitzgibbon before Paul Mitchell arrived at the transport cafe, once in the person of an elderly lorry-driver who obviously feared that she was running away from home, and advised her against seeking her fortune in Central London, and the second time by a leather-jacketed youth of indeterminate age who obviously hoped she was running away from home, and offered to bear her to the bright lights on the back of his Kawasaki.

So she had been forced to re-animate Marilyn briefly, first to shake her head at the lorry-driver and then to send the Kawasaki owner about his business—

"Bug off! I'm waiting for someone."

"Suit yourself, scrubber!"

"You're late." The lorry-driver's concern and the youth's knowing contempt combined with the strains of the morning to fray Frances's nerves.

"Christ! You look awful!" Paul planted a kiss on her cheek before she could avoid him. "And what's more—you smell awful too!"

"And you're still late. I thought there was an emergency of some sort?"

"There is. But I'm not James Hunt—and if I was it wouldn't have made any difference. I've come all the way from Yorkshire this morning, non-stop except for the times the Police flagged me down for breaking the speed limit on the motorway—they should have sent a chopper for you, but all they had to spare was me. So get moving, Frances dear—" Paul picked up her cup and finished off its contents "—Ugh! Because there are leagues to be covered 'ere 14.30 hours."

He held the door open for her. The lorry-driver frowned and the Kawasaki youth gave her a jeering look.

"Where are we going?"

Paul pointed to the yellow Rover directly ahead of them. "Back to

Yorkshire again double-quick, if Jack Butler's new car holds together so long. I would have preferred mine, but like you say—it's an emergency."

She waited until he had settled down into the traffic. "What's the emergency in Yorkshire?"

"Ah . . . now there you've got me, sweetie. So far as I was concerned, everything was going according to plan. By now there's probably total confusion, without Mitchell to put things right. But when I left everything was A-Okay."

Frances thought for a moment. "You know they pulled me off a job?"

Mitchell shook his head and put his foot down. "Nope. Or, at least, I didn't know you were working until I saw you just now . . . and from our past acquaintance I'm assuming that you don't normally spend your free time dressed like a two-bit dolly-bird. Not that it doesn't suit you—"

"Don't be offensive."

"I wasn't being offensive. I was just admiring the skilful way you have thrown yourself into your cover, whatever it may be, respectable Mrs Fitzgibbon. In fact, if I hadn't have known you, I wouldn't have known you, if you see what I mean—even apart from the smell, that is."

Frances took hold of her temper, recalling Paul's technique of old. Once upon a time he had fancied his chances, and this was his juvenile response to being brushed off; but she must not let it blind her to the knowledge that he was clever and efficient, and ambitious with it.

The effort of exercising will-power was steadying and soothing. They hadn't pulled her out of British-American because anything had gone wrong there, but because something more important had come up elsewhere. And, by the same logic, they wouldn't have wasted Paul on a chauffeur's job without good reason when he was involved in that same more important something.

"Are you supposed to be briefing me—is that the idea, Paul?"

He grinned at her. "Good on you, Frances! That's Jack Butler's idea exactly."

"Colonel Butler?"

"*Colonel* Butler as ever is, yes. Fighting Jack, no less—the Thin Red Line in person."

"He asked for me?" Frances frowned at the road ahead. She knew

Colonel Butler by sight, and a little by reputation, but had never worked under him.

"No-o-o. Fighting Jack did not ask for you." This time he grinned privately. "Not for this little lark, he wouldn't."

"What lark?"

"What lark . . ." Paul tailed off as he waited to leave the slip-road for the motorway proper. The Rover coasted for a moment, then surged forward across the slow and fast lanes straight into the overtaking one. Frances watched the needle build up far beyond the speed limit.

"What lark." Paul settled back comfortably. "I take it you've heard of O'Leary, Frances?"

"Michael O'Leary?"

"The one and only. Ireland's answer to Carlos the Jackal."

"The Irish Freedom Fighters, you mean?"

"Sure and begorrah, I do. De Oirish Fraydom Foighters—yes."

Frances swallowed. "But I'm not cleared for Irish assignments, even in England."

Paul nodded. "So I gather. But apparently there's a Papal dispensation in the case of Michael O'Leary and his boyos. And on the very best of grounds, too, I'm telling you, to be sure."

"On what grounds?"

There was a Jaguar ahead hogging the overtaking lane—far ahead a moment ago, but not far ahead now. Paul flashed his lights fiercely.

"Get over, you bastard! Make way for Her Majesty's Servants, by God!" Paul murmured. "You're breaking the bloody law, that's what you're doing."

The Jaguar moved over, and flashed back angrily as they swept past him.

"On what grounds? . . . Well, for a guess, on the grounds that O'Leary is about as Irish as—say—the Russian ambassador in Dublin. Or if, by any remote chance, there is a drop or two of the old Emerald Isle stuff in his veins . . . then because he's not really concerned with foightin' fer Oirish fraydom—at a guess, quite the reverse, if you take my point."

Frances took his point. It was what her poor romantic Robbie had always maintained, she recalled with a dull ache of memory: to him the Irish had always been more vicitms than villains, even the psychos whom he hunted, and who had hunted him—hog-tied by ancient history which was no longer relevant, financed by Irish Americans who had no idea what was really happening to their dollars, but ultimately manipulated by some of the very best-trained KGB cover-men in the business. It didn't help the ache to recall that she hadn't believed him, because he found Reds under every bed; though at least she hadn't argued with him, because it helped him to fight more in sorrow than in anger, even after three beastly tours of duty; she'd even been oddly relieved, that last time, to learn that they hadn't been responsible, his victims—at least not directly—for what had happened to him.

"It's not surprising, really," mused Paul, taking it for granted that she had taken his point. "Whenever there's trouble in Ireland, someone else has to cash in—you can't blame the buggers. The Spaniards did, and then the French, and the Germans. The KGB's only bowing to history."

Frances thrust Robbie back into his filing cabinet in the furthest corner of her memory, where he belonged. "We know that for sure?"

"Not for sure. Nothing Irish is for sure. But it was the IRA that told us."

Frances waited. Because she wasn't cleared for Ireland she didn't know much about the tangle of Irish security beyond what she had read in the weekly sheets in the department in her secretarial days, when she had had to type them out. But in those days the IFF had amounted to little more than an abbreviation for Michael O'Leary's expertise with the booby-trap and the high-velocity rifle.

"They don't quite know what to make of O'Leary. They smell sulphur, if not Vodka—though Vodka doesn't smell, does it! Say caviare, then . . ." He nodded to himself, watching the road. "They've been prepared to take the credit for his hits—in Ulster."

"But now he's come to England?"

"That's right. 'To take the war into the enemy country', as he puts it. We think *they* think he may make the war a bit too hot for them—so they've dropped us the word. Only they don't know where he is, and nor do we."

"He's pretty elusive, then."

"The Scarlet Pimpernel's got nothing on Michael O'Leary. But we do rather think he's using some of the KGB ultra-safe houses in Yorkshire, as a matter of fact. Just a hint, we've picked up."

Back to Yorkshire double-quick.

Frances nodded. "And just what is his war, exactly?"

"Ah . . . well, you see he's got a little list. Of Criminals Sentenced by Military Tribunal for Crimes Against Ireland, as he calls it."

"But that's old hat."

"Sure it is. So everything in Ireland is old hat—it's all just a re-run of the same old late-night films we've seen half a dozen times before. Only this time maybe the KGB has bought the natural breaks to advertise their product."

And that did make a difference, thought Frances grimly. It might even change the end of the film itself.

"I see. And the top name on the list is to be found in Yorkshire, presumably—is that it?"

"Yes . . . and no—" Paul stopped as he glanced in his mirror.

"What does that mean—yes or no?"

"It means . . . hold on to your seat-belt, Frances dear. We are about to be flagged down by the police—" Paul gave her a quick reassuring smile as he decelerated and began to pull across the lanes towards the hard shoulder "—but nothing to worry about."

The car crunched on loose gravel. The silence inside it was suddenly unnerving, punctuated as it was by the intermittent roar and shock-wave of passing lorries labouring their way to the industrial north. Frances watched the sleek police car pull in just ahead of them, a Rover identical to their own except that it was white and ornamented with a dashing blue-red-blue stripe along its flank.

A tall young constable got out cautiously and came back to them. Paul wound down his window and fumbled inside his jacket.

The policeman bent down and peered in at them. Frances saw his eyes widen and was instantly aware that Marilyn's split skirt had divided to an indecent level.

"Paul Mitchell," said Paul, opening his identification folder. "And I'm in an official hurry. Please check with your superiors as quickly as you can."

The young policeman's eyes glazed over with the effort of not looking at what they were looking at, and then switched to Paul's identification.

"Mr Mitchell—yes, sir." The young policeman swallowed bravely. "We have been informed about you—"

A derisive hoot cut him off: the Jaguar they had elbowed out of the road flashed by triumphantly.

"If you would be so good as to follow us, we'll clear the way for

19

you, sir. There's a hold-up about six miles ahead . . . we'll get you past it."

"Thank you very much, officer." Paul's politeness to the Civil Power was impeccably according to the regulations. "We've a scheduled stop just beyond Wetherby, at the Crossways Motel. We shall be there for fifteen minutes. If you can give us ten miles after that it will be sufficient, thank you."

"Very good, sir." The policeman saluted. "Just follow us."

Paul turned to Frances. "Well, at least the system is working now. I was supposed to be cleared all the way down, but I nearly got arrested for reckless driving instead." He glanced down. "And if I'd had you with me I probably *would* have been arrested—the view isn't conducive to careful driving. Not that it isn't enchanting also . . . though I thought suspender belts were strictly for the kinky trade."

"Keep your eyes on the road."

"Pull your skirt together and I'll try to."

Frances draped her plastic raincoat across her knees. "You said 'yes and no'."

"Eh?"

"The top name on the list."

"Oh, yes . . . in Yorkshire. Well, it isn't normally, but it is today."

"Is where?"

"At the University of North Yorkshire, for the conferring of honorary degrees and the opening of the new English Faculty Library."

"You mean . . . he's receiving a degree?"

"That's right. A Doctorate of Civil Law, to be exact. For trying to make peace in Ireland, a doctorate in England . . . and a death sentence in Ireland. He shouldn't have tried so hard."

"The Minister?"

"Ex-minister . . . no, the Minister, that's right. It's the ex-minister who's conferring the degree—he's the Chancellor of the University now. He tried hard too, so he's also on the list. A damned unforgiving lot, the IFF, putting him on the list is purely vindictive if you ask me. And the IRA's not much better—I can't help thinking that they leaked this to us in the first place just to screw us up in knots." Paul shook his head. "Which, of course, is what it's doing."

He shook his head again, and Frances observed him with a mounting sense of disquiet. This wasn't the cool analysis that accompanied proper security, it was more like an acceptance of the inevitable, the sort of fatalism she imagined soldiers in the very front line must have on the eve of an enemy offensive.

But if that was so then the doubling of the targets didn't make sense.

"But Paul—d'you mean to say we've let two people on the list get together in the same place?"

"Three, actually."

"*Three?*" Frances heard her voice rise. "You're joking!"

"No." Paul appeared to concentrate on the police car ahead. "The Lord-Lieutenant will be there, and he was General Officer Commanding in Ulster a few years back. Now he's one of the top advisers to the Minister's opposite number on the shadow cabinet—which puts him right at the head of the list, alongside the Minister himself in fact. Because he's a smart fellow."

Frances found herself staring in the same direction, at the flashing hazard lights of the police car, as they overtook a clot of traffic which had formed behind two juggernaut lorries racing each other up the motorway. With Michael O'Leary on the loose it was nothing short of insanity to assemble three prime targets on one spot; or, at least, on one spot away from the maximum security zone of Westminster and Whitehall where such assemblies were acceptable.

"I know what you're thinking," said Paul.

But Frances was by no means sure what she was thinking. There was obviously some sort of emergency, no matter what Paul had said to the contrary. It was difficult not to jump to the conclusion that it was directly related to the insanity—the irresistible bait which some fool had dangled in front of O'Leary. Perhaps they were panicking now because they'd only just realised what they'd done.

"Huh!" She simulated contempt. If Paul thought he knew what she was thinking she had to encourage him to think aloud.

He gave a quick nod. "That's the way I felt, exactly. But then I thought—North Atlantic, '43–'44—U-boats versus escorts—same problem, same answer."

"North Atlantic—?" Frances caught herself just in time. Not so very long before Paul Mitchell had been a budding young military historian, and one hangover from that lost career was his irritating habit of trying to reduce every situation to some obscure military analogy which could then be solved by the application of Clauswitz or Liddell-Hart. But this time, instead of deriding his theories, she could use them to establish what was really going on.

"I don't see how the North Atlantic comes into things, Paul. Enlighten me."

"It's simple. The Atlantic is very big and a U-boat is very small."

"And it spends most of its time underwater anyway."

He looked at her quickly. "You've got the point?" He sounded a little disappointed.

"No. But I thought that was how submarines behaved. Go on."

"Ah . . ." He brightened. "So of course they're awfully difficult to find, unless you're lucky."

"I thought we had radar for that."

"Don't complicate matters. That isn't the point."

"Sorry." Frances curbed her impatience.

"The point is that you don't have to find a submarine. Because if it's any good it's going to find you—you being a convoy." Again he glanced at her quickly. "And don't start telling me it's the convoy's job to avoid the U-boat, I know that. I'm simplifying things, that's all." He turned back to the road. "There's no avoiding O'Leary, anyway."

"I see. So O'Leary's a U-boat, and we're the convoy escorts—and we just sit around and wait for him to turn up?" Frances frowned at the banality of the image. "That doesn't seem very profound, either as a metaphor or as a piece of naval tactics."

"Uh-huh? Well, that's where you're wrong. . . . In fact, it's a typical armchair critic's mistake. Everything's simple when you know how to do it."

His patronising tone galled Frances. "Well, I don't pretend to be an expert on naval tactics, Paul."

"You don't have to be. It's just elementary geometry: double the size of the convoy and you don't double its circumference—it took the admiralty years to discover that allegedly simple fact."

"So what?"

He gave her a pitying look. "So you haven't actually doubled the size of the target. But you have doubled the number of escorts. . . . We've trebled the target on the university campus this afternoon—but as they're in the same place we can concentrate three times as many counter-terrorism experts in the same place. The mathematics are more favourable for guarding human beings than they are for ships, so we can put more than half our people on the look-out for O'Leary. They're the equivalent of what the Navy used to call 'hunter-killer groups' attached to the convoys—so instead of just guarding the bloody targets for once we've actually got the man-power to hunt the bastard as soon as he comes in range."

"Always supposing that he chooses to oblige you by turning up."

This time it was a half-grin. "Oh—he's coming right enough."

Frances started to add up the facts. If Paul was so sure that an attempt was going to be made then there was inside information, and it would probably have come from the IRA itself. . . . And it was undeniably true that there was always a chronic shortage of skilled manpower—and womanpower—because so much of it was needed for protection of high-risk targets that there was always too little left over to do the better job of eliminating the risk; that was the penalty which inflation imposed on internal security and law enforcement alike along with the stresses it inflicted on the mortgage repayments and the groceries bill. So there was a certain logic in the analogy of Paul's 'big convoy' theory, she could see that.

But it was also an appallingly cold-blooded logic, because for all his high-flown naval history in reality they were doing no more than set an old-fashioned domestic mouse-trap, with three human beings as the piece of cheese.

"You're deliberately using them for bait, for God's sake!"

"Oh no we're not, Frances dear." Paul shook his head decisively. "The Chancellor wanted to give the Minister his degree, it wasn't our idea. And the Minister wanted to come—and the Lord-Lieutenant wanted to be there to talk to them both about the latest Government initiative in Ulster. We didn't set them up." He shook his head again. "The security hazards were pointed out to them too—in writing. I saw the departmental minute myself."

There was a lump of ice in Frances's stomach: that was the absolute give-away, the written warning which the top security bureaucrats issued to protect themselves when they weren't sure they could protect anyone else. She could protest now until she was blue in the face that the ceremony should have been delayed, if not vetoed altogether, but it wouldn't do any good. What was more, Paul knew it, and had known it from the start.

This was the moment, ordinarily, when she might have been tempted to a small controlled explosion of anger, which Paul would shrug off as a piece of feminine temperament, male chauvinist pig that he always pretended to be in her presence. But she did not wish to give him that satisfaction; and besides, the lump of ice had a decidedly cooling effect on her responses.

"I see. So everything in the garden's lovely."

"As much as it ever can be. At least we've got enough men and equipment for once, so we won't fail for lack of resources."

Resignation again. Basically, Paul Mitchell was quite a cold fish under the boyish charm.

"And yet I'm required as a reinforcement? Doesn't that strike you as odd?"

He shrugged and grinned. "The more, the merrier. Not that Fighting Jack is exactly merry at the moment. In fact, he's decidedly feisty at the moment, is our Jack."

"Colonel Butler's in charge?" Frances had never operated under Colonel Butler's direction, and when she tried to conjure him up in her mind's eye all she could manage was the memory of two other very blue eyes registering disapproval. Either the Colonel didn't approve of young women in general, or (since he could hardly disapprove of her personally) he objected to women in this type of work in particular; neither of which conclusions suggested that he would welcome Mrs Fitzgibbon with open arms as a reinforcement.

She realised that Paul had nodded to the question.

"But he's not satisfied with things?"

"That would be an understatement, I suspect."

"What things?" Frances remembered also that the formidable Dr Audley, who was one of the department's heavyweights, had a high opinion of Colonel Butler; and a choice between David Audley's opinion and Paul Mitchell's was no choice at all.

"Oh, he doesn't say—not in front of the hired help. Fighting Jack's a bit old-fashioned that way. Not quite 'Damn your impertinence—do your duty, sir', but near enough."

"He sounds rather admirable. A pleasant change, even," said Frances tartly.

Paul thought about the Colonel for a moment. "The funny thing is . . . that he *is* rather admirable in many ways. He's got all the old pre-1914 virtues, you might say. Like . . . he'd never pass the buck to anyone else, it wouldn't even occur to him. And he'll ball you out to your face, and then defend you behind your back—real officer-and-gentleman stuff." He smiled at her. "Except I suspect he wasn't born to it."

24

"What d'you mean?"

"Well, there's the faintest touch of broad Lancashire under his Sandhurst accent I rather think. Not quite out of the top drawer, is our Jack."

Frances grimaced at him. "I never knew you were a snob, Paul."

"I'm not. Nothing wrong with dropping your aitches—Field Marshal Robertson 'adn't got a 'haitch' in 'is vocabulary, and 'e was none the worse for it. It's the same with Fighting Jack, except that he's learnt the language better. But he does seem to be playing a part."

"Aren't we all?" Frances looked down at Marilyn's platform shoes on her feet. Against all her expectations she'd found them easy to wear. Indeed, when she thought about it, she'd found everything about Marilyn disconcertingly easy, almost disturbingly easy.

"Oh, I know. 'All the world's a stage' and all that. But just a minute or two back you were disapproving of this university lark of ours, and it's my belief that Fighting Jack feels the same way. Only the difference is that if he'd got really bolshie about it he might have scuppered the operation." Paul kept his eyes on the road ahead, but he was no longer smiling, Frances noted. "But he didn't," he concluded grimly. "He didn't."

This was the true face concealed behind the front line fatalism and the naval tactics, thought Frances. With Colonel Butler playing a 1914 Colonel, Paul had naturally chosen a 1914 subaltern as his model. Yet beneath the role the real Paul didn't like the situation one bit either.

"Why didn't he?"

He shrugged. "I suppose . . . because his idea of Colonel Butler is of someone who obeys orders and gets on with the dirty jobs that other lesser breeds and bloody desk-wallahs wouldn't touch with a barge-pole. Which is a noble thought, but maybe not really what the late 1970s require." As though he'd suddenly realised that he was giving himself away he glanced quickly at her and grinned his subaltern's grin at her. "So instead he just exudes disgust and disapproval at the world, and bites my head off every time I open my mouth. I suppose I'm just not his type, really."

If she'd ever had a chance of asking the real Paul what in particular scared him about the operation, other than the actual prospect of encountering Comrade O'Leary round some unexpected corner, she'd lost it now, realised Frances irritably. At the best of times he disliked admitting human weaknesses, and he certainly wasn't going to do so this time.

"But then neither are you, Frances dear." The grin broadened. "So it didn't exactly cheer him this morning when they told him you were coming, believe me . . ." He trailed off.

Whereas now . . . thought Frances, contemplating the plastic mac and the platform shoes . . . whereas now he'd probably burst a blood-vessel at the sight of her. The memory of the Colonel's reaction to her proper mousey self, casually encountered in the corridor, was vivid enough. She blanched at the prospect of his reaction to Marilyn.

"I can't possibly turn up like this at the University," she snapped.

"Very true," agreed Paul. "Not that there aren't some proper little dollies among the students, and you could still pass for one, believe me, with your looks . . . Except we're not infiltrating the delectable student body on this one—so your station this afternoon is inside the new Library, and that's out of bounds to students today. Which means we've got to do a quick respectability job on you at the Cross-ways Motel—a de-tarting process, one might call it in the circumstances."

"What d'you mean?" The prospect of another cover identity alarmed Frances. Covers were not to be taken lightly, they required detailed and careful preparation. Even Marilyn, who had been a rush job, had been allowed a week's cramming.

"Oh, nothing elaborate," Paul reassured her. "Nothing you can't do with your eyes closed. And they've supplied me with a suitcase full of your own clothes—I picked it up twenty minutes before I picked you up. You'll be playing yourself, near enough."

They had been to the cottage, thought Frances. Some stranger had gone to her wardrobe and the big old chest-of-drawers, and the dressing table, and had sifted through her belongings, choosing her own personal things. She shivered involuntarily at the thought.

You'll be playing yourself, near enough.

There was something creepy about that, too. After the last three years that was a role she was no longer sure she wanted to play ever again, always supposing she could recall the character and the lines clearly.

"You can wash that muck off your face at the motel," went on Paul. "We can't do anything about that ghastly hair-do except put a wig on it—there'll be a selection waiting at the motel by now. There

26

isn't time to do anything else, but you'll be wearing an academic cap anyway—and a gown, because it's full academic battle-dress this afternoon. Perhaps a pair of spectacles to make you look a bit more scholarly, instead of your contact lenses. Then you'll pass all right."

"Pass for what?"

"Post-graduate research fellow. There are a couple of dozen new ones in the English faculty, and as term's only just started they hardly know each other—and you are an English graduate yourself, Frances, aren't you? Bristol, was it? Or Durham?" Paul's Cambridge superiority surfaced momentarily. "You should be able to speak the language."

"That was seven years ago." Frances ignored the gibe.

"So long? Well, your supervisor will vouch for you—Professor Crowe. He has full clearance and knows the score." Paul gave her another reassuring look. "Don't worry, Frances. All you're doing really is releasing one of Fighting Jack's blue-eyed boys for a more sensitive job. We're not expecting any trouble in the library."

Famous last words, thought Frances. Apart from being male chauvinist pig patronising words. Obviously Colonel Butler and Paul Mitchell had mentally relegated her to *Kirche*, *Kinder* and *Küche*, as being sexually equipped for nothing else.

But she would not give him the satisfaction of observing her anger. Not so long as there was a chance of catching him out.

"I see . . . And might an English post-graduate research fellow know what she is supposed to be researching? That's the first thing she'll get asked."

Paul nodded. "Ah . . . now as it happens I had a hand in that little detail, as I've been a research fellow myself in my time, you see."

There was nothing more insufferably pompous than an insufferably pompous young ex-Cambridge male pig, decided Frances.

"Indeed? And your research included me, did it?"

"Let's say, I know where your special interest lies in literature. That one time you invited me down to that little cottage of yours I took a look at your bookshelves, Frances."

"My—bookshelves?"

"That's right. You can tell a lot about a person by the books on their shelves. Their books don't lie about them."

"But—" The words dried up on Frances's tongue.

"You've got all the books I'd expect an English graduate to have—Chaucer to Hemingway, by way of Fielding and Hardy. And

27

the usual spread of poetry." He paused. "But you've also got three full shelves of folk-lore and fairy stories . . . *La Belle au Bois Dormant* in the original French, and a nineteenth-century German copy of *Dornroschen* . . . right down to *The Lord of the Rings* and a first edition of *The Hobbit*. All well-thumbed and dust-free—a dead give-away."

All well-thumbed and dust-free. Frances stared at him helplessly.

Of course they were well-thumbed and dust-free. Dusting Robbie's favourite books was one of her compulsive habits. Once she'd decided not to throw them out it had seemed obscene to let them gather dust.

He took her silence for speechless admiration, or something like. "So all I did was to tell Professor Crowe about your collection, and he jumped at the idea. By now he'll have put it around that the title of your thesis is 'The Land of Faerie: From Spenser to Tolkien'. He's putting in Tolkien because with *The Silmarillion* just out, and the Carpenter biography, Tolkien-lore will be all the rage."

She had read *The Lord of the Rings*, all three volumes of it, because Robbie had adored it, and was always quoting from it. Its awful poetry apart, it had seemed to her an absolutely marvellous adventure story for romantically-inclined 14-year-olds. But since Robbie had been a 24-year-old SAS lieutenant she had never said so aloud for fear of offending him. And if Professor Crowe thought otherwise perhaps Robbie had been right and she had been wrong, in this as in other matters.

Paul looked at her expectantly, with just the faintest touch of innocence waiting for approbation. But she couldn't think of anything to say. She had seen that look on Robbie's face.

He turned back to the road in disappointment. A big sign bearing the legend 'The North' flashed by.

"Well . . . I thought you could probably have a ball in the new Library, talking Tolkien, while Fighting Jack and I sweated on the outside—that's all." He sniffed.

Frances swallowed. "Yes, I'm sure I shall, Paul."

"That's the ticket." He grinned at her, quickly reassured that he'd been right all the time. "You can be our Sleeping Princess in the Library, and I shall come and wake you with a kiss when we've killed the wicked O'Leary."

III

THERE WAS MORE than one faerie kingdom, Frances decided nervously as she followed Professor Crowe up the main staircase of the new English Library: hardly ten minutes before, she had left Colonel Butler in one such kingdom of magic and illusion, and she had been profoundly sorry for him; now she herself was entering another, and she would need all her wits about her to play her part in it.

"Frankly, Mrs Fitzgibbon, I don't know why you are here."

To which she had wanted for a moment to reply *Well, that makes two of us, Colonel,* except the way he had said it had somehow suggested to her that he really wished they were both somewhere else, and that had been the beginning of sympathy.

Or perhaps the sympathy had already germinated as she passed through the banks of chattering, flickering surveillance equipment which had been established on the top floor of the half-occupied Science Tower of the new—or fairly new—University of North Yorkshire, and which reminded her of nothing so much as a television studio girding itself to provide live coverage of a Third World War.

In the midst of which sat Colonel Butler.

He wasn't exactly brooding over it all, if anything he seemed to have its operators rather well under his control, from what Frances could observe. But his face, as he glanced past her at them from time to time, bore the same expression of heavily-censored contempt which she had noticed on the face of the American air force general who had once lectured her on the development of one-way remotely-controlled pilotless vehicles (he, who had three times brought back a damaged Phantom from the Hanoi bridges) and the psychological hang-ups of the 'pilots' who 'flew' the RPVs from the depths of their concrete bunkers ("Those goddamn pinball wizards get to like being briefed by computers . . .").

"But since you are here I'm putting you into the library, to take James Cable's place."

No, it wasn't quite contempt. (She had studied the Colonel's face carefully. All the features which had gone to make Charlton Heston a box office idol—the forehead, and the bone structure of cheek and jaw, and the artfully broken nose—added up on his face to ugliness, like a miss that was as good as a mile; yet, at the same time, it was an oddly reassuring ugliness, without any hint of cruelty or brutality.)

Not contempt, but rather resigned acceptance of another inevitable change for the worse. So might the 1914 Colonel Butler of Paul's imagination have contemplated a war of machine-guns and trenches, so unpleasantly different from the jolly manoeuvres of Salisbury Plain, but which had to be accepted and mastered nevertheless, and that was that, damn and blast it, with no time for tears.

He was watching her, too—a little warily, as though he was half expecting her to complain about taking over from James at such short notice, or simply because she was a woman, and women tended to be troublesome.

"Very good, sir," said Frances.

"Ah-urrumph. . . . The Library has been designated a safe and secure area. Which means, as a result of action already initiated, that the probability of an attempt there is . . . statistically low."

Frances remembered what Paul had said, which Colonel Butler was now repeating in the approved jargon as though the words hurt his mouth. And recalling her own first reaction to it she wondered if he was waiting for her to make a liberated protest at being fobbed off, as a mere woman, with a dull job while lucky James was given an opportunity to distinguish himself.

"Yes, sir," said Frances.

"Detective-Sergeant Ballard is in charge of the practical arrangements there, and he will report to you. Your function is . . . to assess behavioural deviations—"

The machines hummed and hiccupped and whirred and bleeped at Frances's back, and she knew exactly how Colonel Butler felt as they computed their probabilities and behavioural deviations: the more godlike the technology made him, the more powerless he felt.

"Do you think I'm talking tommy-rot, Mrs Fitzgibbon?"

Frances realised that she had raised an eyebrow at 'behavioural deviations'.

"No, sir. It just sounds that way." He had enough troubles without a tantrum from Mrs Fitzgibbon. "I can translate it."

"*Quite right.*" He would have smiled, she felt, if it hadn't been a frowning matter. "*The experts say the library is clear. I say that's the time to start worrying. I have to act on what they tell me, but you mustn't—is that understood?*"

"Yes, sir." Frances decided that she approved of Colonel Butler.

"*Any questions, then?*"

Yes, Colonel Butler, thought Frances.

You don't know why I'm here, and neither do I. And it doesn't make sense to pull me off one operation, where I was halfway to becoming useful, in order to waste me on another.

So what am I really doing here, Colonel Butler?

"No, sir," said Frances.

Professor Crowe opened the Common Room door for her.

An immensely tall young man with a shock of uncombed fair hair and an Oxford D.Phil. gown did a double-take on her, coffee cup halfway to his lips, and then pointed at her.

"Good God, Hugo—is this your Amazonian blue-stocking?" he said.

"Another of your false assumptions, dear boy," said the Professor. "I said no such thing."

The fair hair was shaken vigorously. "Not an assumption at all—an incorrect assertion perhaps, predicated on criminally misleading information. I merely extrapolated 'Amazonian' from 'formidable', I admit no more than that." The coffee cup wobbled dangerously on its saucer as he thrust out his free hand. "Miss Fitzgibbon, I presume? That is, if a presumption may be allowed in place of an assertion."

For one fleeting second Frances was reminded of Gary's undressing stare, but in her best Jaeger suit, and with the support beneath it which Marilyn had scorned, she was armoured against such stares. And besides, she was even more strongly reminded of other far-off days by the young man.

"How do you do?" The same strong memory cautioned her against smiling at him. Robbie had always maintained that her gap-toothed smile, which she had first smiled at him on just such another occasion as this—or superficially just such an occasion anyway—was the most promisingly bedroom invitation he had ever encountered, and she had never smiled so readily thereafter; at least, not until just recently for Marilyn's advancement, and this was certainly no place for Marilyn's tricks.

"How do I do?" The young man examined her face intently, almost as though he sensed the smile's absence. "I think I do not so well—thanks to Hugo . . . Thank you, Hugo . . . But you know, Miss Fitzgibbon, he said you were formidable, and I think perhaps he was right. You might even be perilous."

"Perilous?" It was an oddly archaic word, even allowing for the fact that he was striving for effect.

"Of course. 'Faerie is a perilous land, and in it are pitfalls for the unwary and dungeons for the overbold'—isn't that right?"

She couldn't place the quotation, though it sounded like one which any formidable research graduate ought to have cut her milk-teeth on. Damn!

"And no one could accuse you of not being overbold, dear boy," cut in Crowe drily, rescuing her. "Trying to catch an expert out in her own field—and with one of *his* books too . . ."

His books?

"And a thoroughly unreadable little book at that—based on a lecture he gave at St. Andrews before the war, wasn't it?" Crowe looked to her for confirmation, but then did not wait for an answer. "In fact, if I remember rightly, it first turned up in a collection of essays—about ten years after—and not as a book at all. It was an indifferent essay, and it must have been an appallingly dull lecture."

Whose lecture? She had admitted to Crowe that she might be rusty, but she hadn't expected to be put to the test so quickly.

"Not that I ever heard him lecture," concluded Crowe.

Frances felt that she had to say something. "But you knew him?" she asked, radiating proper interest.

"Ronald? Ah . . . well, of course. But chiefly through my supervisor—"

Ronald?

"—who didn't wholly approve of him."

"Sour grapes," said the fair-haired young man. "The favourite food of the only mythical monster commonly found in Senior Common Rooms—the one with green eyes."

"No, I think not." Crowe shook his head. "This was well before he became a cult figure—before even the first volume was published."

Idiot, Frances admonished herself. John *Ronald* Reuel Tolkien.

"Ah—but he'd already done well with *The Hobbit*, hadn't he?" the young man countered. "That was republished directly after the war—" He looked at Frances, then over her shoulder. "'Ullo, 'ullo, 'ullo. Someone's wanted by the Law."

Frances turned towards the door. The Law was grizzled and stocky, but unmistakeable. And it was trying to catch her eye.

"I think he's looking at you, Miss Fitzgibbon," said the young man. "He probably wants to frisk you for infernal devices."

Frances looked at him questioningly. "For what?"

"But don't worry," the young man reassured her. "We've all been through the process, and it's surprisingly painless. The whole place is absolutely crawling with security types—it's getting more like Colditz University every day."

"Oh?" said Frances.

"The Minister for Ulster is collecting his honorary degree today." The young man shrugged. "Presumably they do this wherever he goes, poor devil. He must lead a dog's life—no wonder our revered Chancellor retired from the fray."

"Oh . . ." Frances trailed off nervously. "Well, I suppose I'd better go and see what he wants. Excuse me."

The Law held the door open for her, and then followed her into the ante-room.

"Mrs Fitzgibbon?"

"Sergeant . . . Ballard?"

They examined each other's warrant cards.

"I am just about to make my final check before the count-down, Madam."

I am in charge. In theory anyway, and because of the unit's place in the hierarchy, *I am in charge*.

"Very good, Mr Ballard."

There was no need to panic. The building was a detached one; it had been thoroughly searched several times over a forty-eight hour period; there were two men and a woman officer on the main door, and two men on the back door, with scanners. There were two men on the roof; there was Sergeant Ballard himself; the outside approaches to the building were covered by four monitors. There was no need to panic.

As a result of a sequence of events which neither she nor Colonel Butler understood, there was Mrs Frances Fitzgibbon in charge of all this—the late Marilyn Francis, *vice* ex-Lieutenant James Cable, R.N., who had expressed himself satisfied with it. There was absolutely no need to panic, therefore.

Sergeant Ballard was looking at her, and Frances realised how young officers felt when put in command of old soldiers vastly senior to them in years and experience.

"Very good, Madam." Sergeant Ballard paused. "Then I shall report back to you when the check is completed."

Simple routine. And if the Sergeant felt any distaste at being subjugated to a woman half his age who was drinking coffee socially while he was doing all the work, he didn't show it.

"Thank you, Mr Ballard."

She watched the broad back disappear, knowing that she hadn't asked the crucial question—*Are you satisfied with the precautions?*—because it was also meaningless. No precautions could ever be foolproof. It all depended on whether Colonel Butler's computer could out-think O'Leary.

". . . he was a philologist really, and a very fine one. And he had a good ear, too—he could place a man by his accent with uncommon accuracy. Almost as good as Higgins in *Pygmalion*."

Frances's heart sank: they were still discussing John Ronald Reuel Tolkien.

"Is it true he was obsessed by the '14–'18 war?" The fair-haired young man's voice was no longer bantering. "Are the Dead Marshes in volume two—and the whole of Mordor, for that matter—are they based on his experiences in the trenches?"

"Hmm . . . I don't know about that. But he was fascinated by trenches, certainly . . . I can remember meeting him in the High once—at Oxford. He was standing in the rain watching workmen digging a trench in the road, absolutely transfixed by them—" Crowe broke off as he saw Frances. "Ah, my dear! We have obtained a cup of coffee for you, even though it is almost time for tea, I shouldn't wonder." Crowe looked at his watch. "The Chancellor's party is evidently running behind schedule."

"Thank you, Professor." Frances accepted the cup. There were, of course, two schedules: the official one, and the actual one which fluctuated according to predetermined times and deviations required

smelt of old age as well as Chanel No. 5, even though she was by no means ugly and misshapen. But no prince in his right mind was going to kiss *those* lips willingly.

Except in a fairy story, of course—

"Well, the first prince who kissed her was consumed by fire and burnt to a crisp the moment he touched her lips, because he was only after her father's kingdom.

"And the second prince was frozen into a solid block of ice, because he didn't love her, he was just sorry for her."

The fair-haired young man grunted derisively. "That's a bit rough. But I suppose he should have known that the first two princes never win the coconut. It's amazing how stupid princes are."

"Do be quiet, dear boy—otherwise I shall magic you into the sociology department of a certain London polytechnic for a hundred years." Crowe raised a warning hand. "Do go on, Miss Fitzgibbon. The hot kiss of greed and cold kiss of pity. And now the third kiss?"

He was doing his best to repair the damage done by the young man's interruption, Frances realised. But the spell was broken.

"I'm sorry," said the young man contritely, as though he'd caught a sudden glimpse of her embarrassment. "I didn't mean to spoil the story—please go on."

Frances was momentarily aware of the hubbub of conversation and the clink of coffee cups eddying around them.

". . . an altogether tedious man, without the least pretension. . ."

". . . so I told him to read *Henry Esmond* instead. A far more impressive novel than *Vanity Fair*, and just right for television . . ."

". . . first he put his hand on her knee. And then . . ."

"Please go on," repeated the young man.

At least they weren't asking her awkward questions about Ronald, anyway.

She took a deep breath. "The third prince . . . he'd been on the road for years, ever since he'd first heard how beautiful the princess was—he didn't know anything about the spell. And when he reached the castle where she lived he asked to be taken straight to her. And he kissed her, and she was instantly transformed back to her true self again. And they lived happily ever after."

The young man frowned at her. "Yes . . . but I don't quite see how . . . ?" he trailed off.

She smiled her careful tight-lipped smile at him.

But, Granny, I don't quite see . . .

"Neither did he, of course," she said. "Because—can't you guess?"

"He was blind," said Professor Crowe.

Frances looked at him in surprise. "You know the story?"

"No." Crowe shook his head. "And you say your grandmother told you the story? And she'd had it from her grandmother?"

"Yes. Why d'you ask? Is it important?"

"No. But it is significant, I fancy." He nodded thoughtfully at her. "I rather think it isn't a true fairy story, though. It has elements of the traditional folk-tale, of course—the original enchantment sounds typical enough. And the test-kiss, or kiss-test, is straight out of Perrault, so you'll probably find it classified in Thompson's *Folk Motif Index*. But I suspect they've all been grafted on to a very much darker superstition—a pagan-Christian tradition, possibly . . ."

The young man laughed. "Oh—come on, Hugo—"

"It's no laughing matter, dear boy. In fact, it reminds me of nothing so much as one of the superstitions associated with the Madonna del Carmine at Naples—or with the Madonna della Coléra herself even . . ." He nodded again at Frances. "In which case you were quite right to be scared, my dear—which is itself an interesting example of a child sensing the truth of something she didn't understand and couldn't know. Because even the telling of the Neapolitan story is considered to be unlucky except under special circumstances, and if I were a Neapolitan and a good catholic I should be crossing myself now, I can tell you."

Frances stared at him. She had always felt there was something in Granny's tale of the blind prince and the ugly princess which had eluded her, and Robbie too. Yet now she felt an irrational reluctance to collect the answer simply by asking the Professor to retell the Madonna's story. She knew that she still wanted to know, but that she didn't want to find out.

The young man experienced no such qualms. "Your grandmother wasn't from Naples by any remote chance, I take it?"

"No." Frances, still staring at Crowe, caught the hint of a reluctance similar to her own.

"A pity! Well . . . tell us about the Madonna del Carmine, Hugo. Or, better still, the Madonna della Coléra—she sounds positively fascinating!"

Crowe regarded the young man distantly. "That, my dear Julian, you must find out for yourself. Those are two ladies whose acquaintance I have not the slightest desire to make at present. You may inquire of *Professore* Amedeo in the Languages Faculty, though I doubt that he will choose to enlighten you, prudent fellow that he is."

The hint of reluctance was overlaid by the donnish repartee, so that Frances was no longer sure that Crowe had ever been serious, or whether he had merely been fencing with a favourite young colleague—and 'Julian' was almost too good to be true, anyway. Yet she could have sworn that there had been something there more than mere erudition in that withdrawn look, a touch of an older and humbler instinct, a different wisdom.

Julian gaped at the professor. "Good God, Hugo! Are you asking for cold iron and holy water and the Lord's Prayer?"

"Or bread and salt, and rowan berries . . . and if you must resort to the Lord's Prayer—" Professor Crowe craned his neck and gazed around him as though he had just remembered an important message as yet undelivered to someone who ought to be in the room "—don't forget to pray aloud, dear boy . . ."

That, at least, was one allusion Frances could place accurately: Robbie himself had once explained to her, at a Stratford-upon-Avon *Macbeth*, how both spells and counter-spells only worked when spoken out loud or traced in blood because the Devil could never see into a human soul and consequently required verbal or written undertakings, like those she had given at the marriage ceremony.

"I see that the long arm of the law is back," murmured Crowe to Frances. "And I rather think it is reaching out towards you again, Miss Fitzgibbon."

And not a moment too soon, decided Frances as she smiled at them both. "I don't think I'm on their list, or something like that," she said vaguely.

"Really . . ." Julian grimaced at the Professor. "You know, Hugo, if we had a proper trade union this sort of thing wouldn't happen, you realise that?"

"Dear boy—if we had a proper union we should probably be out of a job by now. Or reduced to time-serving impotence by the National Union of Students under a closed shop agreement, which would be well enough for me, at my age, but which you would find altogether insupportable—off you go, my dear."

"Well, I think that's damned unchivalrous of you, Hugo—"

Frances ducked away from them as they started to chase this new hare.

As before, Sergeant Ballard held the door open for her.

"Yes, Mr Ballard?" As he squared up to her she sensed that the civilian 'mister' was no more to his liking than his formal 'madam' was to her. So they were both equally disadvantaged by protocol.

"Madam . . ." The Sergeant focused on her. "Two faculty members have left the building in the last half hour. Dr Penrose and Mr Brunton."

The names meant nothing to her, so that when he showed no sign of elaborating on this information she was unable to decide whether Messrs Penrose and Brunton were exhibiting behavioural deviations, or whether Sergeant Ballard was a man of few words.

"You were expecting them to stay?"

"They were both on the invitation list for the unveiling, madam."

The unveiling. At her back Frances could hear the noise of scrambled conversation in the crowded Common Room. In a few minutes' time they would all troop down dutifully to witness the Minister unveil the marble plaque in the foyer which declared the building open; that ceremony, together with his acceptance of the honorary degree, was the main event of his visit. But as the building had actually been in use for more than a month this hardly rated as an earth-shaking occasion in the brief annals of North Yorks University; so that, short of Comrade O'Leary adding his own brand of excitement, Messrs Penrose and Brunton were not passing up anything interesting by absenting themselves.

On the other hand, if O'Leary had somehow managed to outsmart the computer then any departures from potential target areas were highly suspicious.

"Anything else of significance?"

"One of the university staff on the desk in the foyer received a rather curious phone call, madam."

He was overdoing the 'madam' bit. "What sort of phone call, Mr Ballard? How was it curious?"

"It was on the pay box in the foyer, not to the desk. But that's happened several times before—the numbers are similar. Only, when he took the call he was cut off before the caller could say anything."

"You mean he never established the origin of the call?"

"That's correct, madam. The telephonist at the other end said 'I have a call for you, Mr Dickson—I'm trying to connect you'. So he waited, and the telephonist repeated that she was trying to connect him. And then finally the line went dead."

"He wasn't expecting a call—this Mr Dickson?"

"No, madam. He phoned his wife to check, but she said she hadn't phoned him."

Frances bit her lip. Knowing the Post Office, she could not see anything particularly curious in an abortive phone call. But it would be better to be safe than sorry.

"How many university staff are there on the desk?"

"Two madam. Mr Dickson and Mr Collins."

"What's their job—today?"

"They are checking coats and belongings into the cloakroom, madam. No coats, or brief-cases and hand-luggage is allowed beyond the foyer today—it's all being checked into the cloakroom." The Sergeant spoke as though he was reciting a brief he had learnt by heart. "And of course they're also doing their usual duties, running the information desk and working the switchboard."

"You mean—they are searching people?"

He gave her a long-suffering look. "No, madam. All the search procedures are being carried out by our personnel at the entrances." He paused. "But the advantage of having university staff on the foyer desk is that between them they know everyone on the invitation list personally, by sight and voice. And they also know the building—Mr Collins has accompanied me on each of my security checks. If there had been anything odd, he'd have spotted it."

That made sense, thought Frances. But she had to do *something*.

"Well ... we'd better inform Control about Penrose and Brunton." If there was a behavioural deviation there, maybe the computer could spot it. "Did they have any hand-luggage?"

"One brief-case each." Sergeant Ballard forgot the 'madam' for once. "Searched at the door, checked in by Mr Collins and Mr Dickson respectively. Checked out by Mr Dickson, searched at the door again on leaving."

Everything would have been listed, naturally. Today no absent-minded professors were permitted in the new English Faculty Library Building, searched and scanned and sniffed as they had been by the Special Branch, and booked in and out by Mr Dickson and Mr Collins, vigilant of eye and ear—

Respectively.

Respectively?

"But if Mr Collins was doing the rounds with you, Mr Ballard—"

"Yes, madam?"

"—then Mr Dickson was on the desk *alone* for a time."

"Yes, madam." Sergeant Ballard looked down on her as from a great height.

Frances stared at him.

"I'll have everything in the cloakroom checked again, madam," said Sergeant Ballard heavily. "And we'll have a word with the exchange about that call to Mr Dickson."

"Thank you, Mr Ballard." Frances looked at her wristwatch. "Then we shall be joining you in about . . . ten minutes?"

The Sergeant checked his own watch. "Fifteen minutes exactly, madam."

It was almost a relief to return to the Common Room, where she was hardly less inadequate as an expert on Faerie than she was as the nominal madam-in-charge of a Special Branch anti-terrorist section which clearly functioned just as well, or better, without her, thought Frances miserably. Because where ex-Royal Navy Lieutenant Cable had no doubt quickly established a working man-to-man relationship with the world-weary Sergeant Ballard, she had just as quickly revealed herself as a Girl Guide amateur. The Equal Opportunities Act to the contrary, it was still a man's world, that was for sure.

She caught Professor Crowe's eye directly.

"Dr Brunton and Mr Penrose—I mean, Dr Penrose and Mr Brunton . . . Who are they?"

Crowe looked round the room. "I don't see them here—"

"They aren't here."

Crowe gave her a quick glance. "Penrose's a crafty fellow from Cambridge who knows a little about the Romantic Poets and a great deal about student psychology. He should make professor in about ten years' time. . . . Brunton is a dark horse from McGill University, allegedly pursuing the Great American Novel, there being no Great Canadian Novelists—"

"Did I hear the ill-omened name of Brunton?" cut in a short dark man with pebble-thick spectacles.

"You heard the ill-omened name of McGill," said Julian.

"Your insular prejudices are showing, Julian, dear boy," said

Crowe. "If Dr Pifer hears you he will simply roll on you, and that will be the end of you, I fear."

A man's world, thought Frances. But today was the man going to be the Minister, or Professor Crowe, or the handsome Julian—or Colonel Butler, or Comrade O'Leary?

"Whatever the ample Dr Pifer may do to me does not alter the sum of what McGill has given to the world," said Julian.

"Stephen Leacock?" suggested the pebble-spectacled man.

"Stephen Leacock *and* the geodesic dome," said Julian with an arrogantly dismissive gesture. "Why are you pulling that hideous face, Tom? Or should I say that *more* hideous face?"

Tom peered at him seriously through the thick lenses. "Eh? Oh . . . I was pondering why 'geodesic' with an 's', that's all."

"It's the science of geodesy with an 's', that's why."

"Ah . . . but those imaginary lines which the geodisists draw—or perhaps they are properly geodesians—those are geodetic lines, with a 't'. So why not 'geodetic domes'?" Tom frowned at Julian as though the fate of the English Faculty, if not the nation itself, hung upon the answer to his question.

"Well, Tom, you'll just have to look it up in your Shorter Oxford." Julian shrugged and grinned mischievously at Frances. "Did you know, Miss Fitzgibbon, that the Shorter Oxford Dictionary weighs thirteen pounds—six-and-a-half pounds a volume? That is, Tom's 1950 edition does. He had occasion to carry them from one set of lodgings to another recently, and when he arrived in an exhausted state the first thing he did was to weigh them on the kitchen scales." He looked down at Tom benevolently.

Tom blinked, found himself looking at Frances, and flushed with embarrassment.

"More to the point—" Professor Crowe intervened quickly "—has the egregious Brunton discovered the Great American Novel yet?"

More to the point, thought Frances, has the egregious Brunton exhibited behavioural deviations recognised by Colonel Butler's computer, always supposing they had any data on him at all?

"Perhaps he ought to borrow Tom's scales and judge them by weight, like vegetable marrows at a horticultural show," murmured Julian. "Eh, Tom?"

"Well . . ." Tom ignored Julian ". . . he does show signs of appreciating William Faulkner."

"Faulkner?" Julian refused to be ignored. "I find him unreadable. That convoluted style—sentences going on for pages, and then ending with a semi-colon! Quite unreadable!"

"Oh—nonsense," said Frances involuntarily.

"Indeed?" Julian regarded her with a mixture of interest and surprise, as Doctor Johnson might have viewed a dog walking on its hind legs, thought Frances angrily. "Nonsense?"

All three of them were looking at her now, and she was aware of the chasm at her feet. Her preoccupation with O'Leary had finally betrayed her into expressing a genuine literary opinion.

But it *was* nonsense all the same. If fairy tales were about unreality, or other reality, or God only knew what, then her beloved Faulkner was about the problems of living in a real world and somehow making it work, even when it was unbearable.

Suddenly all Frances's fear evaporated: where Frances Fitzgibbon was out of her depth, young Frances Warren was in her element: as always, the secret of a good cover was self-discovery.

"Utter nonsense." She smiled up at Julian. "Can you find a contemporary English novelist—*British* novelist—to put in the same class as Faulkner?"

"John Fowles." The light of battle flared in Julian's eye.

"*The Magus?*" The last vestige of Miss Fitzgibbon fell away from Frances: Miss Warren was in charge, and she was as arrogant as Julian. "*Daniel Martin?* You dare put them up against *Sanctuary?* Or *The Bear?*"

"Hah!" said Tom. "Hah!"

"Not that Fowles isn't good," said Miss Warren magnanimously. "Some of the so-called critics need their heads examining. But to compare Faulkner with Fowles . . . Do me a favour!"

"Do us all a favour," said Tom. "Start with *The Bear*, Julian."

He smiled at Frances, cowlike eyes swimming joyfully behind the thick lenses. Gary had smiled at Marilyn like that, ready and hoping to die for her.

Forget Marilyn. Marilyn was with her useless father and her dying mother, somewhere in South-East London.

Detective-Sergeant Ballard was standing in the doorway.

"Well . . . I'm not an expert in the hunting of bears with mongrel dogs in Yoknapatawpha County," said Julian.

"It isn't about hunting bears," said Tom.

"It's about slavery," said Frances. "Faulkner's got more to say

44

about the negro problem in the South than all other American writers put together."

"He has? I've always thought his approach was a bit Schweitzerish myself," Julian prodded her gently. "But then perhaps you have insights into slavery denied me?"

It was a pity that they were settling down to a good argument just when the expression on Sergeant Ballard's face suggested that the computer had choked on one of the names fed into it, thought Frances.

"No more so than any woman. We have some of the same problems the freed slaves had in searching for an identity . . ." But she could no longer ignore the Sergeant's signals. "I'm afraid you'll have to excuse me . . ."

"An identity—?" Julian turned as she pushed past him. "Oh, for God's sake—not again! Hugo, do be a good chap and tell the fuzz either to arrest her or let her alone—"

"Yes, Mr Ballard?"
"We have a suspicious object, madam."
"Suspicious?" Frances repeated the word stupidly.
We're not expecting any trouble in the library!
"Yes, madam."
"Where?"
"In the cloakroom. Almost directly under where we are standing."

Frances looked at her wristwatch.
Damn Paul Mitchell! And Colonel Butler. And the computer.
She had six minutes.

IV

THE CLICK-CLACK of Frances's high heels echoed in the high open space of the entrance foyer as she descended the stairway alongside Sergeant Ballard.

"I have informed Colonel Butler, madam," said Ballard.

Except for the two civilians on the desk, Dickson and Collins, the foyer was still empty. The three Special Branch officers were still in position outside the glass doors, but through the expanse of glass wall on the other side of the doors she could see that a large crowd of students and hangers-on had now assembled outside the entrance.

God! There was altogether too much glass, thought Frances with a swirl of fear.

"We'll have to get those people away from the front of the building, Sergeant," she said.

Ballard cleared his throat. "Instructions are to stand fast, madam."

"Instructions?" Frances frowned at him.

"The moment we start clearing them away they'll know we're on to them," said Ballard. "Otherwise . . . the odds are they won't detonate until they've got the targets into the blast zone."

Frances realised that she had been foolish. If the suspicious object really was a bomb then detonation would be by remote signal, activated from some visual vantage-point in the surrounding campus, and not by any old-fashioned time mechanism. So long as the crowd didn't scatter they were theoretically safe until the Chancellor's party came through the doors.

Above the heads of the crowd and away across the open space between the new Library and the nearest great white tower she caught a momentary flash of academic scarlet.

"Colonel Butler will have to hold the Chancellor's party, Sergeant." With an effort she kept her voice steady.

"He's doing that, madam."

"And the people upstairs must stay where they are."

Ballard nodded. "Mr Collins, sir! I wonder if you would be so good as to go up to the Common Room and prevent the ladies and gentlemen there from leaving? You can tell them there's been a slight delay in the schedule."

Collins and Dickson exchanged glances.

"Perhaps they'd both better go," said Frances.

Ballard cleared his throat again. "Mr Dickson found the—ah—object, madam," he said. "I thought you might want to have a quick word with him."

Frances could feel the seconds ticking away from her life.

"Of course . . . Thank you, Mr Collins . . . Mr Dickson?" Frances attempted to exude confidence. "I won't keep you a moment, Mr Dickson."

Dickson nodded to his friend. "Off you go, Harry."

They both looked old enough to have seen war service, thought Frances gratefully. Certainly they were behaving like veterans.

Collins bobbed his head. "See you upstairs then, Bob."

Frances watched him depart for five heart-beats before turning back to Dickson. "You found this thing, Mr Dickson?"

"Briefcase, madam. Dr Penrose's briefcase."

"Briefcase?" Frances looked at Ballard. "But all the briefcases were checked."

"This one *was* checked," said Dickson quickly. "I saw it checked myself." He pointed to the glass doors. "Then I took it off of Dr Penrose, and labelled it up like the rest, and took it into the cloakroom." He indicated the door on his left with a nod of the head.

"Yes?"

"Officer there asked me to check out the cloakroom again, just now—" another nod, this time at Ballard "—so I reaches up to the top shelf, to make sure there's nothing else there but the cases, just to make doubly sure, like. And Dr Penrose's case—I can't hardly move it. 'Fact, it took me all my time to lift it down."

"To—lift it down?"

Dickson sniffed. "I put the heavy cases on the lower shelves, and the light ones up top. Dr Penrose's was light as a feather, like there was nothing in it. Now it's *heavy.* . . . And, what's more, it's *locked*. And it wasn't locked when I put it in—because I saw Dr Penrose close it up right here, on this desk-top."

Frances found herself staring at the door towards which Dickson had nodded, which bore the legend GENTLEMEN.

Heavy—but still on the top shelf—and locked, when it should have been light and unlocked. Those plain facts disposed of the faint hope that Dickson and Ballard had raised a false alarm with good intent, it didn't take a computer to produce that unpalatable print-out of the statistical probabilities for her. But how—

"Madam!" said Sergeant Ballard sharply.

Someone who was certainly no gentleman had somehow got into the cloakroom, so that now there was only one inadequate thickness of brick between whatever he had left behind him and her own shrinking flesh and blood. But Ballard was right: this was not the time to inquire further into that particular mystery.

"Thank you, Mr Dickson." Frances swallowed a quick lungful of air. "You'd better go and help Mr—Mr—"

"Collins," supplied Ballard, stepping towards the cloakroom.

Frances had never in her life been inside a gentleman's cloakroom.

Once, by accident and in semi-darkness, she had taken the first few steps down towards a men's lavatory in London, at which point the atrocious smell had warned her of the error she was making.

She had never expected to have the door of a gentleman's cloakroom held open for her.

There was a strong smell in the new English Faculty Library gentleman's cloakroom—a smell so cloying that it rasped on Frances's dry throat.

But its dominant ingredient was lavender, not ammonia.

And there was also a large, ruddy-faced man clutching a walkie-talkie to his cheek and sweating profusely.

As well he might sweat, decided Frances with a sudden sense of detachment which surprised her as her eyes were drawn instantly to the briefcase at his feet. It was enough to make anyone sweat.

"Mrs Fitzgibbon is here now, sir," said the sweating man in an unnaturally steady voice.

He had never set eyes on her before, thought Frances, but it was an entirely reasonable deduction in the circumstances.

The man offered her the little walkie-talkie. "Colonel Butler for you, Mrs Fitzgibbon," he said in the same matter-of-fact tone.

It was curious how fear took different people in different ways, thought Frances analytically.

"Fitzgibbon here, sir—"

Her knees were trembling, and the Special Branch man was sweating, but they both had their voices under contol. It was only their bodies which reacted to the imminent threat of dissolution.

48

"Hullo there, Mrs Fitzgibbon. Over." Colonel Butler sounded positively casual, almost sociable.

Frances frowned at the row of innocent briefcases, each neatly labelled, on the shelf directly in front of her. This wasn't the harsh-voiced Colonel Butler she had last met, who had no time for women and even less for pleasantries, beyond the bare necessities of good manners. From another man, *Hullo there*! would have meant nothing. From Colonel Butler it was practically an improper suggestion.

What did he want her to say in reply? 'Meet me tonight behind the ruins of the library?'

Suddenly she knew exactly why he'd said *Hullo, there*: he was scared witless—and with good reason—that at any moment she was going to let the side down by slumping to the floor of the gentleman's lavatory in a dead faint.

"Sir—" She looked from the briefcases to the sweating man, and then to Sergeant Ballard. The Sergeant regarded her with fatherly concern, and he wasn't sweating. "Sir, I have Sergeant Ballard and one of his men with me. And one highly suspect briefcase. I suggest that there are too many men in the gents' at the moment. Over."

Her knees were still trembling, and what she'd just said did not at all reflect how she felt—the sense of it, if not the actual words, had a curiously Marilynish cheeky ring about it, not like Frances at all. (Marilyn would have made a joke of going into the gents'; she wished Marilyn was here now, and not Frances!)

"Hah! Hmm . . ." After a brief silence the voice crackled in her ear. "Ballard's man came off the back door. Send him back there. Over."

Frances nodded the reprieve at the sweating man.

"I've done that. Over."

"Good. Now give me Ballard for a moment. Over."

Frances handed the radio to the Sergeant.

"Sir?" Ballard barked. "Over!"

Frances didn't want to listen. The silent majority of her wanted to be treated like a weak and feeble woman, and sent to a place of safety to sniff sal volatile. But there was a small vociferous Liberated minority which was outraged at the prospect of being passed over—so much so that it made her stare quite deliberately again at the briefcase, which was something she'd been trying very hard not to do.

It sat there, black and bulging and malevolent, four feet away from her on the brown quarry-tile floor. It seemed to get blacker and to bulge more as she watched it. The silent majority insisted on exercising its democratic rights, and for a fraction of a second the quarry tiles swam alarmingly.

"Madam!" Ballard handed her the radio. "I have my instructions. The Colonel is transmitting to you now."

He was going. She was about to be left alone with the briefcase. She wished Sergeant Ballard hadn't looked at her so sympathetically.

"Fitzgibbon?" Pause. "Over."

Now she really was alone with the sodding thing.

"Sir." Pause. "Over."

Ridiculous jargon. But he had said *Fitzgibbon* as he might have done to his poor bloody second-lieutenants in battle, and somehow that was enormously gratifying to the idiotic Liberated minority.

"Listen to me, Fitzgibbon. I've got people here with me who press buttons, and they tell me that that briefcase of yours is the decoy they've been waiting for—don't worry about this transmission being picked up, they've got a black box that scrambles it . . . that's one thing they can do, by God!"

And they'd be listening to him too, and he didn't give a damn. Against the run of play her heart warmed to him.

"They say it's a brick, or a book, or a couple of telephone directories, to make us look the wrong way. And I should tell you that—"

They sounded eminently sensible, thought Frances.

"—and we should ignore it, and wait for the right one."

Frances looked at the briefcase again, and her knees advised her that the button-pushers were not themselves in the gentleman's lavatory.

"But I say it's the real thing—d'you hear, Fitzgibbon? Over."

There wasn't a clever answer to that. "Yes, sir. Over."

"Good."

Not good. Bad.

"They also say the moment we start clearing people from outside the Library, we start playing O'Leary's game. And I agree with them there. But by the grace of God, because that fool of a porter moved it, we know there isn't a trembler in it. *So pick it up, Fitzgibbon.*" Pause. "Over."

She knew she had to do it at once, or she would never do it. That was what he intended, too.

Two steps.

She picked it up.

It was heavy.

"I've picked it up—sir. Over."

"Good. Now put it down again—gently." Pause. "Over."

Ming vases. Dresden china. Nitro-glycerine.

"Sir." Croak. "Over."

"That's very good, Fitzgibbon. Now you know you can pick it up. Because we can't move a bomb-handling team in there—if I'm right he'll be watching that place like a hawk, and he can blow it any time he likes. But we *can* do what he won't be expecting: in a few minutes from now, when I'm good and ready, you're going to carry that briefcase out of there, Fitzgibbon."

Frances closed her eyes.

"We can't move the people. I can only delay the Chancellor's party so long—are you listening, Fitzgibbon? Over!"

The sodding briefcase was imprinted on her retina. She opened her eyes and looked at all the other cases.

"Spare me the details." Jargon. "Over."

"I want you to understand what you're doing. You've got the best chance of carrying it out. You're new here, they haven't had time to spot you—you've never been on an Irish job. You're wearing an academic gown, and you have a perfect right to carry a briefcase. Take some of the papers out of one of the other cases—and some books, and carry them too. Look like a student."

It was beginning to make some sort of sense, she just wished someone else was going to do it. But, undeniably, Sergeant Ballard did not look like a student.

"Professor Crowe will be waiting for you at the door, Ballard's getting him. By then he will know what's happening. Let him see you off the premises. Don't hurry—gawp around like the rest of them out there . . . then walk to your right, and bear right as you reach the corner of the building—Crowe will direct you. There's a wide open space, with a few trees and shrubs in it, and then there's a big pond in a hollow—it's a duck-pond, you'll hear the ducks quacking. . . . Put it down on the edge of the pond and leave it—that's all you have to do."

All?

"Have you got that? Just talk to Professor Crowe—as though you were one of his students. Act naturally."

51

Act naturally—don't scream and run. Just talk to Professor Crowe about Ronald and the eucatastrophic endings of fairy stories.

"Colonel Crowe will be waiting for you—Professor Crowe. Over."

Colonel Crowe? Well, there was a once-upon-a-time, thought Frances.

"I repeat. Professor Crowe will be waiting for you. Have you got that, Mrs Fitzgibbon? Over."

There was a suggestion of steel in that last *Have you got that?* which in turn suggested to Frances that the soldier inside Colonel Butler would not have thought twice about giving James Cable or Paul Mitchell the same orders, but was still only half convinced that *Mrs* Fitzgibbon could be trusted with a bag of laundry, never mind a briefcase. But that he was giving her the benefit of the doubt because he had no other choice.

"Loud and clear, Colonel Butler. Over."

Grunt. "Leave the button on receive. Out."

Silence.

But they must surely be running out of time now, with the original six minutes long gone. And the longer they waited, the more likely it was that O'Leary would smell a rat..

She looked down at the briefcase.

How heavy was heavy?

Five pounds? Ten pounds? Twenty pounds?

Not that it would matter to her because, at the range of one yard, half a pound would be sufficient to spread her all over the cloakroom.

But it would be more than that: it would be calculated to blow the brick wall against which it had been placed into ten thousand lethal fragments in the entrance foyer on the other side of it. By which time, of course, she would already have been dissolved into unidentifiable fragments herself.

The silence began to ring in her ears. There were small sounds in the distance beyond the ringing, but she couldn't distinguish them. It almost seemed to her that the very sight of the briefcase had a muffling effect on her hearing; that somehow, just as noise spread out from an exploding bomb, so silence was spread by a bomb before it exploded.

And yet when it did explode she wouldn't hear it: she would be dead before the sound reached her brain. There would be no brain to receive the message. No brain, no ears, *no Frances*.

She looked at her wristwatch, and was astonished at the short space of time which had elapsed since she had last looked at it, outside the Common Room upstairs.

Julian would still be arguing the toss with the short swarthy don, Tom.

Professor Crowe ought to be downstairs by now.

Mrs Simmonds would be typing Mr Henderson's afternoon letters—and probably Mr Cavendish's letters too, in gratitude for her deliverance from the unspeakable Marilyn.

Gary would be dreaming of rescuing Marilyn from the Comanches.

O'Leary would be—

Mustn't think of O'Leary.

On the wall in front of her there were three shelves.

On the shelves there were eighteen briefcases, an untidy little pile of type-written papers, a copy of the *Guardian*, and a solitary book, *The English Novel: A Critical Study*.

Eighteen briefcases plus one—

And, for a bet, those papers, that *Guardian* and that fat volume were the original contents of Dr Penrose's case, which had made room for whatever was in there now—

Everything brought her back to that sodding briefcase—

Why didn't Colonel Butler give the word? What was delaying him?

She must think of something else. Anything else.

The short wall on her left was made up mostly of frosted glass through which she could see only vague shapes and colours—that was bad, all that glass—

The wall on her right was even more alarming: between two vending machines there was a full-length mirror in which a young woman wearing an MA gown and her best Jaeger suit was staring transfixed at her, white-faced and frightened out of her wits—

She turned away hastily from the image before it had time to scream at her.

Behind her was a double line of coat-hooks and a scatter of coats, ending in an open doorway through which she could see a gleaming white tile wall. That was obviously the source of the lavendery smell which had hit her as she entered the cloakroom: if she had ever had any curiosity about the furniture of a men's lavatory she now had the chance of satisfying it in perfect safety.

Except that she didn't have any curiosity left about anything, least of all about men's lavatories, even when they smelt of lavender—

Perfect safety?

The perfect inaccuracy of the words struck her: they were so perfectly and utterly ridiculous that she didn't know whether to laugh or to cry at them.

It would be more appropriate to laugh. After all, not even the three old ladies in the rugby club song could rival her predicament—they hadn't been trapped in a gentleman's lavatory—

Only she was desperately afraid that once she had started to laugh she would never be able to stop.

"Fitzgibbon—are you receiving me? Over."

Now she had missed her chance: there was no time now either to laugh or to cry, or to see the rest of the gents'.

"Loud—" The word again came out as a husky croak "—*Loud* and clear. Over."

"We're ready to go. Over."

A moment ago she had been begging him to give the word, but she felt differently now. Being left alone suddenly seemed preferable.

"I repeat—we're ready to go. Do you read me? Over."

Well, at least he sounded a bit more like his old irascible self.

"I read you loud and clear—" In fact he was probably thinking *Bloody women*! under his breath. So this reply she had to get right, even though the cloakroom floor heaved under her feet. And to get it right she could not do better than to resurrect Marilyn again "—I thought you'd never ask, that's all. Over."

Pause. Evidently Colonel Butler wasn't accustomed to cheek from flibbertygibbet young girls.

"Right . . ." The distortion cheated her of any absolute certainty that Marilyn had scored a point. "Off you go then. And good luck. Over and out."

Just like that: *Off you go then*, and *good luck*!

But he was right all the same, thought Frances: there was no point in thinking about it—thinking would just make it more difficult. The only way to do it was not to think about it, simply to do it.

She settled the strap of her handbag comfortably in the crook of her left arm, put down the walkie-talkie on the shelf beside the type-written papers, scooped up the same papers and the *Guardian* and the critical study of the English Novel and tucked them under her left arm above the handbag strap, and picked up the briefcase.

It was heavy—

She tensed her arm against its weight as the muscles of her right breast pulled tight against it.

It mustn't look heavy—

The white-faced young woman in the mirror walked towards her, and then turned outwards into the doorway without giving any sign of recognition.

The entrance foyer was huge and empty, and the click of her high heels echoed off the polished floor.

Detective-Sergeant Ballard and Professor Crowe were waiting for her just inside the glass doors.

Crowe smiled at her.

In fact, he positively beamed at her—

"There you are, my dear! We've been wondering where you'd got to—"

So they hadn't told him what she was carrying, thought Frances, undecided as to whether that omission was kind or unfair. And yet he hadn't raised his eyebrows as she had shouldered her way out of the gentleman's cloakroom, so maybe—

Ballard moved in front of her, blocking her path. And also blocking any view of their encounter which an observer might have from any distant vantage point across the campus outside.

"If you would be so good as to have a brief word with Colonel Butler, madam, after . . ." Ballard searched comically for a suitable description of what was coming before the brief word "after . . ."

"*After*wards," said Crowe, still smiling. "And after that, my dear Frances—it is Frances, isn't it?—come and have tea—or maybe something stronger, eh?—in my rooms in the old Dower House. . . . If you have time, of course."

He did know?

But if he did know, how could he smile at her like that?

Ballard opened one of the glass doors for her.

"Thank you, Sergeant," said Crowe reaching over her head to steady the door.

Cold autumnal air enveloped her. There were lots of people round about, but a clear path stretched out ahead of her.

Turn to the right.

Crowe was still beside her, one hand on her elbow gently steering her in the right direction. Out of the corner of her eye, away to the left over the heads of the crowd standing on the slight slope in front of the new building, she caught another flash of the same colour she had seen earlier, of scarlet doctoral robes.

"There they are now," murmured Crowe in her ear. "So they did go into the Student Union after all—if it had been the Minister of Education that would have been a place to steer clear of, even though our present young things are rather more . . . motivated— is that the word?—motivated . . . than some I have encountered. Hah!"

The crowd was thinning around them. It wasn't fair that she should carry him along with her a yard more than was necessary.

"I—I can find my own way now, I think," said Frances.

"Of course you can!" Crowe nodded, but continued to walk by her side. "But . . . I was wondering, now, whether you knew an acquaintance of mine—a Cambridge man—in your line of work. The name eludes me—now what was it?"

The hand was on her shoulder now—her left shoulder. The right shoulder was beginning to ache.

"Mitchell?" hazarded Frances.

"No-o . . . That name doesn't ring a bell . . ." He shook his head. "Big fellow—played rugger, but for some reason never got his blue. History scholar—medievalist—clever fellow, but eccentric—"

David Audley, thought Frances with absolute certainty. The specification fitted like a glove.

It was no business of Professor Crowe's to know the names of her senior colleagues, nevertheless. Paul Mitchell, by any other name, was fair enough, since he was here on the ground. But David Audley, somewhere else, was another matter.

"I think you must have him mixed up with somebody else," she smiled back at him.

"Very probably—very probably!" He returned the smile with another smile. "Well, Frances my dear—here we are, then."

They had passed the corner of the building long since, following the curve of a gravel path into an open parkland thick with fallen beech leaves. Directly ahead of her she could hear the subdued conversational quacking of ducks undisturbed by human beings and the need to compete for free handouts of bread.

Crowe squeezed her arm gently. "I must get back to my dull duties now, my dear. And you must complete yours. But you've only a yard or two to go."

He had talked her far beyond any possible requirement of Colonel Butler's, Frances realised as she looked around her. And he had also talked her out of remembering to be terrified until this moment.

Even now he wasn't in any hurry to leave her.

"Thank you, Professor." In other circumstances he deserved to have a kiss planted on his cheek, but in these ones she could only give him every last extra second back in return for the minutes he had freely given her.

It really was only a few yards: the pond was in a natural hollow in the parkland, and she could already see the far side of it, with the near side, hidden by the slope just ahead, no more than a dozen strides away.

Which was just as well, for her last shreds of nerve were running out with time and distance.

One step after another—three, four, five, six—

Now the convenient path she'd been following obstinately refused to take her any closer, dividing to sweep round on each side of it. But that no longer mattered—

But it did matter.

As she stepped off the path on to the carpet of leaves her high heels sank through into the soggy ground beneath. The fall of the slope made the going even more treacherous, and she teetered wildly as first one foot and then the other became trapped, unbalanced equally by the weight of the briefcase and the fear of what might happen if she dropped it.

The cruising ducks on the pond caught sight of her and instantly changed course, quacking loudly in anticipation of food. Their cries awakened other ducks ashore on the far bank, which at once threw themselves into the water, hydroplaning towards her across it on beating wings and feet. The whole pond exploded into a frenzy of greed.

Frances lost contact with one of her shoes. *The English Novel* slipped out of her grasp and slithered down the slope, followed by the rest of Dr Penrose's possessions.

The ducks hurled themselves towards the scattered papers.

With a convulsive effort Frances freed her other shoe. But as she did so her foot came out of it and her already shoeless foot slid out from under her. She sat down heavily on her bottom, just managing to clasp the briefcase to her breast before she hit the ground. Both her stockinged feet rose in the air as the weight of the case pushed her on to her back and she instantly started to toboggan down the slope towards the chaos of squabbling ducks and mud-stained papers.

She cried out in terror, but the sound was lost in a crescendo of panic-stricken quacking and wing-beating as she crashed into the ducks.

For a moment there were ducks everywhere: ducks running over her legs, ducks clumsily trying to climb the slope beside her, ducks attempting impossible vertical take-offs, ducks colliding and snapping and splashing in the shallows.

Their panic infected her. She thrust the case away from her, down between her legs into the filthy duck feathered water in which her own feet were immersed ankle-deep.

Then she was scrabbling feverishly back up the slope on her hands and knees—

Her shoes—*she must have her shoes*—even if there was no time to put them on.

She was running in her stockinged feet—free from the briefcase at last—sobbing and running as lightly as a deer—

Paul Mitchell appeared from behind a beech tree in her path.

"Hold on there, Frances!"

She swerved to avoid him, but he caught the flying edge of her gown and swung her round.

"No—damn you—" she struggled instinctively, gasping for breath, but he caught her wrist.

"Hold on there!" Now the other wrist was caught. "It's all right, Princess—it's all right. We're far enough away if it goes bang . . . and it probably won't go bang anyway. But we don't want to create a disturbance, so just calm down—okay?"

Far enough away?

Frances looked back.

She hadn't run away in the same direction by which she had reached the pond; somehow she had veered to the right, away from the main buildings.

And she had also run much further than she had imagined: she couldn't even see the pond now, and the unspeakable quacking was muted.

Paul released her wrists. "Better put your shoes on, Princess. The ball's not over yet."

Frances looked down at her feet. Her tights were soaking and muddy. There was a duck-feather—several duck-feathers—stuck to her ankle. Her knees were muddy too. And her hands.

She caught her breath. "Sod it!" she said feelingly.

"That's better," murmured Paul.

By the grace of God she still had her handbag—somehow its strap had never left the crook of her arm. She extracted a handful of tissues from it and tried to wipe her hands.

"Here—" Paul knelt down and wiped the worst of the mud from her feet with a large handkerchief. "Now give me the shoes."

Her relief began to evaporate. She still had her handbag, but she had left her self-respect behind her by the duck-pond, together with the briefcase.

"Foot, please," said Paul.

Humiliation choked her. She had panicked, and what was worse, she had panicked in front of Paul Mitchell.

"It fits! It fits!" He grinned up at her. "You are the true princess, and I claim your hand in marriage—"

There was a rustle of leaves beside them. Balancing on one stockinged foot, Frances turned towards the sound.

"Hullo, Frances," said James Cable.

And in front of James Cable, she thought desolately. And there was someone else with him too; and beyond them both lay the prospect of reporting to Colonel Butler in the control centre.

"Too late, old man," said Paul from ground level. "Cinderella is mine."

"Sorry you had to carry my can, Frances." Cable ignored him. "But the library was supposed to be clean."

"Clean!" Paul grunted contemptuously. "Fighting Jack is going to have your guts for garters, James—to use his own inimitable phrase. . . . Give us the other shoe, Princess."

Frances looked down at him. She was never going to be able to outlive that nickname now, not in a thousand years. Even when the exact details of her disgrace had been forgotten she would still be 'princess', Paul would see to that.

"I can do it, thank you." She slipped her cold, wet foot into the other shoe.

"Suit yourself. One glass slipper is enough." Paul returned the ruined handkerchief to his pocket and rose to his feet. He looked at the man who had accompanied Cable. "You've got your chaps out round the pond, Jock?"

Frances put a name to the face.

Maitland.

"Aye." Maitland considered Frances shrewdly. "A black briefcase, Mrs Fitzgibbon. Approximate weight?"

Maitland, Technical Section. Late Royal Engineers.

Weight?

A million tons, the ache in her shoulder advised her. Or was the pain in her imagination?

"About ten pounds—I don't know exactly. Maybe more." She looked at him helplessly. "It was heavy."

"Not the way you were throwing it around," said Paul. "I thought you were going to heave it in, the way you were swinging it about. . . . I tell you, Jock—whatever there is in the case, it's certainly shockproof."

"Oh, aye?" The shrewd eyes settled on Paul momentarily. "Well, that's something then. And you just be glad it wasn't you that found it out the hard way, laddie."

"Oh, I am, believe me." Paul was unabashed by the jibe; it would take a lot more than anything Maitland could say to dampen him, thought Frances enviously. He wore his self-confidence like a wet-suit.

He winked at her. "I've much too much imagination for a nasty job like that. In your shoes—or out of them—I'd have been running long before you, princess."

"Aye," agreed Maitland. "You might have been at that."

"But that still wouldn't make it the real thing."

"No, it would not." Maitland eyed Paul thoughtfully for a couple of seconds before turning back to Frances. "Ten pounds, you say. And the case would be three . . . maybe three and a half pounds."

"It could have been more."

"It would be enough. And you left it by the water's edge as instructed?"

Frances's toes squelched inside her shoes. "Half in the water, actually."

"No matter." He came close to smiling. "It'll do no harm where it is for the time being, thanks to you. It will bide its time, and so shall we." He nodded to her. "Thank you, Mrs Fitzgibbon, for your help."

"Aye," murmured Paul as Maitland moved away. "But Fighting Jack will no' bide his time for us—and especially for you, Frances. You remember where to find him?" He glanced at Cable. "Or are you here on escort duties, James?"

"Me? No—I'm carrying the glad tidings to the library." Cable gave Frances a lop-sided grin. "I just came this way round to apologise to you, Frances."

"It wasn't your fault." She frowned suddenly. "What glad tidings?"

"Ask Paul. I've got to go—ask him—" he pointed at Paul as he started to turn away "—he's been in with the Colonel."

Frances transferred the frown to Paul. "What glad tidings?"

He shrugged. "Oh . . . owing to unforeseen circumstances there will be no Sarajevo this afternoon. All assassinations have been postponed indefinitely, by order of Colonel Butler."

"What d'you mean?"

He pulled his don't-blame-me face. "I mean, dear Princess, that if James has overlooked any more infernal devices in the privies there, only innocent bystanders are now available to act as casualties."

"Don't be—" she bit off the word as she saw his face change.

"Flippant? I'm not being flippant. The Chancellor and the Lord-Lieutenant are already off the premises—in different directions. And I—I am on my way to the playing fields to check in the RAF chopper Fighting Jack has summoned for the Minister. 'Called away on urgent state business'—that's the official word."

"You mean . . . there's no opening ceremony?"

"Correct. No opening—no ceremony. No VIPs—no big bangs. No O'Leary. Operation aborted, and that makes two for you in one day. If I didn't know better I'd think you were jinxed, Fitzgibbon."

He'd been listening in to her dialogue with Butler, Frances realised. But then Cable had said as much with his parting words. So the powers above were evidently breaking in Paul early to the control of the latest surveillance technology. There were to be no psychological RPV hang-ups allowed to develop in him.

"But . . . you know better?" At the last moment she converted the opening words of an angry jibe into a respectful question. Of course, he habitually cloaked his true feelings under flippancy and irreverent chatter about his superiors. But this time it was a thermal covering for anger, and the temptation to throw *We're not expecting anything to happen in the library* at him was outweighed by her curiosity about that anger.

"Oh, I do—yes." He glanced at his watch.

"Tell me." It was no good turning on the charm, he'd never fall for that from her. But just the very faintest suggestion of professional admiration might serve. "Tell me, Paul."

He looked down at her. Quite deliberately she rubbed the end of her nose with a muddy finger.

He grinned at her. "Now you've got mud on your nose. . . . Hell! I guess you're owed it, at that."

"Oh . . ." She removed the mud with her handkerchief. "Yes?"

"Well, I told you he didn't like things—"

"Colonel Butler?"

"Fighting Jack, so-called—yes. Only it seems I made a mistake about his methods of fighting."

"What methods?"

"That's right. . . . He hated the whole operation, but he didn't turn it over to anyone else—"

"So you said on the way up." She nodded. "A matter of duty."

"So I had the wrong answer."

It was anger which was making him talk. Being wrong didn't sit well with his ambition. All she needed to do was to keep him burning.

"And what is the right answer?"

"Huh! The right answer . . . is that he had to stay in charge of it so he could screw it up at the one time when nobody could stop him—when it was actually in progress."

If he was right that was shrewd thinking on Butler's part, thought Frances. An operation like this was like an old bombing mission in World War Two: up to the moment of take-off the pilot could always be replaced, but not when he was half-way to the target.

Only it also entailed the same risk too: he had to come home with his bombs wasted or still on board, and with an explanation.

"All he needed was an opportunity. And you gave it to him with your briefcase, Princess—'The Princess and the Wicked Briefcase', by Jack Butler. The ultimate fairy story!"

"But—"

"He had this chopper on stand-by at Driffield, and nobody even knew about it! He was just waiting for one thing to go wrong—that's all he wanted, just one deviation."

Behavioural deviation? Even now, after everything that had happened to her, she couldn't trust herself to echo the jargon out loud.

"The briefcase—?"

"The Library was a designated safe area." Suddenly the shape of his mouth changed, both corners drawn down. "'If a designated safe area isn't safe, Mitchell, then the basic assumptions of this operation are equally unsafe. And that changes our parameters.'"

Parameters? One thing was for sure: Colonel Butler knew how to fight technology with its own jargon.

"What does that mean?" She watched him consult the time on his wrist. "Or what did it mean?"

"'I don't mind risking Fitzgibbon, that's what she's paid for—' That's you dealt with, Frances. 'But a Minister of the Crown is entitled to adequate protection'—it meant he didn't even phone London. He aborted on his own authority, that's what it meant."

Frances found herself on Colonel Butler's side. Or at least partially so: he had done her the compliment of treating her like anyone else, uncomfortable though the treatment had been. She owed him something for that.

"Well, it wasn't a safe area, Paul." *And I've got the wet feet, ruined tights, muddy suit and damaged self-respect to prove it*, she thought miserably.

In the distance the ducks quacked their agreement.

"It wasn't?" For a second he looked through her. Then he focused on her. "You know, you were never in any danger, Princess. He just let you sweat to prove a point."

"He—*what*?"

"That's right. Just to prove a point. You were his grandstand play."

Frances clenched her teeth. "You mean—there was no bomb? How d'you know that?"

"For sure, we don't know. But I'll give you ten to one against. Or twenty to one, if you like."

She remembered the look Maitland had given him when he implied almost as explicitly that the bomb was imaginary. "You know something that I don't know."

Her anger was defusing his. "I know we picked up those two chaps of yours—Brunton and Penrose. Brunton was all set to score

63

with a Moral Philosophy student in his rooms—a female student, nothing queer about Brunton . . . And Dr Penrose was on his way back to the Library. He'd been posting a letter. He didn't need his briefcase for that."

Frances swallowed. "Someone else could have tampered with it. The cloakroom wasn't out of bounds, damn it."

"With those two old watchdogs looking on? And they were watching for anything suspicious—and since they would have caught the first blast you can bet your sweet life they *were* watching."

"But somebody *did* tamper with it all the same," Frances persisted.

"So what if they did?" His lip twisted. "The only person who was ever at risk was whichever of those two picked it up first . . . that's what Brunton's girlfriend would call empirical verification."

She had to stop being angry. "If there was a bomb it would be remotely-controlled—Butler said as much."

"Is, not was. We know that—he couldn't say anything else. All the O'Leary bombings in Ulster have been copy-book remote-controlled jobs, it's his speciality. This whole operation was based on that, for God's sake, Frances—" his voice sharpened "—this whole aborted operation, that is." He consulted his watch again. "Over which obsequies I must now go and preside, while you go to receive your accolade from the butcher."

Accolade?

She had never been in any danger—?

"No—wait, Paul!" She reached out a dirty hand to stop him. "I still don't understand."

He grimaced at her. "Christ, Frances ! Don't you ever read any of the technical hand-outs? Or the daily papers, come to that?"

"What d'you mean?"

"Didn't you read about the local radio-taximen screwing up the Delta rockets on Cape Canaveral?"

"Yes. But—" Frances stopped. Any radio-controlled device could be set off by any signal on the right frequency. But that was old hat. "You can jam the signal—"

Again she stopped. It wasn't good enough. . . . They had brought three of O'Leary's prime targets together not simply to save them, and certainly not to ensure that she would never be in any danger, but to ambush O'Leary.

"Of course we can jam it." He swung half round and pointed towards the university buildings through the trees away to his right. "With what we've got up there we can jam half of Europe—the cream of Signals Intelligence raring to go, all the latest West German-American equipment the SIGINT boys have been begging to use—Top Secret U equipment."

Frances stared past the finger at the high rise concrete towers. Top Secret U put her way out of her league.

"We can not only jam it, we can *trace* it." The finger was part of the hand again, and the hand was an exasperated fist six inches from her face. "A ten-second trace within ten feet over a one mile radius, and enough manpower to hit the source of the signal within half a minute on the campus—"

For a moment she thought he was going to hit her too.

"—and that bloody stupid old woman up there backs his prejudice against that *certainty*—"

In that instant, when Frances was just beginning to object to the term 'bloody stupid old *woman*', when 'bloody stupid old *man*' would have served just as well, the briefcase exploded.

V

THE FIFTH SUCCESSIVE match flared, licked the already-charred edge of the newspaper but failed once again to ignite it, and went out, leaving Frances in darkness.

She prodded blindly through the wire mesh of the incinerator, cursing her own irrationality. The matches were damp and the paper was damper, and it would have been far easier and much more sensible simply to have dropped the whole pathetic bundle into the dustbin to await the next garbage collection; and even if she could induce the newspaper to smoulder it probably wouldn't generate enough heat to burn up Marilyn's suspender belt and almost-see-through blouse and plastic raincoat; and even if they did catch fire then the flames would fail to consume the bits and pieces in the cheap handbag, the Rose Glory and Babe containers, which would survive to clog the bars at the bottom of the incinerator, to the annoyance of old Mr Snow when he burnt the next lot of garden rubbish unsuitable for his beloved compost heap.

And now she had dropped the sodding matches . . .

Yet even as she groped for the torch which was also somewhere at her feet, she recognised the necessity of Marilyn's destruction.

Marilyn was dead and gone—her fingers touched the cold metal of the torch—and Marilyn had never been alive anyway. But there was something about Marilyn which frightened her nevertheless.

She clicked the torch button.

In the beam of light she saw clearly for the first time the stick of wood with which she had been poking the incinerator. Only, it wasn't a stick of wood, it was a cricket stump.

It had been the first thing that had come to her hand in the garden shed, she hadn't bothered to look at it, it was just a stick to push down the bundle into the incinerator. It hadn't been a cricket stump then, because there was no way a cricket stump could have got into the garden shed.

And yet now it was unquestionably a cricket stump.

There had been a bag, an ancient scuffed leather bag, full of cricketing gear which she had inherited with the rest of his worldly goods—

With all my worldly goods I thee endow—

In fact, there had been a weird and wonderful collection of sporting equipment scattered through the tin trunks of clothes dating back to his prep school days. In his short life Robbie seemed to have tried his hand at everything from fives to fencing by way of boxing and badminton.

All of which she had given outright to the Village Sports Club.

Not, repeat *not* . . . *not* with the intention of eliminating him from the reckoning, as she now purposed to obliterate Marilyn. She had known from the start that there was no way of doing that—had known it instinctively, and because of that instinct had set out to embrace the inevitable by accepting it and making use of it.

Making use of it—

That was why his dressing gown, which was good and warm and only needed its sleeves turned back, enfolded her now.

That was why, although she had given away all his adult clothes to Oxfam, she had kept the orange-and-black striped rugger shirts and white sweaters he had worn as a fifteen-year-old, which fitted her perfectly; all of which, with the Cash's name tapes identifying them as the property of R. G. FITZGIBBON, could hardly be more explicitly memorable every time she touched them—

Robbie, not in the morning and at the going down of the sun shall I remember you, but beside the washing machine, and on the clothes-line, and at the ironing board, and in the airing cupboard, where I shall be expecting you and you cannot take me by surprise.

She stared down at the cricket stump in her hand.

Marilyn and Robbie.

But Robbie wouldn't have fancied Marilyn at all, she wouldn't have been his type—

Or would she?

Or would he?

The snap of a twig underfoot and the polite warning cough and the powerful beam of another torch caught Frances almost simultaneously, crouched over the incinerator like a murderess disposing of her victim's belongings, clad in nothing but her underwear and a dressing gown which obviously did not belong to her.

She turned quickly, swinging the feebler beam of her own torch to challenge the intruder, but his light blinded her.

"Mrs Fitzgibbon?" There was only half a question mark after the name; it was as though he was as much concerned to reassure her that he was not a night prowler as to confirm her identity to his own satisfaction.

"Yes—" She realised that she knew the voice, but there was something which prevented her from bridging the gap between that knowledge and full recognition; also, in the same instant, a breath of cooler air on her body warned her that the treacherous dressing gown was gaping open in the light. She dropped the stump hurriedly and pulled the folds together at her throat.

"Who—" She managed at last to direct her own beam on his face. "Oh!"

She knew why she had not been able to put a name to the voice.

Messenger: *The king comes here tonight*.

Lady Macbeth ....Frances Warren (Upper Sixth)

Lady Macbeth: *Thou'rt mad to say it*!

Except there had been no messenger to warn her of his coming, so that he had caught her in total disarray, with no words—without even any coherent thoughts—to conceal her surprise.

"My dear—" He snapped off his torch, leaving only hers to illuminate him "—I do apologise for appearing like this, without warning . . . and at this time of night too."

Without warning, and at this time of night: the politeness rang hollow inside Frances's mind. With or without warning, more like, and at any time of the day or night—here—for God's sake, *here*—that required more than an apology.

"And I'm afraid I startled you . . . But I was walking up the path to your front door, and I saw your torch, you see . . ."

He was talking like a casual caller, or as a friendly neighbour might have done if she had had any friendly neighbours, or even as dear Constable Ellis would have done on one of his fatherly don't-worry-I'm-keeping-an-eye-on-the-place visits, which invariably occurred within twenty-four hours of her return from whatever she'd been doing if she was away more than a week—it had even been in the back of her mind before he had spoken that it might be Constable Ellis behind the light.

All of which somehow made it worse, because of all people *he* was furthest away from being a casual caller or a friendly neighbour or a fatherly policeman, and the comparisons only emphasised that infinite distance.

"That's quite all right, Sir Frederick." But that was a lie, and a palpable lie too, in spite of the cool voice she could hear like an answering tape played back to her: if he knew anything he must know that she was surprised half out of her wits at his sudden appearance out of the dark in her back garden, away from his own proper setting which was as much part of him as was the heavy gilded frame a part of the portrait which hung above the fireplace in his office. And, Christ! If it had been old Admiral Hall himself who had stepped out of the darkness with a polite 'Mrs Fitzgibbon' on his lips she would have been hardly more disconcerted!

A lie, then—to be qualified into a half-truth at the least.

"I didn't recognise your voice for a moment, though," said the coolly taped voice, her own voice.

Well, that was closer to the truth, because in the four years—or nearly four years—that she had worked for him he had hardly spoken to her four times directly; when she had been Group Captain Roskill's secretary the year before those nearly-four-years, carrying and fetching between them, he had talked to her more often than that, and smiled at her too.

As he was smiling at her now, if she was reading the shadow-lines on his face correctly in the feeble light of her own torch; but this time the smile frightened her, shaking her torch-hand so that the other shadows danced and crowded round behind him, like the uninvited ghosts from her own past whom he had disturbed—Robbie and Mrs Robert Fitzgibbon, and Frances Warren (Upper Sixth), and even the new half-ghost of Marilyn Francis which she had been trying to exorcise in the incinerator.

She didn't want him to smile at her, because whatever had brought him here could not be a smiling matter, but she couldn't turn off the smile.

"In the circumstances that's hardly surprising." He chuckled briefly, and the sound seemed to her as far from amusement as the shadow-smile had been. "For a moment I hardly recognised you, my dear Frances. They've made you blonde again—and frizzed your hair. And you're wearing those contact lenses, of course." He nodded as though he could still see her clearly. "Well . . . I wouldn't quarrel with the lenses, but I can't say I like your hair that way."

"No?" She put her hand involuntarily to her head, which she had forgotten was still outwardly Marilyn's. "Well, I can't say that I like it much either, Sir Frederick, to be honest."

Or not to be honest, as the case might be, the still-unexorcised Marilyn whispered in her inner ear; and that involuntary gesture had been pure Marilyn, too. A dead give-away, in spite of the cool Frances-voice.

She switched off her own torch, enveloping them both in total darkness, and for a moment total silence also.

"Ye-es . . . But it was entirely right for British-American at the time, nevertheless, as I recall now. And as I'm sure you appreciated very well. That is to say, you understood . . ." He trailed off, as though the related subjects of her appearance and her assignment in British-American were of no great interest to him any more. "What an absolutely marvellous night-sky you have out here in the country! You know, we have nothing like this in central London, or very rarely—galaxies like grains of sand—and I cannot help thinking that it's a bad thing for us Londoners. . . . The stars . . . without them one is inclined to lose one's sense of . . . not proportion so much as insignificance, I suspect—wouldn't you say?"

Insignificance?

Was entirely right for British-American at the time.

A statement of fact—*was*: with that he eliminated the possibility that she had been taken off British-American because of some mere administrative stupidity. He knew all about that, just as he knew all about her, and all this was as near to an apology for seeming to push her around as he could bring himself to make.

Away in the far distance, beyond the immediate circles of darkness and silence which surrounded them both, she could hear the faint drone and snarl of cars jockeying for position on the long pull up Hammond's Hill on the motorway. And she fancied that if she listened carefully enough she ought to be able to hear the computer-whine of her own brain merging the non-information she possessed already with the non-information he had just given her, and, more than that, adding to it his presence here now—a very large and significant mountain come uninvited to a very small and insignificant Mohammed.

After the bomb there had been Colonel Butler—

"Thank you, Mrs Fitzgibbon. . . . Well, there's nothing more you can usefully do here, so you'd best go home, and I'll call you if I need you. . . . When Mitchell has seen the Minister off he'll give you one of the cars."

He was good, was Colonel Butler, she had decided at that point, observing him control the ant-heap confusion without fuss, without raising his voice, without a nuance of I-told-you-so: it had been like watching a re-enactment of Kipling's *If* by one quiet, ugly-handsome, totally decisive man who somehow made the time and had exactly the right word of reassurance or encouragement or command for everyone, from the slightly panicky ministerial security officer, whose minister had been whisked away from him by Paul Mitchell, to a Jock Maitland drenched with muddy water and plastered with feathers and flying duck entrails but still—or even more—dourly and gloriously Scottish—

"—ye wairr rright, sairr—and a lateral charge too, of aboot six poounds . . . But that doesna' make a nothing of the otherr—he's a trricky one, this fella'. . ."

"Happen you're right too, major—" Colonel Butler had smiled at him, and it was that rare and private change in his own expression which purged his ugliness; and at the same time the Lancashire which Paul had noticed peeped through the Sandhurst accent, so that for a moment it was like speaking with like *"—so you get yoursel' over to t'other, an' doan't let that young chap Pirie lay a finger on it. He wants t'be a hero. I rely on you not to let him make his wife a widow—"*

The other and *t'other* had confused her for a moment, but then she had disentangled them:

There had been a second bomb.

"Oh sure, Princess, there were two of them . . . hold on a sec while I fix the seat for you . . . James's legs aren't as pretty as yours, but they are somewhat longer. . . . Because that's Comrade O'Leary's modus operandi when he's expected. And the trick is . . . There! I think that will do nicely . . . the trick is to distinguish which is the diversion and which is the real killer. Is A intended to set you up for B? Or is B intended to divert you from A?"

71

(Under his Chobham-armoured assurance Paul was still angry, but there was something odd about that anger after Colonel Butler had made such a fool of him; and therefore, while one part of her wanted to slip away in the car's nicely-adjusted seat, as far and as fast and as quickly as possible from the University of North Yorkshire, there was another part which wanted to stay and find out why Paul was still angry when he should be humiliated; because, to give him his due, Paul was usually ready to admit when he was wrong.)

"Well, I suppose I should be glad that Colonel Butler got it right." (She had to find the chink in the armour to make him say more.)

"Well . . . that we don't really know, do we? And now we'll never know, because he changed the rules." (He had looked at her curiously then, and she knew she had found the chink: there was always something which Paul knew that no one else knew, and which he shouldn't have known.) "But I tell you this, Princess — there's something very odd going on, and that's a fact."

"I wouldn't dispute that." (After swapping British-American for the new Library, and Mr Cavendish's letters for O'Leary and *The Land of Faerie* that was an understatement of the truth.)

"I don't mean your little bomb, duckie—"

"It wasn't little." (She had shivered at the memory; even *duckie* was a painful reminder of things best forgotten.) "And don't call me . . . that."

"Okay, Princess. But I mean . . . they hauled you off a job to come up here, didn't they?"

"So what?"

"So I've got news for you. They took me off a job too."

"I thought you were Colonel Butler's Number Two?"

"His Number Two? That's a laugh." (But he hadn't laughed.) "More like his errand boy. He didn't know what to do with me—he didn't want me under his feet, but he didn't trust me out of his sight either."

"He sent you to collect me."

"Oh sure. And to brief you. So I was safely away from the stake-out here, and he knew exactly what I was doing. An errand boy's job. . . . And when you got here he didn't know what to do with you either—right?"

(She had had no answer to that: it had been no less than the truth.)

"Come on, Frances—don't be dim! This isn't our scene—you

72

weren't selected and trained at great expense to carry bombs from one place to another, and I'm not a glorified taxi-driver-cum-public-relations-man. Forty-eight hours ago I was all packed for Washington, to be David Audley's Number Two—packed and briefed. And I don't know what you were tarted up for, but I'll bet it wasn't for a fancy-dress ball. But whatever it was, it was bugging you when I picked you up, so it has to be bugging you a lot more now—what the hell we're supposed to be doing here?"

(Of course, it had been bugging her. So now it was all the more important to find out what he made of the nonsense.)

"I thought we were here to catch O'Leary, Paul."

"Is that what you've been doing? All I've been doing is watch how Fighting Jack does his thing—I know a lot more about him than Comrade O'Leary, as of now, Princess. Which may be highly educational, but hardly makes up for not being in Washington, I tell you."

"Well, don't look at me, I don't know—" (He had been doing just that: looking at her narrowly, really looking *at* her, not so much to check whether she was saying less than she knew but rather as though by adding her to himself, like two individually meaningless jigsaw pieces, he might catch a glimpse of the whole design.) "—and anyway I'm going home, thank God!"

'Oh, no! He's sending you home—Fighting Jack is. And that's a very different thing. . . . You're missing the point, Princess. And that's not like you."

"Flattery will get you nowhere."

"Not flattery. It's just that I need straw to make my bricks."

"And I don't?"

"Sometimes you don't, I've noticed. I was hoping this might be one of those times."

"Not this time. Why don't you ask Colonel Butler?"

"Ask Fighting Jack? You're kidding!"

"No, I'm not . . . kidding." (She had heard the anger in her voice under the weariness, but had no longer cared to conceal it.) "You seem to have some sort of bee in your bonnet about him, but I think he's pretty damn good, what I've seen of him. So why don't you stop bitching—" (Sod it! She had used that word again!) "—stop complaining and just ask him straight out?"

(He had laughed then.) "Oh, Princess—you *are* under par! That's the whole point—that's what is *really* odd about us being here, and we don't know why—that's bad enough. It doesn't seem to make sense, but it has to somehow, that's all . . . we just can't work it out."

"Yes?" (She had shivered again: the aftermath of fear was this bone-deep chill, a déjà-vu of the grave.) "So what?"

"Christ, Frances! *He doesn't know the answer either*—like, he's a convoy commander, and they've sent him a couple of battle-cruisers—"

"Oh, for heaven's sake, Paul . . . spare me the naval history."

"What?"

"I don't even know what a battle-cruiser is—and I don't want to know."

"Oh—sorry, Princess. But what I mean is—"

"Marvellous!" said Sir Frederick Clinton. "That must be Orion—the belt with the little dagger . . . and that reddish star in Taurus—"

"—what I mean is, Butler doesn't know why we're here either. As if he hasn't got enough to worry about as it is . . . But then he's a crafty old devil—which is why he's packing you off home, Frances dear."

"What d'you mean, Paul?"

"Top brass sends you up—he sends you packing. If we're meant to be a team he's splitting us up before we've got started. So if they send you back again they're going to have to do some explaining. I tell you, he may look like the the very model of an old-time major-general, but he's one smart operator, believe me. I've been watching him—I haven't had anything else to do but watch him—and I've changed my mind about him. He's bloody smart."

"—and that reddish star in Taurus must be Aldebaran. And there's the Plough, bright as anything—quite splendid! Do you know about stars, Frances?"

Butler, thought Frances. She had learnt precious little about Comrade O'Leary (in fact, she had learnt more about John Ronald Reuel Tolkien than about Comrade O'Leary), and even less about surveillance technology, but she had had a grandstand view of Colonel Butler in action, and so had Paul Mitchell.

"No, Sir Frederick."

It was no longer totally black. Her eyes had become used to the darkness, so that she could make out the loom of him against the darker mass of shrubbery.

"A pity, with this sky of yours."

Butler. But why Butler? It didn't make sense.

The darkness which remained was a comfort to her: it not only equalised Robbie's old dressing gown with what would surely be an immaculate overcoat, but it also concealed her bewilderment.

"Yes. But do you know about battle-cruisers?"

"Battle-cruisers?" She could hear his surprise, the darkness seemed to magnify it. *"Battle-cruisers?"*

She had the initiative now, but she would have to work hard to keep it.

"They're no good for convoy work, I believe."

"Yes . . . that is to say, no . . . unless the enemy was using some powerful surface ships as commerce raiders, I suppose . . ." He trailed off uncertainly.

"So what were battle-cruisers used for?"

"What were they used for?" He paused for a moment. "Well, if I remember correctly, the theory behind them was big guns plus high speed, but not much armour. So they could catch anything, and run away from anything they couldn't sink. . . . Though I don't think it worked out quite like that in practice . . ." He paused again. "But I thought you were an expert in fairy stories—I didn't know you were interested in naval matters."

"I'm not." Frances decided to let the negative serve for both subjects; it would be too exhausting to explain away the first misapprehension, and it really didn't matter any more, anyway.

"No?" The single word was heavy with curiosity and caution, carefully packed in his habitual politeness. He had decided to concede the initiative, and was waiting to see what she would do with it.

"But Paul Mitchell is."

"Paul Mitchell? I thought military history was his special subject. In fact, I'm sure it is."

"Well, he's into naval history now, Sir Frederick."

"Is he now? With a particular emphasis on battle-cruisers?"

"Not particularly. He has some extremely complicated theories—mathematical theories—about the size of convoys in the last war."

"Indeed?" He was smiling at her again. She couldn't see the

smile, but she could sense it. "That would be like him, of course—he has an insatiable appetite for facts and figures . . . and for facts in general. It's the historian in him. . . . And you get on well with Paul, do you, Frances?"

If we're meant to be a team he's splitting us up before we've got started, thought Frances.

He meaning Butler—

It was time to stop sparring.

"So where did the battle-cruisers come in?" Sir Frederick jogged her obligingly.

"Yes. Well—" Frances drew a long careful breath "—he was wondering—Paul was wondering . . . and so am I, Sir Frederick . . . what a pair of battle-cruisers were doing in Colonel Butler's convoy, where they were absolutely useless—where they weren't needed and they weren't even wanted."

"Ah—I see . . ." For a moment there was silence between them. "Yes . . . and where one of the battle-cruisers was very nearly sunk without a trace this afternoon, to no very good purpose too—so it seemed to you, eh?"

There was no answer to that, only a memory which would have been ridiculous if it had not been still so terrifying: *sunk without a trace in a duckpond, HMS. Fitzgibbon.*

"And did you come to any conclusion about this . . . incomprehensible piece of naval strategy, Frances?"

Frances swallowed. "Not at the time. I think Paul was close, but he didn't have enough to go on."

I need straw to make my bricks.

"But now you have enough to go on?"

He was here, standing in the darkness of her garden, that was all she had to go on, thought Frances. And if that was enough to make her reach for a conclusion, that certainty, it was still not enough to make the conclusion a believable one.

"I require an answer to that question, Frances."

That was a direct order, as direct and explicit as he could make it short of grabbing her by the shoulders and shaking an answer out of her; *require*—she could remember David Audley defining the difference between 'request' and 'require' in a way which made time stand still over two centuries of military and diplomatic semantics—*require* left a subordinate not a millimetre of choice, one way or another.

76

"Yes, sir."

"Then why do you think you and Paul were sent to Yorkshire?"

"To watch Colonel Butler."

"What makes you think that?"

Require was still in force.

"Because that's what we did, in effect."

"Yes?"

"Because nothing else makes sense."

"Go on."

"And you are here now."

"Which you think makes it a matter of internal security. *Go on.*"

She was tired, and the thick serge material of the old dressing gown no longer kept the night chill from her shoulders.

"Which still doesn't make much sense . . . sir."

"And do you think Colonel Butler could reach the same conclusion—that you were sent to watch him?"

"I don't know Colonel Butler well enough to answer that. I didn't have long enough to watch him."

"But I require your opinion."

Require.

"I think . . . no, I don't think so. I think—Paul thought—that he wanted to know why we'd been sent to him, and that was why he sent me back home. If you want me to go back again to watch him I'll have to have a much better cover story."

"He smelt a rat, then?"

"I wouldn't put it as strongly as that." Frances thought hard for a moment. It occurred to her that Butler would have to be damn good to have worked out what they had been doing, since they hadn't known themselves what they were doing.

But then Butler *was* damn good.

"Yes?"

"I think he simply didn't know what to make of us. . . . I suppose it depends whether or not he's expecting to be watched. If he is, then . . . yes. If he isn't . . . then I don't think so. He had a lot of other matters on his hands."

Silence.

"Good."

More silence. It was almost like being blind: she could sense the presence of the things she knew were around her. Sir Frederick two yards in front of her, the incinerator on her right, the cricket stump at her feet, and on her left the scatter of Marilyn's proofs of identity bulging out of the plastic handbag—Birth Certificate and National Insurance card, Post Office Savings book and Agency references . . . even the misspelt letter from 'Dad' and the holiday snapshot of Marilyn in her bikini, posed self-consciously against the alleged beach unbrellas of Torremolinos. So much effort for nothing!

"What is your opinion of Colonel Butler?"

It was a logical question after her last answer. And it required—required—the truth. Nothing else would do.

"I think he's good."

Well, that was nothing more than the truth, anyway. If she was expected to have noticed more than that it was their hard luck, they'd have to go to Paul for that.

"But you said you didn't see very much of him really, did you?"

"No, I suppose not." The truth requirement roused her obstinacy. "But I liked what I saw."

"Yes. But that wasn't a great deal, was it?" He pressed the point again, like a man committed to pushing a door marked 'Pull'. "I'm afraid things didn't go quite according to plan there. We were expecting him to keep you alongside him a little longer—as he did with Paul."

If by 'things' he was referring to a certain briefcase, then things had certainly not gone quite according to plan, thought Frances. Yet she had never observed such insensitivity in him before, and he wasn't the sort of man who pushed 'Pull' doors. So he was after something else.

"I think he sent me to the library because it was supposed to be safe, Sir Frederick."

"Because you were a woman, d'you mean?"

He was goading her, quite deliberately.

"Possibly. I gather he doesn't altogether approve of women, that's true. . . . But I'd guess it was also because I'd never worked for him before, so he didn't want to have to worry about how I'd perform."

"Yes?" He'd wanted more, and now he knew it was coming.

"You can check with Paul—as you say, he saw more than I did . . ." And what would Paul say? she wondered. Well, Paul was no fool, and even with no straw for his bricks he'd been way ahead of her this time. In fact, he'd had the answer in the palm of his hand—he'd grasped it, but he simply hadn't recognised it. Which

78

wasn't really surprising, because it was an almost unbelievable answer.

The enormity of it—her answer, her conclusion—hit her again.

They had been watching Colonel Butler.

And it was a matter of internal security.

She knew she was right. Even if Sir Frederick hadn't yet confirmed it in so many direct words, she knew she was right, just as she knew that Colonel Butler was formidably good at his job even though she had observed him directly for only a few minutes. But she also knew that there was something not right—something not wrong, but nevertheless not right either—with her conclusion.

And part of that not-rightness lay in the way Sir Frederick was waiting so patiently for her to put her thoughts together, too patiently for the circumstances, as though he had all the time in the world; time which he couldn't have, otherwise he wouldn't be here, in the dark of her garden.

"I don't know . . ." What he wanted her to explain couldn't rationally be explained; even in the dark it would be like taking her clothes off in public before an eager and critical crowd. Yet his patience hemmed her in on all sides. "I suppose you could say I saw him when he was up against it—first on a job he hated and then when everything was going wrong . . . and you can't measure time in minutes at times like that."

"So you had enough . . . of that sort of time to observe Colonel Butler to your satisfaction?" He sounded unsatisfied.

"I thought so, yes." She knew it wasn't going to be enough.

"Thought?"

"After what you've said—"

"Forget what I've said." He cut her off quickly. "I haven't said anything."

"But you have."

"Then you must consider the possibility that you may have misinterpreted it." He paused. "You were very impressed with Colonel Butler's performance under stress. That's understandable—he's an extremely competent man. He wouldn't be where he is, doing what he's doing, if he wasn't. You're only telling me what I already know, Frances."

"What else do you want?" She heard her voice sharpen defensively. "What else do you expect?"

"From you—I don't want sentences beginning 'I suppose you

could say'. I know what I'd say. I want to know what you can say. I want to know what you *felt*."

Now he was spelling it out, what she had already sensed. And now she could also sense the urgency beneath his patience, like blast-furnace heat through thick asbestos.

But how did he know that she had *felt* anything about Colonel Butler? And even if he thought he knew—he couldn't know a thing like that, it wasn't possible to do more than think it—why did he want to know what she felt? Of what conceivable value would that be to him?

"Come on, Frances—" the voice out of the dark was gentle, but inexorable "—just tell me what you felt about him. It's quite simple."

"It isn't simple—" Her own voice sounded harsh and uncertain by comparison. "No, I don't mean that—it's very simple. But it isn't rational. I mean, I can't explain it rationally."

"Then don't explain it. Just describe it."

"But it's too fanciful."

"So . . . you wouldn't put it in a report to Brigadier Stocker—I accept that. But you are not reporting to Stocker now, you are reporting to me. And I want an answer."

Frances felt a stirring of fear again, but this time it was a fear she could handle. Indeed, it was almost—or not almost, but actually—a sensation she found pleasing: if fear was a habit-forming drug then there were some varieties of it to which she was immune, like the briefcase fear; but this variety was indistinguishable from pure excitement, like the recurrent dream of bird-flight she had had in the old days—in Robbie's days—when she had not understood how she could fly, or why she was flying, but only that the ground was falling away from her and she was free of it.

So now she was in the middle of something she didn't understand, something which was very perilous—to be off the record with Sir Frederick must be altogether perilous: if she was flying, then it was as Icarus had flown, towards the sun—but at least for a moment she was free of restraint, and of the shyness which always clogged her opinions.

"You want me to be—you require me—to be fanciful?"

"Require? Oh yes, I see—'require' according to David Audley—is that it?" The smile was there in the darkness again. "Well, then—yes. I require it, Frances."

"All right. Then I had a feeling—a fancy—about Colonel Butler. If you like . . . an instinct."

"An instinct . . . Yes?"

"I said I thought he was good." She hesitated.

"So you did."

"It was a Freudian choice of words. I didn't mean simply good at his job—efficient, formidable—I meant *good*."

This time she understood his silence. It was an awkward word to digest, even an anaconda might think twice before trying to swallow it whole.

"Good . . . meaning virtuous?" He surprised her by not even attempting to belittle the word down to manageable size with an easier one.

"Yes."

"I see. Which accounts for your disquiet—whatever side a virtuous man is on, that's the right side. Do you think that is invariably the case?"

"Of course not."

"But in this case you hope so—even if it makes your other guess wrong?"

"Is it wrong?"

"A good question. Do you often have instincts like this about people?"

He was playing with her, thought Frances bitterly. And yet she could have sworn that a moment before, when he had required her to tell him what she felt about Colonel Butler, he had been deadly serious.

But that moment was over. "Why are you so interested in my so-called instinct, Sir Frederick?"

"Not only yours, my dear."

"But mine in this instance."

"True. . . . Then for two reasons." He paused. "You see, everyone has the faculty of instinct, more or less—it's a survival from our animal past. Our pre-prehistoric legacy, if you like."

"And I have a special legacy, do I?"

"As it happens, we think you do, Frances. Unfortunately, however, it's a legacy in a very doubtful currency. Because in modern human beings it is heavily devalued—grossly distorted, more accurately . . . by reason in the first place—the Darwinian essential of instinct is independence from reason—and by emotion

81

in the second. In the male of the species reason is the main problem, and in the female it is emotion—generally speaking, of course."

Chauvinist! thought Frances.

"Is that so?" she said coldly.

"Now in your case, Frances, reason and emotion are probably both problems. Whereas in Paul's case reason is undoubtedly by far the larger problem—"

They had probably been unable to find any emotions at all in Paul, except possibly anger and pride, decided Frances.

"—so much so that he'll probably have to make do without instinct altogether, and manage with experience and knowledge. But then fortunately he has an exceptional memory, and very considerable powers of observation. . . . But that's beside the point. In *your* case, Frances, it's almost as though reason and emotion sometimes cancel each other out, and you are left . . . as it were . . . with pure instinct."

"Sometimes?"

"Yes. In the controlled tests we gave you a few years ago—and as confirmed by subsequent field observations—we gave you a score of four out of ten on a notional scale."

"Four?" Frances felt deflated. If she was a pre-prehistoric female animal under the skin, she wasn't a very efficient one, clearly. "Four?"

"Four out of ten."

"So I can't rely on my instinct, then."

"You certainly cannot. If you could you'd be an animal, my dear—you wouldn't be talking to me here in the dark, you'd be hunting me for supper. There's a million years of evolution, not to mention a few thousand years of civilisation, between nine-point-nine out of ten and four out of ten."

She stared at him. Four-out-of-ten lacked night-vision too. And four-out-of-ten was cold and confused.

"Then . . . if my score is so low . . . why—"

"Low? My dear Frances, it isn't *low*. The consistent mark for instinct—among experienced officers—is *two*. And anything near three is exceptional."

The chilly fingers between her shoulder blades were not those of the night. "And four?"

"Four is phenomenal. Literally . . . because we've never had a four. Which means sometimes—no, I'm not going into the details.

82

One day I'll arrange a meeting between you and our psychological people. Only you'll have to be careful with them—four years ago they wanted to keep you and take you to pieces to see how you worked. Huh!"

Frances frowned into the darkness between them. Four years before there had been a lot of tests—everything from conventional I.Q. papers and ink blots to weird guessing games and an elaborate version of hunt-the-thimble. They had seemed to go on for an unconscionable time; in fact, hers had gone on longer than anyone else's, which she had assumed was either because she was a woman or because she was a borderline candidate. But she had nevertheless taken them all for granted.

Well, her phenomenal four-out-of-ten instinct hadn't worked then, that was for sure! she decided grimly.

"The fact was—and is—that you are more valuable to us, my dear," concluded Sir Frederick. "But let's go inside—you must be perished with cold. It was altogether thoughtless of me to keep you out here in the dark, beautiful though it is, your night sky."

In the dark, thought Frances. She had been in the dark and she was still in the dark.

"No—wait. You said there were two reasons, Sir Frederick." In the light she would be over-awed by him: out here the odds were evened up.

"So I did. Very well . . . you had never served under Butler before. If we'd told you to go and observe him then I believe your instinct would have been distorted. You would never have had that one clear vision you had today. And that was what I wanted you to have, Frances. It was the first thing you had to have."

The first thing?

"But I was wrong. It wasn't a clear vision."

"Have I said that?"

"You've implied it, Sir Frederick."

"I've implied no such thing. You've doubted your instinct, and that's good. You must never rate it higher than a suspicion—but that's a very different thing."

"Are you telling me I'm right about Colonel Butler?"

"No, Frances. I'm telling you I *think* you're right. I think—and I rate two-point-five—I *think* that in a few minutes . . . a few of your out-of-time minutes, Frances . . . in a few minutes you came up with an instinctive certainty which our top personnel selection experts couldn't give me in a year. Because they'd be afraid to—they don't have the equipment to do it, the equipment doesn't exist—so I couldn't require them to do so. Do you understand now?"

Top personnel selection experts.

Personnel selection.

Selection.

They had been watching Colonel Butler.

And it was a matter of internal security—

She had had the right answer, almost. Prompted by Paul, and spurred on by Sir Frederick's presence, she had had the right answer, only she had got it back to front.

"You're going to promote him."

"Not quite. We may promote him. We are contemplating his promotion. But there are questions to be answered first." Sir Frederick emitted a sound which she couldn't identify in the dark. Perhaps it was a back-to-front laugh. "My dear Frances, you are doing something now which the workers of the world want to do . . . and what the democratic principle is supposed to do . . . although looking at the back benches of the Commons—and the front bench too in places—I have my doubts about that. The only thing you can say for it is that it works better than behind the Iron Curtain, a lot better. . . . You are participating in the election of your boss. Indeed, you have the veto."

"The veto?"

"In effect—very possibly." The back-to-front sound reached her again. She decided that it wasn't a laugh: whatever he was doing, he wasn't laughing. "And you'd better get it right, for everyone's sake, including your own."

"But I don't know—" Frances was suddenly aware that she was hugging the dressing gown to herself so fiercely that the torch was digging painfully into her left breast "—I don't know enough about him to make that sort of decision."

"You haven't finished yet. You've only just started, in fact."

No, thought Frances. *No.*

"Sir Frederick . . ." She had to get it right. "I don't have the experience—I don't have the qualifications. And sod the instinct."

"Excellent!"

That wasn't right, then. "Paul would do it better. He'd enjoy doing it."

84

"Enjoying it isn't a qualification. Not enjoying it—that's a qualification. That happens to be one of Jack Butler's best qualifications for the job we may give him, in my opinion: he'll hate doing it, but he'll do it all the same. And so will you, Frances. So will you."

The torch was hurting her again.

"What will I do?"

Acceptance was painful too. It even hurt to know that he was right—that he had been right all along. How did he know more about her than she knew herself? Was that two-point-five? And if it was, then what use was four-out-of-ten?

"First you'll read a special report on him. Then you'll decide what you wish to do—who you wish to see, where you wish to go. All that will be arranged for you. All you have to do is to ring a number which I shall give you." He paused. "As of now you're a VIP, Frances."

Dry mouth, fast pulse, cold back. What clinical symptoms were they?

"To whom do I report?"

"The same number."

"Can I ask for advice?"

"Whom have you in mind?"

"David Audley." No question about that. In fact, now she thought about it, it was a mystery why they weren't giving this job to David, rather than to her, because David knew Colonel Butler better than anyone else.

"David's in Washington. He's busy."

"But I'd like his advice."

"No. Not David."

Categorical negative. There was information there, of a sort. She would need to think about that.

"Group Captain Roskill, then."

No back-to-front sound this time. Just nothing.

"I think you'd better read the report first."

I don't feel like a VIP, thought Frances. But there was no percentage in asking that question. Come to that, she wished now that she hadn't asked the question about David Audley . . .

She'd have to be more careful about asking questions in future.

There was one question which couldn't be avoided, though.

"What job is Colonel Butler in line for?"

"Don't you know?" He seemed almost surprised. "As yet you don't really need to know, anyway."

So she ought to know. So Paul Mitchell, if he thought about it, was bound to know—and the sooner she extricated herself from the question, the better, before he embargoed Paul too. She hadn't taken her own advice quickly enough.

"It doesn't matter," she shrugged the words at him.

"No. But I tell you what I'll do." He paused. "What was that thesis you were allegedly writing at North Yorkshire University? Something about Tolkien—?"

"It doesn't matter." She switched on the torch. "Let's go inside."

He ignored the light. "*Fairyland*—that's it. It was *Fairyland: From Spenser to Tolkien*."

"'Faerie' actually—'The Land of Faerie', not 'Fairyland'. There's a considerable difference," she said pedantically, directing the beam into his eyes and wishing it was brighter.

"Of course—I beg your pardon! You know your Tolkien backwards?" He blinked at her. "Naturally."

"Naturally." She could hardly deny that now.

"Good. Then I can perhaps let Tolkien explain for me much better than I could." He lifted his hand up into the light, so that for a moment she thought he was shielding his eyes from it. "*The Lord of the Rings*, he called his book, didn't he? 'Rings' in the plural."

A flash of gold caught her eye as he lifted one finger from the others. There was a signet ring on it.

"Rings of power, Frances. The Seven, the Nine, the Three . . . and of course the One. Right?"

She could just about remember that, but obviously he had read the book—the three volumes of it—more carefully than she had, so she'd better keep quiet.

"An interesting concept—rings of power. Fortunately we don't have to contend with the One . . . or at least not in the way the other side has to. Because we do still have machinery for changing the hand that wears it. . . . But we do have other rings, Frances. And like Tolkien's rings they confer great power, and not least the power to bring out either the best or the worst in the wearer."

The gold glinted as he moved his hand in the torchlight.

"So before we give Jack Butler a ring of power we have to know as much about his worst as about his best, that's what it amounts to, my dear."

"His worst?" The question came out before she could stop it.

"That's right. You see ... we know his best—which is very good, no doubt about that, no doubt at all. . . . But there is—how shall I put it?—a loose end which does worry us a bit." He paused, as though 'loose end' was not quite how he wanted to put it. "It's nothing to do with security, really."

No more questions. At least, not until she'd read that report, and maybe not even then, decided Frances.

"A ghost—we want you to lay a ghost from the past, Frances." He nodded, to himself as well as at her. "Can you lay a ghost, do you think?"

"I don't believe in ghosts, Sir Frederick." And in this garden that was just as well, she thought. "So they don't frighten me."

"Very sensible. That is, so far as the ghosts of the past are concerned."

"Are there ghosts of the future?" Damn!

"Oh yes—they are the frightening ones, my dear. When you get to my age you see tomorrow's ghost in the mirror. Tomorrow's ghosts are still alive, but on borrowed time—your job will be to lay those ghosts too, before it's too late. Let's go inside."

After he had gone, which was after she had read and re-read the report, and he had taken it away with him, Frances sat in front of the electric fire, which warmed the sitting room but did not warm her.

There is a loose end which does worry us a bit.

Well, there was a loose end, of course. But there was more to it than that—the very fact that it had been Sir Frederick himself who had come to her, and that he had briefed her in such an eccentric way, so very differently from Brigadier Stocker, aroused her deepest suspicions (the more so as David Audley had always maintined that 'Fred' was the most devious old sod of them all; though, again, since she had never been briefed by him before she had no previous experience there to judge by).

We want you to lay a ghost.

Well, there were ghosts enough in Colonel Butler's file, and not merely his hecatomb of the Queen's enemies either.

General Sir Henry Chesney was an old ghost, rich and benevolent.

And Leslie Pearson Cole was a classified ghost, probably off limits now for ordinary mortals, even temporary VIPs.

But Patrick Raymond Parker was a very public ghost, with a whole string of his own ghosts in attendance; any newspaper morgue would deliver them up to her.

And there were tomorrow's ghosts there too—

Trevor Anthony Bond was still alive somewhere.

And Major Starinov of the KGB was also probably still alive, though for her purposes he might just as well be dead for all the information he could give her.

But the little Misses Butler would be very much alive, though not so little now. Very much alive, and very promising too.

Sir Frederick hadn't told her everything, they never did. And the file hadn't told her what she most wanted to know about the most important ghost of all.

Madeleine Françoise de Latour d'Auray Butler, née Boucard.

Frances stared into the uninspiring glow of the electric fire.

Madeleine Françoise had not originally been a loose end—if she had been then Colonel Butler would never have got this far in the promotion stakes. Madeleine Françoise had been tied up to everyone's sufficient satisfaction, and now something (or someone) had untied her—had raised her ghost, which had not walked for nine years . . .

(A devious old sod, so she had to think deviously too.)

(An old man near retirement; but it couldn't be his job Colonel Butler was lined up for, that was out of the Colonel's league, she was sure of that.)

(Whatever job it was, Sir Frederick wanted him to get it too, but obviously wasn't prepared to fight openly for the Colonel, to risk trouble for him. Was it Paul who had said the Old Sod was sitting tight for his pension and his life peerage? It was certainly Paul who had hinted that the Old Sod was losing his grip, no longer holding off the Minister and the politicians and the Civil Servants as he had once done.)

(She must talk to Paul as soon as possible. Short of talking to David Audley . . . short of disobeying orders . . . Paul was her best bet. Paul wouldn't be frightened of tomorrow's ghosts.)

She was tired, but she didn't want to go to bed.

She got up and crossed to Robbie's side of the fireplace, where Sir Frederick had sat while she read the report, and lifted the three Tolkien volumes out of Robbie's bookshelf.

Then she went back to her own side and sat down again, and

started reading at random, flipping from place to place, picking out the names from the past of her original reading.

Rings of Power . . .

It was dead quiet in the cottage, as always.

There was a letter from her Robbie between the pages of the first volume. She felt no curiosity about its contents, they wouldn't be interesting. She wasn't even very surprised that it was still there; she had dusted the book a dozen times, but she hadn't opened it. Bits of the old days like this were always turning up, she had long since ceased trying to look for them, they didn't matter.

She screwed the letter up into a tight ball and dropped it into the wastepaper basket, and went on reading.

The men of Carn Dûm came on us at night, and we were worsted. Ah! The spear in my heart!

Well, it was still a fairy story—it hadn't changed, and neither had she. There was no spear in her heart for Robbie.

Wizards and trolls and elves with bright eyes and sharp swords, and rings of power . . .

She knew she wasn't really concentrating. Rather, she was wondering how it was she already knew that Colonel Butler hadn't murdered his wife on the morning of November 11, 1969.

VI

As PROMISED, THE side-door of the publican's snug of the Bear and Ragged Staff public house was unlocked one hour before licensed opening time, and ex-Detective Chief Inspector William Ewart Hedges was waiting for her on the other side of it, sitting comfortably beside a newly-lit fire with a copy of the *Daily Telegraph* and a pint of mild.

Telephone Number 01-836 20066, Extension 223, might have the sort of fat, self-satisfied, establishment voice she always found most off-putting, but at least he knew how to deliver the right man to the right place at the right time at short notice, thought Frances.

Predictably, the right man wasn't quite as quick to recognise her, though his double-take as she entered was so fleeting that she wouldn't have noticed it if she hadn't been half expecting it, and his moment of surprise when she dropped the catch behind her was so well camouflaged that it was hardly noticeable at all except as a cautious nod of greeting.

"Mrs Fisher?" He rose to his feet with the characteristic stoop of a tall man accustomed to low beams in old pubs.

"Mr Hedges?" The question was altogether superfluous after he had doubly identified himself by knowing her latest identity, but good manners and a modest demeanour were what the occasion demanded. "It's very good of you to see me, to give me your time like this."

He studied her in silence for a moment, as though taking her to pieces and then reassembling her to see how the parts fitted together.

"That's all right, Mrs Fisher. I've got all the time in the world."

And so he had, thought Frances, and that was the trouble: if he'd still been a serving policeman it would have been in his best interest to co-operate with her to the full, and she could lean on him if he didn't. But a retired man was beyond her reach, he could keep his mouth shut and there was nothing she could do about it.

She smiled.

No smile in return: Ex-Chief Inspector William Ewart Hedges was a man's man, not a ladies' man, that litmus paper test indicated.

"May I see your warrant card, Mrs Fisher, please?" said ex-Chief Inspector William Ewart Hedges.

And a cautious man.

"Of course." Frances opened her bag. For an instant she couldn't remember which compartment held which identity. It would never do to give him Marilyn in her bikini.

"Thank you."

He took his time comparing the Fitzgibbon photograph with the Fisher illusion. And at the end of his time he frowned at her.

"Yes, Mr Hedges?"

"Why the wig, Mrs Fisher?"

Frances blinked at him. "Is it so obvious?"

"No." He shook his head. "It's very professional."

He was making a point: he was informing her that ex-Chief Inspector William Ewart Hedges wasn't to be trifled with. But if he wasn't already a hostile witness, why did he have to make that point?

Hostile as well as cautious?

"Then—why the question, Mr Hedges?"

He nodded. "You're not wearing a wig in your photograph. But it's the same style, and the same colour, your hair. Young ladies don't usually wear mouse-brown wigs . . . But perhaps I shouldn't ask?"

Frances made the connection. The implication of her presence was the re-opening on a nine-year-old case which had never been solved. And that could either mean that there was new evidence, or that Inspector William Ewart Hedges hadn't done his job properly nine years before.

Hostile, then. So at least she knew where she was.

She smiled again. "That's all right . . . As it happens, I'm blonde underneath."

"Blonde? Good gracious!"

"Why 'Good gracious', Mr Hedges?"

He pursed his lips disapprovingly. "You haven't got the face for it, if I may say so . . . without wishing to be personal—the figure, but not the face, Mrs Fisher."

He was telling her that blonde, on her, would be vulgar. (Which, of course, was the exact truth: Marilyn had been nothing if not vulgar.)

He was also establishing his superiority, and that would never do.

She took the warrant card from him, and as she did so Mrs Fisher was born. Marilyn Francis would have laughed, and would have given him something to look at. Mrs Fitzgibbon would have been embarrassed, and might have blushed. But the arrogant Miss Warren would have been angry, and Mrs Fisher and Miss Warren were sisters under the skin.

"I have my job to do, Mr Hedges." She put the card into her bag and snapped the bag shut. "The Assistant Chief Constable has told you why I'm here, I take it?"

He started to nod, but Mrs Fisher didn't give him time to admit that the ACC (Crime)—or maybe it was the ACC (Operations)—had indeed disturbed his leisurely retired breakfast with a phone call.

"What did he tell you?" asked the frowning Mrs Fisher.

"Not a lot," said Hedges defensively.

Attack, attack, attack!

"Nine years ago. You were in charge of the case."

"Yes."

"Do you recall it?" Mrs Fisher pressed her point.

"Yes."

"You recall it? After nine years?"

"Yes—" His eyes clouded momentarily "—I remember it."

Sod Mrs Fisher, decided Frances instinctively. After a very short acquaintance she didn't like Mrs Fisher. What was more important, this man would remember nine years ago and Colonel Butler for his own reasons, and not because Mrs Fisher was a hard little bitch with a wig and a warrant card and the ACC's blessing. It would be Frances, not Mrs Fisher, who made William Ewart Hedges talk.

"It's a long time, Mr Hedges," said Frances. "But it's important that you do remember."

He looked at her strangely, as though he was seeing her for the first time—and seeing Frances, and not Mrs Fisher, or anyone else out of her bag.

The fine art of interrogation David Audley had always maintained, *It's a game, and it's a duel, and it's a discipline, and it's a job like any other. But in the end it's an art. And that means, in the end—or it may be the very beginning—you may have to risk losing in order to win.*

"It's important for Colonel Butler," said Frances.

Hedges frowned at her. "Colonel—?"

Nine years ago, thought Frances. It had been Major Butler then, and although the ranks hadn't mattered after that, it would be Major Butler that Inspector Hedges remembered.

"Major Butler," corrected Frances.

"Would you like something to drink, Mrs Fisher?" Hedges gestured to the chair on the other side of the fire. "I'm sorry—I'm forgetting my manners."

She needed a drink. "A whisky—would that be possible?"

Why had she said that?

"Any particular brand?" he smiled at her. "They have some very fine malt here."

Frances sat down, and without waiting for an answer he swung round to the empty bar counter behind him. "Isobel! One large Glenlivet, if you please!"

He turned back to her. "Nine years ago . . ."

Malt whisky. Nine years ago she had never even heard of malt whisky, thought Frances. Nine years ago she had never tasted whisky in her life, in her nineteen sheltered years. And now she didn't know (except that it was a cold day, and she was colder still) why she had asked for whisky—or why he had offered, of all whiskies, the one she knew how to drink, from the years between.

He nodded at her, a nod for each year. "A year or two back—maybe not . . . Or not so well. But now . . . yes, I can remember it."

Was that how it was? thought Frances bleakly. In the end, was it the ones that got away that came back to mind, yesterday's ghosts?

"I'm glad to hear it," she lied. Or, at least for the time being, didn't lie. "This one bugged you, did it?"

"Bugged?" He winced slightly at the slang. "No—"

He cut off as Frances stared past him, and then turned towards the bar. "Ah . . . thank you, Isobel."

It was the publican's lady—and she was looking at Frances with considerable surprise.

"Thank you, Isobel," repeated Hedges.

Isobel looked from Frances to the tumbler in her hand, and Frances understood the raised eyebrows. It was not a ladylike measure.

"Would you like some water, madam?"

As Frances estimated the tumbler's contents—more like three fingers' generous measure than two—memory twisted inside her. Robbie had taught her to drink malt, but she had also learnt bitterly what his own measures signified: one for pleasure and relaxation

93

over his books and his music, two for sleep and forgetfulness, and three to nerve him again to fumbling passion with his unresponsive partner. And for all the good it did him, he might have doubled the dose.

"No, thank you." She smiled mechanically. Perhaps he'd have done better to have doubled hers, three had only tightened every nerve in her to do what he had wanted, but hadn't helped her to deceive him in the doing; and that had been a disaster out of which not even Marshal Foch could have attacked his way.

Isobel gave her one last, very old-fashioned, glance, and ducked back into the depths of the pub; Hedges swept the glass off the bar and presented it to her.

"Thank you, Mr Hedges."

She sipped the fiery stuff, and thought as she did so how very strange it was that the spirit itself—this ardent spirit which had always failed to arouse any ardour in her—the thing itself hadn't instantly reminded her of Robbie, but only the quantity of it which had been poured into the tumbler, a purely visual memory. But then ever since Marilyn had been terminated—or perhaps it was ever since the bomb, as though its concussion had shaken loose some defensive shield in her head—her memory had been playing tricks on her, reminding her of what she didn't want, and didn't need, to remember.

Hedges was staring at her, and with a start she realised that she had been staring at him across the rim of the tumbler, and not seeing him at all.

"Do you want to know about her . . . or him, Mrs Fisher?" Being looked through seemed to have disconcerted him slightly, the tone of his voice told her. "The wife or the Major?"

The Major.

The nine years fell away from Frances at last. Nine years ago (she had been a student nine years ago, and a spinster, and a virgin, and the secretary of the University Labour Club, and an admirer of Anthony Wedgwood-Benn; and now she was none of those things and nine years might have been nine million) . . . and nine years ago Colonel Butler had been a major, and before that a captain, and before that a lieutenant, and before that an officer-cadet, and before that a corporal, and before that a private, and before that a schoolboy, and before that a child and a baby and a glint in his father's eye in a backstreet house on the wrong side of the tracks (Paul had been right

94

there—right as usual); but for her he would always have been *Colonel* Butler if it hadn't been for ex-Detective Chief Inspector William Ewart Hedges (who, nine years ago had been Detective Inspector Hedges), who had suddenly put *Major* Butler in another perspective of time, his own perspective—with Butler pickled forever in the aspic of a police report as *Major*—but one which opened all the other perspectives to her . . . even the perspective of the future, in which (although rank didn't really matter in the department, and she didn't even understand what her own grade of assistant-principal meant)—in which they would surely promote him to Brigadier if . . . if she, Mrs Fisher, Mrs Fitzgibbon and Miss (nine years ago) Frances Warren, the student-spinster-virgin-admirer, gave him a clean bill of health, pronouncing him fit to wear one of Sir Frederick's Rings of Power for better and not for worse, whatever that might mean.

The Major—

Even the deferential way he had pronounced the rank told her something: *Et tu*, William Ewart Hedges, and she must make an allowance for that.

But there was no more time to think of that now. There would be time for that later.

At least it had all flashed through her mind quickly: after he had said *The wife or the Major?* he had reached for his pint of mild, hitherto untouched, and now he was just setting it back on the table, two inches drawn from the brim.

The wife or the Major?

Major and Mrs Butler.

Major John (but always Jack) Butler, MC (General list).

Mrs Madeleine Françoise de Latour d'Auray Butler, née Boucard.

Lord! thought Frances, still staring at Hedges but thinking a carbon copy of the thought she had had the night before when she had first encountered the name—*Lord!* If there was a story in the losing of her more than that in Sir Frederick's file there must also be a story (which the file had totally omitted) in the winning of her, if she was anything like her name. The very idea of Butler married was hard to swallow, but Butler carrying off a *Madeleine Françoise de Latour d'Auray Boucard* took her breath away before she could swallow the idea. It sounded altogether too much like a romance from a woman's magazine, and even if the truth would surely be prosaic and dull she could no longer resist the temptation of asking the question she hadn't dared to put to Sir Frederick the night before:

"Was she beautiful, Mr Hedges?"

It wasn't the answer, or the form of the answer anyway, he had been expecting.

"Didn't they show you a picture, then? There were a lot of 'em about at the time, as I remember. Hundreds."

Of course there would have been, thought Frances.

"No."

"I expect they could find one for you."

"Was she?"

"Beautiful?" He took another pull of his beer, but more slowly, as though he had decided that just as she had made him wait while she surfaced from her own deep thoughts, so he had a right to make her wait for his own to come up from the past. "Have you seen the daughters?"

She shook her head.

"No? Well, they say the eldest girl—the one that's at college now—they say she's the spitting image of her mother." He drew a vast snowy handkerchief from his pocket and wiped his mouth with it. "I couldn't see it at the time, I must say. Except for the colouring, of course . . ."

The one at college *now*. So he had already done some checking of his own. But naturally.

"The colouring?"

"Red hair." He nodded. "All of 'em had it—the Major, the wife, and the three little girls. Like peas out of the same pod, they were, the girls."

"She had red hair?" Frances conjured up Colonel Butler's short-back-and-sides, which had been clipped so close that it was almost *en brosse*. Yet when she thought about it now it had been not so much red as grey-faded auburn.

"More like chestnut—what they call 'titian', I believe." That candid look of his was back again as his eyes flicked briefly to the mouse-wig covering her blonde crowning glory. "Very striking, it was."

"But you never actually saw her, did you?"

"No, I never actually saw her. None of us did." He paused. "But there was this picture of her, colour picture." He paused again. "They say it didn't do her justice."

96

"Who said?"

"The milkman. The postman." He shrugged. "The shopkeepers in the village . . . the woman who cleaned the house and kept an eye on the little girls when she was out."

She had been beautiful. He hadn't said it out loud, but he had shouted it nevertheless, more loudly than if he had actually said it. And she, Frances, had known it all along—the certainty had been there in her original question: not 'Was she *pretty*, Mr Hedges?' but 'Was she *beautiful*, Mr Hedges?' Not a four-out-of-ten certainty, but a ten-out-of-ten certainty.

But how?

The fire blazed up and she felt its heat on her face, and she shivered.

Wife to Colonel Butler: *Madeleine Françoise de Latour d'Auray Boucard, born La Roche Tourtenay, Indre-et-Loire, 4.8.28.*

"She was forty-one years old," said Frances.

He gazed at her impassively. "Was she now? I suppose she would have been about that, yes . . . But she didn't look it." The light of the flames flickered over his face, emphasising its impassivity. "You'll have to look at the eldest daughter—that's your best bet, Mrs Fisher, if you want to know what she looked like . . . and add a few years."

A few years. The eldest daughter—Diana, Sally or Jane? Diana for choice. . . . The eldest daughter would be 19 now, maybe 20, thought Frances irritably, struggling with the mathematics. Diana Butler, the Art student, but with the dominant de Latour d'Auray Boucard genes which made her the spitting image of her mother. It was hard to imagine the John (but always Jack) Butler genes not being the stronger ones.

"So if she's alive she'd be fifty now," thought Frances aloud, the maths falling into place at last.

"If."

Death and decay and dissolution coffined the *if*, buried it deep and erected a headstone over it.

"But she's not, you mean?"

"You've read the reports, Mrs Fisher." Just a shade testy now, he sounded.

"Yes, Mr Hedges. And the Assistant Chief Constable's submission." She was losing him, and she didn't know why. "In effect—'missing'. But you think she's dead?"

97

He drew a deep breath through his nose. "There's no proof."

"But you think she's dead, all the same."

"What I think isn't proof." He looked at her steadily. "What do you want me to say, Mrs Fisher?"

Now she was fighting for an answer, and it was almost as important to know why she had to fight for it as to win the answer itself. So although it would be the easiest thing in the world to say, simply: 'I want you to say what you think, Mr Hedges', that wasn't good enough any more, because it would only win half the battle, and she needed to win both halves now.

So again it had to be instinct, the heart and not the head.

"Mr Hedges . . . I've got a difficult job to do. I'm not sure that it isn't impossible—to be honest."

Bad word—wrong word. She wasn't being honest.

"A dirty job."

Better word. And ex-Detective Chief Inspector Hedges knew all about dirty jobs, too.

"She walked out of the front door. And she disappeared off the face of the earth—"

She could have put it better than that: the deadpan police reports, the dozens of minutes of inquiries by dozens of different policemen, all had the garlic smell of death on them, the smell of killing.

"Did he kill her, Mr Hedges? Could he have killed her?"

Even that wasn't enough. But did she have to give him everything, leaving herself nothing?

"He could have, Mrs Fisher. Physically, he could have." He stared at her. "Unless you have an alibi for him."

"But you think he didn't?"

Still he wouldn't give her anything.

"Yet you treated it as murder from the start, Mr Hedges."

"No." He relaxed. "We got to it quickly, that's all."

She had made a mistake—she had let him get away from her.

He shook his head. "Cases like this, Mrs Fisher—you have to bear in mind that a lot of murders start with missing persons. Or, to put it another way, every missing person is a potential murder victim. So every report, it's not just kicked under the carpet—it's taken seriously.

"On the other hand, having said that, it is a matter of the actual circumstances. With a young kid, for instance, even if there's a history of his running off, I used to get moving straight off. But with a woman . . . saving your presence, Mrs Fisher . . . you get quite a lot of women just sloping off, one way or another, and there are inquiries you've got to make first. Like, if there's been a row . . . or if there's another man—you can't just jump straight in."

"But this wasn't like that."

"No, it wasn't—precisely. She just went off for a bit of a walk, and she said she wasn't going for long." He paused, staring reflectively at a point just above Frances's head. "She didn't even take her bag with her . . ."

"And it started to rain."

"That's right. . . . It came on to rain quite heavily, and she only had a light coat with her." Another reminiscent pause. "It was the cleaning woman phoned us in the end—she'd waited long past her time, and she wanted to get home. But she couldn't leave the little one all by herself."

Jane Butler, aged six. One of the identical peas. Not at school because she had flu. Mother had sat up with her part of the night, which was why she had wanted a breath of fresh air . . .

He focused on her. "But you know the details, of course."

And there weren't really many details to know at that, thought Frances. In fact, that was the whole trouble, the beginning and the end of it: Mrs Madeleine-and-all-the-rest Butler, aged 41, had stepped out for a breath of air after having spent a disturbed night with a sick child, and it had started to rain, and she hadn't been seen again from that November day to this one, nine years later. And so far as the local CID and the Special Branch had been able to establish, she hadn't met anyone, or even been observed by anyone. She had taken nothing with her, no money, no cheque book, no means of identification; and she had left behind her no debts, no worries, no fears. She had turned a quiet piece of English countryside into a Bermuda Triangle.

"How did you get on to it so quickly, Mr Hedges?"

He half-shrugged, half shook his head. "Routine, really. Like I said . . . we don't take missing persons lightly."

"Yes?"

"Well . . . in a case like this it's usually the uniformed patrol officer who answers the call, and he's likely to be a sensible lad. . . . He'll talk to the person who called us, and have a bit of a quick scout-round, maybe. And if he doesn't like what he finds he'll phone his sergeant pretty sharpish—because if there is something badly wrong then time can be important—and he'll say 'I don't like the look of this one, guv'nor', like as not."

"And in this case he didn't like the look of it?"

"That's right." He nodded. "You see, he knew there hadn't been any local accidents that morning—road accidents involving personal injury—which was the most obvious answer. And she wasn't the sort of woman to just go off and not phone back if she'd been delayed anywhere. . . . There was the kiddie in bed, see . . . And although it had stopped raining by then there isn't much cover on those country roads at that time of year—it'd be about the same time as now, with most of the leaves off the trees. So she'd have likely got quite wet, with just a light coat and a head-scarf . . . It just didn't smell right to him."

"Yes?"

"What did it smell of, you mean? Well . . . he thought it might be a hit-and-run, with her in a ditch somewhere maybe . . ." He trailed off.

There was something else, something left unsaid or something not yet said. Frances waited.

"Or maybe worse . . ." He drank some more of his beer, and then wiped his mouth again with the table-cloth handkerchief. "You see, usually, whether we're really worried or not, the first thing to do when a woman goes missing is to get on to the husband. If there's any trouble of any sort . . . if he isn't part of the trouble himself, then nine times out of ten he knows what is, or he's got some idea of it. Or he knows where she'd go, anyway—to her mother, or her sister, or even to some friend of hers nearby . . ." He trailed off again.

There had been no mother, no sister and no nearby friend. But what was more interesting was that Hedges didn't like talking about Colonel—Major—Butler, so it seemed.

"But we had a bit of a problem there at first—or our lad did. Because the cleaning woman had told him the Major had gone up north on business—driven off at the crack of dawn, the wife had told her—but the woman didn't know where. And she didn't know what his business was, of course. . . . She thought he wasn't in the army any more, she said, and she thought he maybe worked for the Government in London. But she didn't know what at."

The cleaning woman had been a smart lady, thought Frances.

"Normally this isn't a problem." Hedges shook his head. "You just ask the neighbours. But there weren't any neighbours, and they hadn't been living there long——not near neighbours, anyway. So the sergeant got the constable to find their address book, and told him to try the London numbers in it." He gave Frances an old-fashioned look. "There was one of them in the front with no name to it, so he tried that first."

01-836 20066, thought Frances. Or its 1969 equivalent . . . The cleaning lady and the constable had both been smart.

Hedges nodded at her. "So that was when we really got our skates on—the CID *and* the Special Branch. But that's all on record, of course . . . what we did, and what they did. You probably know more about that than I do, Mrs Fisher." The old-fashioned look had a sardonic cast to it now. "Like what the Major's business up north was, that day. We never got a 'Need to Know' clearance for that."

"What were you told?"

"Verbally . . ." Hedges blinked and paused, as though for a moment the memory eluded him. "I was told to discount him from my inquiries—that was at first. Then later on I was told that I must check for sightings of him, or of his car, in the vicinity at the material time. Which we would have done as a matter of routine by then if we hadn't been warned off in the first place, of course."

Frances was tempted to ask him what he had deduced from that change of instructions, but then quickly rejected the temptation. He could only have made the wrong deduction, that the Major had provided an alibi which had not in the end seemed water-tight to the Special Branch; and by telling him how the actual facts had been so very curiously and inconclusively different she might colour his memory.

She waited.

His lips compressed into a tight line. "There were no such sightings, Mrs Fisher."

In that moment Frances decided that she would have to investigate the circumstances of Colonel Butler's not-alibi herself, and not merely ask for them to be re-checked as she had intended. It would mean another wearisome, time-consuming journey north, with little promise of further enlightenment because they had never seemed to have an rhyme or reason to them in the first place, let alone any connection with Mrs Butler's disappearance. But nevertheless, they remained as a small, strange inconsistency, like an irrelevant but mysterious footnote at the bottom of the Special Branch report.

She pulled herself back to the more pressing problem. "Is that what you meant by 'Could have', Mr Hedges? He could have been in . . . the vicinity at the material time—in another car, say?"

"We never traced another car. He would have had to have hired one from somewhere, and left it somewhere." Hedges paused. "When he finally arrived that evening he was driving his own car, anyway. And we never turned up any unaccounted car hirings for that morning." He stared into the fire for a second or two, and then glanced up sidelong at her. "Assuming he couldn't prove his movements for that morning—where he was, or where he should have been . . . if he didn't go north, as the cleaning woman said . . . if he'd waited around somewhere until his wife came out . . . if he knew where she was going . . ."

He was building up the 'ifs' deliberately, as though to demonstrate what a flimsy edifice they made.

"If he'd had a confederate, of course . . . but then no one saw any strangers hanging around, and in a country district like that it's surprising what people notice . . . it's possible, but the timing would have had to be good if they didn't want to risk being noticed . . . But it's possible—anything's possible."

But not likely, he meant. For a moment Frances was reminded of her own dear old Constable Ellis, who prided himself on knowing everything that moved on his own rural area beat by day, and most things that moved by night. Though, of course, he was a very old-fashioned copper, altogether different from the wild boys of the Met. with whom she had worked in the spring, the new-fashioned coppers who had unashamedly fancied their chances of extending inter-departmental co-operation into the nearest convenient bed.

Well—*sod it!*—this was inter-departmental co-operation too, but at least he wasn't looking at her with that calculating, undressing stare which already had her on her back staring over his shoulder at the patterns of light and shadow on the ceiling.

Possible plus Unlikely equals Could Have.

They had given him a possible suspect in a possible murder case. But then, for security reasons, they had stopped him carrying through any investigation of Colonel—Major—Butler's not-alibi, and had left him only with the suspicion that there might be something he'd missed somewhere; and although he was speaking now without any apparent rancour, nine years after the event, that rankled still.

Only it didn't rankle in the way she'd expected: whatever was in his mind now, it wasn't the nagging doubt that his Major had got away with murder in his patch.

Suddenly and vividly Constable Ellis came into her mind again: Constable Ellis sitting opposite her across her own fireplace, just as Hedges was sitting across from her now—Constable Ellis on one of his paternal visits to her, with a steaming mug of cocoa in his hands—she had heated the water for it on the primus stove: it had been during the power workers' strike, when he'd called on her every time it was the village's turn to be blacked-out. . . . Constable Ellis telling her how—

God, but she'd been slow! He'd even told her himself, had William Ewart Hedges—once directly, and half-a-dozen times implicitly—and she'd failed to pick up the message.

What was worse, it had also been there between the lines of the report she'd read the night before. Hedges had merely confirmed it.

"Would you like another drink, Mrs Fisher?"

Frances looked down at her empty glass with surprise. She had drunk the stuff without noticing it, and now the warm feeling deep inside her was indistinguishable from the excitement that tightened her muscles and made her throw out her chest almost as far as Marilyn had once done for Gary.

Cool it!

"Good heavens!" Girlish smile. "No, thank you, Mr Hedges."

David Audley: *The time to be extra careful is when you think you've won—when you think you know.*

"I don't want to be breathalysed before midday."

Because she hadn't won. There simply hadn't been a duel: the duel had been in her imagination, because of her own slowness and stupidity. Simply, because she hadn't known which side he was on, she hadn't understood that Mrs Fisher and ex-Chief Inspector William Ewart Hedges had been on the same side from the start.

So she had to get it exactly right now.

"But can I get you something?" She pointed at his empty tankard.

He shook his head, his eyes never leaving hers. Although he hadn't admitted it, he knew, just as well as she did, that they'd moved on from *Could have* to *Didn't*.

Get it right. Chest in, extinguish girlish smile.

"Patrick Parker, Mr Hedges."

Patrick Raymond Parker, born Liverpool 11.7.41. s. Michael Aloysius Parker and Margaret Helen McIntyre—

Again, he knew. And this time he knew if anything even better than she did: the print-out from the Police National Computer, the circular, the telex, laying it on the line that the North Mercian Police Force had turned a fatal crash on the motorway and six missing women into an Incident Room, complete with a possible murderer and victims, and even a hypothetical *modus operandi*.

"Uh-huh. Patrick Parker, of course." This time he didn't nod, he merely acknowledged the fatal name with a single lift of the head, pointing his chin at her. "But that was never proved."

Never proved, like everything else, thought Frances bitterly.

Patrick Parker, *born Liverpool 11.7.41.*—a blitz baby, conceived in emergency, carried in fear and born twenty-eight years before to the sound of air raid warnings and bombs to *Michael Aloysius Parker and Margaret Helen McIntyre*—Patrick Parker had slammed into the back of a lorry (which had braked to avoid a car, which had skidded to avoid another car, which had swerved to avoid another car which had overtaken another car without giving a signal—it happened all the time, but this time fatally) four weeks after Madeleine Françoise de Latour d'Auray Butler née Boucard had said 'I won't be very long' to her cleaning woman. And although they'd never traced either the car that had given no signal (perhaps there were no such cars, anyway: there had only been the first car driver's word for that chain of events. But it didn't matter, anyway), they had found Stephanie Alice Cox, spinster aged 26, as well as Patrick Parker, bachelor aged 28, in the wreckage of the maroon Ford embedded in the back of the lorry.

Only, while Patrick had been where they expected him to be, safety-belted and transfixed by his last moment of agony in the driver's seat, Stephanie had not been found in the passenger's seat beside him; she had been travelling less conventionally and far more uncomfortably in the boot of the car; though not really uncomfortably, since she hadn't felt a thing, even at the moment of impact, because she'd been strangled ten hours before the lorry-driver jammed his foot on the air-brakes.

"I agree. It was never proved," Frances nodded.

Madeleine Françoise Butler, not proved.

And Julie Anne Hartford, not proved.

And Jane Wentworth, not proved.

And Patricia Mary Ronson, not proved.

And, not quite proved, Jane Louise Smith—

Only Stephanie Alice Cox, *proved*.

(Stephanie Alice Cox hadn't even been reported missing when the car in front of the lorry had skidded, but then Stephanie Alice Cox's mother didn't count one night's absence as anything out of the ordinary for Stephanie Alice.)

"But she could have been one of them, couldn't she?"

Hedges rocked on his seat. "Yes . . . she just could have. He picked up one of them in the morning. Of the likely ones, that is."

"And not all of them were scrubbers. Jane Wentworth wasn't."

"She was the one whose car broke down? That's true. And she wasn't so young, either—that's also true." He had raised an eyebrow at 'scrubber', as though it wasn't a word he expected from her. But then he could hardly be expected to know that yesterday she—or at least Marilyn—had been a card-carrying member of the National Union of Scrubbers, thought Frances.

In fact, Marilyn would have fitted into that list of likely pick-ups for a free-spending psychopath, as to the manner born.

She shivered. He'd been good-looking, nicely-spoken with just a Beatles-touch of Liverpool, and—so his mates had recalled—surprisingly gentle for a skilled operator of such a big earth-moving machine. But also a murderer.

"And the date fits too, Mr Hedges. It was a Tuesday, and he wasn't back at work until the Wednesday." The shiver remained with her as she thought of the long stretches of embankment on Patrick Parker's ten miles of motorway extension, now busy with the thunder of traffic, under which (if the North Mercian Police and the Police National Computer were to be believed) Julie Anne Hartford, Jane Wentworth and Patricia Mary Ronson would lie until Doomsday, and maybe Jane Louise Smith and Madeleine Françoise Butler as well.

He shook his head. "The date helps, but it isn't conclusive. If he did kill them, he never killed to a recognisable cycle. And the distance is right on the very edge of his radius—maybe a little beyond it."

"But you don't know how far he went. You never knew where he went."

"North Mercia put him next to a couple of them—in the same pub as one of them on the night she disappeared."

"He was an opportunity murderer. Lack of opportunity—say on the Monday night—that might have pushed him further out."

"Lack of opportunity?" His mouth twisted. "You don't know modern girls."

"I'm a modern girl, Mr Hedges."

"Would you accept a lift from a stranger?"

"It was raining," said Frances.

"She wasn't far from home." He pressed his advantage. "Would you have accepted a lift?"

"I'm not her."

"She was a lady."

A compliment. The blonde hair was forgotten.

"So was Jane Wentworth. Maybe you don't know modern ladies."

He shrugged. "Maybe."

"But . . . you don't think it was Parker, then?"

He looked at her warily. "I didn't say that at all."

Then he was playing devil's advocate. "So you *do* think it was Parker?"

"I didn't say that either. It could have been Parker. But the circumstantial evidence wasn't strong—it was never strong enough for a coroner's inquest, not for her. And that's a fact."

It was indeed a fact, thought Frances. And it was also a fact that Hedges was well-placed to state: no CID officer of all the forces liaising with the North Mercian Incident Room had worked harder than he had done to connect Patrick Parker with any of their missing women. He had really pulled out all the stops.

And in vain.

"But strong enough to write the case off, Mr Hedges."

"It's still open, Mrs Fisher." He spoke as though his mouth was full of liquid paraffin.

"Of course." She smiled at him innocently. "But Parker remains on your books as the strongest suspect . . . particularly as you'd written Major Butler off the list long before— before Parker's name came over the telex."

Something flickered in his eyes that wasn't a reflection of the flames in the grate. "What makes you think that, Mrs Fisher?"

Frances checked herself just in time. It was as if the ground had trembled beneath her, warning her of a hidden pit in front of her.

Another step—another word, another sentence or two—and she would be over the edge: she would be telling him how clever she was, she would be patronising him, and that would close his mouth just when she needed him to tell her not *what* he thought about Major Butler, but *why* he thought it.

She put her empty glass carefully down on the hearth. It had been David Audley—again, and always, David—who had said in his interrogation lectures that *truth is the ultimate weapon.* So it was time to pretend to drop her guard again. And this time it had to work.

"Of course, my name isn't really 'Fisher', Mr Hedges—as I'm sure you will have guessed."

His face blanked over with surprise.

"But the 'Mrs' is genuine. My husband was killed in Ulster a few years back."

It was more than a few now, strictly speaking. How time accelerated with its own passage! In a year or two Robbie would be ancient history. But in the meantime he surely wouldn't mind helping her, anyway.

"I'm sorry."

"There's no need to be. It was an accident, actually—not the IRA. He was on foot patrol one day, and he slipped on the edge of a pavement just as an armoured personnel carrier was passing. It was a road accident, I always think of it as that, now."

Was that how Major—Colonel—Butler remembered his Madeleine Françoise? If it had been Patrick Parker cruising by . . . she might just as easily have been knocked down by his car on that country road as by the unknowable madness that had driven him.

"We had bought a cottage on the edge of a village, about an hour's run from here. I still live there."

His mother had thought that was a mistake, and that a flat in London, near her work, would be far more sensible, far less lonely. But she would have been just as lonely in London; or even more lonely, since the loneliness of the cottage had been—and still was—something natural and inevitable which she could accept, and with which she could come to terms. And which, if she faced the truth (that ultimate weapon), was what she wanted. (Mother-in-law only wanted to get her married off again as soon as decently possible, anyway; gaining an unwanted daughter-in-law had been bad enough, but then losing a son and gaining only the responsibility of a young widow was unbearable—the more so when the widow had made it abundantly plain that once was enough.)

Mustn't think of all that again though, sod it!

"—but I'm away a lot of the time, so the local police keep an eye on the place for me."

He nodded to that. Keeping an eye on places was also something he understood; and since there was more that he had to understand that was encouraging.

"There's a policeman who comes to see me regularly. He's an old chap, and he's pretty close to retirement—he's very nice and kind, and he knows everything that goes on in the village . . . Like, an old-fashioned bobby."

Was that the right word?

"A dying breed," said ex-Chief Inspector William Ewart Hedges.

It was the right word.

"Yes . . . well, it's got so he's keeping an eye on me as well as the cottage. We drink cocoa together, because he doesn't like coffee. And he tells me I should get married again and have a houseful of babies."

Constable Ellis and Mother-in-law were strange allies, when she thought about them.

"So you should," said William Ewart Hedges.

"Chance would be a fine thing!" A maidenly blush would have been useful, but that wasn't within her histrionic range. "Anyway, he came to see me regularly during the power workers' strike last year, every time it was our turn for a black-out—he'd drop in of an evening to see how I was coping . . . To chat me up, or to cheer me up."

He seemed for an instant to be on the edge of saying something, but then to have thought better of it, closing his mouth on the unspoken words. Perhaps he had felt the ground tremble under him too, thought Frances; perhaps he had been about to say *You seem to be coping well enough, Mrs Not-Fisher. Well enough with power cuts and widowhood both—perhaps too well for your own good, Mrs not-Fisher.*

So the Fitzgibbon façade was on the top line today.

"But one night he was the one who needed cheering up."

(More and more it had been Mrs Fitz who had been cheering up Mr Ellis, and not vice-versa; because Mr Ellis could remember an older world in which he had lived, and which he liked very much

108

better; whereas Mrs Fitz didn't know any better, so that for her the worse was only a small decline from the bad, and the better was just a legend.)

"Yes?" Hedges was looking at her with intense curiosity.

"Sorry." Frances concentrated her mind again. There really was something wrong with her today, the way her thoughts were wandering into irrelevances. It must be post-Cinton (and post-Marilyn) shock, if not post-bomb malaise.

"There was a break-in at the church. . . . Well, not really a break-in, because it wasn't locked properly. The thieves got away with some rather beautiful seventeenth-century silver."

"Yes . . ." Hedges nodded reminiscently. "We've had the same thing hereabouts. It's like taking chocolate from a baby."

Frances nodded back. "They never caught the thieves—the local police didn't."

"Never caught ours either. Long gone, they were. It was four days before we even knew they'd lifted the stuff, and—" He stopped abruptly. "I'm sorry. Go on, Mrs . . . Fisher. Not coppin 'em was putting him down, your old chap, was it?"

"No, Mr Hedges, it wasn't that at all. Quite the opposite, almost." She paused deliberately.

"The opposite?"

She had him now. "Yes. The local CID thought it was one of his local tearaways—a boy they'd had their eye on already. But they couldn't prove it, you see."

"Uh-huh." And he did see too—she could see the seeing of it in his eye. "But he didn't go along with them, eh?"

"It was something he said to me, Mr Hedges. They'd been leaning on the boy—"

"But if they can't prove he did it, Mr Ellis . . . They can't arrest him if they can't prove it, can they?"

"Nor they can, Mrs Fitz. But 'tisn't the point, that isn't. Point is, I can't prove he didn't, neither."

"—and he said that it was just as much a policeman's job to prove innocence at to prove guilt, and that sometimes the innocence was more important than the guilt—the more difficult it was, the more important it was likely to be."

"It's like the Parson says, Mrs Fitz—'Number Nine: Thou shalt not bear false witness against thy neighbour', and that's easy to know when you're doing it. But what price 'Thou shalt bear true witness for thy neighbour'? That's not so easy, I can tell you. Because half the time you don't know what the true witness is—an' the other half, you can't prove it."

(She remembered, as she spoke, that it had struck her as incongruous—not funny, certainly not funny; but incongruous—that her fatherly Constable Ellis should see young Mickey Murphy as his neighbour; Mickey Murphy who might not have lifted the church silver, but who looked at her as though given half a chance he would lift her skirt; but then that was before she herself had declared Colonel Jack Butler to be her neighbour, which was equally incongruous.)

"I see." Hedges sat back in silence for a moment. "You think . . . you believe . . . that for some reason I never really rated the Major as a suspect. Is that it?"

"No, Mr Hedges—I don't mean that." She smiled at him. "I think you came round to it quite quickly. But that wasn't quite what I meant, not really."

"Came round to it?" He seized on the phrase as though determined not to let its meaning escape.

"Oh yes." She nodded. "I agree entirely with your assessment: of all the men I've ever met, the . . . Major is—he seems to me—the least likely to commit a murder. But I have no new evidence to prove it, either."

He frowned at her.

"Proving the negative case is one of the most difficult Intelligence exercises—it always has been," said Francis.

This time he nodded his acceptance. "That's true."

"So I know why I don't *think* he did it, Mr Hedges. But I can't put what I *think*—what my instinct tells me—in a negative report. If I write 'Major Butler seems to me to be of all men the least likely to murder his wife' they'll just laugh at me. They want facts, Mr Hedges—not fancies."

The corners of his mouth drooped. "But I can't give you any facts, Mrs Fisher."

"No. But I want to be sure. So you can tell me what you never put in any report—which was what made you lay off the Major and concentrate on Patrick Parker before you'd ever heard of him. That's what you can give me."

He stared at her for a moment, then through her, and then at her again. "All right . . ." Then he looked at his watch, and then he put his glass back on the bar counter. "Isobel!"

Frances waited.

"It was the little girls—him and the little girls, that night. The way he was."

Isobel appeared, took the glass, and looked expectantly at Frances. "Madam?"

"No thank you." Frances hated to look away from him, even for a second.

"I was there when he came back. He didn't know anything—he saw the police vehicles, of course, so he'd have known something was up, but he couldn't have known what, exactly . . ."

Unless he did know, exactly, thought Frances heretically.

"At that stage I'd been told to count him out. Otherwise I'd maybe have been suspicious—with a wife missing, and you don't like the look of it, it's the husband you look at first . . ." He tightened his lips ". . . I still looked at him pretty sharp, but more out of curiosity than suspicion. Because by that time I knew he was Military Intelligence, and I wasn't sure that his wife going missing might not have something to do with that . . . even though your people said that it didn't, and it was a CID job, not a Special Branch one.

"We had our Special Branch man there, of course. But on a 'Need to Know' basis—he didn't do the talking, I did . . .

"So I gave it to the Major straight, all the details. And why we were worried—we'd already had the dogs out, in the late afternoon, while there was a bit of daylight, and they hadn't found anything."

Isobel appeared at his shoulder. "Here you are, Billy."

'Billy' didn't seem right.

"How much do I owe you, Isobel?"

"Get away!" She disappeared before he could argue.

He took a long pull of the beer, produced the huge handkerchief again, and went through the mouth-wiping ritual.

"He didn't say anything, he just listened. And the questions I asked him, all I got was 'yes' or 'no', nothing more. He didn't say a thing until I'd finished, and then he simply said 'Where are my girls?'

"And I told him we had a policewoman with them. . . . You see, Mrs Fisher, there wasn't anyone locally they knew, having moved in not long before. And the cleaning woman had her own family to look after—and there weren't any relatives, not on either side, that we could trace. So my WPC had given the kiddies their tea, and had looked after them—she'd even helped the eldest one with her bit of homework from school—"

Diana. Now at university, and beautiful like her mother. But then ten or eleven years, and with her bit of homework to do.

"—and then put them to bed—"

That 'bit of homework' at ten years of age was a reminder that they'd all been privately educated from the start, Diana and Sally and Jane, the three peas in the pod.

"—but she couldn't get the little one, that'd had the flu, to go to sleep—"

Jane. Aged fifteen now, but only six then . . . Jane, then at St. Bede's junior preparatory house and now at famous and exclusive St. Bede's School five miles down the road, with her sister Sally (eight then; now seventeen and coming up to her A-levels).

Mathematics. Even as day-girls they'd leave no change from £1,000 a year each at St. Bede's, plus taxi fares if there weren't any buses, which there probably weren't. Plus university keep for Diana. Plus wages for a full-time housekeeper. . . . All that drove home, as nothing else could, the curious fact from the record that Major (then Captain) Butler had been the sole beneficiary of the late General Sir Henry Chesney, sometime owner of Chesney and Rawle Printing & Publishing; and that whatever problems Colonel Butler had (and Major Butler had had, and Captain Butler might have had), they hadn't been—and weren't—money problems.

Sole beneficiary of General Sir Henry Chesney (no relative) equals private means.

Private means equals girls' public school education multiplied by twelve years multiplied by three (plus housekeeper multiplied by nine years).

'No relative' made all that worthy of closer scrutiny. And the more so because although the young (and newly-rich) Captain Butler had sold up Chesney and Rawle's for blue chips—ICI and Marks and Spencer's, but not Rolls-Royce (someone had advised young Captain Butler well)—and had shaken the dust of Blackburn (or the dirt and the grime), which Chesney and Rawle had turned to gold, from his feet . . . nevertheless he had been in Blackburn that November morning, when his wife had disappeared, and not in Harrogate, across the Pennines, where he should have been.

It might be nothing, it might be something. And it might be everything.

"Mrs Fisher?"

"She couldn't get Jane to go to sleep. I'm listening, Mr Hedges." Frances amended her expression to one of close attention.

"Jane?" He frowned.

"The littlest one." She must be more careful. "Jane."

"Yes." He grudged her the knowledge of the smallest Butler's name. "It was Jane—that's right."

Frances kicked herself. He'd been ready to tell her what he'd never told anyone else, and now she was on the cliff-edge of losing him because of her own stupid inattention.

"Yes?" She willed him back from the edge.

Where are my girls?

"He said 'I must go and see them'. And I said 'Is there anything you can tell us, that may be of assistance?' But he didn't seem to hear—he just went to the door, and then he turned back and said 'Do they know that she's missing? What do they know?' like it was something he'd just thought of.

"And I said we couldn't very well keep it from them, but we'd said she'd had to go away. So he looked at me for a moment, and then he went out. And I heard him pause at the bottom of the stairs, as though he was thinking—or as though he was looking at himself in the mirror there, for a moment. And then he went up."

Not looking at himself, that didn't ring true, thought Frances. Of all men, Colonel Butler would be the least likely to need to straighten his regimental tie or smooth his regimental hair, which was too short to need smoothing, before going up to his girls.

"Looking at himself?"

Hedges ignored the question. "A little while after that I heard her laughing."

Frances blinked. "Laughing?"

"I went to the foot of the stairs and called the WPC down. I asked her what they were doing up there.

"She said he'd looked into the elder girls' bedroom, just for a second or two, then he'd gone into the little one's. 'He's reading to her', she said. 'He's got this book, her favourite book. I was reading it to her—it's called *Felicity Face-maker*. I think he's making faces at her.'"

Hedges stared at her, as though he expected her to make a face at him. "Do you know why I'm telling you this?"

There was no answer to that.

"Perhaps you think I've got a remarkable memory—nine years ago?"

There was no answer to that either. 'No' would be a lie, and 'yes' would be a mistake.

"I haven't. Not more than the next man, anyway."

That wasn't a question, it was a challenge.

"There are some things no one forgets," said Frances.

Hedges nodded. "So . . . when I told him how she'd gone missing—his wife—he knew what I was telling him. He knew what I thought, it was in his face. I suppose it must have been in mine, come to that.

"Except there wasn't anything in his face. Not a thing.

"We had a man once—a constable on point duty who went to pull a woman out of a car that'd run into the back of a petrol tanker. It went up just as he was trying to get the door open.

"He didn't get her out. A nice-looking boy he was, too—" he looked away from her for a moment, into the heart of the fire which was burning up nicely in the grate "—and they did remarkably well with him, the surgeons in the hospital. What they couldn't give him back was the muscles, in his face. He had his face back, more or less, but not any expression to go with it.

"And that was the way it was with the Major—Major Butler. No expression for me—and then he went up and made his little 'un laugh . . . and he read to the other two as well . . . took about half an hour, thirty-five minutes—and then back to me. Like he was in shock, and the shock had burnt out the muscles . . . Or as if he was holding himself steady, and if he didn't he'd burst into tears. And he wasn't going to do that in front of a stranger, not ever.

"I had him for about an hour, too. He went through her clothes, just to make sure what she'd been wearing. Or that she hadn't taken anything else to wear."

At that stage he still hadn't been quite convinced: it might have been foul play or it might have been deep design.

"And a couple of days later, after they'd told us we could check on his movements locally, I went through the house with him from top to bottom—because there've been cases we've looked everywhere, and then the missing person's been found dead up in the loft, and been there all the time . . .

"Her private affairs as well—the money and the cheque-book and suchlike; and the passport too—I went through all that with him as well. That's where something turns up, if they've gone off of their own free will, because they've got to live somehow . . . and that way we've traced them sometimes, the wives, but they don't want the husbands to know where they are. And we don't tell on them either, except that they're alive. It's not our job, that."

He shook his head at her. "But we turned up nothing, of course—as you well know.

"But *he* was the same: not moving a muscle . . . Except with the children, and then he didn't care who saw it. He never pretended for me, right from that first evening, only for them— and if one of them came in while I was with him it was like I wasn't there. I've never seen anything quite like it."

"He switched on for them."

"Yes. Switched on is right. He lighted up for them, like a Christmas tree. And each time he did, it damn near fused him."

Character assessment, not proof. But then she'd never expected proof, thought Frances. And who better than Hedges to provide the assessment?

"Then he would have done anything for them—his girls?"

"Yes, Mrs Fisher. He would have done anything for them." Hedges conceded the possibility with the air of a man who was ready for the question behind it. "So long as it didn't hurt them."

There it was, the built-in limitation: three little girls with no relatives, no matter how rich they were, couldn't afford to lose one parent, never mind two. And that had been the risk, if the deed was Butler's.

"He's a clever man, Mr Hedges."

"Aye. And a hard man too, Mrs Fisher. And a trained man."

One of us, he was saying.

"So?"

Hedges took a slow, deep breath. "I was there. I talked to him, I watched him. And I listened to him, what little he said. . . . A very tough customer—and I've met some tough customers in my time, believe you me, Mrs Fisher. So if what you wanted to know is *could he kill*, then the answer is obviously *yes*. He's been a soldier, and he's trained to do it—and he's had enough opportunities, I don't doubt. All of which you probably know about already, anyway."

True enough, thought Frances. In his time Butler had been nothing if not a fighting soldier, and there were graves in his record to prove it, all the way from Northern Europe in '45 to Korea, and back via Aden and Cyprus.

"But killing is one thing—killing under orders—and murder is another. What I saw of him . . . murder, even under orders . . ." His eyes hardened as he stared at her, the moralities of the police and the security service dividing them ". . . I'd say *doubtful*. Or even *very doubtful*."

The eyes accused her.

"And when it comes to the murder of the mother of those little girls of his, no matter how he may have felt about her, then my answer is *no*, Mrs Fisher. Not him. Not in a thousand years."

He paused.

"I can't prove that—I never could prove it. But even if you'd got proof that says otherwise, that you haven't told me about, my advice to you, Mrs Fisher, would be to go back and double-check it. And then check it again.

"And I'll give you three reasons for that, two other reasons.

"The first is that Patrick Parker did it. I couldn't prove that either, but for my money it was his work.

"And the second is . . . if I'm wrong about everything else—about what sort of man he is, and about Parker . . . then you and I wouldn't be here now, Mrs Fisher. If it had been premeditated murder—and for him to come back and do it three hours after he drove away it would have to be premeditated—then he'd have fixed it so there wouldn't be any doubt hanging over him then or now. I'd stake my pension on that. He didn't know about Parker, and he wouldn't have left it hanging in the air like that. He would have had an alibi.

"And the third reason . . . the third reason, Mrs Fisher, is that the second reason is a load of nonsense—the third reason is the best one of all, to my way of thinking.

"I've known a lot of villains in my time, young woman. And one or two good men I'd stake more than my pension on. And the Major was one of them."

116

VII

FRANCES WAITED FIVE minutes after William Ewart Hedges had gone before buying time on Isobel's private line.

01-836 20066.

"Whitehall Trust. Can I help you?"

The voice reminded her unbearably of Mrs Simmonds.

"Extension 223, please."

Click. Scrambler on. Clickety-click-click. Wait.

"Extension 223." The self-satisfied voice.

"This is Fisher. I've talked to Hedges. Have you arranged Brookside House for me?"

"Hullo Fisher. Of course. The Police are there now."

"The Police?"

"Brookside House has had a break-in. Three houses in one morning in the same area—shocking! Nothing valuable stolen, but as the Colonel is on the list we have to send someone down to liaise with the local Special Branch man. Just a simple matter of following the routine—they called us." Smug chuckle. "I'm afraid you'll have to be the one, Fisher dear. Sorry to disturb you, and all that . . . but you're not busy at the moment, so it'll have to be you."

"Why me?"

"I said—you're not busy. Officially you are still part of the Colonel's group. But as he packed you off home you're twiddling your thumbs. So you are the obvious choice—it stands to reason. Right?"

As a short-notice cover story it wasn't bad, but the superiority of the voice roused forgotten memories within Frances—echoes from the past she had never remembered before—

'*Frances Warren and Samantha Perring—fighting in the gym.*' (Miss Widgery's voice had been as sexlessly superior as Extension 223's.) '*I am aware that you did not strike the first blow, Frances. But violence is always inadmissable. And in a young lady it is unpardonable.*'

But Frances Warren had learnt differently since then.

"It doesn't sound simple to me."

"Don't be awkward, Fisher. It's the best we can do in the time available, with the housekeeper there."

"I want her out. I want the house first, and then the children. I want to be alone there."

"Like Greta Garbo . . . You know, you don't ask for easy things, Fisher. The housekeeper is like a limpet, she never leaves the children on their own except on her day off. And then the cleaning woman stays with them—stays the night, too."

Frances waited.

"All right—so we've managed something . . . just so you don't think it's easy, that's all. And it will still require some ingenuity on your part. Or some respectability, I should say—you're not still blonde, are you?"

"No."

"Thank God for that." Extension 223 sniggered knowingly, as though he had the bikini snapshot of Marilyn before him. "It's cost us a favour, too—quite a sizeable one."

"Yes?" Frances just managed to take the waspish note out of her voice. There was no point in letting old angers betray her.

"All right." He sounded disappointed at her subservience. "You must be there shortly after 1400 hours, as our representative—the Police will meet you. Right?"

"Yes." After the first time it was easy.

"At about 1430 the housekeeper will receive a phone-call—they call her 'Nannie', by the way . . . Butler striving for bourgeois respectability, I shouldn't wonder, eh?"

"Yes." Now it was harder again.

"'Nannie' will receive a call from the Matron of the Charlotte Tyson Nursing Home, a Miss Prebble—"

"Who?"

"Miss Prebble. Just listen, Fisher. Matron Prebble is Nannie's best friend, they nursed together in the QARANCs years ago, when Nannie was an army wife. Prebble runs this nursing home, and on her day off Nannie takes over—it's on Nannie's day off too, and night off . . . Just a small place, run on a shoestring. And at the moment it's badly understaffed, so Matron Prebble has no one she can hand over to except Nannie—at short notice. And that's what we've arranged: short notice. Nannie will have to take over tonight."

"How?"

"The home is nearly bankrupt. We've arranged for the Ryle Foundation to offer Prebble a grant—they're an Anglo-Arab group, and they owe us a favour. And they've got money to burn."

Frances had heard of the Ryle Foundation, it had been one of Hugh Roskill's responsibilities.

"Yes?"

"Prebble will phone Nannie. She's got to go to London, and there's no one else she can turn to at short notice, we've made sure of that, too. So that's where you come in, Fisher—you have to convince Nannie you can baby-sit for her. You have to earn your keep, Fisher."

The voice stung Frances. "I've already earned my keep—" she caught herself. "I'm just afraid Butler will be suspicious, that's all."

"Of course he'll be suspicious. It's his business to be suspicious. But he's got a lot on his plate with O'Leary at the moment, and it seems he approves of you, Fisher." The voice was smugly approving. "And I like that—I like that a lot, it's good for us. And I also like the sound of you earning your keep—I like that even more if it means you obtained something from that awkward policeman of yours."

That was interesting. Whether Hedges had originally been awkward because he hadn't been allowed to do his job properly, or because he hadn't done his job properly anyway because he liked his Major Butler, she hadn't time to decide. Nor, for that matter, could she decide whether he hadn't been awkward with her because he liked her, or because he hadn't changed his mind about the Major in nine years.

But that was something she could think about. What mattered now was to sting Extension 223 into confirming her suspicions of him.

"He thinks Colonel Butler's clean."

"Oh?" Extension 223 sounded sceptical. "Indeed?"

"He liked him, too."

"Don't we all! The Thin Red Line in person, of course! But what did he give you, the policeman?" Extension 223 didn't quite slaver over the inference that William Ewart Hedges had revealed something to Colonel Butler's disadvantage, but it was plain to Frances that whatever it might be, it would be received with intense satisfaction.

So Colonel Butler had an enemy where he ought to expect an impartial judge.

"I can't say for sure yet." That was all the more reason why she must play hard to get: it was the least she could do for Colonel Butler, to offset Extension 223's bias against him, and it was also what she wanted to do.

"Not sure?" Now his voice was positively seductive.

"I gave him a dozen chances of saying one particular thing, and he never said it. And then, at the very end, he suggested it—by accident, I think. But I have to be sure, which is why I must get into the house . . . and talk to the children without the housekeeper being there after that."

"Now you're being oracular."

"I could be mistaken, that's all."

Silence at the other end. If she was right about him he'd be thinking now of a way of encouraging her to come back with Colonel Butler's scalp, or not at all.

Still more silence.

"I could be mistaken," repeated Frances, rearranging the emphasis to suggest that she didn't think she was, nevertheless.

"Of course. And we must be absolutely fair—that's essential." The voice changed. "This isn't a witch-hunt. That's the very last thing it must be."

Frances felt confused, even a little disappointed: it was as though another man had taken over, calm and businesslike, and quite unlike the first one.

"We also appreciate that any sort of truth will be difficult to establish now, Fisher," the Number Two voice continued. "But what you in turn must appreciate is that you'll never have a more important assignment than this one. I'm sure you do understand that—you must forgive me for sounding pompous after I may have seemed . . . a little flippant, perhaps."

"Not at all," said Frances.

"And you're right—absolutely right. We cannot afford to make any mistake about Butler. If we do, we'll live to regret it. And some of us may not live to regret it, too. It's up to you—and I shall be at the end of this line twenty-four hours a day to help you. As of now, nothing's too big and nothing's too small if you want it. All you have to do is ask."

The big league.

Sir Frederick had said as much the night before: *As of now you're a VIP, Frances.*

"What's more, nothing goes on the record until you are ready to put it there. You are the boss, Fisher."

Well, there was a Ring of Power, thought Frances. And it was on her finger, to use as she wished.

"You've already done well. To have picked up anything at all from that file . . . and from that policeman. You're not the first one to have tried, believe me."

Frances had the feeling that she'd been tested—

"You are the first one to succeed."

—and that she'd passed the test. No wonder she'd found Hedges so hard to thaw!

"But that's no accident. You were chosen for this. And what's more, I recommend you, Mrs Fisher—off the record." He made the recommendation sound like an unpaid debt she had contracted, but which he expected to collect, with interest, soon enough.

"So . . . what do you want us to set up for you next—after you've finished in the house, that is?"

He was already taking for granted that whatever it was she was looking for, it was there and she would find it. And she didn't know whether to be flattered or frightened by such confidence.

Also, in a strange way, there *was* something about this voice that she recognised. Although she could still swear to herself that she had never heard it before—even allowing for the distortion of the telephone—there was something in it which jarred her memory. But how could she remember hearing something that she had never heard?

"Fisher?"

"Yes . . ." Caution replaced her momentary euphoria. And in any case the prospect of *after you've finished in the house* had a sobering effect: if she found nothing then she was in trouble, yet if her one nagging suspicion was confirmed then Colonel Butler would be in trouble.

"Yes?" He prodded her gently.

"Yes. Well . . ." Frances grasped the nettle. "What is Colonel Butler doing at the moment?"

"Why . . . he's still pursuing O'Leary, of course." There was a frown in his tone, as though he was disappointed in her. "Why do you wish to know, Fisher?"

"Up in Yorkshire?"

"Yes. That's where he thinks O'Leary is."

"Where, exactly?"

"This morning I believe he is pursuing his inquiries in the town of Thirsk." Extension 223 sounded as though he had no great confidence in the inquiries bearing fruit. "Why do you have to know exactly where he is, may I ask?"

He was warning her off. They were keeping tabs on Butler now, naturally, but that was someone else's job, not hers—hers was Butler in '69, not Butler this morning, he was politely telling her.

And, for a guess, that might be Paul Mitchell's job, he would be good at that . . . Paul Mitchell the watcher of Colonel Butler, the pursuer—Butler, in his turn, would be better at *that*, pursuing rather than waiting in ambushes festooned with computerised electronics. A hunter and a fighter, was Colonel Butler, not a trapper.

"Fisher?" Extension 223's patience was exemplary.

"I'd like to see the file on Trevor Anthony Bond."

"Ah!"

Frances breathed a sigh of relief. There was a file on Trevor Anthony Bond, she knew that because it had been cross-referenced in the file on Colonel Butler. What she hadn't known was whether it was an active or a passive file—it might well have been passive with effect from 11.11.69, from the afternoon when Butler had first and last quizzed Trevor Anthony on his KGB contacts. Indeed, it might very well have been passive from 11.11.69, but that *Ah!* told her it wasn't passive now; that it was—one will give you ten—within reach of Extension 223's right hand on his desk, maybe.

"He's still alive, I take it?"

"Oh, yes—alive and kicking."

"And living in Yorkshire?"

Pause.

"Yes." Pause. "Thornervaulx Abbey."

"He's still there?" Frances shivered. Why had she assumed—why had she known before she asked—that Trevor Anthony Bond still worked for the Ministry of Public Building and Works at Thornervaulx?

"Yes."

Fountains, Kirkstall, Jervaulx, Byland, Rievaulx, Thornervaulx—the great ruined abbeys of Yorkshire.

They were all a blur in her recollection of the things past in another life.

Fountains, Kirkstall, Jervaulx—

Fountains had been full of people picnicking on the grass, leaving their Coke cans and sweet papers and tinfoil . . .

She closed her eyes.

Frances Warren, aged 10, had had a green-flowered dress with a velvet bow for dinner—dinner with Uncle John in the immense Victorian vicarage—a dress which had flared out gloriously when she pirouetted in front of the mirror . . . except that she had had no breasts at the time, when the unspeakable, rebarbative Samantha Perring had already owned a bra—

Kirkstall, with the marvellous museum across the road, with the Edwardian street and the penny-in-the-slot machine that reconstructed a murderer's last hours, right down to the six-foot hanging drop—

"Frances! Stop working that gruesome machine!"

Kirkstall and the Hanged Man.

Jervaulx had been too ruined and dull, without the carefully manicured lawns of Byland, with its ruined pinnacle; and the wooded beauty of Rievaulx, where they had lunched on the hillside—

Chicken legs and white wine.

"John darling, don't give the child another glass—you'll make her quite tipsy!"

"Nonsense, m'dear. It's important for a girl to hold her liquor these days. Hold your glass steady, wench."

And she had thought thereafter, and still half thought, that holding her liquor was really only a question of keeping her glass steady in her hand.

But Thornervaulx was still misty in her memory, mixed and confused with Fountains and Rievaulx . . . in another wooded valley (*"Dale, wench, dale—you're in Yorkshire now, not your muggy Midlands!"*)—in another wooded dale—hidden from the outside world of the flesh and the devil, as the old Cistercian monks planned it to be.

Perhaps that was the effect of that second glass of Uncle John's white wine, pale gold remembered through the sleepy warmth of a little girl's summer afternoon, already rich with the prospect of grown-up dinner and the wearing of the new dress—perhaps not surprisingly the old abbeys had become as jumbled in the little girl's recollections as their own tumbled stonework, while the taste of chicken legs and wine and the crisp feel of the dress were as well-remembered as yesterday—

"Mrs Fisher!"

Frances found herself staring fixedly at the whitewashed wall in front of her nose.

Thornervaulx Abbey, where Major Butler had questioned Trevor Anthony Bond on the afternoon (repeat afternoon) of 11.11.69 about his recent contacts with Leslie Pearson Cole (q.v. deceased, restricted) and Leonid T. Starinov (q.v. restricted).

"I'm sorry. I'm still here—I'm just thinking . . ."

"About Trevor Bond? There isn't much in the file, I can tell you. He didn't have much to say for himself."

No, thought Frances. But what he had said had been distinctly odd.

"He gave Colonel Butler an alibi at first, though—didn't he?"

"Which Butler promptly contradicted. And when the Special Branch went back to him, Bond simply said he'd got it wrong—that he made a mistake. What's the point of double-checking that, may I ask?"

No point, of course, thought Frances.

And that was the point.

"It seems a funny sort of mistake—to say 'morning' instead of 'afternoon'. It couldn't have been more than a week afterwards, when they came to check up on him again, probably not so long. He must have a very short memory."

For a moment he said nothing. "I don't think it was quite like that."

He'd read the file quite recently, but the details hadn't registered with him as being important. It had merely been a minor matter of routine for him, just as it had been for the Special Branch originally. So minor that now he couldn't recall the details precisely.

"What was it like?"

"Hmm . . . Hold on a minute, and I'll tell you . . ." His voice faded.

It wasn't quite fair to Colonel Butler to say that he'd contradicted Bond, reflected Frances. He would have put in his report independently, in which the afternoon interview with Bond had been recorded. And almost certainly the Special Branch men who had subsequently checked it out with Bond would never have seen that report, which must have had a security classification. The discrepancy between Butler's 'afternoon' and Bond's 'morning' would only have been spotted when the two reports reached the same desk.

And then, quite naturally, it would have been re-checked, because all discrepancies had to be resolved. But it would still have been only a minor matter of routine because it had been Butler himself who had established that he had no alibi for the material time of his wife's disappearance:

Although I had originally planned to interrogate Bond in the morning I decided on reflection that the afternoon might be more productive. Having approximately three hours on my hands, and there being no other duties scheduled for the day, I adjusted my route to take in my home town of Blackburn, arriving there at 1020 hours and departing at 1125. While in Blackburn I spoke to no one and recognised no one. I then proceeded to Thornervaulx, via Skipton and Blubberhouses, purchasing petrol at the Redbridge Garage, near Ripley (A61), at 1305 hours, arriving at 1425 after lunch at the Old Castle Hotel, Sutton-on-Swale.

As a not-alibi that could hardly be bettered, Frances concluded. If the Colonel had been trying to set himself up, that change of plan plus *I spoke to no one and recognised no one* had done the job perfectly. Trevor Bond's conflicting 'morning' stood no chance against such an admission, and once Bond had obligingly changed his tale to conform with it there had seemed no point in the Special Branch men treble-checking him any further. It was 9 o'clock in the morning that they were after, not 3 o'clock in the afternoon, 200 miles north.

"Hullo there, Mrs Fisher."

"Yes?"

"You're quite right. He does seem to have a remarkably poor memory, does Master Bond. Even worse than you thought, actually."

"Yes?"

"It was only two days. Butler visited him on the 11th—Tuesday the 11th. And the Special Branch checked him two days later, the first time, November 13th, when he said Butler was there in the morning. . . . And then they did the re-check on Monday the 17th, when he changed it to the afternoon. . . . So—only two days . . . But they do appear to have been perfectly satisfied with his explanation."

Yes, thought Frances, but it had just been routine for them. For Butler, on the 11th, Trevor Bond had been a suspect in a security matter. But on the 13th and the 17th, for the Special Branch, he had merely been an alibi witness in a missing persons case in which they were only indirectly involved—and in which Bond himself was also only indirectly involved, come to that.

"Is there a verbatim?"

"For the 13th? There's a statement for that . . . a very brief statement. But to the point, nevertheless: '*A man came to see me on Tuesday, morning, when I was having my tea at about 11 o'clock, and asked me a lot of silly questions about people talking to me. I never did understand what he was on about.*' And there's a note from the detective-sergeant to the effect that Bond couldn't actually remember Major Butler's name, but only that it had been a red-headed man in a brown check tweed suit with a red Remembrance Day poppy in his lapel who'd been a 'Major someone or other'. Which they took to be a positive ID in the circumstances."

"What circumstances?"

Extension 223 coughed. "The sergeant thought Bond was a near-idiot. 'Apparently of low mentality', to be exact." He paused. "A judgement subsequently confirmed on the re-check. Do you want to hear it?"

Frances's heart sank. Low mentality's natural travelling companion was a bad memory.

"Yes."

"Very well. I quote—or rather a certain Detective-Constable Smithers quotes: '*In the morning—yes, as I was having my tea. Oh bugger, I tell a lie. It was in the afternoon I was having my tea, not the morning. I was sweeping up the leaves by the high altar, they blow in there from the trees at the back, where the wall's down at the corner there. In the morning I was repairing the wall of the infirmary cloister, I had my tea there in the morning. It was when I was having*

126

my tea in the afternoon when he comes up to me. I'd been sweeping the leaves round the altar. It's all these questions. Why are you asking all these questions? Haven't you got anything better to do? It was the afternoon, not the morning. But I put my name to that bit of paper. I was mixed up, that's all. I have a thermos in the morning, for my elevenses, and I make another thermos for the afternoon in the winter, when it's cold . . .' Do you want me to go on, Mrs Fisher?"

'Oh bugger' was right, thought Frances. Her tentative theory on Trevor Anthony Bond looked to be as much in ruins as Thornervaulx Abbey, where the autumn leaves blew in over the site of the great golden altar under which the bones of St. Biddulph had once rested.

"No." But there were still two questions to be asked, the answers to which had not been in Butler's file, and no matter how dusty the answers they still had to be asked. "Was anything ever established against Bond?"

"You mean . . . other than the fact that Pearson Cole and Starinov each spoke to him on consecutive days? Actually, it was Starinov who spoke to him first, then Pearson Cole. . . . That was established, certainly. They were both being tailed."

"Did they know they were being tailed?"

"That's anybody's guess." He sniffed. "Pearson Cole . . . probably not . . . Starinov was a pro of course. But then so was the man who set up the surveillance on him. . . . That makes it anybody's guess."

"And they did make contact?"

"Pearson Cole took the high jump just as we were about to pick him up. Starinov was diplomatic—he took the next plane home. It's fair to assume those two events weren't unconnected, that was the official view." Pause. "But whether Bond was the link man . . . that was never proved, one way or the other. And he's never stepped out of line since, so far as we know. Nothing known before, nothing known since."

The old Scottish 'non-proven': Trevor Anthony Bond, apparently of low intelligence, had been left pickled in doubt, innocent but unlucky, guilty but lucky, or guilty but too damn clever by half, and nobody knew which.

Just like Colonel Butler, in fact.

And, in the matter of Madeleine Butler's disappearance, just like Patrick Raymond Parker too.

Sod it!

Question Two, then.

"What did Colonel Butler have to say about him, Trevor Bond?"

"Ah . . . now Butler was not entirely converted to the Special Branch view, you might say. Because, although he didn't get anything out of him, he didn't think the fellow was as stupid as he made out."

Frances perked up. "In what way?"

"In what way . . . Well, reading between the lines . . . say, perhaps not a traitor, but possibly an artful dodger. But he wasn't sure after only one stab at him."

Only one stab at him. That had never occurred to her, and it was a bonus she hadn't expected. She ought to have thought of that before, but better late than never.

And the bonus gave her cash for another question.

"What was Pearson Cole doing?"

Pause.

"Sorry, Fisher. Classified."

Frances frowned at the wall. "'All I have to do is ask'. I'm asking."

"That means within the limits of the job."

Then—it's within the limits."

"I'm afraid it isn't, Mrs Fisher. Colonel Butler is your concern—Colonel Butler and his lady—not Pearson Cole. I'm sorry, but that's the way it is."

His voice was very gently chiding, almost silky, so far as she could make out, and once again it struck a chord in her memory which she still couldn't identify. The telephone was worse than last night's darkness, in which she had at least been able to pick up Sir Frederick's tone without distortion, even with heightened perception.

"Unless I can prove otherwise, you mean?"

"That would change things, naturally."

It was a Catch-22 situation, thought Frances bitterly. "And Trevor Bond?"

"You can have his file, I'll have it sent to you—or a flimsy of it . . . But you haven't really justified your obsession with him, either, you know."

"It isn't an obsession." Frances's resolve to keep her own counsel weakened: although he hadn't said as much he obviously didn't rate

128

her chances. "If he wasn't a contact, then of course it doesn't matter . . . But if he *was* . . ."

"That's a very big if. Do go on though—if he was?"

"Then he wouldn't have made any mistake about the time of day. It would have been pointless. So on November 13 he lied—deliberately."

She paused to give him time to work out the different interpretations of that: if it was a lie, then it hadn't done Butler any harm—on the contrary, if he had confirmed it, then it would have given him an alibi for the time of his wife's disappearance.

But in fact the Colonel had rejected any idea of an alibi with his own detailed—but unsubstantiated—account of his own movements that morning.

And yet, if it was a lie, then it also hadn't done Bond himself any good—on the contrary, it had put him at risk again by bringing the Special Branch back to him when he ought to have been keeping his head down; which would only have been justified if it had done Butler harm.

Which it hadn't . . . (Indeed, if Bond had actually stuck to his original lie, and had cast doubt on the Colonel's own account by insisting on giving him an alibi, that might have been more embarrassing. But he hadn't done that, either.)

The possibilities went round in circles, but they always came back to the same point: not one of them made any sense.

Suddenly, a vivid memory of Dr David Audley surfaced in Frances's mind.

David—theorising on the pitfalls of action based on faulty intelligence in the lecture room of Walton Hall—

David—dear David, with his expensive suit typically in disarray, one fly-button undone ('Dishevilled urbanity', whispers Paul Mitchell, already star pupil in the awkward squad)—

Dear David—typically illustrating bitter experience from the advice of 'my old Latin master' on the hazards of translating the Orations of Cicero: *Since Cicero can be relied on to make sense and your translation does not make sense, then it is prudent to assume that the error is yours, not Cicero's.*

"Hmm . . ." Extension 223 sounded sceptical, but cautious. "So . . . why should he do that, Mrs Fisher?"

In short, nonsense must be wrong. . . . And by the same token, even though our adversaries are rarely men of Cicero's calibre, when your interpretation of their actions does not make sense it is prudent to assume that the error is yours—and that you have been taken for a bloody ride according to plan. Until proved otherwise, therefore, nonsense must be wrong.

"I haven't the faintest idea—I don't know." But what she did know, thought Frances, was that she missed David Audley's counsel now; and more, that in the matter of Colonel and Mrs Butler she missed it twice over. "But I think that nonsense must be wrong until proved otherwise."

For a moment there was no sound from the telephone, and then it emitted an odd crackling growl, as though the source of the nonsense theory was known, and disliked.

"All right, Fisher—" Extension 223's voice was strangely harsh: the growl had definitely been his, not the phone's "—but I think that you're clutching at straws—"

"Straws are all I've got," said Frances.

"Don't you believe it! Keep plugging at Mrs Butler, that's my advice. But I'll do what I can with Bond in the meantime." The harshness was gone, like a distant rumble of summer thunder only half-heard and far away, and the voice was all velvet encouragement again. "The flimsy of the Bond file I can get to you today . . . and I think I'll run a quick present-whereabouts-and-status check on him too, just in case—so as not to risk wasting your time. The last one we've got is nearly three months old, I see."

Frances felt complimented—so as not to risk wasting her valuable time, indeed!—and then the last words registered as significant.

They had never proved anything against Trevor Bond, but they had nevertheless run PWS checks on him for nine whole years—three-monthly checks for nine blameless years. And although PWS checks could safely be left to the local police that confirmed what she had already begun to suspect about Pearson Cole from Extension 223's reluctance to talk about him: that whatever he'd been up to once upon a time, all those years back, it must have been something red-hot—and so hot that it had even kept the dull Trevor Anthony Bond file warm, so it would seem.

And that was decidedly interesting—

"And Pearson Cole?" Nothing venture, nothing gain.

"I can't promise anything there, Fisher. The odds are against, but I'll pass the word on. . . . That's the most I can do, and the best . . . just for you, Fisher, I'll do that."

"Thank you," said Frances meekly. David Audley would know because he knew almost everything, but David was out of bounds; and Paul Mitchell *might* know, because he often knew what he wasn't supposed to know, but he was out of reach, at least temporarily. And if Extension 223 really was doing his best for her such thoughts were treasonable, anyway.

"You just concentrate on Colonel Butler in the meantime. And on the wife." Pause. "On this hunch of yours, whatever it is."

Promotion, riches and fame, the voice promised her: *not a witch-hunt*—perish the thought!—*but if you bring Colonel Butler's head on a platter, Fisher, the world is at your feet.*

"I'll do my best." Frances felt seduced, on her back.

"That's fine, then. And now I have one little bit of good news for you: those expensive gloves of yours have been found."

Gloves?

Those expensive gloves of yours?

Those expensive gloves of yours have been found?

"Oh—" The white-washed wall blazed in front of her. "Oh?"

Gloves? She had a pair of black gloves at home, bought for Robbie's funeral and never worn since; she could remember clenching ice-cold hands in them as the rifles fired over the grave. Once she had had a pair of grey woollen mittens, when mittens were all the rage in the Fifth Form. . . . And Robbie had bequeathed her a pair of dirty white-and-green cricket gloves and a well-worn Fives glove . . .

She never wore gloves.

"Yes?" She stared at her left hand, with its short life line on the palm. Mustn't be superstitious—and don't let him ask her to describe them until she knew more about them, these expensive gloves of hers which had been found, but never lost, never even possessed.

"Young Mitchell found them . . . somewhere in the Library, in the Common Room, I think he said. Khaki-colour—are those the ones?"

Frances looked at her sleeve. Paul had seen this suit yesterday, and it would be like a man—and particularly like Paul—to describe this beautiful new Jaeger green so insultingly.

131

"Green—yes." She committed herself to Paul and the gloves.

"Good. I'll get him to post them on to you—not to worry."

Frances worried furiously. That couldn't be what Paul intended with the mythical gloves. But what the hell did he intend?

It could only be communication. Since he couldn't know where she was, he had to tell her where he was.

"Where are they?" Was that the right question?

"Where are they?" For a moment he was thrown by the sheer triviality of the present-whereabouts-and-status of Mrs Fitzgibbon-Fisher's expensive khaki-green leather gloves. "They're in his hotel—the Royal Europa, Harrogate. But I'll get him to post them."

"No. I can make time to pick them up tomorrow." Frances curbed her excitement: if it wasn't the right question it had been near enough. But what she had to do now was to reinforce its triviality. "Those are my very *best* gloves. They cost a *fortune*—" (That was safe. Anything made of leather cost a fortune) "—and the colour-match is *perfect* . . . I'm not trusting them to the Post Office. I shall pick them up *myself*!"

"All right, Fisher—if you must!" He chuckled. *"Mulier est hominis confusio."*

"What?" She pretended not to understand the chauvinist jibe.

"Nothing . . . As I said, just so you concentrate your energies on Colonel Butler, m'dear. Because . . . none of this has gone on record, but we're relying on you to come up with something, make no mistake about that. Understood?"

Promotion, riches and fame—or demotion, penury and oblivion.

"I understand."

Click.

Wait ten seconds.

"Directory inquiries, please. . . . I'd like the number of the Royal Europa Hotel, Harrogate, please."

She rummaged in her handbag for her wallet. With phone charges what they were at peak times, how much did she owe Isobel?

"Royal Europa Hotel."

"May I speak to the Head Porter, please." (For a guess, Paul would start at the top.)

"Head Porter. Can I help you?"

"My name is—" (Frances experiences a moment of confusion:

what was her name?) "—Fitzgibbon. I believe you have a pair of gloves for me. Left by a Mr Paul Mitchell?"

"Ah . . . Miss Fitzgibbon—yes . . . And that would be Miss *Frances* Fitzgibbon, I take it?"

"Yes." Frances licked her lips. "You have my gloves?"

"Yes, madam. We have your . . . gloves." He placed a curious emphasis on *gloves*, turning the word into a conspiracy between them, and a pass-word too. Suddenly Frances felt hand-in-glove with him, and part of all the rendezvous in which he had played the role of go-between—his discretion and loyalty bought for a blue fiver—for other Paul Mitchells and Frances Fitzgibbons over the years.

And, just as suddenly, the knowledge was painful to her, that there was no one now who would wish to buy that discretion for her and anyone else, for what Paul would have led this Head Porter to believe: a night in one of his double rooms—*Where love throbs out in blissful sleep/Pulse nigh to pulse, and breath to breath/Where hushed awakenings are dear . . .*

If that had been the case, what would she say now?

"Was there a message . . . with the gloves?"

"Ah . . . Would you hold the line for a minute, madam?"

What was he doing? Turning on the tape? Putting the extension through? Or moving the Receptionist out of ear-shot?

"Thank you, madam . . . Now, if you please, on one side of your fireplace there is a book-shelf—am I right?"

"What?"

He cleared his throat. "I am instructed to ask you, madam: on one side of your fireplace there is a book-shelf. What sort of books would there be on that shelf, now?"

Frances closed her eyes. The fireplace—to take precautions like this Paul had to be scared—the fireplace had books on each side of it, she'd made the bookcases herself during Robbie's second tour in Ulster . . . Robbie's books on one side, hers on the other—her Faulkner and Hardy and Fielding, and all her poetry anthologies—

God knows 'twere better to be deep/Pillowed in silk and scented down—but why was she thinking of those lines, from one of Robbie's favourite poems, and of all poems that one, the death one?

She opened her eyes. Paul had only noticed Robbie's books at his side when he had sat at that fireside, in the empty chair.

"Fairy stories and folk-lore."

133

"Fairy tales—that's correct. Thank you, madam." He drew a five-pound breath of relief. "If you have a piece of paper and a pencil handy, I have a message for you, madam."

There was a pad by the phone, with a biro on a string.

"Yes?"

"'Ring 0254-587142'. Have you got that, madam?"

It may be he shall take my hand/And lead me into his dark land—
Damn! "Yes. 0254-587142."

"'Ask for the Adjutant'."

"Yes. Ask for the Adjutant."

"'Exercise caution'."

Paul really was scared. And as of this moment, since Paul didn't scare easily—never had been scared in her experience—then Frances was frightened, thought Frances.

"Yes?"

"That's all, madam. Just that."

"Thank you." She waited, but he didn't seem inclined to hang up. "Yes?"

"The gloves, madam. What shall I do with them?"

"Oh." So there really was a pair of gloves. But of course there was: Paul wouldn't make that sort of error. And, by the same token, she must play her part in the charade. "I'll be coming by to pick them up, probably tomorrow."

"Then I'll leave them in Reception for you . . . And . . . good luck, madam."

Click.

One good thing about being frightened, thought Frances analytically, was that it dissolved both poetry and feminine vapours—that would be Wing Commander Roskill's famous adrenalin overriding the central nervous system, making a super-woman of her.

0254-587142. Poor Isobel's phone bill!

"Guard Room."

Frances frowned at the wall. "I beg your pardon?"

"You've got the Guard Room, love." The owner of the voice appeared resigned, though not unkindly, to explaining what was bound to be a wrong number. "Queen's Lancashire Regiment, Blackburn Depot—Salamanca Barracks. Is that what you want?"

The adrenalin pumped. No need to wonder now what Paul was

doing, of course; while she was excavating Colonel Butler's marriage, he was turning over Colonel Butler's military career, or some unresolved question mark in it—and who better than Paul Mitchell, the ex-military historian, to dig into that history?

(And who better than Widow Fitzgibbon, the ex-military wife, to dig into that marriage? Ugh!)

"I'd like to speak with the Adjutant, if you please." Frances heard her most county voice take over, turning the request into an order. "He is expecting a call from me." Haughty sniff. "An urgent call."

"Very good, madam." The Guard Room came smartly to attention at the word of command.

The past flooded back painfully, surging over her and then carrying her forward before she could check it into the might-have-been present. Robbie would have made captain now, and if they'd still been together she'd have been an established regimental wife—even maybe a wife-and-mother, with a son down for Wellington—

If.

No!

Think of Colonel Butler—*Major* Butler, Captain Butler, Lieutenant Butler, Officer Cadet Butler . . . even Private Butler.

Paul had been right: *not quite out of the top drawer, our Jack*—she ought to have noticed that, if not noted it (what did it matter where he came from?), because her ear was sharper than Paul's (but maybe it did matter now, remembering how Colonel Butler—Captain Butler at the time, it had been—from the wrong side of the tracks had carried off Madeleine Françoise de Latour d'Auray Boucard, of Chateau Chais d'Auray, which sounded a long way beyond the other side of those tracks).

(Because that had been as out-of-character for the dour Colonel Butler she knew, or thought she knew, as for the Private Butler who had risen from the ranks of his Lancashire regiment, out of the back streets of Blackburn . . . somehow inheriting the fortune of General Sir Henry Chesney *en route*.)

(There was more in Colonel Butler than met the eye, much more and very different. But how much more, and how different?)

"Miss Fitzgibbon?"

The Adjutant. Widow Fitzgibbon could tell an adjutant when she heard one. Wellington and Sandhurst. Or any public school and Sandhurst; Johnnie Kinch, who had danced rather closely with not-yet-Widow Fitzgibbon, had been Eton and Sandhurst and Robbie's adjutant, and that could have been Johnnie Kinch's voice, down to the last inflection.

"Could I speak to Mr Mitchell, please?" said Frances cautiously.

"Ah . . . jolly good!" Caution met caution. "Would you hold the line for a tick?"

For a tick she would hold the line.

(But it wouldn't have been Private Butler, of course—his had been a rifle regiment, or was it a fusilier one? An Army wife ought to have made that important distinction—it would have been Rifleman Butler, or Fusilier Butler . . . Except, the truth was, she had never been a very good Army wife, imbued with the proper attitudes, but just a very young one full of learning and politics out of step with her situation, in which there was also more than had met her eye—more and very different.)

"Princess?"

That was Paul—no doubt about that.

"Yes?"

"Where are you phoning from?"

"Does it matter?"

"Where-are-you-phoning-from?"

"A pub in the back of beyond."

"The pay phone?"

"No. The publican's private line. What's your problem?"

"You got my message. Did Control phone you? Or did you phone Control?"

"What's the matter, Paul?"

"For Christ's sake, Princess—answer the question!"

"I phoned him. For Christ's sake—what's the matter?"

Silence. Clever Paul was assessing the chances of putting himself on someone else's record. Clever *scared* Paul.

"Okay then, Princess. We've got things to talk about."

"Like what?"

"Like . . . how you're going to smear Jack Butler, maybe?"

"What d'you mean—smear?"

136

"Have it your own way—'investigate', if you prefer. Just so you keep on digging until something starts to smell. Choose your own euphemism, I don't care."

"I seem to recall, last time we met you weren't so pleased with him," Frances snapped back defensively.

"Hah! Nor I was. But that was . . . let's say professional disagreement, tinged with envy. This is different—and don't tell me you don't know it. . . . Come on, you tell me you're not digging dirt. If you can do that then okay. But if not . . ."

The challenge hit her squarely. That was the way it had seemed to her when Extension 223 had first talked to her, but somehow she'd forgotten her initial reaction. And now that he wasn't talking to her—now that his voice wasn't seeping into her ear—she could recall how she'd felt—

"Come on, Frances. Take me seriously just this once—is that what you're doing?"

Digging dirt—? Well, crudely put, that was exactly what she was doing, even if she didn't want to find any.

The voice of Extension 223 had been the voice of Saruman, Tolkien's wicked wizard, who could always daunt or convince the little people.

"Yes."

"Good girl. Because that's what I'm supposed to be doing too—digging dirt. My problem is your problem."

A moral Paul? Frances didn't have to test the possibility in order to reject it. A delicate conscience had never hampered him in the past, and it wasn't likely to be spiking him on one of its horns now. Paul's dilemmas were always strictly practical ones.

"So what? It won't be the first time either of us has dug dirt, Paul."

"Very true. That's where the gold is, in the dirt—I know."

"Then what's so different now?"

"Hah! The difference, Princess, is that then we were digging in the national interest. What old Jack would call 'the defence of the Realm' . . . not as part of a bloody palace revolution."

"A—what?"

"You heard me. A bloody-palace-revolution. The Ides of March in the Forum. A quick twist of garrotting wire and a splash in the Golden Horn. The Night of the Long Knives. And us in the middle of it, up to the elbows in gore."

"Paul . . . are you out of your mind?" Frances stared at the white wall in dismay.

For a moment the phone was silent. "Paul?"

"All right . . . so I'm exaggerating. We do these things in a more civilised manner, of course. . . . But if I'm crazy, Princess, then I'm being crazy like a fox, I tell you. And . . . you start thinking for yourself, for God's sake. Have you ever taken part in anything as whacky as this before?"

Frances started thinking.

'Whacky' was a typical Paul word, but it wasn't too far off the mark. There had been something decidedly odd about this operation from the start, she had been telling herself that all along.

"Who briefed you, Frances?" He paused only for half a second. "Top brass? And off the record?"

"Yes." *Exercise caution.* And that applied to her dealings with Paul as well, because if there really was a major security shake-up in progress—'palace revolution' was also typical Paul—then two things were certain: there would be rival factions jockeying for power, and Paul Mitchell intended to be on the winning side, regardless of the interests of Frances Fitzgibbon, never mind Colonel Butler. "But I wasn't told to smear Colonel Butler, Paul."

"Don't be naïve, Princess. Whose side are you on?"

He was being unusually direct or exceptionally devious, decided Frances. But which?

"My side. Whose side are you on, Paul dear?"

"Hah! I deserved that!" He chuckled at his own self-knowledge. "Okay, Frances *dear*—Princess mine—my off-the-record top brass set me to inquire gently into two small areas of doubt about our Jack's warlike career . . . gently and discreetly, but I'd better get the required answer if I value my civil service pension *bien entendu.* Namely, if he was so bloody good at his job, why was his promotion so slow? And was the late glamorous Madame Butler the pillar of wifely chastity—or wifely virtue—that the official records suggest? To which I strongly suspect the required answers are *He wasn't really any good, so he wasn't promoted,* and *He wasn't any good because Madame B wasn't so virtuous while he was away at the wars, and he found out and that screwed him up.* Right?"

Frances stared at the white wall. "Damn you, Paul—"

"I said required—hold on, Princess—I said required. I didn't say

138

'correct'. Those are the answers they want me to come up with, not the answers I may come up with."

"Damn you! I haven't started yet!"

"Well, hard luck! You wanted to know which side I'm on, and I'm telling you. Though it's not easy on this bloody instrument—David Audley's right: the telephone is the devil's device, and God rot Graham Alexander Bell or Thomas Alva Edison, or whoever. You may be a female Bachelor of Arts in English Literature, Princess, but I'm a Master of Arts in History, where facts still count for something . . . and I'm not getting the *right* answers. Which worries me more than somewhat."

"I'm sorry to hear that, Paul." Beneath the froth he did sound worried, and that purged her anger. "I really am."

"So you should be. Because you should be worried for yourself too, my girl. And worried on two counts, also. Or at least two."

"And what are they?"

"Oh, you can laugh." He didn't sound his casual self, and that equally purged any shred of humour from their situation. "It's Jack Butler's promotion we're supposed to be superintending. Has it occurred to you . . . that might be true?"

"I assumed it was. Isn't that why it's important?"

"Too true. But I think I know what the promotion is."

The Ring of Power, thought Frances—and then backed off from the image. Whatever power Colonel Butler was in line for, it had nothing to do with fairyland, or Middle Earth, or Cloudcuckooland; it was life-and-death power here on earth, her earth.

"And what promotion is that, then?"

"I'm not telling you—on this line. Four hours from now, where will you be, Frances? We have to talk, you and I."

He really believed his 'palace revolution' theory, she believed that now. And, allowing for paranoia being an occupational hazard of their profession, she was beginning to believe in his belief.

"I'll be at Colonel Butler's home this afternoon—and this evening, I hope."

"Why there, for God's sake?"

"I have some answers to get, like you, Paul."

"Christ! I'm dim, aren't I! Madame Butler, I presume?' He breathed out. "They're really pushing it, aren't they!"

"Has it occurred to you that they could be right?" she pushed him deliberately, even though she knew the answer: Paul's distinction between right and wrong was always strictly factual, not ethical. Neither cheating nor any other morality came into it.

"You better believe that I have, Princess. That's the main thing that worries me. And that's why I need to see you. *We have to talk*."

He wasn't going to go further on his own account. But he might go further on hers. "So what's the second thing that should worry me? You didn't actually get round to telling me."

"Nor I did . . ." He left the answer hanging in the air for a moment. "They gave you *carte blanche* for the job, did they? They said you're the boss?"

"Yes."

"Me too. So who was the first person you wanted to talk to about Jack Butler?"

David Audley—

Paul hardly waited for an answer. "David Audley, of course. Because he's known Jack from way back—even before that file started, if my scuttlebut is correct. . . . Only *carte blanche* doesn't include David Audley, does it? Right? Or Hugh Roskill?"

Now he was pushing her.

"I'll bet you tried, Frances—because you've got some pull with Hugh Roskill from your happy little secretarial days . . . And did they tell you that your handsome Wing Commander just happens to have winged off somewhere on business, where you can't pick his brains—did they tell you that?"

She hadn't even got as far as a refusal on Hugh, thought Frances: she hadn't even understood what she was into at that stage. "So what?"

"Roskill doesn't matter much, but David Audley does—did you know that Jack Butler is godfather to David's daughter, the apple of his eye?"

"Yes—"

"Of course, David makes no secret of it. And I bet Jack Butler's a damn good godfather too. He's a great one for anniversaries, so he'd never forget a birthday—and he probably checks on the poor kid's catechism too, I shouldn't wonder."

"Get to the point, Paul."

"Don't be dim, Frances—that is the point. Among other things David Audley is almost certainly the greatest living authority on the life and times of Jack Butler."

"But also a friend of his."

"After a fashion. It's more of a love-hate relationship, actually—old Jack doesn't altogether approve of some of David's professional attitudes, David's too much of a maverick for him . . . But even if I grant you friendship—and admiration—it wouldn't make a jot of difference if it came to a security crunch. Because under the skin our David is a real hard bastard—which you should know as well as anyone, Frances, having seen him in action."

That, undeniably, was true, thought Frances. In professional matters David was not, decidedly not, a follower of the Marquess of Queensbury Rules.

"Hell, Princess—" Paul's voice was suddenly edged with anger "—doesn't it strike you as bad medicine that neither Hugh nor David are here just when we need them most? And we can't even damn well *talk* to them either—and there are such things as communications satellites . . . David's only in the embassy at Washington, not on Mars—we could have him back here in the flesh by Concorde for tea-time, taxi-time included. But . . . *neither of them*—you can call that bad management, if you like. Or bad luck. Or coincidence. But if you do, you'd better remember also what David taught us about them, Frances."

Bad luck is what the Other Side wishes on you.
Coincidence is very often a damned liar.
And bad management—

Then Frances knew exactly what Paul was up to, why he was going to so much trouble to spell everything out, and—above all—what he intended her to do about it.

(She could recall not only the words, but the occasion; David, fairly tanked-up after dinner, and James Cable and Paul and herself, all relaxing after a hard day's work . . . and Paul, very carefully not tanked-up at all, playing his favourite game of capping David's quotations, or anticipating them, and gently needling him.)

("And bad management," David had said, "is when you find yourself taking unnecessary risks.")

("And good management," Paul had said, "is presumably when you find someone else to take those risks?")

"All right, Paul, I take your point. We do have to talk." She

141

thought hard for a moment. "You better make it after dark, quite late
. . . and by the back way, if there is one. And if there are any
complications I'll park my car pointing out of the driveway."

"There's a careful princess, now! And just as well too, maybe . . .
if your friend Hugo is right."

"My friend—who?"

"Hugo. Hugo Crowe."

"Oh—Professor Crowe, you mean. He's not my friend, I've only
met him once."

"Well, he regards himself as your friend. He says you are a
darling—even a Grace Darling, combining heroism with beauty.
Just another passing conquest of yours, Princess . . . but obviously
you've stopped counting them—fairy princesses are traditionally
cruel, of course."

He was pleased with himself now that she had taken his point.

"If he's right? How should he be right?" Frances frowned. "Right
about what?"

"You told him a story—about a blind prince? A fairy story,
presumably."

The skin between her shoulder-blades crawled suddenly. "Yes.
Yes?"

"He says you shouldn't have told it. But particularly he says you
mustn't point at anyone. And on no account must you kiss the third
prince—you're to choose one of the other two. And don't ask me
what all that means, because I don't know, and he wouldn't tell me.
For my own good, that was, he said. A very superstitious fellow,
your friend Hugo . . . though no one has a better right to be, I
suppose."

Frances closed her eyes. "I'm not with you at all, Paul. Why
is—why has he the right to be superstitious?"

"You havn't done your homework. He's the author of *The
Psychology of Superstition* . . . why people won't walk under
ladders, and all that stuff. Huh! But please don't worry about me,
Frances dear—you can point at me any time, I'm not superstitious.
And you can kiss me too, I'm not blind—it'll be a pleasure, I assure
you. . . . Maybe tonight, and make an honest princess of you." A
kiss sounded down the line. "Watch out for yourself, Frances—save
all your kisses for me."

ON THE OUTSKIRTS of Colonel Butler's village there was a big new garage, with a showroom full of gleaming Japanese cars and an unbeatable offer on its petrol.

Frances pulled on to the forecourt, just short of the pumps, and sat thinking for a moment, hypnotised by the empty phone box beyond the car-wash at the far end of the buildings.

All she had to do was to go to that box and lift the phone and dial the number and put the money in, and then say a few words. It would be just another phone call, and even if the Mossad line at the Saracen's Head was no longer secure it would be untraceable if she was quick.

Except it wouldn't be just another call, because once she'd made it she'd be more than halfway committed to one side of Paul's palace revolution and not to the side with the better odds at the moment. Not even, come to that, to the side that had the right on it for certain, notwithstanding her instinct—and William Ewart Hedges' blessing.

A tousle-headed young man came out of the petrol kiosk and stood staring towards her.

Paul, on the other hand, was hedging his bets with a vengeance. Though (to be fair to him) he'd gone a lot further than she might have expected him to go, with his ambitions, and with the promises of advancement they would have made to him, like those which had been made to her in return for results.

The young man pointed towards her, and then to the pumps.

Mustn't point at anyone.

What Paul hadn't done, and what he wasn't going to do (because of those ambitions), or at least not yet, until he was sure which way the tide was flowing (also because of those ambitions), was to risk disobeying a direct order.

(Good management is finding someone else to take the risks; namely, Mrs Frances Fitzgibbon.)

She rolled the car forward to the five-star pump.

The young man looked at her, and then the car, and then at the pump. And finally back at her. He was young and beautiful, and he wore an incredibly patched pair of jeans which appeared to have been poured on him, and a dark blue sweat shirt bearing the legend 'Oxford University'.

Frances looked down at the fuel gauge: it had registered under half-full when Paul had turned over the car to her yesterday, a long way north, but it was still not quite on empty. It was that sort of car.

"Can I help you?" He smiled, and was more beautiful, and the accent went with the sweat-shirt.

"Do you take Barclaycards?"

"Barclay and Access—not American Express, for some obscure reason. But you won't get any Green Shield Stamps, they're only for hard cash, I'm afraid." Still smiling, still looking down at her, he tossed his curls towards the great garish poster above his shoulder. "It's all in the small print. Though actually our petrol is cheap at the moment—you're supposed to come in for our extra special offer, plus quintuple stamps for cash, and then think better of it and buy a new car instead, with a full tank and a million stamps, or something."

He really was lovely, thought Frances uncontrollably. But he was ten years too young for her—in another ten years she'd be old enough to have a son his age—and as unattainable as a shaft of sunlight.

"Should I be tempted?" She knew that it was the temptation of make-believe, if only for a moment, to which she was surrendering.

The smile compressed itself with mischief. "There's a couple of salesmen back there just waiting for me to give them the signal. . . . Actually, the cars aren't bad at the price, though the spares are a bit pricey. Myself, I'd rather have a Honda Four-hundred-four."

"A motor-bike?"

"A bike, yes." His eyes glazed at the thought, blotting her out, and when they saw her again they were no longer interested in her. "Four star, you want?"

The gossamer moment was over. She was just a woman customer in a nondescript car and he was a young petrol pump attendant, a strange face glimpsed for an instant in passing, and then gone forever.

Yet, in a stange cold way, Frances had the feeling that she was the stranger, the unreality, not this boy. For he belonged to the warm-blooded world of friends and car salesmen, and pay on Friday, saved towards his Honda Four-hundred-four, which was a real world beside which hers was a shadow country of ghosts and memories. Simply, she had caught his warmth for an instant, as any ghost might warm its pale hands on the living, and that had made her substantial enough for him to see. But now she was fading again, and the sooner she faded away altogether, the better—the safer—for them both.

"Five star, please." She reached decisively into her bag for the right Barclaycard, neither Fitzgibbon nor Fisher, but her own very private, untraceable Maiden Warren.

"Five star?" He controlled his surprise just short of disbelief. "How many gallons?"

She no longer saw him. It was curious that she had pretended to herself for so long that she was in two minds about the phone call, even that she'd half-blamed Paul for setting her to it, when she'd intended all along to make it, since last night. Paul had merely added reason to her instinct for disobedience.

"Fill her up." She passed the card across without looking at the boy, and opened the car door. "I'm going to make a phone call."

She pressed the button and the coins dropped.

"Saracen."

It was a rough East End voice. But then, the Saracen's Head was a rough East End pub, David Audley had said, where the beer was as strong as the prejudices and it didn't pay to ask the wrong question or support any team except West Ham.

"I'd like a word with Mr Lee." Out aloud 'Mr Lee' sounded rather Chinese, or even Romany, certainly not Israeli.

"'Oo wants 'im?" the rough voice challenged her.

"A friend of a friend of his," replied Frances obediently.

"Oh yus? Well, 'e ain't 'ere."

Recognition sign.

"Mr Lee owes my friend six favours, for services rendered." She wondered as she spoke whether that meant anything or nothing; with David's quirky sense of humour it might even be a genuine reminder.

"Is that a fact, now? 'Old on a mo', luv."

Frances waited. Through the smudgy window of the phone box she saw the young man take the nozzle of the petrol hose out of the tank. He peered at the numbers registered on the pump, and then back at the car. Then he scratched his thatch with his free hand. Then he bent down and looked underneath the car. Then he straightened up and stared towards the phone box. Then he reinserted the nozzle into the tank again.

Frances cursed her carelessness, which had quite unnecessarily turned him from an uninterested, disinterested young man into an interested young man. And more, a sharp young man (as it was November, and term had started, for a guess a sharp young man serving out his free year before Oxford, earning enough on the pumps for that Honda of his dreams?). And, most of all, a young man who would remember her now, right down to the Warren Barclay-card, if anyone came to unlock his memory. *Sod it!*

"'Ullo there?"

It was a different voice, but only marginally different, and not what she had expected even though she had never expected Colonel Shapiro himself.

"Mr Lee?"

"Naow, 'e ain't 'ere. I'm a friend of 'is. Do I know you, darlin'?"

"No—" Frances floundered for a moment as she watched the young man filling the tank. When he had done that, if he was the young man she took him to be, he would look under the bonnet on the pretext of checking the oil. "No. I'm a friend of a friend of his."

"Oh ah?"

The young man replaced the hose in the pump, taking a sidelong glance at the phone box as he did so. Then he walked round to the driver's window and leaned inside to release the bonnet catch.

"You still there, darlin'?"

"Yes."

Sod it! He was lifting the bonnet now. She had never made stupid little mistakes like this before, never taken big risks like this before . . . never disobeyed direct orders like this before, or almost never. And it was making mistakes, taking risks and disobeying orders which killed people, and more often than not other people too. That had been what David himself had said; and, in a very creepy way, that had been also what Professor Crowe had told Paul Mitchell— *you shouldn't have told that story.* And the queer thing was that she had always known there was something malevolent about Grand-mother's fairy story, even before she'd told it to Robbie that last time, by the fireside, on his last leave.

"Come on, darlin'—spit it out, get it off yer chest."

Superstition, sod it!

"Is this line secure?"

"You arskin'? It was until I 'eard your voice, ducks!"

Superstition: if she pointed her finger at the young man with his head under the bonnet of her car, then that would solve one of her problems. But that would be too cruel . . .

"My friend said . . . if I ever needed to get a message to him, Mr Lee would do it. And Mr Lee owes him six favours, he said. But is this line secure?"

"Hah-hargh! If you ain't blabbed—if my pools comes up this Saturday . . . an' if my old auntie 'ad two of 'em she'd be half-way to being my uncle—if you 'ain't blabbed, then you pays yer money an' you takes yer choice, darlin'. And I ain't promisin' nothin', mind you. But if you was to give me a message then I might pass it on to Mr Lee if I sees 'im. An' then it'ud be up to 'im, like—wouldn't it, if 'e owes yer friend like you say 'e does. Right?"

The young man closed the bonnet, pressing it down to engage the lock and carefully wiping his paw-marks from the cellulose with a rag from his back pocket. Beyond him, on the edge of the forecourt, there was an old break-down truck, looking rather broken-down itself, like a sick doctor waiting for emergency calls he couldn't attend; and beyond the truck a line of dead elms with the bark peeling from their diseased trunks; and beyond the elms a great bank of rainclouds from whose advance-guards above her the first spots of rain spattered on the dirty window, as she stared out of it, blurring the scene.

He was flannelling her, of course: he was Mr Lee, because there was always a Mr Lee in the Saracen's Head during opening hours, David had said—one Mr Lee or another, it didn't matter who—to take messages for Colonel Shapiro, that was Mr Lee's job.

And she, equally, was flannelling herself, still pretending up to the very last moment and beyond it that maybe she would, and maybe she wouldn't, give Mr Lee her message.

"Right, darlin'—" He knew it too "—speak up, then."

"All right. This message is for Mr Lee. He must contact our mutual friend, the one to whom he owes six favours—" Frances launched herself into space; time would tell if there were rocks far below, or too little water "—who is at present in our Washington Embassy. The contact must be indirect, but soonest."

"'Indirect, but soonest', I got that. And whose embassy would that be, now?"

"Mr Lee will know. The message then is 'Return to U.K. immediately. I will contact you through Mr Lee'. Have you got that?"

"Ah, I got it. But I ain't makin' no promises. If—"

"If nothing. Do it now. Or find another pub." She hung up before he could contest the threat, which was empty and childish and self-defeating, but the best she could manage in mid-air at short notice.

She reached up and swept the remains of her small change into her purse. One thing was for sure, anyway: she had burnt her boats with a vengeance. If Mossad's line into the Saracen's Head public house wasn't secure—David had thought it was okay, but David wasn't infallible; and the Israelis were damn good, but they weren't infallible either—then even if the eavesdroppers didn't manage to trace the call back to this forecourt (and they'd had enough time, it had lasted far too long for safety) there'd be enough on that tape to identify her, and David too, once the right people got round to listening to it.

The plus factor was that that would take time, because it would be a plain different section evaluating the tape, who certainly wouldn't be able to place her or her embassy straightaway, the more so as their heads would be full of their own Arab-Israeli hassles; it would have to travel through the proper channels, and because money and manpower were short some of those channels were so choked with material that it might take days . . . even weeks. There was even just a chance that it would sink altogether in some backwater.

But that wouldn't do at all, she chided herself: putting a smile on the face of a risk was a bad habit, it was always safer to assume the worst. And the worst . . . allowing for collation and transcription—and from her own typing pool days she could estimate that closely enough: as a semi-friendly, semi-civilised foreign agency Mossad wouldn't rate high on the pile at the moment—allowing for all that, the worst could be forty-eight hours before the balloon went up. . . . And then it would be back to that same ignominious typing pool, maybe.

She stared again through the window at the rain-distorted figure of the young man waiting for her under the canopy above his petrol pumps. She was deluding herself again, of course: breaking a direct instruction, and using a foreign intelligence service to do it, wasn't on a par with breaking school rules, as posted on the assembly hall notice-board for all to see. (*Everyone must keep to the LEFT in corridors and on staircases, and Forms must move in single file.*) It was big time stuff, like being caught with a boy in the shrubbery, *deshabillée*, which needed no written rules to indicate the likely punishment.

So, once they'd added two and two together it would be bread-and-water for some unspecified period, and then out on her shell-like ear, and back to her widow's pension with a framed copy of the Official Secrets Act, the relevant passages heavily underlined in red.

Unless, of course, it was Colonel Butler himself who was by then in charge of hiring and firing.

Irony, irony . . . all she had to do was to give him a clean bill of health. And although she could argue—and it was true—that she was only making contact with David Audley because it was the truth she was after, it was also true that the truth she was very much predisposed to uncover would give Colonel Butler his promotion, his Ring of Power.

She snapped her bag shut and stepped out briskly into the rain.

The young man looked at her with undisguised curiosity now: he was bursting to ask her about the souped-up engine under the bonnet.

"I've checked the oil, it's okay." He rubbed his hands on his bit of rag. "And the tyres—they're okay too . . ."

"Thank you." Frances stared at him discouragingly. The final irony would be for the promoted Colonel Butler to decide—being the man he was—that however grateful he might be for her disobedience he couldn't possibly overlook such unstable behaviour, such unreliability, in one of his agents. And a female agent too, by God!

"I—I've filled her up, too." He was nerving himself to pop some sort of question. "Fourteen gallons—or just under fourteen and a quarter, actually."

That was at least six gallons more than the normal tank of this make of small family car was designed to take, Frances computed. The only car they'd had spare when the Colonel had banished her from the university had been a tailing special, she'd known that the moment she put her foot down on the accelerator, though without any particular gratitude. But now it was certainly a convenient vehicle to possess.

"Thank you." She looked through him as she felt in her purse for a tip. Twenty pence would be enough, but a Honda Four-hundred-four sounded expensive, and he'd remember her whatever she gave him, so . . . say fifty, because he was so beautiful. "Could I have my receipt, please."

"Oh . . . yes, of course!" He blushed becomingly too. "Thank you very much."

"There's a Colonel Butler who lives just outside the village. Brookside House, I think the name is?"

"Brookside House . . . ?" Either the fifty-pence piece, or the engine, or the foxy lady Fitzgibbon seemed to have dried up his mouth.

"Colonel Butler. Brookside House."

"Yes." He nodded quickly. "Runs a Rover—a yellow Rover. And . . . he's got a daughter . . ." His eyes glazed again, exactly as they had done for the Honda Four-hundred-four. If that was for Diana Butler, she must be quite a dish, thought Frances.

"Three daughters."

"Yes. Three daughters—Brookside House." He focused on her briefly, and then pointed down the road towards the houses. "You go straight through the village, and then bear left at the junction, down the Sandford road, towards the motorway. It's about half a mile on, all by itself, with a long drive to the house, on the edge of the woods—you can't miss it."

"Thank you."

She wanted to give him a smile, to leave him with something that was really hers, but her mouth wouldn't obey orders, and there was no more time. The wipers swept the screen clear, but when she looked back in the mirror the first of the dead elms had blanked him out of sight, and she was alone again in her shadow country.

IX

TWENTY-FOUR HOURS earlier, before she had studied the edited highlights of the file on Colonel Butler, Brookside House would have ambushed Frances with surprise, even shock.

Now, of course, the opulent rhododendron tangles at its gateway and the manicured quarter-mile of gravel drive between trimly-fenced horse paddocks amounted to no more than a gloss on the file, computed at compound interest over the years since Captain Butler, *sole beneficiary (no relative) of General Sir Henry Chesney*, had capitalised on his inheritance.

The mathematics of the scene confirmed her previous estimate: Chesney and Rawle's had been an old-established, deeply-entrenched and almost disgracefully prosperous business, which had been sold when the pound was still something to conjure with (which was when little Frances Warren had been not long out of her push-chair). Even allowing for the depredations of a quarter of a century's taxation and inflation, and throwing in a full-time gardener and maybe a stableboy with nannie and the school fees of the last ten years, and adding them all to Brookside House, which had been purchased when the Colonel—then the Major—had finally quit his regiment . . . subtracting all this (and the running costs of Madeleine Françoise de Latour d'Auray Boucard) from the Chesney-Butler inheritance and there would hardly be a scratch in it, much less a dent.

The drive curved ahead, alongside a stable block. A horse poked its head out of a loose-box, returning her frown incuriously.

Add horses to the list . . . although of all people Colonel Butler was no horseman, surely . . . but add horses, nevertheless.

Still only a scratch, not a dent.

The daughters, then. Obviously the daughters. For girls the horse was as potent a symbol of power and glory as the motor-cycle was for boys—as the Honda Four-hundred-four was for that magnificent young man on the petrol pumps.

Quadruple garage ahead, beyond another great rhododendron jungle, and a collection of cars to be categorised: Nannie's Allegro in one open garage, under cover; a Police panda, white and pale blue; a gleaming Marina and another gleaming Marina, with close registration marks—both smelling of the Fuzz too, CID and Special Branch, for a guess . . . by their cars shall ye know them!

In a way, it wasn't just a disappointment, it was a surprise, all this. And it wasn't simply that it was hard to adjust Colonel Butler to this state of wealth and comfort which had not come to him either by right of birth or as the spoils of success, but rather that the product of it all—this house, this property, that horse—was not Butler.

Simply, but inexplicably, they cast the wrong shadow from her sharp memory of the man.

Colonel Butler—her Colonel Butler—was not stockbroker mock-Tudor and horse-paddocks. He was solid Victorian red brick, gabled and respectable and rooted in all the lost certainties of the nineteenth century, when the sun never set on his flag. His house, his true house, would be a house with good bone structure and secrets of its own, not a thing like this, with no past and no future, but only an endless ephemeral present.

This wasn't his house, it was *her* house—Madeleine Françoise's house—out of which she had stepped, across this gravel, down that drive, on to that road, to nowhere, nine years ago, almost to the very day if not to the actual hour.

"Mrs . . . Fisher?"

She had caught the footfall crunching on the gravel behind her. It had been more important to think that thought through than to turn towards the sound. Now she could come back to it later.

Fisher was careless of them. Here, where she could be remembered and described by Nannie, she could only be herself.

Nannie.

Mrs Elizabeth Mary Hooker, S.R.N., widow of Regimental Sergeant-Major Alfred Charles Hooker, Royal Mendip Borderers (killed in action, Korea 1951).

Nannie.

"Yes." She felt inside her bag for the Fisher credentials.

He studied them only briefly, because he had already stared his fill at her, taking in face and colouring, height and weight.

"Geddes, Mrs Fisher. Detective-Sergeant, Special Branch."

She took her details back from him, and his own. He was short for a copper, and long-haired, and swarthy enough to pass for a Pakistani. Which, all of it, might be not without its Special Branch uses, reasoned Frances.

"Thank you, madam." The dark eyes were bright with intelligence, assessing her but not stripping her. Storing her away for future references, too.

"But . . . for today's purposes I shall be Mrs Fitzgibbon, Mr Geddes." Because she liked the look of him, and also because she needed him on her side, she smiled at him carefully, without opening her lips. "Colonel Butler already knows me as Mrs Fitzgibbon."

"Very good, Mrs Fitzgibbon."

"You've met Colonel Butler?"

"Yes, madam. In the way of routine, that is. Not today, of course."

Like her own cottage, this was a house on the list. Which meant that the Special Branch would have checked out its security and the Uniform Branch would keep an eye on it, regularly but unobtrusively, day by day. In the way of routine.

She nodded. "Tell me about the break-in."

"Nothing to worry you." He smiled white teeth at her. "That's my guess, anyway . . . for what it's worth."

"Yes?"

"Small time job. No precise information—just looking for money and jewellery." He nodded over his shoulder towards the house. "This is the sort of place where it's usually lying around for the taking . . . easy pickings nowadays. Except that the Colonel doesn't leave it lying around, except on the walls."

"On the walls?"

"Some nice water-colours. Samuel Atkins, Copley Fielding, Paul Sandby . . . a couple of William Callows . . . a Labruzzi, rather a striking one. And the Turner, of course . . ."

"A Turner?" She was torn between surprise at his appreciation of art—a *rather striking* Labruzzi—and this new insight into Colonel Butler, whom she could no more place in an art gallery, catalogue in hand, than she could on a horse, bridle in hand. "You mean, J. M. W. Turner?"

"Only a minor drawing." He bobbed his head. "But very nice of its kind—the only thing of substantial value in the house. The only thing I'd take. Only not to get rid of. Probably too difficult to hock anyway . . . not rich enough for the hot market, but still easily traceable. Not worth the risk, in fact."

Her surprise had adjusted itself. There was no reason why a copper shouldn't know his art, and no reason why Colonel Butler shouldn't collect, with his money. It was no more surprising—rather, much less surprising—than Robbie's obsession with fairy stories.

Her nails dug into her palms. Why, just since yesterday, was she continually thinking of Robbie?

"Was anything taken?"

"So far as we can make out . . . three christening mugs—modern silver. One carriage clock, gilt. One transistor radio, plastic . . . Just small stuff, like the other places."

"The other places?"

"Didn't they tell you—no? This is one of three. The other two down the road, over Sandford way—" He pointed "—same sort of jobs: all done between eight and nine-thirty this morning, when the kids were being taken to school. Then the mothers went on to do a bit of shopping . . . here it was the house-keeper . . . and when they came home the back door had been forced. The other two places chummy found some cash—not much—and a bit of costume jewellery in one." He shook his head. "He didn't do very well for himself at all."

"I see." Frances exhibited relief which was only partly feigned. In fact the department's resident break-in artist, if there was such a person, seemed to have done quite nicely at short notice. "So it looks like a local job, then?"

He nodded. "That's what the DI thinks, and I can see no reason to disagree."

"Nobody saw anything?"

"Not a thing, so far. Each of the houses backs on to woods—he almost certainly came in that way, specially here, with the long drive. Plenty of cover at the back, and it's only half a mile from the side road to Winslow. Most likely a local boy with local knowledge. So . . . nothing to worry you, Mrs Fitzgibbon."

She smiled at him. "I think you're right, Mr Geddes." To one smile add a small sigh and a pinch of resignation. "But I shall have to go over the place all the same."

He cocked his head interrogatively, not quite frowning. "Is that really necessary, in the circumstances?"

"Probably not, in the circumstances. But Colonel Butler is engaged in extremely sensitive work and we haven't been able to contact him yet. So . . . he's entitled to the full treatment."

There wasn't much he could say to that, still less object to. Every service looked after its own vulnerable next-of-kin, and their service particularly, as a matter of security as well as routine commonsense enlightenment. And when something was actually amiss the job couldn't be skimped, he should know that.

All the same, there was no percentage in seeming to teach him to suck eggs, a woman who did that in a man's world only encouraged chauvinism. A little calculated femininity paid better dividends.

She spread the smile. "Besides, the Colonel's by way of being my boss most of the time. When he sees my signature on the release he'll talk to his housekeeper, and if I haven't impressed her with my devotion to duty I shall be cast into the outer darkness."

"Ah! That does make a difference—I take your point, of course." The corner of his mouth twitched. "I didn't know that you were . . . acquainted with the lady."

Frances regarded him curiously. "I'm not."

"You're not? Ah . . . well, then—" he gestured towards the house "—I'd better not keep you from your duty, Mrs Fitzgibbon."

He hadn't produced any of the reactions she'd expected, thought Frances as she walked beside him to the iron-studded mock-Tudor door in the mock-Tudor porch. In fact, except for the momentary twitch, he hadn't produced any reactions at all, expected or unexpected.

The heavy door was ajar, opening for her at the touch of his fingers on it. Beyond it, the entrance hall was high and spacious, with a great carved oak staircase dominating it, and gloomy in the November overcast except for the high-gloss polish of the parquet floor and the stair treads, which reflected a daylight hardly apparent outside. Frances corrected her first impression: not so much mock Tudor as Hollywood Tudor, art imitating art.

All it needed for an echo of *Rebecca* was the beautiful Mrs Butler on the staircase. But the woman on the staircase certainly wasn't the beautiful Mrs Butler.

Frances stood her ground as Nannie—it could only be Nannie—advanced toward her. It struck her as odd that she should feel she was holding her ground, but that was how she felt.

Then, as her eyes grew accustomed to the gloom, she knew that it wasn't odd at all, her instinct had simply been ten paces ahead of her eyesight.

Nannie wasn't much above average height, and she wasn't fat either, but she was . . . solid. Her battleship-grey twin-set matched the colour of her hair, and her hair matched the colour of her eyes. A large nose dominated her face: she levelled the nose at Frances and stared down it with all the friendliness of a gamekeeper come upon a poacher in the covert.

Frances opened her mouth in the hope that the right words would come out of it.

"I have absolutely nothing to say to you," said Nannie pre-emptively. The grey eyes flicked up and down Frances once, then nose and eyes swung towards Detective-Sergeant Geddes. "You gave me to understand, constable, that you would not tell the local newspaper anything about this."

"Yes, Mrs Hooker—"

"Indeed, you promised. You gave a positive undertaking—"

"I'm not a reporter," said Frances.

The nose came back to her. Nannie peered towards her, sighting her at point-blank range. "No? Well, you are exactly like the young woman who misreported me at the last parish council meeting." She scrutinised Frances's face again, then her suit. "You still look like her . . . but you are better dressed, it's true . . . Hmm! Then if you are not a reporter—what are you?"

"My name is Fitzgibbon—"

"You are not a policewoman. You are far too little to be a police-woman."

Detective-Sergeant Geddes cleared his throat. "Mrs Hooker—"

"You are not too young to be a policewoman—and you are not that girl who misreported me, I can see that now, she was much younger . . ." Nannie conceded the point on the basis of her own scrutiny, not on their denials. "You are older than you look too. It's in the eyes, your age is. Old eyes in a young face, that's what you've got. And also—" She stopped suddenly.

"Mrs Hooker, this is Mrs Fitzgibbon, from London—from the Colonel's department." Geddes seized his chance. "She's the person we've been waiting for, that I told you about."

"What?" Nannie frowned at him, then at Frances.

"I'm a colleague of Colonel Butler's," said Frances.

Disbelief supplanted the frown. "A colleague?"

"A subordinate colleague," Frances softened the claim.

Nannie transferred the disbelieving look to Geddes. "You didn't say it would be a woman," she accused him. "I expected a man."

Like master, like housekeeper, concluded Frances grimly:

Colonel Butler and Mrs Hooker had the same ideas about the natural order of things. Perhaps that coincidence of prejudice had been an essential qualification for the job nine years ago, when he had been casting around for someone to take charge of his motherless girls.

So now, although Nannie obviously disliked having policemen tramp over her highly-polished floors almost as much as she hated thieves, she might just have tolerated one of her employer's colleagues—any of his colleagues except this one, who added insult to injury by being the wrong shape and size.

Hard luck, Nannie, thought Frances unsympathetically. But more to the point, hard luck, Frances. Because here was an unfair obstacle on the course, the only clue to which had been that twitch of the detective-sergeant's just half a minute before it had loomed up in front of her. And more than an obstacle, too, because obstacles could be removed, or climbed, or jumped, or avoided.

Nannie was watching her intently, no longer with naked hostility, but without either approval or deference. And that was the problem: somehow, and very quickly, Mrs Hooker must approve of and defer to Mrs Fitzgibbon.

Small smile.

"Sorry, Nannie. But I'm afraid I'm the best they could manage at short notice. You'll have to make do with me." 'Nannie' was a risk, but she had to take a short cut to some degree of familiarity. And also, at the same time and without seeming too pushy—too unfeminine—she had to assert herself.

She turned to Geddes. "Who else is here?"

"Inspector Turnbull and his DC, madam. And the uniform man." Geddes gave her a glazed look. "I think they are out the back somewhere, in the garden."

She wanted them all out. She wanted Nannie to herself, without interruptions.

"Then would you be so good as to tell the Inspector that I'm here. please?" No smile for Detective-Sergeant Geddes. "Don't let him stop what he's doing. I'd just like to have a word with him before he goes . . . before you all go . . . will you tell him?"

"Very good, madam." Geddes moved smartly towards the door.

"And wipe your feet when you come back in," admonished Nannie to his back.

"Yes, madam." He sounded happy to be getting out of her way. What was more important, however, was that the foot-wiping

157

admonition offered one possible short-cut to Nannie's heart: the sooner Mrs Fitzgibbon got rid of the police, the better for Mrs Fitzgibbon.

"Now, Nannie . . . I take it the Colonel hasn't phoned, or anything like that?" She padded the question deliberately.

"No, Miss Fitzibbon." Nannie declared neutrality.

"Are you expecting a call from him? Does he call home regularly when he's away?" Frances decided to let the 'Miss' go uncorrected for the time being.

"No, Miss Fitzgibbon." Armed neutrality.

"I see . . . Well, we're doing our best to get in touch with him." Not true. "It's only a question of time."

Nannie stiffened. "There's no call to worry him."

Frances wondered how much Nannie knew about the nature of her employer's work. Probably not a lot, the Official Secrets Act being what it was, though enough to accept that a break-in at Brookside House could never be treated at its face value.

"I'm sure there isn't," she agreed gently. "But the rules say that we have to, for everyone's protection. So you must look on me as just part of the rules, Nannie."

Nannie thawed by about one degree centigrade. "Very good, Miss Fitzgibbon."

It was going to be hard work.

"At least I can get rid of the police for you, anyway," she offered her first olive branch with a conspiratorial grin. "There's no need for them to hang around now that I'm here."

As an olive branch it was not an overwhelming success: Nannie simply nodded her acceptance of the lesser of two evils.

More than hard work, decided Frances. "In the meantime, perhaps we could go somewhere a little less . . . public?" She looked at her watch: it was two o'clock already. "Somewhere where there's a telephone?"

Nannie glanced at the telephone on the table at the foot of the staircase, then back at Frances.

"There is a telephone in the library," she admitted grudgingly, indicating a door to Frances's right.

Frances followed her to the door. There had to be a bridge between them somewhere, or a place where the bank was firm enough to construct a bridge. Or even a ford where she could cross over to Nannie's side without drowning in the attempt.

The library really was a library: a long, high room entirely walled with books from floor to ceiling except for its two immense mullioned windows. The wooden floor shone with the same high gloss as that of the hall, but here there was no smell of polish, only the dry odour of accumulated knowledge on paper, compressed between old leather and matured over dozens of years. At the far end was an immense mahogany desk, in the direct light from one of the windows. All its drawers were open, one of the top ones pulled out so far that it rested at an angle on the one beneath it. A silver-framed photograph lay on the floor, face down.

Frances heard Nannie draw in her breath sharply beside her.

Suddenly Frances remembered how hot her own dear Constable Ellis had been on the subject of burglary—

"But I've nothing worth taking, Mr Ellis. I might just as well leave the cottage unlocked. They wouldn't find anything, no matter how hard they looked."

"Don't you believe it, Mrs Fitz. They'd take something you wouldn't want to lose, even if they left empty-handed."

"Now you're being too clever for me, Mr Ellis. Shame on you!"

"Oh no. If it happens to you, you'll know sure enough. And it'll make you sick, too. Because breaking into a woman's house—goin' through her private things, like the flimsy things she wears next to her skin, if you'll pardon me, like her knickers and her silk slips an' such-like—that's almost like rape when a stranger does it. So . . . breakin' into a house is like raping it. Raping its privacy, you might say. It isn't changed, not really. But it isn't the same, even if they don't take a thing."

Frances looked at Nannie. "Have the Police been through here?"

"Yes." Nannie continued to stare at the desk.

"Right, then." Frances walked across the library to the desk. First she fitted the displaced drawer into its runners and pushed it back into its proper place, and then slid back the other drawers, one after another (very neat and tidy was Colonel Butler; his letters held together with elastic bands, still in their original envelopes; his receipted bills in their appropriate folders—*School Fees* was the topmost folder in one drawer, *Insurance* in another; a place for everything, and everything in its place, that was Colonel Butler). Then she methodically straightened the desk diary and the pen-holder and the leather-bound calendar. And last of all she set the silver-framed picture in its proper place, on the left. The photograph was of Nannie herself and the three children at the seaside; judging by the size of the largest child it dated from the early 1970s.

"It's all right now—everything's all right. He—they were only looking for money, Nannie. The picture glass isn't broken."

"There wasn't any money in the desk," said Nannie, not to Frances but to the library itself, as though the thief was still hiding in it.

But then, of course, she was right: the thief was still hiding in it. A different thief, yet one who knew what she was after even if she didn't know what she might find. Not a conventional thief, who would take the water-colours off the walls and leave the drawers gaping, but certainly a thief within Constable Ellis's definition.

A thief, no doubt about that.

The thought was painful to Frances, but the pain helped to concentrate her mind on the job just when she'd been in danger of letting sympathy cloud her judgement.

"Don't worry, Nannie." She touched Nannie's arm reassuringly. Just a touch—a Judas touch; a pat would have been too much. "It won't happen again, we'll see to that."

Nannie looked down at the slender hand, then up at Frances.

"You know, I think we probably have friends in common," said Frances, testing the bridge cautiously. "Isn't the Colonel one of Cathy Audley's godfathers—David Audley's little daughter?"

Nannie regarded her for the first time with something approaching recognition.

"David Audley is another of my bosses." Frances smiled. "And I know his wife too. Have you met them—the Audleys?"

Nannie blinked, and her nose seemed less aggressive. "You know Dr Audley, Miss Fitzgibbon?"

"One of my bosses—my first, actually . . . Though I'm assigned to the Colonel at the moment. Which is why I'm here now, of course." Frances nodded encouragingly. The bridge—a totally false structure, but built with convenient pieces of genuine truth—was beginning to feel solid beneath her. It even occurred to her that she was building better than she had intended: if Colonel Butler himself didn't altogether approve of David Audley—at least if Paul Mitchell was to be believed—it looked as though Nannie differed from that view; and that coincided with her own observation, that while

Audley was generally rather rude to his equals, who were usually male, he was unfailingly courteous to women.

(The first time she'd encountered David Audley he'd been having a blazing row with Hugh Roskill, who hated his guts, when she'd been Hugh's secretary; and he—David—had apologised to her next day (but not to Hugh!) with a big box of After Eights.)

But she was losing momentum with Nannie now—and she only needed another few steps to be over the Bridge of Lies. Already she was so far over and committed to the crossing that the last worst lying truth, the truest lie, was no longer too outrageous to use.

"It's 'Mrs', not 'Miss', Nannie . . . actually."

"'Mrs'?" Nannie frowned, yet somehow more at herself than at Frances. "Oh . . . I'm sorry, Mrs Fitzgibbon . . ."

"Yes?" Frances hooked on to Nannie's uncertainty. One way or another she had to fish the right cue out of her. "Yes?"

"I'm sorry. I didn't quite catch what the constable said when he introduced you . . ." Nannie wriggled on the hook.

That wasn't the right cue. But it also wasn't what was really in Nannie's mind, Frances sensed. There was something else.

"Yes?" Frances jerked at the line. Given time she would have played Nannie gently, that was the whole essence of the art of interrogation, even with a hard-shell/soft-centre subject like this one. But time was what she hadn't been given, this time.

She looked down at her wrist-watch, and as she raised her eyes again she saw that Nannie was staring in the same direction.

She looked down again: Nannie couldn't be interested in the time; Colonel Butler's girls—*my girls*—didn't get home until 6.20, they did their two preps at school after tea, just as she had done once upon a time, a thousand years ago.

Nannie had looked down at the same angle—nose at the same angle—a few moments before, at the hand on her arm.

At the hand.

Frances looked at her hands. There was nothing to catch Nannie's interest, or her disapproval either (yesterday morning Marilyn's unspeakable Rose Glory red would have aroused that, but now the talons were trimmed and clear-varnished—now the hands were hers again).

Nothing—they were simply hands and fingers, unadorned.

Nothing!

Oh, beautiful! thought Frances—like the mention of David

Audley, it was better than she had designed, the ultimate true-lie handed to her—*handed* indeed!—on a plate, steaming hot and appetising!

She ought to have spotted it more quickly, the thing that she always looked for in other women. But now she mustn't spoil her good fortune by looking up from her third finger in triumph: and to get the right expression all she had to remember was what a dirty, despicable, millstone-round-the-neck unforgiveable lie she was about to tell.

The lie twisted under her breasts as she met Nannie's eyes.

"No wedding ring, you mean?" She spread the empty hand eloquently without looking down at it again. "No wedding ring?"

She clenched the fingers into a small fist as soon as she was sure that Nannie was looking at them.

"The ring is with my husband. He was killed in Ulster three years ago. Three years and six months and a week. He was with the SAS at the time, but he was a Greenjacket really. And we were married for seven months and four days." Frances plucked all the years and months and days out of the air for effect: she might as well be hanged for a sheep as a lamb, and lies that couldn't be checked ought always to be fully-grown and vigorous, and hard-working.

Now there was pain in Nannie's eyes, and that was good.

So . . . it was time for a little more truth.

"I was a secretary in the department—" Hugh was on good terms with Butler, as near a friend as the Colonel had among his colleagues "—Group-Captain Roskill's secretary. Do you know Group-Captain Roskill, Nannie?"

Nannie knew Hugh Roskill, she could see that. And since Hugh was also no slouch with women, young or old (though not in the David Audley class), that was good too.

In fact, she was home and dry now: Nannie knew enough to make all the necessary connections and deductions from the Fitzgibbon saga. Which was a merciful deliverance from the need to use the ultimate weapon, the last truth that was itself a deliverance of a sort; the little Robert, or little Frances, who hadn't made the grade, accident (or too much gin) cancelling out accident.

That wasn't even in the records, anyway, it was one of the few private things left, and she'd given enough by now to expect to collect on her investment.

"Your husband served with the Colonel, didn't he?" Frances

changed the subject unashamedly, as of right. It was Army widow to Army widow now, sister to sister in misfortune although separated very nearly grand-daughter-grandmother in years.

Nannie nodded. "Yes, he did."

"I thought so." Frances let the answer appear to confirm what might have been an intelligent guess; it would never do to reveal how much she knew about RSM Hooker and his lady, from the Butler file.

Unfortunately, Nannie didn't seem disposed to enlarge on the relationship. It was depressing to find that even the home-and-dry ground was still hard going.

"In the Lancashire Rifles?" There was no way Nannie could let that misapprehension go by, she had to correct it.

"No, dear—"

No, dear! That 'dear' had been dearly bought, even haggled over, but she had it at last.

"No, dear. Mr Hooker was a Mendip—the Royal Mendip Borderers. The Colonel came to us in Korea, *from* the Rifles." The nose moved eliptically between them, half correcting and half confirming. "And he was a captain then, of course, when he came to us."

(To us. It was still *us* after more than a quarter of a century, the family *us* of RSM Hooker's long-time widow; it could have been *us* with the Widow Fitzgibbon just as easily, if she'd indicated the need; they would probably have found her another subaltern if she'd indicated that need—probably given the poor sod his courting orders, they were old-fashioned that way; even as it was there was often something waiting for her in the accumulated post at the cottage, like the regimental newsletter, and always a Christmas card.)

(Even Nannie here in front of her was a proof of the durability of the system: all those years after Korea—*us in Korea*, when Nannie had never been within five thousand miles of the place—Butler had remembered the widow of the RSM of his adoptive regiment when he'd needed someone for his girls.)

"Of course—I understand now." Frances nodded wisely, and decided to change the subject again. She had the vague memory, from one of Robbie's attempts to explain how the army had been reorganised—massacred—in 1970, that the Mendips had been swallowed up in the Somerset and Cornwall Light Infantry. But it really was a vague memory, and it wouldn't do at all to exhibit a lack of military knowledge in such an area, when there was nothing more to be gained there.

She glanced around her. She could ask about this library, which had more books in it than ever Colonel Butler could have read. But that question would sound too obviously chatty, even though she genuinely wanted a quick answer to it; and she could get the answer easily enough for herself, though not so quickly, simply by looking at those books—always providing she remembered how completely Paul had mis-read the ones by her own fireside.

Better to get down to business, that was something Nannie would accept without suspicion.

"Now, Nannie . . . what I have to do—is to decide what sort of break-in this has been. This is because . . . of the kind of work the Colonel does." She gave Nannie half a smile. "It's just a precaution, that's all—a sort of double protection, in addition to what the Police provide."

As soon as she'd said it, she wished she hadn't, because in the circumstances of those open drawers and missing christening mugs it was gobbledygook, and from the slight lift of the eyebrows over those grey eyes it was quite clear that Nannie knew it was, too.

Then the eyebrows went back to normal, and the half-smile was returned.

"Yes, dear—I understand that," said Nannie. "The Colonel has been through the routine with me. You don't need to explain. If it's all right you sign a form and give it to me, and the Police carry on a normal investigation." She nodded helpfully.

It occurred to Frances that she hadn't got a release with her. Maybe Detective-Sergeant Geddes had one—maybe he had a whole pocket full of them. But it really didn't matter now that Nannie was on her side.

It didn't seem to matter much to Nannie either, suddenly; she had her sang-froid back, though it was a subtly-altered coolness, now a benevolent neutrality more concerned with Frances than herself, even to the extent of accepting that garbage about double-protection without irritation.

Just as suddenly Frances felt ashamed of what she'd done, what she'd had to do. It wasn't lying about Robbie—the ring, that little circle of white gold, wasn't with him, it was in the bag on her shoulder, to be used as necessary; she simply hadn't bothered to put it on today, it hadn't been important—if there was deceit there, it didn't matter because it betrayed nothing of value. But deceiving Nannie was something different.

"And it *is* all right, dear," said Nannie solicitously. "You don't need to worry. Because this is just . . . an ordinary robbery, the constable said so." She nodded. "He said there have been two others just like it this morning.

"But of course . . . of course, you have your job to do, and so you must talk to the constable for yourself, dear. But I've been all over the house with him—the constable thought the burglar didn't have very long in the house, because Mr Rodgers was cutting up the elm in the home pasture, and he came back to the workshop to get the bushman-saw at 9.15—the constable thinks the burglar saw him coming, and that scared him off . . ." Nannie piled non-event on non-event in an attempt to reassure the young Widow Fitzgibbon that there really was nothing to worry about in Brookside House, banking up the coals-of-fire on the widow's head.

"Thank you, Nannie."

"The Colonel *could* come back tonight. He does try to be here as often as possible, you know . . . though as tomorrow is the 11th he'll be off early if he does come—"

The telephone on the desk pealed out, cutting her off in mid-flow to Frances's overwhelming relief.

"I'll take it—" Frances was halfway to the desk before Nannie could react.

She lifted the receiver.

"Is that you, Bessie?" said a voice quickly.

Frances glanced down at the number. "Wilton Green 326."

"Sally?" The voice sounded surprised. "Is that Sally?"

Sally?

Sally equals *Sarah*—equals *Sarah Butler, born 1961.*

"Hold on a moment." Frances looked at Nannie "I think it's for you, Nannie. . . . Who is that speaking, please?"

"Hullo?" The voice, which had been excited before it had become surprised, now became dauntingly well-bred. "This is the Matron of the Charlotte Tyson Nursing Home. If that is Wilton Green 326—3-2-6—may I speak with Mrs Elizabeth Hooker, please?"

All that was a far cry from *Is that you, Bessie?* But it was the right cry, nevertheless.

"It's the Matron of the Charlotte Tyson Nursing Home, Nannie."

"Oh . . . yes." Nannie took the receiver from her. "Don't go, dear—it's a friend of mine."

Frances estimated the distance between the desk and the door and the phone in the hall, and the time needed to get from one to the other.

"I'll wait outside, Nannie."

As Nannie put the phone to her ear she stepped out smartly towards the door.

"Don't go—there's no need to go—"

She reached the door, and then turned back to Nannie. "It's all right—I'll come back when you've finished."

That was five seconds gained—and add another five seconds for Nannie's embarrassment. Then, close the door and subtract five seconds for the time it took to reach the table at the foot of the staircase.

Click.

Frances found herself looking at herself in the mirror at the bottom of the stairs as she lifted the phone.

Would Nannie know what that *click* signified?

"Are you there, Muriel—hullo?"

The mirror at the bottom of the stairs.

"Bessie—hullo, is that you, Bessie?"

I heard him stop at the bottom of the stairs, as though he was thinking—or as though he was looking at himself in the mirror there—

"—quite awful. And the Police traipsing round makes it worse, because I'm sure they'll never catch anyone—"

Sod it! She was missing the dialogue!

"How absolutely beastly for you, dear. And are they still there? The police, I mean? Because that wasn't Sally who answered the phone, was it?"

"No, dear. Sally's still at school, she doesn't know anything about it yet, neither does Jane. It all happened after I took them to school this morning, while I was in the village."

"I didn't think it was Sally. . . . Did they take anything?"

"The children's christening mugs, and the clock in the lounge. And my radio from the kitchen . . . nothing important . . . the Police think Rodgers may have disturbed them."

"Rodgers saw them?"

166

"No. *Disturbed* them. No one saw anything."

"That wasn't Mrs Rodgers on the phone, was it?"

"No."

"It wasn't Mrs Rodgers?"

"No. She's never here on a Thursday."

"I didn't think it was Mrs Rodgers. Who was it?"

There was a pause while Nannie considered how to deal with her friend's curiosity.

"It was a policewoman. Why do you want to know, Muriel?"

"Oh . . ." Muriel sounded disappointed. Then she perked up. "Is she staying with you, Bessie?"

"Staying with me?" Nannie was clearly mystified. "Why should she stay with me?"

"Well . . . with the Colonel away . . ." Another thought occurred to Muriel. "Or is he coming back now, after the robbery?"

"Is he—?" Nannie graduated from mystification to suspicion. "Muriel, why are you phoning me? What's the matter?"

Now it was coming, thought Frances. The trouble was that Muriel—Matron Prebble—was a lot less formidable than she'd bargained for.

"Look, Bessie—" The voice hardened: it was less like Muriel and more like Matron Prebble, thank God! "—something important has come up . . . I hardly know how to put it to you, with what's happened, my dear, but it truly is important. In fact, it's a life-line, the one we've been praying for, Bessie."

"What?"

"I've just had a call from Sir Archibald Havergal—"

"Who?"

"Sir-Archibald-Havergal. He's chairman of the grants committee of the Ryle Foundation, my dear—enormously rich—"

All the perfumes of Arabia—the Ryle millions and the smell of oil—were enough to sweeten almost any hand. But were they enough to sweeten Nannie's?

"We're in line for a grant, Bessie dear—a big one! We'd have to take some post-operative recuperation patients from the Middle East, of course . . . but that would be no problem, we could have a new wing for them. And the work we could do for the elderly—it's what we've prayed for."

"That's wonderful news, Muriel!" exclaimed Nannie.

"I've got to go to London as soon as possible—this very afternoon. If I phone back directly they'll send a car for me. I'm to meet Sir Archibald and a representative of the United Gulf Emirate at a hotel—an hotel. And they want me to stay the night to sign the papers in the morning. They even want Mr Toynton of the solicitors to come up with me, he's to stay the night, too. All paid for by the Foundation."

Nannie said nothing to that, even though Muriel waited desperately for her to react.

"I've tried everyone, Bessie. Mrs McGuffin can't. And Matron at St. Elfrida's can't. And the Cottage Hospital can't supply anyone until tomorrow morning. You've just got to come, my dear—I can't leave everything to Gloria, she's not nearly up to it. She'd panic at the first emergency. You've *got* to come—at least until 9 o'clock tomorrow, when Sister Bellamy says she can be here."

Nannie was thinking now—Frances could hear her thinking. And she was thinking 'no', and that had to be prevented from reaching her tongue, at all.

She ran back to the library door, tiptoe on tiptoe, skidding dangerously on the polish, grabbing the door-handle for safety.

"Finished, Nannie?" She just managed to catch her breath.

Nannie frowned at her distractedly.

"Er . . . no, dear."

"Trouble?" She didn't have to be the Department's hot little female property, Sir Frederick's Four-out-of-Ten girl, to chance that insight: it was written all over Nannie Hooker's face.

"What's the problem?" There was no time for delicacy. "Can I help?"

Nannie held the receiver against her corseted chest. "No, dear. A friend of mine wants me to . . . to help her. But of course it's out of the question."

"Help her how?" Frances advanced towards her, all interested innocence.

There was nowhere for Nannie to go: she was trapped at both ends of the telephone. "She wants me to . . . to look after her nursing home tonight. It's what I normally do for her one day every week, and one night. But I can't do it tonight—" she started to lift the receiver to her mouth.

"Is it important?" Frances persisted.

Nannie nodded, suddenly irresolute. She knew what was coming, Frances sensed.

"Then of course you can help her. I can stay for the children—" Frances sprang under her guard "—I'd *love* to—and I can stay the night, too—no problem. I haven't got to be anywhere until midday tomorrow, no one's waiting for me . . . And if the Colonel comes back I can report to him, it'll actually save me a lot of trouble—"

That was a mistake: Nannie wouldn't approve of doing the right thing for the wrong reason. She had to make it an appeal, not just a convenient duty offered, but also an act of kindness to her.

"Please. I'd much rather look after the children than go back home . . . to a cold home."

Good one, Frances! Lonely little Widow Fitzgibbon.

"And I do like children, Nannie—"

Another good one.

"I can even cook, you know. All you have to do is to tell me what their favourite supper is—I'd *so* enjoy cooking for someone again."

She was even beginning to convince herself, even though she hated cooking. The phone in Nannie's hand chuntered impotently. Nannie raised it to her mouth without taking her eyes off Frances. "Hold on a moment, Muriel."

"It would be an adventure for them, too. Getting used to me, it would take their minds off the robbery, Nannie." Frances nodded. "What time do they get back from school?"

"A quarter past six," replied Nannie automatically.

If they didn't like anything too elaborate that would still leave her enough time, thought Frances. And, for a guess, they probably preferred a quick fry-up anyway—bangers and beans, or bacon and eggs—and she could manage that. "What do they like?"

The corner of Nannie's mouth lifted.

And pancakes to follow. The entire human race liked pancakes; and they were not only a treat, they were easy to produce—even Robbie had never faulted her pancakes.

Nannie was still observing her closely, and suddenly Frances knew that Nannie was almost listening in to the menus which were running through her brain.

"What do they like, Nannie?"

The phone came up again. "Muriel—"

Detective-Inspector Turnbull left at five to three.

(Detective-Inspector Turnbull had decided that it was a routine job, a quick in-and-out semi-professionally executed by a borstal graduate with more technical skill than intelligence, whom they would pick up sooner or later asking for thirty-seven other offences to be taken into consideration, and who would be patted on the head by the judge, given five pounds out of the poor box and told not to be a naughty boy again, and who would promptly do it again since it was more fun than working and a useful addition to the unemployment benefit; but Detective-Inspector Turnbull was also relieved that Mrs Fitzgibbon agreed with him instantly, with no awkward questions and an equally quick signature on the release, and he was happy to leave Detective-Sergeant Geddes to deal with that and to do anything else Mrs Fitzgibbon required, no matter what.)

And Nannie left at ten past three in her uniform, half excited for the gold future of the Charlotte Tyson Nursing Home, but still half worried about leaving her charges to Widow Fitzgibbon, and consequently also leaving very precise instructions to the Widow—

("Jane can watch the Nine O'Clock News on BBC-1, if she wishes to, *in her dressing gown*—the Colonel likes them both to keep up with world affairs. And Sally can watch the first half—the first half *only*—of the ITV news at ten o'clock . . . And don't take any argument from either of them, dear. Tell them that you know the rules, they are good girls really, so you won't have any trouble with them, but they will argue—")

—and a letter conferring her power-of-attorney on the Widow, pending her return or the return of their father, whichever might be the earlier.

("I'll mention the Colonel, dear, that will give them something to think about, so they won't play you up—they *are* good girls, but they are half-way between being girls and being young women, and that can be awkward, believe me.")

And Detective-Sergeant Geddes left at quarter past three, with his release signed and sealed in its envelope (*For the attention of the Chief Constable* ready-typed on the latter).

("Is there anything else I can do for you, Mrs Fitzgibbon?")

("Yes, Mr Geddes. There's a Chinese take-away restaurant on the edge of town, a new one opened about two months ago." The Widow Fitzgibbon consulted the price-card Nannie had given her. "The Wango-Ho, in Botley Street . . .

("Here's seven pounds, Mr Geddes. I'd like two sweet-and-sour pork, one chicken-and-almonds, and one beef-and-green-peppers. Plus three portions of rice—two fried and one boiled—and three spring rolls. And I would like it delivered here at 6.30 sharp this evening—if there's any change, put it in the police charities' box.")

Twenty past three.

The sound of Detective-Sergeant Geddes' car had faded away.

Rodgers, the house-horse-and-garden handyman, who so fortunately hadn't seen anything this morning, had faded away too.

("Three o'clock is his time on a Thursday, dear. But if you'd rather not be alone I can ask him to stay on, and I'm sure he will—I can stop by Mrs Rodgers' cottage and leave a message to say that he'll be late home . . . Thursday is her day at the Vicarage, but I can give the message to the woman next door.")

("No, Nannie, it's quite all right. I don't mind being alone, it doesn't worry me.")

It was still not absolutely quiet in Brookside House: she could hear the distant rumble of the central heating boiler.

That at least had been the truth: she didn't mind being alone—even if it hadn't been necessary she wouldn't have minded it, it wouldn't have worried her. Aloneness was now her natural habitat, whether she was by herself or in a crowd. Originally she had set herself to get used to it. Then she had become accustomed to it. And now she preferred it.

The boiler stopped, and its echoes quickly died away.

Frances stood in the middle of the empty hall and listened to the silence begin, waiting for it to reassure her.

She imagined it forming in the top of the house, where at the noisiest of times there would always be a secret yeast of it, ready to grow the moment the front door slammed shut. From there it would seep down, from floor to floor and room to room, until it had filled every last corner.

Roof space, carefully lagged (Colonel Butler's house would be carefully lagged); attics and box-rooms; bedrooms one by one, master bedroom (there would be one single bed), children's bedrooms, guest bedrooms, Nannie's self-contained flat; bathrooms and dressing rooms and lavatories; then down the staircase, tread by tread; into the hall, into the breakfast-room and the dining room, and the kitchen and the pantry and the laundry room; into the library, curling round the desk; into the playroom and the study room; into the television room, into the sitting room, into the conservatory (how a conservatory fitted into Hollywood mock-Tudor remained to be seen, but a conservatory there was, nevertheless).

Now she could hear it all around her. The house was ready for her at last.

X

"IF I WAS your mother, Jane," said Frances deliberately, coldly seizing her opportunity, "I would say that you've just put a great deal too much in your mouth."

Jane attempted for a moment to manipulate her spring roll, which was collapsing greasily down her chin.

"If . . . if you were my mother—*oops!*—" A tangle of bean sprouts dropped out of the roll on to the spectacular mound of sweet-and-sour-pork, chicken-and-almonds and beef-and-green-peppers which Jane had arranged in an enormous crater of rice "—*if* you were my mother, then you would have been ten when Father married you—no, ten when you had *me* . . . and eight when you had Sally, and six when you had Di. Which, according to the sex talks Baggers gives us at school, is just not on."

"No." Sally raised an elegant morsel on her chopsticks. "She's about twenty-eight. She could just have had you—if she was exceptionally unlucky."

Frances wondered whether that *unlucky* was a purely biological judgement, or whether Sally was referring specifically to her sister. At the great age of seventeen Sally Butler handled her chopsticks like a Chinaman and was too clever by half, or maybe by three-quarters. Fortunately for the human race—the male half of it, anyway—she was also homely and horsey, apart from the superb hair; but to have been beautiful and that smart would have been unfair on both her and mankind, the contest would have been totally one-sided.

"Twenty-eight?" Jane examined Frances with the appraising eye of a second-hand car dealer. "Yes, I suppose you could be right at that."

Frances felt the need to keep her end up, to join them if she couldn't beat them. "And that would make Sally your step-sister," she observed. Mother would have to wait for another opportunity.

"And that wouldn't be bad, either," said Jane, who was obviously accustomed both to her elder sister's accuracy in guessing ages and also to the need to keep her own end up also. "Are you really as old as that? You don't look it, you know, Frances."

"I don't think I could be your mother, quite," Frances parried the question. *Not that I wouldn't like to be*, she thought quickly. At fifteen Jane was beginning to lose her puppy-fat and to exhibit the red-gold beauty of her eldest sister, if the portrait in the master-bedroom hadn't lied.

In fact, where Sally had diverged from the mould somewhere along the line to become a true Butler daughter, Jane might well end up more like Madeleine Françoise than the fabled Diana.

Sally stared at her for an instant, catching her in the act of projecting her sister's face into the future.

"You know about our mother, don't you?" Sally selected a sweet-and-sour pork ball from its fellows. "It'll all be in Father's print-out, of course."

God Almighty! thought Frances—Father's print-out!

"Twenty-eight is quite old," said Jane, to no one in particular. "Relatively old, anyway. Not *too* young, anyway."

Frances looked from one to the other. Jane munched complacently; Sally lifted the pork ball on her chopsticks and popped it into her mouth.

"Your Father's . . . print-out?" Not too young for what?

"Computer print-out. Everything's on computer, obviously," Sally informed her.

Jane stopped munching. "What sort of computer?"

Sally ignored her sister. "Isn't it?"

"Oh—I get you," said Jane. She nodded to Frances. "You know our mother's dead, that's what she means. Well . . . not strictly speaking dead—strictly speaking she's missing. But after all these years it's like the war—like Nannie's husband. He's still missing, although they know he was killed, because Father was there. But they lost him after that." She made it sound almost like carelessness. "He wasn't there when they came back, anyway—there was just a shell-hole."

On one level they were both being incredibly cold-blooded, almost to the point of childishness much younger than their actual years, even allowing for the retarding effect of an English private girls' school education; but they had been just as cool over the break-in—or, at least, Jane had been just as cool, and Sally had been cool once it had been established to her satisfaction that the thief had not put a sacrilegious hand on either of her horses.

However, that hadn't surprised Frances, from her own memories

174

of a similar education. The order and discipline of their school lives, with its well-defined rules and regulations, emphasised the disorder and indiscipline of the jungle outside, so that they were able to take the break-in as something like a misfortune of war. Also, she recalled that petty theft was more or less endemic at school (*Money must NEVER be left in the cloakrooms or in the desks*), and an endless subject for rumour and speculation. To have been burgled would provide them both with an exciting tale next day which would lose nothing in the telling.

What was disturbing all the same—or tantalising, anyway—was the suspicion (also out of her own memories) that they were also operating on another level, the nature of which she had not as yet fathomed. But children like this, who were immature in some areas, were apt to be precocious in others.

They were waiting for her to say something.

"Your Father is very much my senior." That was a statement they could both understand. "So I don't get to see his . . . print-out . . . any more than you see your reports."

Jane swallowed her mouthful. "We do see our reports," she said. "And I bet Father's seen your print-up—print-out, I mean."

"I expect he has." And now to business. "I'm sorry to hear about your mother."

"What does your husband do?" Sally's hitherto impeccable manners suddenly deserted her. "Does he work for Father?"

"My husband is dead."

"How?" said Jane.

Nannie was prettily revenged. "He was a soldier."

"A soldier—?" Jane regarded her with interest. "Like Father, was he?"

"*Tais-toi!*" snapped Sally. "I'm awfully sorry, Frances."

"So am I," said Jane quickly. "What rotten luck!"

"Shut up," said Sally. "Our mother died nine years ago, that's what the Police think. After seven years a missing person is presumed to be dead, anyway."

Frances was beginning to feel out of her depth. "Is that so?" she said inadequately.

"That's right," agreed Jane in a totally matter-of-fact voice. "Like in the war. There's 'Missing, believed killed in action', and there's 'Missing, presumed killed in action', and there's just plain 'Missing'. Maman was 'Missing', but after seven years it's the same as 'Missing, presumed killed in action'." She nodded at Frances. "'Presumed' is really when they don't actually know, but it's the most likely thing. When they've got some evidence—like with Nannie's husband, Father was there in the trench with him when the Chinese attacked, and saw him get shot, but then he had to go to another bit of the trench, and then they were shelled, you see—" she nodded again "—our side shelled them, Father called them up on his wireless and said 'There are hundreds and hundreds of Chinese here, and only a few of us, so if you shell us you're going to kill a lot more of them—'"

"He didn't say that at all," cut in Sally. "Father had built this sort of tunnel, and he retreated into it with his men. It was what they'd planned to do if things got really bad. Father had it all planned, exactly what they were going to do, Frances."

"Well, it was still jolly brave—they gave him a medal for it," said Jane.

"I didn't say it wasn't. I just said it was *planned*."

"All right, all right! Anyway . . . when they came out of the tunnel and drove the Chinese off the hill—it was a hill they were on, just above a river—when they got back to the trench there was a shell-hole where Nannie's husband had been, so they had to make it 'Missing, *believed*', that's all I'm saying."

Frances groped for a suitable reaction. Jane was clearly determined to inform her, apart from the fine distinctions of the military casualty list, that her father was a gallant officer; while Sally, for her part, favoured intelligence above bravery, and was equally determined to establish that. Unfortunately it was not the information she required from them.

"I see." Yet she didn't really see at all.

A hill in Korea, a quarter of a century or more ago: how many children—how many adults, for that matter—knew anything about that old war? How much did she herself know?

She shook herself free of it. She wasn't concerned with RSM Hooker, of the Mendip Borderers, or even with Captain Butler, Mendip Borderers (attached). She was concerned with Major and Mrs Butler.

But she still couldn't think of anything to say.

"So that was what happened to our mother," said Jane.

'I'm sorry' would hardly do. And in any case, she'd already said it once. If anything, she was now further away from the vital question than before these unnerving children had re-opened the Korean War.

"But then, it was probably all for the best," continued Jane philosophically. "It probably wouldn't have lasted, the way it was going."

It wouldn't have lasted. It was all for the best—the way it was going?

It wouldn't have lasted?

"Lots of the girls at school are in the same boat," Jane nodded at her. "Baggers says the one-parent family is going to be the big social problem of the 1980s, with the present rate of divorce."

It wouldn't have lasted.

"But that doesn't take account of re-marriages." Sally rested one elbow on the table and looked intensely at Frances. "What do you think of second marriages, Frances?"

"I haven't really thought about them." The question momentarily unbalanced Frances just as she was zeroing in on Jane. "I don't know . . . What do you mean, 'it wouldn't have lasted', dear?"

"I think second marriages are a good thing," said Jane. "I mean, it stands to reason that you know better what to look for the second time round—'Marry in haste and repent at leisure' is what Baggers says, and she could be right for once. I think I shall almost certainly get married twice: the first time will be a terrible mistake—it'll be a purely physical thing, an animal passion I won't be able to resist . . . Or it may be plain lack of experience, like David Copperfield and Dora. I can never imagine David Copperfield in bed with Dora, it must have been an absolute disaster. The mind boggles—at least, my mind boggles. What d'*you* think, Frances?"

Frances's mind wasn't boggling, but it was hurting her more than she could tolerate. Unlike Jane, she could imagine exactly what had happened in David Copperfield's bed, down to the last humiliating detail.

Jane didn't wait for an answer. "So the first time will be a ghastly mistake—but the second time I shall get it right. And I'll be an absolutely super step-mother too. I shalln't try to be a mother, I'll be like an elder sister, only better . . . And my step-children will be the most marvellous aunts to *my* children, if I decide to have any. It'll be an extended nuclear family—all for one, and one for all, like the Three Musketeers!"

It was fair enough for those who could identify themselves with the King's Musketeers, thought Frances—and the set books at school hadn't changed much, obviously. But Jane's sharp little sword was making her feel like one of the Cardinal's Guards.

"What did you mean, 'It wouldn't have lasted'?" She hung on grimly to her original question.

"Oh . . . they didn't get on, Father and Maman," said Jane off-handedly. "That's all."

"You don't remember," said Sally. "You were only a baby."

"I was six—"

"And a baby."

"And you were an old-age pensioner, I suppose. I was there just as much as you—in fact more, because you and Di were at school. I can even remember the day Maman went—she was furious with Father, I can still remember that. Because he wanted to go early, while it was still dark, and she said he didn't have to. And he said he had to."

"Had to do what?" Frances felt the old excitement, the old drug, heighten her perception: suddenly she was a fly on the wall in the past, on that other November day nine years ago, because of this child's total recall; which, in spite of the boastful words, was the total recall of a deep wound still raw inside her, which wouldn't heal until somebody who understood its nature set about treating it; and Nannie could never do that, and her Father couldn't either, because he didn't know about it, because there was no way the child could tell him about it, not in a million years.

Well, that wasn't her job. Her job was to re-create that moment and to observe it—the moment which William Ewart Hedges had suspected—'no matter *what he thought of her*', he'd let slip—and which she had also suspected even before he'd let it slip.

Not Four-out-of-Ten, Frances—Frances Warren, Frances Fitzgibbon—and not Five-out-of-Ten, or Six, or Seven, or Eight, or Nine. This was the real thing, the Ten-out-of-Ten monster inside her, which had no rational explanation, which was frightening when she thought about it.

"Had to do what?"

Jane's eyes clouded—

God! There was another Ten-out-of-Ten, except it should have been obvious to her long before, what they were about with their well-rehearsed dialogue, why they were at such pains to tell her such secrets!

No. She mustn't even think of that, it was ridiculous!

"Oh . . . he had to get somewhere by 11 o'clock—he had an

appointment, or something. And he wasn't going to break it for any-thing, no matter what she said, he said—Maman shouted at him on the stairs, I heard her, I was sick in bed. He didn't shout, of course—he never shouts. But he was quite *loud* for him." She nodded. "He said he had to go, and he jolly well went. It was duty, I expect."

Having approximately three hours on my hands, and there being no other duties scheduled, I adjusted my route to take in my home town of Blackburn, arriving there at 1020 hours and departing at 1125 hours. While in Blackburn I spoke to no one—

No appointment . . . which Major Butler wasn't going to break for anything. Or anyone—angry wife or sick child.

"Well, that was jolly unusual for them, they didn't row like that very often. It was mostly they were simply cold and uptight—or Maman was, anyway," said Sally, conceding a trench she could not defend, but standing fast on her main position. "I think the whole trouble was that they didn't shout at each other enough—Maman went one way, and Father went another, that was the trouble. She didn't like cricket, for example."

"Cricket?" Frances tightened her jaw quickly, before it could fall off.

"Cricket is a very interesting game, you know," said Sally. "It isn't as exciting as show-jumping, but in some ways it *is* quite scientific. You ought to watch it, Frances. Father will explain it to you—he's terrific at explaining."

"Cricket is a dull game," said Jane.

"Don't be stupid, Jay." Sally's voice slashed at her sister. "Frances would enjoy cricket if Father explained it to her."

Frances glanced side-long at Jane: she knew with a terrible certainty that the child was about to stand her opinion of cricket on its head.

"I don't mean *dull*—" There was a slight flush to the peach cheeks "—it only seems . . . I mean, it only seems *difficult* if you don't understand it. Like . . . like additional maths. But once you've got the hang of it . . . then it has an inner poetry all of its own, cricket does."

Another of the *obiter dicta* of the redoubtable Miss Baggers (or whatever her real name might be, Baggott, Bagnall or Bagley for choice) was being hurriedly conscripted for service outside its original context.

"It does?" Frances melted in the heat of the desperation the child was striving to hide under false enthusiasm. "Yes, I'm sure it does."

She could well afford to be merciful now; she had what she wanted out of them, they had given it to her without any effort on her part, freely out of their own need. And she could get more, anything she liked, for the asking simply by giving them the tiniest bit of encouragement.

"Our mother was foreign, of course—she was French. You can't expect a French person to understand cricket," said Sally suddenly, as though prompted by a stirring of older loyalty. Then she frowned. "Not that it really is difficult—Jane's quite wrong there."

She was recalling herself to her duty, to the more important business in hand, which had to be done, thought Frances bleakly.

The business of imparting information about the virtues and interests of Colonel Jack Butler;

The business of discovering, at the same time, information about the background and character of Mrs Frances Fitzgibbon;

And, on the basis of the latter, and also on Mrs Fitzgibbon's reactions to the former, the business of deciding whether Mrs Fitzgibbon would be a suitable wife and step-mother for Brookside House.

"Have you ever watched cricket?" asked Jane. "Or do you ride horses?"

Frances thought: *The poor little things must be pretty hard-up for eligible females to grab me so quickly.*

And then: *They probably are hard-up. Mostly they'll only meet their friends' mothers (was that where the one-parent-family interest came in? Had they already looked over that field and found it wanting? Or didn't they fancy step-sisters as well as a step-mother?).*

And then: *Or their friends' elder sisters, who would be too young (and she herself was almost too young).*

And then: *Yet maybe not so unsuitable, at that: an army widow (one tick there), in the same line of work (so she'd know the score there—two ticks), who liked Chinese take-away meals and obviously didn't actively dislike cricket.*

Poor little things indeed! Diana going off to University, the first bird to fly the nest, would have brought home to them that they were getting older and the world wouldn't stand still; and that Father was travelling a lonely road which could only become more lonely as they followed Diana—in their place would she have thought that far ahead, like this?

And then, brutally: *Sod it! She wasn't in the business to solve teenage girls' family problems—her business wasn't to be either merciful or cruel.*

"I've done both, as a matter of fact, Jane. And I wield a mean hockey stick, too." *And I play dirty, too, Jane dear.* "But I didn't know your mother was French. Tell me about her—how did your father meet her, for a start—?"

XI

PAUL MITCHELL CAME to Brookside House like a thief, very quietly, after dark and by the back entrance, following her instructions to the letter, but arriving inconveniently nevertheless, just as Frances was demonstrating her pancake-tossing expertise to a devoted audience.

Because of that it was Jane who answered the knock on the door.

"There's a man for you, Frances."

"A man?" The kitchen was separated from the back-door by a lobby, and the fizzling of the pancake mixture in the frying-pan had drowned the back-door dialogue. "What sort of a man?"

Jane sniffed—not a pancake-sniffing sniff, a disapproving sniff. "A young man. Not a policeman."

"How d'you know he's not a policeman? Policemen can be young."

"He smiled at me." Jane didn't elaborate on the significance of that, but doubtless Baggers had warned her against smiling strangers. "He wants to talk to you, he said."

"Have you let him in?" Frances toyed with the notion of sending Paul—it had to be Paul—away until the girls had gone to bed. But there was always the possibility that Colonel Butler would come back later, and that might be why Paul had come earlier than she had bargained for.

"No fear! I didn't like the look of him, so I put the door on the chain."

"We always put the door on the chain," supplemented Sally. "I think we ought to have dogs, myself. A pair of Rhodesian Ridgebacks—'Lion-dogs'—and we'd be as safe as anything . . . and we wouldn't have been burgled today, either. But Nannie doesn't like dogs, worse luck."

"I bet you like dogs, Frances," said Jane with perfect confidence. "Of course, we'd look after them—and take them for walks, and everything, if you didn't want to."

The chickens were already being counted, thought Frances sadly. The poor little things would probably spend half the night now planning how to sell the suitable Mrs Fitzgibbon to Father, that knight *sans peur et sans raproche*.

But Paul was in danger of being forgotten.

"Ask him what his name is, dear. If it's Paul, then let him in—he is a sort of policeman."

Jane sniffed again. "Okay—if you say so, Frances." The desire to appear an obedient potential step-daughter/younger sister outweighed her disapproval.

Frances served Sally with the final pancake. It was (though she said it herself, as shouldn't) an absolutely perfect example of its species.

"That's gorgeous, Frances!" Sally rubbed her stomach guiltily. "But you've made us eat too much, you know—we've got to watch our figures." She looked down at a figure which, if it was going to be watched, would only be watched with approval.

"Nonsense. You're just right." Irresistibly, Frances found herself slipping into her allotted role in response to their prompting. "Eat it up."

The sad truth was, of course, that she'd become such a chameleon that there wasn't a real Frances left to argue the toss, she cautioned herself. And when the role was as easy as this—when the other actors were as determined to make her a success (for all she knew, they might both hate pancakes, but they would eat anything she cooked tonight until it came out of their ears, she knew that)—no other Frances had a chance.

"Hullo, Princess," said Paul. "Pancakes? Is there one for me by any chance?"

Sally looked up from her pancake with an expression of undisguised hostility.

"And who might you be?" The influence of Nannie at her frostiest was apparent.

"Paul Mitchell—at your service, Miss Butler." Paul wasn't used to such immediate feminine disapproval, guessed Frances. But he rallied as gamely as any man might have done who encountered a barbed-wire fence in what he had assumed would be open country. "At everyone's service, in fact."

"Indeed?" As Sally considered him her sister circled round to stand behind her. For the first time Frances could see their father in both of them: when those stares had matured they would be able to stop a grown man in his tracks at twenty paces.

Even as it was their combined effect rocked Paul. He looked to Frances for support as much as for a pancake.

"I'm afraid not." Frances was torn between conflicting loyalties, but for once her sympathy was marginally on Paul's side, with the odds he was up against. She tilted the empty mixing bowl for him to see. "You're just too late."

"My luck!" Paul didn't look at the Misses Butler. "I hope I'm not disturbing you, Princess?"

"No. We're just finishing."

"Why do you call her 'Princess'?" Curiosity got the better of Jane's disapproval.

"Because she is a princess." Paul didn't smile this time. He was learning. "Through how many mattresses could the true princess tell there was a pea under her?"

"How—" Jane frowned at him. "It was twelve, I think."

"Twelve it was." Paul nodded towards Frances. "She can manage thirteen, no trouble . . . Also, the last time I met her, she'd lost a shoe . . . Also, she tells fairy stories, so I gather. She's an expert on them."

Jane looked at Frances. "Are you really?"

Frances regretted her marginal sympathy. "Mr Mitchell works with me—" she embraced them both with the same look "—so I have to talk to him on business now. You'll have to start the washing up without me, I'm sorry to say."

"But you won't be going?" asked Jane. "Not tonight?"

"No." Frances smiled, reassuring herself as much as the two girls. "I will be staying. And Mr Mitchell will be going."

"Well . . . that's all right," said Sally.

"I could help with the washing up," offered Paul.

"No," said Sally. "Thank you."

"It wouldn't be fair," said Jane. "You haven't dirtied anything."

"That's unfortunately true," Paul turned his charm on to full strength. "But—"

"After we've finished washing up we'll go and watch TV, Frances," said Sally. "There's a programme we like at quarter to."

"What about your prep?"

"We did that at school. First prep before tea, second prep after—that's why we stay till six," said Jane. "After we've watched our programme we shall read. I'm reading *The Lord of the Flies*—it's one of our set books."

"I shall do some biology," said Sally. "I'll make some coffee after the Nine O'Clock News. But if you'd like something to drink before, there's sherry and stuff in the cabinet in the sitting room—"

Paul followed Frances to the library.

Just as she had done, he looked round curiously. By the time she had finished drawing the curtains he was halfway along one section of shelving, running his eyes over the titles. He stopped suddenly, while she watched him, and drew a book from one of the shelves.

"*Winged Victory*—" he opened the book "—*Ex libris Henricus Chesney* . . . so it has to be a first edition." He flipped a page. "And signed by the author, too! A nice little collector's piece . . . and I'll bet there are a few more like it hereabouts." He replaced the book. "All the old General's books, of course."

Frances waited. She knew he was going to say something more.

"You know, that was the only thing of the old man's that he kept," said Paul. "Sold up the house and contents. Gave the papers and the diaries to the Imperial War Museum—matter of fact, I've actually read some of them . . . when I was researching there. Beautiful copperplate hand, the old General had . . . Not a bad commander, either, come to that—kept his men well back when the Germans attacked in 1918—not at all bad . . . And the old man's medals and portrait to the Lancashire Rifles' Museum . . . Just kept the books, that's all."

And the money, he didn't bother to add. They both knew that, it didn't need to be said.

"You've been researching the General, then?" That didn't really need to be said either, but she didn't want to trade anything of value yet, before he'd offered her something worth having in exchange.

"Uh-huh. The General and the Colonel both." He seemed engrossed in the titles of the books. "Or the General and the Captain. And the General and the Rifleman—hard to think of Fighting Jack as an Other Rank, but that's how he started . . . in the army, that is. With the General he started out even lower down the scale. The social scale."

"Yes?"

"Yes. He was odd-job boy to the General's gardener in his school holidays—did you know that, Princess?"

"Wasn't his father the General's sergeant-major in the First World War?" Frances encouraged him.

"That's right. Regimental Sergeant-Major. And RSM Butler was . . . 'a proper tartar', so I am reliably informed. Like the General, in fact—both hard as diamonds, one with a bit more polish than the other. But both hard as diamonds."

"Reliably informed by whom?"

"One Who Should Know: the old General's gardener, ex-batman. One Private Albert Sands—*Rifleman* Sands, I beg his pardon!" Paul looked at her—through her—suddenly, smiling to himself, his face quite transformed by his memory. "Rifleman Sands, aged 84—a jolly old boy who has all the nurses eating out of his hand. They say he pinches their bottoms if they don't watch out—Rifleman Sands, *sans* teeth, almost *sans* eyes, but not *sans* memory, fortunately. . . . He sits there like a little old wizened monkey, a bit vague about the last twenty years, but before that he's practically got total recall. Just a little old man—but he and Butler's father pulled the old General off the barbed wire at Beaumont Hamel in 1916." Paul's eyes flickered. "Pulled him off the wire—the old General was only a young Colonel then—pulled him off the wire under machine-gun fire in full view of the Germans, and dragged him into a shell-hole." The eyes focused on her. "And you know what Rifleman Sands said, Princess? He said 'It was a bloody silly thing to do, we should have known better—we could have got ourselves killed'."

Frances held her tongue. This was another Paul, a different Paul whom she had only very rarely glimpsed.

"The irony is that after the war they both went in opposite directions, the General and the RSM, and on opposite sides—the RSM was a printer, and he organised the Union in the General's printing works, Chesney and Rawle's. Come the General Strike in 1926 and they fought each other, in fact. Tooth and nail."

He looked at Frances, and Frances began at last to see the direction in which he was heading.

"The General was a pillar of the Conservative Party—a Tory alderman on the council, and he could have had the Parliamentary seat if he'd wanted it, too . . . And ex-RSM Butler was the heart and soul of the local Labour Party."

And little Jack Butler caught in the middle, caught between two men who were both as hard as diamonds, old comrades implacably opposed to each other.

"Rifleman Sands reckoned that if it had been a marginal Parliamentary seat they would both have stood for it, and made a real fight of it. But it was a safe Tory seat, and neither of them reckoned to waste their time in London when they could be pitching into each other where they were. Beautiful!"

But maybe not so beautiful for little Jack, though?

Paul turned back to the books again.

"What about . . . Colonel Butler . . ." She couldn't call him 'little Jack' out aloud ". . . when he was a boy?"

"Ah . . . You mean, what did Rifleman Sands have to say about Rifleman-Colonel Jack?" He reached out for another book, and Frances noted the care with which he extracted it from the shelf, how he pressed the top of its spine inwards first so that he could lift it out from the bottom without straining the binding. "Yes . . . another *Ex libris Henricus Chesney*—but the one next to it—" he exchanged one book for another "—that can't be, because I remember when it first came out, *The Debateable Land* . . . that would be about '69 . . . *J. Butler 1970*, there you are! And the old General died way back in '53 . . . so—quite a lot of these must be J. Butler's, actually. But that figures, as they say . . . that figures."

"Who say?" Frances inquired gently. So far he hadn't given her anything, and now he was teasing her.

"'Always had his nose in a book, young Jack'—Rifleman Sands." Paul nodded at the shelves. "Thought he was going to be a schoolmaster, young Jack, did Rifleman Sands . . . scholarship boy at the grammar school, with his nose always in some book or other when he wasn't working at his odd jobs. And that's really how it happened, I suppose: the General kept an eye on him because he was RSM Butler's son—gave him the job because he was RSM Butler's son, Sands was there when he gave it to him. And then saw how much he read, and gave him the run of the library too. . . . One lonely old man and one lonely small boy—no mother, and Father Butler busy with his politics and his trade unionism when he wasn't working . . . and the old General's only son had been killed by the Afridis ten years before, up in Waziristan somewhere, and his wife had died of 'flu donkey's years earlier, just after the '14–'18 War. One plus one equals two . . . I guess young Jack must have aroused the old man's interest first, because he was his father's son. Then the interest became a sort of hobby, because the boy was intelligent . . ."

More than that under the surface, Frances suspected. There was a familiar enough pattern here: the age gap was such that the two of them would probably have been able to talk to each other in a way that they could never have talked to anyone else. She could remember the confidences she exchanged with Grannie, which went far beyond anything either of them had told Mother. And, for a guess, unspoken love would have followed spoken confidences.

As always, she was surprised how the memory of Grannie still ached. Or not the memory, but the loss.

"And then the interest—the hobby—became an obsession." Paul gazed into space for a moment. "You know, they wrote to each other once a fortnight, Butler and the General—never failed. Sometimes it was only a note from Butler. And sometimes, when he was away at the war, and when he was in the thick of it in Korea, the letters would bunch up and arrive together. But the General would give Rifleman Sands a letter to post every other Monday, rain or shine, every one numbered in sequence. And he'd report to Sands how Butler was getting on—the day Butler's Military Cross was gazetted they both got stoned out of their minds, Sands says. Started with champagne, which neither of them liked, and finished up on 40-year-old malt whisky, and Sands sprained his ankle trying to get on his bicycle afterwards, and was off work for a week." Paul grinned at her suddenly. "Got his money's worth out of our Jack, the General did, in Rifleman Sands' opinion—or value for money, anyway. And so did Sands himself, he was quite frank about it: nice little private nursing home, with pinchable bottoms—not a lot of change out of £100 a week, I should think—all at Rifleman-Colonel Butler's expense. *And* not in the General's will, either—the General took it for granted that Butler would do it, and Butler did it."

"Does that make Sands a reliable witness?"

Paul laughed. "The old bugger doesn't give a damn. With his pension and his investments—he's been a bachelor all his life, and the General made his investments for him—he's got enough to see himself out, no problem. He said so himself."

"Then why does he accept money from Butler?"

"Ah—now that's interesting. He does it to please Butler."

"To . . . *please*—?"

Paul nodded. "That's got you, hasn't it! *Autres temps, autres mœurs*, Princess . . . You see, the way Rifleman Sands was brought up—and the way Rifleman-Colonel Butler, our Jack, was also brought up, just one street away in the same district, also on the wrong side of the tracks, but in the same world as the General—was that if a man did his duty to the best of his ability, then everything would be all right, come what may. You can laugh—"

"I'm not laughing."

"Then bully for you. That makes you a very old-fashioned girl, I can tell you . . . But I've talked to a lot of these old boys, when I was pretending to be an historian, and trying to find out how they stood it in the trenches. And it all comes back to the same thing: they didn't think it was religious, but they were all brought up on the Bible and it's straight out of St. Paul to the Colossians, chapter three: *And whatsoever ye do, do it heartily, as to the Lord, and not to men; knowing that of the Lord ye shall receive the reward of the inheritance, for ye serve the Lord Christ.*"

Good God! thought Frances involuntarily: Paul Mitchell quoting the Scriptures—it wasn't so much surprising that he could recall the words accurately, because his amazing capacity for recall was well-known, as that he accepted their importance in preference for more cynical interpretations.

"So Rifleman Sands considers it *his* duty to let Butler do *his* duty. Which in turn allows Sands to leave his money to Army charities—mostly the British Legion—which Butler himself knows perfectly well, because he's an executor of the will . . . I tell you, Princess, it's all absolutely incredible. And at the same time it's beautiful as well, the way both of them have it worked out between them—where their obligations lie."

He was telling her something now. Maybe he didn't think he was—maybe he was simply blinding her with what he took to be irrelevant facts, however academically interesting—but he was, nevertheless. He was telling her something of enormous significance.

"What about those letters? The General would have kept them—did they go to the Imperial War Museum?"

Paul shook his head. "No way we're going to get a look at them. They're safe in the bosom of the regimental archives somewhere—he didn't include them with the papers he gave to the museum. And I mean safe. Because when he handed them over he slapped a 50-year embargo on them, and only he can unslap it . . . the adjutant made that crystal clear."

He paused for a moment or two, ran his finger over some of the books casually, and then glanced sidelong at her. "A decent fellow, the adjutant . . . didn't know Butler himself, too young, but he produced a couple of old sweats who knew him pretty well, and put me on to a retired half-colonel of the Mendips who was one of his subalterns in Korea. . . . Lives not far from here, the half-colonel, so I took him in en route. And there was another chap I talked to this morning, ex-Rifles . . . I've covered one hell of a lot of ground since last night, and that's the truth.

He was impressing her with how much he knew, and how much he had to offer. And also that he was nearly ready to start trading.

"But he didn't tell me about the letters, the adjutant—I heard about them from Rifleman Sands. And when I phoned the adjutant back he said—ever so politely—that if Her Majesty wanted to see them it'd be a case of *hard luck, Your Majesty*."

"That's a pity," said Frances.

"I agree. Except they would only have given us the beginning of the story, and it's the end of it we really need . . ." He watched her. "That is . . . if we're looking for the same thing, Princess."

"True." The trading had started. "You said Sands thought he was going to be a schoolmaster, not a soldier? Did he really mean that?"

Paul half-smiled. "Takes a bit of effort to see Fighting Jack as Mr Chips, not Colonel Blimp, doesn't it!"

"Did he?"

"I doubt it. I think Rifleman Sands simply thinks that any poor boy who won a scholarship to the Grammar and liked reading books ought to be a schoolmaster, that's all. Just the old class prejudice against the Red Coat . . . plus his own memories of the trenches, I suspect."

"And what did Butler's father make of it?"

"Well, I think . . ." He broke off. "I think . . . that it's about time you stopped asking questions and answered one or two for a change, Princess. Like, for instance, what this sudden interest in Fighting Jack's academic progress means?"

Frances shrugged. "I think he's a complex man."

"Aren't we all?" He gestured towards the shelves of books. "But he carried on the family tradition—adopted family, anyway. They're all military, or military-political. Or political . . . *Ex libris* Butler is the same as *Ex libris* Chesney."

"Not upstairs."

"Upstairs?"

"In his bedroom."

"Indeed? Books in his bedroom? Well, well!" He was interested in spite of himself. "What dark secret have you uncovered there, then?"

Frances thought of the hard, narrow bed and the carefully adjusted reading lamp, as well as the well-thumbed books. And also what the children had said.

"No dark secret, Paul. Just Hardy and Dickens and Thackeray . . . he's re-reading *Henry Esmond* at the moment."

"Re-reading?"

"And Defoe's *Journal of the Plague Year*. And Robert Penn Warren's *All the King's Men*. And Hemingway and Stephen Crane. And Jack London's *Martin Eden*."

"That would be rather suitable," murmured Paul. "But Hemingway—that's a turn-up, I must say!"

"And John Dos Passos . . . Thoreau, Mark Twain . . . and Faulkner—every bit of Faulkner . . ." She trailed off.

"Hmm . . ." There was a frown on his face now. "Not a simple soldier, you mean? But maybe a man after your own heart, perhaps?"

He had seen her books, Frances remembered, even though he had also confused Robbie's with hers to her discomfort.

And then . . . after her own heart?

Well, they both had the same Yoknapatawpha County tales, except that his had been bought new in '55—*J. Butler 1955*—and hers picked up, dog-eared, in the Charing Cross Road fifteen years later.

Heart—

And except his had an underlining in it (and it was his underlining too, in the same coal-black ink of *J. Butler 1955*), and as he had never underlined anything in any other of his books, so far as she could discover, that passage from Faulkner's Nobel Prize acceptance speech had to be strong magic for him:

. . . the old verities and truths of the heart, the old universal truths . . . love and honour and pity and pride and compassion and sacrifice . . .

"You favour the psychological approach this time, then? 'Know the man, and you'll know where to find the facts everyone else has missed'?" At least he was deadly serious and not making fun of her.

"Are there any facts everyone else has missed?"

He didn't reply at once; he was still adding the unsuspected literary Butler to his Fighting Jack, and getting no sort of answer.

At length he nodded. "I think there are, somewhere—yes."

"Why?"

"Because of us, Frances. You and me."

"What d'you mean?"

"I mean . . . I don't believe they would have detached us without a reason—I don't think it can be just because someone high up hopes to block Butler's promotion. I think that a word has been dropped somewhere that there is something. And if they put the same people on it who checked him out before, they think those people will find the same things, which will amount to nothing. But you and I—we start out fresh. That's what I think, Frances."

And we're the best too, he left unsaid.

"Which leaves us with the old 'means, motive and opportunity'— if he killed her, then how did he, and why did he, and when did he?" He paused fractionally. "Only we already know that there could have been a 'when', because he never produced an alibi. And the 'how' hardly matters, because when it comes to killing he's got more notches on his belt than Billy the Kid."

"But only in war."

"But he enjoyed it. That's what the chap who was with him on the Imjin in Korea said. They were in trenches—trenches and dug-outs and wire, and it was bloody cold, and they were overrun by rats. Rats don't like cold, they like nice warm dug-outs. And you can't poison them because they go home to die, and then they smell. And there were plenty of dead bodies to smell, too. . . . In fact, it was like the '14–'18 War—in some ways it was even worse, because there weren't any billets behind the lines, or if there were they were full of rats and lice—and the rats and lice were full of scrub typhus and Songo fever, neither of which Butler senior had to contend with on the Somme. Apart from which there was foot-rot and ring-worm and malaria. *And*, of course, there were a million Chinese who were quite prepared to swop casualties at ten to one—"

This, again, was the other Paul: a Paul transformed by his private military obsession, convoys and battle-cruisers forgotten now.

"Butler admired the Chinese—wouldn't let anyone despise them," said they were damn good soldiers who deserved to be better supported. Said it was unlucky for them they were up against the British Army, who couldn't be beaten in defence if they were properly led, and he intended to see that they were. Absolutely mad on weapon training and leadership and physical fitness—no one in his company was *allowed* to get sick, he'd have a chap's boots off and examine his feet as soon as look at him, he said he could tell when a man had bad feet just by looking at him . . . Absolutely revelled in it—" he stopped short as he caught sight of Frances's expression. "What's that look supposed to mean?"

"You haven't said anything about killing, Paul."

"No. But—"

"You've described the General and the father in *their* trenches, maybe. You haven't described a professional killer," said Frances.

Paul's jaw set hard: he didn't like to be caught out on his own battleground. "There was Cyprus, Princess—his first bit of Military Intelligence. That shoot-out in the Troodos Mountains in '56 wasn't trench warfare. And the I-Corps sergeant's automatic jammed, so those were all his kills."

He was into the small print now. And obviously he knew a great deal about the military Butler—more than she did. But he hadn't mentioned Trevor Anthony Bond and Leslie Pearson Cole, and that could mean that they hadn't exposed that chapter of the Butler file to him, although he'd had the military chapter in greater detail.

"All right, Frances. We've both been digging, and we both know something we didn't know before . . . I know he was a damn good soldier in the trenches. And that he was a one-man execution squad in the mountains. And you know his taste in literature—would that qualify as an old-fashioned hunger for self-improvement, now?"

"Self-improvement?"

"That's right. An old northern working-class passion that's gone out of fashion with the coming of the welfare state." He paused. "I agree he's a complex character. A working-class boy who struck it rich. Maybe a schoolmaster *manqué* . . . a self-made officer and gentleman of the old school, anyway—self-made in someone else's image, or his version of someone, that was maybe two wars out-of-date. Perhaps that was why his face never quite fitted in his regiment: he thought he was conforming, but he was conforming to the wrong pattern." He paused again. "And then out of the blue, in the sort of dirty fighting he'd never prepared himself for, he finds he has a natural talent for counter-intelligence work—unregimental work, just when his regimental career is beginning to go sour on him . . . and also just when they're beginning to cut the army down, and amalgamate the famous regiments out of existence. And he really hated that, I can tell you. No Lancashire Rifles any more, no Mendip Borderers. No family to belong to—or pretend to belong to. Just duty. And Madame Butler."

He stared at her. "We have to put it together and get an answer to our question, one way or another, Frances."

Frances knew that she couldn't put it off any longer. If she did she'd merely delay him, he'd come to it himself eventually.

"He hated her too."

Somewhere deep in the house behind and above her she could just distinguish the thump of pop music.

The means and the opportunity had always been there as a possibility; they had been so obviously there that they'd never really mattered.

Either the girls' TV programme was a Pick of the Pops variant, or they required a background of noise for the assimilation of their set-books.

But no one had ever produced a motive.

"You're sure?" He had been expecting something like it; it was just as well she hadn't flannelled him.

"Yes."

"From the children?"

"Indirectly." It had been close to directly, but the circumstances in which the information had been given made that admission stick in her throat. "They confirmed it indirectly."

"You knew already?"

"By the time I . . . talked with them . . . yes."

"How?"

"This house." Now she wanted to get it over. "There isn't a thing of hers in it. Not an object, not a piece of clothing—not a handkerchief, not a book. Not even a picture. Not a single thing."

He looked around him.

"This was always his room. His books and his desk—they are the same. But the curtains are different. He replaced them."

He wrinkled his nose. "Not in very good taste."

Frances swallowed. "He hasn't got very good taste. She furnished the whole house when they moved in."

"Elegantly, I presume?"

She looked at him interrogatively. "You presume?"

"She was French, wasn't she?"

Deep breath. "Yes. And yes, I think. From what the middle daughter remembers."

"But he chucked it all out?"

"He sold it. The daughters—the two elder ones—are just starting to get him to re-furnish again. The eldest girl has made him sell all the pictures he bought—the paintings—and has replaced them with ones she likes. She's studying Art at college."

"He does what he's told, does he? Well, I suppose he can afford to indulge them, anyway . . . But how d'you know all this? Did they tell you?"

"Some of it. But he keeps very careful accounts—" she nodded towards the desk "—it's all neatly filed in there."

Paul stared at the desk for a moment. "So . . . he blotted her out." He turned back to her. "You knew this before you talked to the girls—that he hated her?"

"Yes."

He frowned. "But couldn't it have meant great love—*la grande passion*, possibly? All reminders unbearable?"

"Possibly."

"But not likely?" The frown became perplexed. "He met her at the end of the war, just before or after . . . the file doesn't say which. But he didn't marry her then—he didn't marry her until he came back from Korea in '53 . . . So . . . he—she was very young when he first met her. And she waited eight whole years for him. That doesn't sound like a passing fancy to me, Princess, you know."

"Or alternatively, she waited until he was rich," said Frances brutally.

"Hmm . . . ye-ess." He rubbed his chin thoughtfully.

"You know something?" She could hear a slight rasping of stubble.

"Maybe." He stopped rubbing. "I haven't picked up the least suggestion that she ever played around."

"No?" There was more to come.

"If anything she was . . . rather un-French."

"Un-French?"

"Rather cold. Say, beautiful but unapproachable."

That was a typical chauvinist judgement: if Madeleine Françoise had been English her coldness would have been unremarked (or not even noticed, as her own had never been noticed). But as a French-woman Mrs Butler was expected to be sexy and available, as well as having good taste in house-furnishing.

"She wasn't affectionate, in fact?"

"Yes. That's about it." The chauvinism had restored some of his confidence. "Is that what you wanted to hear?"

At the same time he didn't sound wholly convinced, and Frances could understand why. That first meeting, in the excitement of the war or the chaos of its aftermath, touched a chord of romance in him. Men, even men like Paul with his calculating-machine passion for facts, very often had foolish romantic streaks in them somewhere which the right stimuli activated. And in his case, with his passion-ate interest in things military, the imagined picture of the young British soldier meeting the young French girl might just do that trick.

Come to that, it might also have done the trick with Madeleine Françoise, she thought with a sharp spasm of memory. In his old pullover and cavalry twill trousers Robbie had been just a very ordinary boy, just another young man, if a little shorter-haired and better-mannered than average. But in his uniform, very straight and very young, he had been something else. . . . The old song was right—there was *something about a soldier* . . . something enough to delude clever little Frances Warren anyway, once upon a time, so maybe enough for Madeleine Françoise too.

But that didn't really fit this case, because it hadn't been a wartime romance. There were those eight years to swallow: had Butler waited until he could afford to marry, or had Madeleine Françoise waited until he was worth marrying?

"Or is that what you expected to hear?" Paul pressed her. "The daughters told you as much—how the devil did you get them to tell you a thing like that?"

That was one thing she wasn't going to tell him. "They had their reasons . . . and I said 'indirectly'."

"And this house." He looked around him again, then back at her. "You're still not levelling with me, Princess."

"Not levelling? What d'you mean?"

"I mean . . . you came here, and you talked to them—and you somehow got them to talk to you, God knows how. But you couldn't have known what they were going to say, or what you were going to find. But you came."

It would be easy to say 'Where else could I start?' It would even be logical, so that he couldn't argue with it.

But it wouldn't be the truth, or the most important part of the truth, and he would know that too. Because there were rare moments when Paul's instinct also operated independently from the data in his memory store, and this was one of them.

All the same, if she could avoid admitting the whole truth—

"It was in the report . . . Or rather, it wasn't in the report, Paul."

"What wasn't?"

"It never stated that they were a devoted couple."

"Would you have expected it to?" He regarded her incredulously. "Hell, Princess—those Special Branch chaps of ours are bright coppers, but they haven't exactly been raised on Shakespeare's sonnets."

"I've talked to the inspector who was on the case at the time . . ."

"Yes?"

"He was quite sharp too. And he liked Butler. I was waiting for him to say it—there were half a dozen times when he could have said it—'It was a happy marriage'. Or even 'There was nothing wrong with the marriage'—anything like that—"

"Or 'It was a bad marriage'? He didn't say that either?"

"He didn't say anything at all, not deliberately."

"So it didn't stick out enough to seem important to him."

"But in this case it was important. Because there was no circumstantial evidence either way, so the motive had to be twice as important."

"Okay, Princess." Paul conceded the point gracefully. "Then he liked Butler—so he didn't push it, you may be right. But, a bit of cold fish is our Jack. And cold fish plus stiff upper lip plus duty—it doesn't make for demonstrations of affection."

"*No!* That's just where you're wrong, Paul. Colonel Butler isn't really a cold fish at all. He's terrifically affectionate with his daughters." Frances swallowed. "And I mean, *physically* affectionate. I mean . . . for example, every night he was home—right up until they started to develop, anyway—he'd insist on bathing them. And they loved it. In fact . . . they still don't mind if he sees them naked—they actually tell him their measurements—"

"—*and Father always has to have the scores when he gets home, Frances. Like 'Australia 356 all out, England 129 for two, and Jane 31-23-31—'*"

"Good God!" Paul sounded not so much surprised as slightly shocked at her intimate revelation of Butler family life. (But then, of course, Paul was an only son of a widowed mother, and a boarding school boy too, so under the Cavalier exterior there was probably a Puritan hang-up or two about adolescent girls, thought Frances nastily.)

"They adore him." She struck at his embarrassment. "They'd do anything for him."

The blow rebounded instantly: anything even included attempting to conscript the wholly unsuitable Mrs Fitzgibbon as a potential Second Mrs Butler. And how many others before her? she wondered, remembering the eager, scheming little Butler faces.

"Uh-huh?" Paul quickly had his hang-up under control. "But mightn't that make them perhaps not so reliable witnesses to the marriage?"

"No, I don't think so." Frances shook her head. He still wasn't totally convinced, and she couldn't blame him. The omission of any judgement of the quality of the Butler marriage, either in the report or in William Ewart Hedges' recollections, was negative evidence; and her own investigation of the house was hardly less subjective, even when added to his own findings. But she could hardly admit to him that all this, plus what the girls had told her, were merely corroborative to the instinct she'd had from the beginning about Butler. How could she ever tell anyone that she knew what she was going to find before she had found it? That the knowledge was like a scent on the wind which she alone could smell? That this house itself still smelt of that old hatred?

"One thing about Maman, though—she always smelt beautiful, I do remember that." Jane had closed her eyes. *"Lançome 'Magie', I think it was—"*

"It wasn't Lançome 'Magie'," Sally had said professionally. *"It was Worth 'Je Reviens'."*

In the circumstances of a nine-year-missing mother, that wasn't funny, Frances had thought—and still thought: Je Reviens was a promise too horrible to think about nine years after a possible encounter with Patrick Raymond Parker, 'The Motorway Murderer' of the headlines which suddenly came back to her. The women who met Patrick Raymond Parker didn't ever come back: they were planted deep—Julie Anne Hartford, Jane Wentworth, Patricia Mary Ronson, Jane Louise Smith . . . and Madeleine Françoise de Latour d'Auray Butler, née Boucard—they were planted deep under his stretch of motorway, compacted by his great earth-moving machines and held down by the thickness of hardcore and concrete and tarmac, and millions of speeding vehicles, until doomsday; and even if the world ended tomorrow, and it took another thousand years for green-growing things to push up through that hard surface, they wouldn't come back.

And yet . . . in another way and in her own sweet vengeful time, she *had* come back, had Madeleine Françoise. And even now she was reaching out to catch her husband's heel from behind, when he least expected her touch.

She shook her head again, decisively. "No."

"No?" He was no longer searching for doubt in her. Instead he was superimposing her conclusion on top of his own knowledge in the last hope that they wouldn't coincide.

Finally he sighed: one thing Paul never did was to argue with inconvenient facts, or not for long.

"Okay. So they adore him, he adores them. And he hated *her*." The corner of his mouth drooped. "So you've got the one bit of dirt no one else came up with—the Reason Why. And they're really going to adore *you* for that. Or *he* is."

"He? Who?"

"Our Control. Our esteemed Control. He who will give us anything we want, everything we want, provided we will give him exactly what he wants. Namely, the dirt on Jack Butler—a dirty knife in the back for Fighting Jack: the Thin Red Line attacked *a tergo*, with no time to turn the rear rank back to back, like the 28th at Alexandria—"

"What d'you mean?" Frances quailed before his summer-storm anger.

"Battle of Alexandria, March 21st 1801. French dragoons caught the 28th—the Glosters—in the rear when their infantry was attacking from the front. So their colonel turned the rear rank round and fought 'em off back-to-back—I know you don't go much for the military, Princess, but you ought to remember that from your Arthur Bryant—" He swung away suddenly, towards the book-shelves, scanning the titles "—and he'll be here somewhere, Sir

Arthur will be, you can bet your life—"

Frances took a step towards him, but he was already moving down the long shelving. "I didn't mean that, Paul."

"No? *The Years of Endurance*—it has to be here, the old General would never have missed it . . . No? Well, perhaps you ought to have meant it—there's something in it you ought to see, by God!"

"Paul—"

But he ignored her, pouncing on a maroon-coloured volume and thumbing through the pages without looking up as he swung back towards her. "Yes—"

"Paul—listen to me, please."

"No. You shut up, Princess, and listen to *me*. Listen to this, in fact—"

Frances opened her mouth, and then shut it again as he looked for a moment at her.

"1801. We beat the French in Egypt. Everyone knows about Nelson sinking their fleet at the Nile, but that was no contest—no one remembers we beat their army, Bonaparte's veterans of Lodi. No one ever gives a stuff for the British Army, they just take it for granted—and pay it wages that would make your average car worker go screaming mad with rage, and rightly so—" His eyes dropped to the page "—now, listen—"

This was the obsessive Paul again, the military historian who had never worn a uniform. But there was something more to it than that obsession this time, thought Frances: something in his mind had connected *now* with 1801, which she could only discover by holding her tongue.

"Abercromby—General Sir Ralph Abercromby, commanding the army that beat the French. Died of wounds a week after—gangrene from a sword-cut—67 years old, but he wouldn't give up until the French retreated from the battlefield . . . they put him in a soldier's blanket and he insisted on knowing the name of the soldier, because the man needed his blanket. . . . Here it is: when he died there was a General Order of the Day published:

'*His steady observance of discipline, his ever-watchful attention to the health and wants of his troops, the persevering and unconquerable spirit which marked his military career, the splendour of his actions in the field and the heroism of his death are worthy the imitation of all who desire, like him, a life of honour and a death of glory.*'"

He didn't look up when he'd finished reading the passage: he was re-reading it, memorising the words for himself, for his own purposes, for the secret Paul, to make sure he was word-perfect.

But where was the connection?

He looked up at last. "Well . . . at least he's not quite dead yet, Princess—our General Abercromby."

So that was the connection: somewhere along the line during the past twenty-four hours Paul Mitchell had finally changed his mind about Colonel Butler, from anger to approval, to admiration. And if it didn't quite make sense to Frances—computers like Paul shouldn't have emotions—it was altogether fascinating that he should in the end have come to the same conclusion as the irrational one she'd had at the beginning.

"I haven't killed him off."

"You're going to give them a motive."

"But no proof."

"They don't need proof. Control doesn't need proof." He shook his head. "They're never going to hang anything on him—even if they could that would be bad publicity. All they want is enough to put the big question mark on him, and means and opportunity never were enough for that. But if you can add a motive to it . . . that'll be enough to swing it."

He was right, of course. If the marriage was on the rocks . . . and nothing could be proved against *her* . . . then Butler wouldn't have got the children—*my girls*. And that, in the whole wide world, was the one thing he might have killed for out of the line of duty, they could argue.

And that would be enough to swing it.

What have I done? thought Frances. *I don't for one moment think that Colonel Butler killed his wife—but if I put in a true report of my conclusions I shall suggest that he did.*

"You agree that there is a motive?" The cold, pragmatic half of her still wanted to know why Paul was so emotional about the job of excavating Colonel Butler's past. Because it couldn't be that Paul simply admired Butler's Abercromby performance in the Korean trenches and the Cypriot mountains—not enough to hazard his own career, anyway.

"A motive?" Paul's voice was suddenly casual—as casual as a subaltern of the 28th echoing the command *Rear rank—Right about—Prepare to repel cavalry*! "Frankly, Princess. I don't give a fuck about motives. Or wives. Or murder—"

That was David Audley speaking: David never swore, except very deliberately to shock, or to emphasise a point by speaking out of character . . . And Paul was a chameleon like herself, taking his colour from those he observed about him.

"—Or anything else, but what matters—what really matters."

"What really matters?"

"What matters is—we don't kill off Fighting Jack. That's what matters."

"Kill off?"

"We don't block his promotion. All we have to do is disobey orders—give him a clean bill of health—lie through our teeth: happy marriage, tragic disappearance, 'Motorway Murderer'."

So Paul had done his homework—naturally. Paul knew reporters and news editors. Like David Audley, Paul was owed favours and collected on them, promising future favours. Paul was born knowing the score, down to the last figure beyond the decimal point.

But did Paul know about Trevor Anthony Bond, and Leslie Pearson Cole (deceased, restricted) and Leonid T. Starinov (restricted)? And the curious not-alibi which lay between grimy Blackburn in the morning and medieval Thornervaulx in the afternoon—did he know about that too?

At the moment he didn't care, anyway: he was bending all his will on bending her will.

Make me an offer, thought Frances cynically. It would have to be either an offer she couldn't refuse or a threat she couldn't ignore, nothing else would serve—that must be what he was thinking, not knowing what she had already done for his Fighting Jack.

"Can you give me one good reason why I should do that, Paul? Why I should risk my neck?"

"Why?" He snapped *The Years of Endurance* shut and reached up to slot it back into its space in the shelf. "Say . . . the best interests of our country—" He glanced sidelong at her, and then straightened the books casually "—would that do?"

That was the offer: the National Interest, with no direct benefit attached for her. Quite a subtle offer.

He faced her. "And in our best interests too, as it happens, Frances."

She had been too quick off the mark: Self-Interest as well as National Interest—that was more like Paul.

"Our best interests? How?"

He grinned. "Didn't I tell you? Nor I did!"

I think I know what his promotion is, Frances remembered. She had been staring at Isobel's white wall when he had said that, deliberately tantalising her.

"You didn't quite get round to that, no."

The grin vanished. "You've been playing pretty hard to get, Princess. It's been all give and no take, don't you think?"

The threat was coming.

"I wouldn't exactly say that." But it was true nevertheless, she decided. She had been a pretty fair bitch to Paul, matching his hang-ups with her own.

"Okay—have it your way . . . I'll tell you." He nodded slowly. "But first I'll tell you something else: if you tell Control that Butler had a motive for chilling his missus . . . then I'm going to phone the Grand Hotel in Blackburn—"

"Blackburn—?"

"That's where Jack is tonight—and I'm going to tell him the score. At least he'll have the chance to face the enemy at his back then—"

"What's he doing in Blackburn?"

He did a double-take on her. "How the hell do I know? I don't know—Jim Cable said he'd be there tonight, until about midday tomorrow—what the devil has that got to do with it? It's his home town, isn't it?"

"You were in Blackburn today."

"Ah . . . Yes. But he's not on my trail, if that's what you mean."

"How d'you know he isn't?"

"Because Jim Cable booked the hotel for him the first day they went up to Yorkshire, more than a week ago. Which was at the start of the O'Leary hunt—long before the Butler hunt started, Princess."

"He's on O'Leary's trail, then?"

"Yes, he is—and very hot too, Jim says." He nodded.

"In Blackburn?" Frances persisted.

Paul frowned. "No, not in Blackburn. What's so all-fired important about Blackburn?"

"You said you didn't know what he's doing there. But you know what he isn't doing."

He shook his head. "I meant that literally. He told Jim he was taking a half-day off on the Friday week ahead, and he'd be spending

203

the night before in his home town, that's all. He'll be back on the job by 1.30 tomorrow, anyway—you can pick him up at the University then if you want him." He continued to frown at her, half puzzled, half suspicious. "We seem to have lost the thread rather, Princess. And you haven't yet revealed what you intend to do."

The heavy door-knocker on the mock-Tudor door boomed out, echoing in the empty hall outside the library.

"Are you expecting callers?" asked Paul quickly.

Frances shook her head, listening intently. Even before the echoes had died away she could hear other sounds mingling with them inside the house.

"Then who—?"

She raised a finger to cut off his question. That first sound had been the clatter of the latch on the TV room door. Then there had been a burst of unmuffled pop music—at that volume it was amazing that the girls had heard anything else, even that thunderous door-knocker—but the music had been quickly muffled again as the door was closed on it. Now there came the distinctive clackety-click of Sally's fashion clogs crossing the parquet floor of the hall, ending with the thud and rattle of mock-Tudor bolt and safety chain on the door itself.

At least it couldn't be Colonel Butler himself, because Colonel Butler was in the Grand Hotel, Blackburn, this night—this Thursday night (that other November night, nine years ago, had been a Monday night).

What was strange was that she wasn't as relieved as she should be that it couldn't be Colonel Butler. Indeed, analysing the strangeness, she came upon the beginning of a day-dream that he had come back, very late, after the girls were safely tucked up and asleep, and she herself was comfortably curled up (in Diana's exotic nightie and warm dressing gown, which Jane had found for her), reading his *Tales of Yoknapatawpha County*—reading in it maybe 'As I Lay Dying', or 'A Rose for Emily', or perhaps 'The Bear', which she had first encountered so unforgettably at college—young Frances Warren as excited as John Keats On First Looking into Chapman's Homer—in 'Go Down Moses'—

"I hope you don't mind me reading your Faulkner." (One hand clasping the book to her breast, the other modestly joining the edges of the gown together at her throat.)

204

"Not at all, Mrs Fitzgibbon." (Very formal, he would be.) *"You like Faulkner, do you, Mrs Fitzgibbon?"*

"Very much." ('The old verities and truths of the heart,' Colonel Butler.) *"I think we've both read him in the same way, you know."* (Deduction: From the dates on the fly-leaves, each meticulously recording the book's date of acquisition, Butler had read his way through Faulkner at break-neck speed, book after book, in the midst of his duel with the EOKA terrorists in the Troodos Mountains, beginning with *Intruder in the Dust*, and then *Absalom! Absalom!* He must have had them flown in, money no object by then, for by then he was a rich man, the ex-poor boy from Blackburn, self-made officer-and-gentleman . . . Maybe lying in ambush all day on those rocky hillsides with his sub-machine gun and his newest Faulkner?)

(Well, in the same way, if not in the same circumstances exactly. Except that it was all in her imagination, every word, every picture. All a dream.)

"Frances," said Sally. "Frances—there's a policeman at the door, for you, he says. Not the one who brought the Chinese grub—food, I mean."

Frances smiled at her, sisterly-step-motherly. "Yes, dear?"

"He says he's a policeman, anyway. He says he'll show you his . . . his warrant card. But he's not in uniform, so I haven't let him in. But he says he knows you."

So it would be Detective-Sergeant Geddes. The delivery of the Chinese take-away had been a constable's chore. But what would Geddes want?

"All right, dear. I'll see him."

"Okay. I'll tell him you're just coming." Sally ducked out obediently, sisterly-step-daughterly.

Frances looked at Paul. "I'll take him into the sitting room."

"Don't take long." From his expression Paul's patience with the hard-to-get Fitzgibbon was close to exhaustion. "I'd like to know what you're intending to do, Frances."

What she intended to do.

What she was doing was also all a dream, thought Frances. Ever since the bomb everything had had an insubstantial quality, fuzzed at the edges, as though she was living out an alternative version of a life which had actually ended beside the duck-pond in a spray of blood and muddy water and feathers.

"I shall be here tonight and in Blackburn tomorrow," she said.

The door was open, but on the chain. She could smell the wet November darkness through the gap, beyond the area of the porch light.

Through the side window of the mock-Tudor porch she saw a long strip of light where the curtains in one of the mullioned windows of the library hadn't quite met. As she watched, the light went out and a second or two later the curtains moved: Paul was observing her policeman.

"Yes?" she addressed the gap.

"Mrs Fitzgibbon?"

"Yes." She peered through the gap. Whoever it was, it wasn't Detective-Sergeant Geddes. The moustache was there, and the rather swarthy complexion too; but this was a stockier and an older man.

"Special Branch, madam. My warrant card."

Frances accepted the card—Detective-Superintendent Samuel Leigh-Hunter. That certainly made him top brass, on a level with their own formidable D. S. Cox in the department; and he had the same heavy-lidded seen-it-all-but-still-learning-from-it look which the best of them had, and which was frightening and reassuring at the same time—that much one glimpse through the gap registered.

Caution, though: she still didn't know him.

"Yes, Superintendent?" The chain remained in position under her hand.

"I'd like a word with you, madam. Inside the house, if you don't mind." The eyes were opaque. "With reference to Dr David Audley."

Frances's legs weakened at the knees. "I beg your pardon?" she heard herself say, in Mrs Fitzgibbon's haughtiest voice.

"Let the man in, Frances," said Paul from behind her.

"What?" she swung round.

"Let him in, you crafty little bitch—or I should say something complimentary really, I suppose!" Paul grinned broadly at her.

"What?"

"Then I'll let him in." He reached past her towards the chain, lifting the nob out of the slot. "Come in, Colonel Shapiro—join the club!"

XII

THE ISRAELI WASN'T pleased. Frances sensed his displeasure the moment he stepped inside, it was like a tiny movement of air setting one leaf quivering on a still day.

"Captain Mitchell." The leaf no longer moved, but it had told its tale: Paul had touched it with his unexpected presence.

"Not 'Captain'." Paul's grin faded to a self-deprecating smile. "The highest rank I ever aspired to was lance-corporal in the Cambridge University OTC, I'm afraid, Colonel."

"Of course. But the first picture we ever took of you was as a captain—France in '74. In an RTR black beret. And first impressions last longest." Shapiro traded smile for smile. "And you are something of a tank expert, 1918 and all that, I believe?"

"But not on your level—1967 and all that . . . the Jebl Libni counter-attack, was it?"

They were crossing swords as well as smiles, and asserting themselves and exchanging professional credentials at the same time.

"And that gives us something in common with David Audley," Paul moved forward smoothly, choosing his ground. "Wessex Dragoons, wasn't he—'43–'44?"

"Well, well!" Shapiro conceded a point. "'Not a lot of people know that.'"

Paul accepted the Michael Caine claim. "He doesn't dine out on it—80 per cent casualties in Normandy, maybe. But then, David plays a lot of things close to his chest . . ." He turned towards Frances. "Like you, Frances. Though the chest is much more worth playing close to, I must admit."

"Mrs Fitzgibbon—" The smile vanished from Colonel Shapiro's face: he came from a race and a generation less crude, far less prone to such juvenile familiarity "—forgive me my deplorable manners. I am sorry to disturb you with not a word of warning, but your phone here isn't secure."

This was the grey country again: that was exactly—almost word for word exactly—what Sir Frederick had said to her twenty-four hours before, to the minute; the old-fashioned courtesy giving her an apology which Paul Mitchell would never have rated, but the new-fashioned equality of the sexes putting her in the front line of necessity, in which a woman could do a man's job to the death.

"That was your man in the woods behind the house, I take it?" said Paul conversationally, but pleased with himself.

"Yes." This time Shapiro's irritation was plain. The poor devil in the woods would soon find himself somewhere even less pleasant than England on a dripping November night after this, said the irritation.

"I thought he might be one of ours. Or just a copper." Paul was merciless: he had been too good for the man in the woods, and he liked being better than Mossad, who were good—and they were good because Shapiro was here now, within hours of one phone call; and that could be either because they were technologically good, or because they had an inside man somewhere; but however good they'd been, Paul had been too good for them, his sight-and-sound in the wet darkness had been better; if it had been a killing matter, he would have killed, and that would have been an end of it, not to be boasted about; but it had only been a passing in the dark, and he couldn't resist exulting in it—

None has ever caught him yet, for Paul, he is the master:
His songs are stronger songs, and his feet faster.

His confidence offended her. If Paul died before his time, it would not be because he wasn't good enough; it would be because he chose to test his excellence to an impossible invulnerability, giving the enemy the first shot because he had to believe no bullet had his name on it. He would die uselessly then, simply to test a theory, not by accident, like Robbie.

She felt the iron in her soul again. She had nothing to lose.

"Have you contacted David, Colonel Shapiro?"

"Yes." The deplorable manners were forgotten now, thank God: now they were on equal terms. "Not personally. But . . . yes, Mrs Fitzgibbon, we have spoken with him."

Our Man in Washington. The Israelis had Washington sewn up tight as a drum when it came to contacts, even if they no longer called the tune in the Administration and Congress.

"And he's coming back?"

Shapiro nodded. "The CIA's bringing him in." Then he smiled, a touch of wolf under the sheep-dog. "They owe him one."

Everybody owed David one: David was both a Godfather and a Godson. Half his strength lay in those unpaid debts.

"He's made a proper bog-up of this one, all the same," said Paul, dryly superior.

Shapiro nodded again, to Paul this time. "Ye-ess . . . I'm afraid that with this one . . . desire has finally out-run performance." Another nod. "As you say—a bog-up. A proper bog-up."

He sounded as though he'd never heard of a *bog-up* before, but that the onomatopaeic meaning of it appealed to him as being self-explanatory.

Frances was aware simultaneously that she was being ignored and that she didn't know what they were talking about. She scowled at Paul. "What d'you mean—David has made a . . . bog-up?"

Paul looked over his shoulder at the door to the TV room.

"Let's go back into the library, Princess."

"A bog-up?" repeated Frances.

Colonel Shapiro looked around him, just as Paul had done—just as she had done. Then he looked at Paul.

Damn them all! thought Frances. The great male conspiracy of knowing too much was in that look.

"David thought he had it all cut-and-dried before he went to Washington?" Paul nodded at the Israeli. "Right?"

Slow nod. "That's about the size of it. Yes."

"Had what cut-and-dried?" snapped Frances at both of them.

Paul thought for a moment before replying. "You drew the top brass last night. Who was it?"

Frances kept her mouth shut. He'd fished for that name once already. He certainly wasn't going to catch anything now.

"All right. Let's put it another way. Who *wasn't* it?"

Who wasn't it?

Frances saw her error of the night before. She had been so overwhelmed by Sir Frederick's arrival, and then by her own cleverness in connecting it with Colonel Butler, that she'd clean forgotten to ask herself one very important question, even though it had been half-formulated in her mind after he had said *You are not reporting to Brigadier Stocker*.

"It wasn't Tom Stocker, was it?" The question mark at the end wasn't a question mark: it was Paul's way of emphasising a statement of fact.

"It wasn't Tom Stocker because Tom Stocker is in an oxygen tent at King George's," said Paul. "And his job's up for grabs."

So that was the Ring of Power waiting for a new finger.

And it was very surely a Ring of Power, no doubt about that: Sir Frederick's Number Two ... chief-of-staff, deputy managing director, first understudy—first lieutenant—and confidant. And more than that, too. . . . All the doors opened to Brigadier Stocker, and all the files unlocked themselves for him. Liaison with other departments and other agencies passed through him, on his signature. He had the day-to-day patronage of hiring and firing and promoting.

He did all the work, including the dirty work.

It should have been Brigadier Stocker's voice out of the darkness in her garden.

"He failed his physical four months ago," said Colonel Shapiro.

God! thought Frances: the Israelis always knew everything. No wonder the Russians were so suspicious of their Jews; and that was more than half the reason why David Audley had given her his homily on cultivating them—why he had openly boasted to her of co-operating with Mossad unofficially. It had even sparked one of his rare moments of crudity: *I'd rather have them inside the tent, pissing out, than the other way round*!

"He should have resigned straight away," said Shapiro. "He already had bad chest pains, even before the physical . . . But the man they had lined up for the job wouldn't take it. Turned it down flat on them."

"David Audley," said Paul. He glanced quickly at Shapiro for confirmation. "It was David, wasn't it?"

"Correct." Shapiro didn't take his eyes off Frances. "We have a copy of his refusal telegram—he'd just started his tour in Washington. Clinton was dining with the Provost of St. Barnabas at Cambridge that night, David's old college. And David actually sent the telegram *en clair* just to let Clinton know he didn't give a damn—typical David. But he also recommended Butler for the job while he was about it."

Paul gave a half-laugh. "Typical David indeed! But he was quite right, of course—on both counts. He'd be an absolute disaster in that job, would David. An absolute disaster!"

Shapiro gave him a sharp look. "Why d'you think that, Mitchell?"

"Paper-work and public relations? Talking to Ministers of the

Crown? Ex-trade union bosses? David has a streak of mischief a mile wide at the best of times. He'd talk down to them quite deliberately—he'd try to make fools of them, and he'd end up making a fool of himself."

He was wrong, thought Frances. Or at least half wrong. David didn't suffer fools gladly, but he had learnt to suffer them. The private fight which he waged endlessly—and lost endlessly—was between duty and selfishness. He had refused the job simply because it was no fun.

"He was right about Butler, though," said Paul dogmatically. "One hundred and one per cent right."

Shapiro lifted one bushy eyebrow interrogatively, silently repeating his previous question.

Paul nodded. "Oh—he's not a genius, is Fighting Jack—our Thin Red Line . . . He's damn good, but he isn't a genius."

"But he knows his duty?"

"That's one strike for him, certainly. He doesn't want the job, but he'll do it." He bobbed his head. "And he'll do it well—and he'll win his coronary ten years from now like poor old Stocker. The crowning glory of a life spent above and beyond the call of duty: one oxygen tent in King George's, with a pretty little nurse to special him on his way out."

Shapiro nodded.

"But that isn't the real qualification," said Paul. "I mean, it *is* the real qualification from our point of view—" He nodded to Frances "—General Sir Ralph Abercromby and all that . . . *ever-watchful to the health and wants of his troops*, Princess: when he sends us over the top, the wire will be cut ahead of us, and the reserves will be ready just behind—you better believe it!

"But no . . . His real qualification is that the bloody politicians won't be able to resist him. Ex-grammar school scholarship boy, risen from the ranks by merit—son of a prominent trade unionist, a friend of Ernie Bevin's—still with a touch of Lancashire in his accent, too. Which he can turn on when he wants, when he needs to . . . no Labour minister can resist *that*. Not for the power behind the throne in Intelligence, by golly!

"And if the Tories have a hand in it . . . by God! all he'll have to do is grunt at them, and all the other qualifications work for them too. They'll see him as a true-blue Tory, risen from the ranks—the very best sort of salt-of-the-earth Tory. Even the fact that his Dad was one of Ernie Bevin's friends will count for him—the Tories dine out on Ernie Bevin's famous last words—*The Buggers won't work!*—epitaph on the Welfare State! A perfect Intelligence profile, either way, for the late seventies—a man for all seasons!"

He nodded again at Shapiro. "But you're right really, in the end . . . about Duty. So they'll all take one look at him, and they'll trust him on sight." He shrugged and grinned at them both, almost as though embarrassed. "Bloody hell! Come to that, *I* trust him—even though he hates my guts—*I* trust him!"

Well, well! thought Frances, in astonishment. Well, well, well, well, *well*! And yet—well again!—all that made the whole thing even more inexplicable.

"But if that's the case, Paul—if that's what everyone thinks of Colonel Butler—how have we ended up with the job of wrecking his chances?" she frowned at him. "And how did David . . . bog it up?"

Paul looked to Shapiro for the answer. "Colonel?"

"Who's got it in for Colonel Butler?" Frances shifted the questions in the same direction. *And come to that*, she added silently, *what the hell are you doing here, Colonel Shapiro?*

Shapiro rubbed the tip of his nose with a stubby finger.

"Yes . . ." He considered her reflectively for a moment, as though he'd picked up an echo of what she hadn't said. "Well, Mrs Fitzgibbon, I would guess that the probable answer to your second question is 'Nobody'. Or it was to start with, anyway." He paused. "And I'm afraid that the answer to your first question is that David wasn't very clever for once. He tried to play politics, and he played foolishly."

"Politics?"

Shapiro sighed. "And . . . very regrettably . . . some of the blame is mine too. I condoned—I contributed to—a most egregious error of judgement. I must confess it. And I have come here tonight to do all I can to rectify it."

Frances began to feel out of her depth. That Mossad should be interested in Brigadier Stocker's successor was fair enough. But although it would have suited them down to the ground for David Audley to take the job they had no reason to expect any favours from Colonel Butler.

"It was such an excellent idea, that was the trouble with it. One should always be suspicious of excellent ideas," said Shapiro sorrowfully. "The better they are, the worse the situation becomes if they go wrong."

Way out of her depth, decided Frances.

"It was such a good idea that Audley came back from Washington to make sure Sir Frederick Clinton acted on it—to make sure nothing went wrong. And while he was here he came to me to enlist my support for it—I have some influence with the West Germans, and also with the Americans over here. He wanted the right people to be primed if there was consultation . . . and we both agreed it was . . . an absolutely excellent idea."

But why did the Israelis think Butler was an excellent idea?

"For quite different reasons, as it turned out," continued Shapiro. "Although at the time I thought differently—I thought David was playing the same game as I was, even though he said he was being entirely altruistic—" he nodded at Paul "—exactly as you claim to be, Mitchell. You say Colonel Butler doesn't like you, but you trust him . . . And that's precisely what David Audley said. And I didn't believe a word of it."

"Why not?" said Frances. "Don't tell me it was just because David is devious."

"You know, I *am* being rather altruistic," said Paul to no one in particular. He sounded suspicious of himself.

"My dear lady—young lady—" Shapiro caught himself just in time. "I told you—I made a mistake. Isn't that enough for you?"

Under the urbanity he was angry with himself—so furious that it required a continuous effort not to burn up everything and everyone around him, not excluding dear young ladies, thought Frances. But one thing he wasn't going to receive from this young lady—and 'young lady' from him was patronising and he ought to have known better: in Israel 'young ladies' were accepted as young soldiers—was any special consideration. Whatever he'd done, there was no way Colonel Shapiro of Mossad would have behaved altruistically.

"I didn't believe him—" Shapiro saw that he wasn't about to be offered an olive branch, and that cooled him down "—for the sufficient reason that Colonel Butler thinks very highly of him, professionally. Which is all that matters."

Yes. And so here was another one who wasn't concerned with motives and wives and murder, decided Frances. For all Shapiro cared, Colonel Butler could be the Motorway Murderer himself, with women planted under the roadway one to every hundred yards for miles on end. Professionally that was of no consequence whatsoever, provided it was done efficiently.

"My God!" said Paul in a hollow voice. "It's Audley that they're after, not Butler!"

"*What?*" For once Frances ignored her own hateful feminine squeak of surprise. "What?"

"Christ—I'm dim—*dim!*" Paul, in turn, ignored her, addressing himself to Shapiro. "I thought Fred Clinton was losing his grip—letting them push Butler out of the way, doing their dirty work for them."

"He *is* losing his grip," snapped Shapiro. "Five years ago . . . even two years ago . . . he would have closed up that file on Butler tight—he would have locked it up and thrown away the key. If Stocker hadn't been a sick man he still might have managed it. But with Stocker the way he was—no help . . . waiting for the next pain in his chest . . . and he's too old to fight the way he used to, Clinton is. The politicians pushed him—you're right, Mitchell: there are people who know all about Audley, and they don't like what they know—he doesn't push around easily, and he isn't polite with it either. Also there's the anti-Audley faction in your own department—they really hate his guts too."

"For a different reason, I hope to God!" murmured Paul.

Audley?

"So do I," said Shapiro grimly. "By God—I hope that too!"

Audley? Audley?

"Clinton's 64. He's retiring next year," said Paul.

Clinton—Audley? Not Butler, not Stocker. But Clinton and Audley?

"In November. One year exactly," Shapiro nodded. "We have one year—to the day, near enough. He'll be at the Cenotaph on Remembrance Sunday, and that'll be the last time."

The irrelevance of the exact dating threw Frances into confusion. Sir Frederick Clinton had always attended the Remembrance Day parade in Whitehall, every Sunday of every November that she could remember, with his medals on his chest. Twice, when she'd been duty officer, he'd quite deliberately taken her too—had put someone else on duty for an hour quite deliberately.

"*You'll want to come of course, Frances. You have something to remember.*"

She'd never seen David there—in spite of the Wessex Dragoons'

80 per cent casualties. But then David wasn't sentimental.

She'd never seen Butler there either . . . And that was much stranger, with his passion for anniversaries and the Lancashire Rifles' battle honours, which must be scattered across dozens of cemeteries all the way to Korea and back.

But that was all irrelevant: she was being diverted from the wood by the bark on the trees.

Paul noticed her confusion at last, and took pity on her.

"Frances—I'm sorry! I am dim-witted." But he was pleased with himself, nevertheless. "Fred Clinton's retiring next year."

"Yes?"

"It's as plain as the nose—" Paul's eye flicked to Shapiro's beak, which almost rivalled Nannie's, and then came back to her "—as the pretty nose on your face. I just didn't get it until I realised that no one would expect me to be altruistic—to want to do the right thing just for once for the right reason, like poor old Thomas Archbishop in *Murder in the Cathedral*.

Exasperation. "Paul, what are you talking about?"

"He turned the job down—David did. Stocker's job. And he pushed Butler for it—" Paul pointed at Colonel Shapiro "—and he lobbied all over the place for Butler to get it. And David doesn't normally play politics, he despises politics almost as much as Fighting Jack does. Right, Colonel?"

"Correct." Shapiro nodded. "And a grave mistake, too. David Audley is a professional who tries to behave like an amateur. He suffers from the gentlemen-and-players syndrome—a common British disease afflicting ex-public schoolboys."

"Very true. But not a common Israeli disease afflicting ex-tank commanders," Paul agreed, deflecting the insult back at the Colonel. "So few gentlemen in that line of business, I suppose?"

Frances looked at them angrily. "For God's sake—both of you—why are they after David, not Butler? What's David done?"

"It's not what he's done, it's why he did it," said Shapiro.

"Or rather, dear Princess, why everyone *thought* he did it," said Paul.

Motive again, thought Frances bitterly. She had already found a motive Colonel Butler had had for something he hadn't done; now all she had to find was a motive David Audley had lacked for something he had done.

It came to her a second before Paul spoke, but too late.

"They thought David was going for Sir Frederick Clinton's job," said Paul.

Just like that. Simple, obvious and self-evident. Like the nose on Nannie's face—plain as the nose, plain as the face.

David Audley for Number One.

Therefore, in advance, to prepare the way for the lord, his old friend and colleague—godfather to his daughter—for Number Two.

"Correct," said Shapiro.

David Audley for Emperor.

But first Colonel Butler for Grand Vizier.

It was safe as well as simple: the Grand Vizier never got the Emperor's job, that required different qualifications as well as *cojones*. But the Grand Vizier was uniquely well-placed to influence the succession . . . and—God!—also to eliminate rivals.

Frances stared at Paul. Was he thinking what she was thinking: that whoever was urging them both on to dig the dirt on Colonel Butler, was acting in self-defence, to avert the possibility that before long, otherwise, Butler would be urging Mitchell and Fitzgibbon to dig the dirt on *them* with his new Ring of Power? Everybody had dirt hidden somewhere, and given time and resources someone else could find that dirt.

(She went on staring at Paul. It wouldn't take him long to find out that Mrs Frances Fitzgibbon's marriage had been breaking up because Mrs Fitzgibbon was rotten in bed; and that Captain and Mrs Fitzgibbon both knew that Captain Fitzgibbon wouldn't come back to her from that last Ulster tour, one way or another. It wouldn't take him long. He might even know already, at that, being Paul.)

(She mustn't think of that. She didn't want Robbie to come back any more than Colonel Butler would want Madeleine Françoise to come knocking at his mock-Tudor door again.)

David Audley for Emperor.

No wonder there was a palace revolution in progress!

"I know what you're thinking," said Paul.

That wasn't possible. She had to head him off, anyway.

She turned to Shapiro. "Is David after the job?"

"I wish he was!" Shapiro scowled at her. "But he's not. He just isn't hungry enough to fight, that's the trouble."

"Maybe this'll change his mind," said Paul. "He may not like to fight, but he doesn't like to be beaten."

Paul was hungry, thought Frances. If Paul thought he was being altruistic, he was deceiving himself.

"I wouldn't rely on that assumption," said Shapiro. "And even if he does fight—even if *we* fight—I wouldn't rely on our chances of winning."

Paul nodded. "No—I agree. This makes it a different ball-game. It's relegation or promotion now."

"It's the bloody Cup Final—I beg your pardon, Mrs Fitzgibbon." Shapiro acknowledged Frances, but kept his eye on Paul. "You think you've been shouting for the wrong team, Mitchell?"

Paul grunted ruefully. "I don't think I've got any choice now—in this company. The trouble is, I don't even see how to win by fighting dirty." He nodded at Frances. "That's what our little Princess was thinking. You're going to have to produce one hell of a magic spell to get us out of this one, Princess. Otherwise it's going to be 'unhappy ever after' for us."

Shapiro saved Frances. "What do you mean?"

"I mean, Colonel . . . that it won't be good enough for Fitzgibbon and Mitchell to give Colonel Butler a clean bill of health. We weren't put on this one to find an answer they didn't know. We were set to find what they knew already—to make it nice and respectable." He shook his head at Frances. "Somebody's already talked—I knew that smug bastard who briefed me was giving me the message, not seeking after wisdom."

"What message?"

Paul's lip curled. "Nine years ago, Colonel—nine years to the day, almost—*our* dear Colonel could have killed his wife. And that was very naughty of him."

"He didn't," said Frances.

"Of course he didn't. Fighting Jack wouldn't do a vulgar thing like that—the old General wouldn't approve. Besides which he knows his Kipling on the subject of service wives—of course he didn't! He couldn't." He paused. "And if he did it would have been a beautiful tragic accident, with an unbreakable alibi built into it, and no comeback nine years later."

So Paul Mitchell and William Ewart Hedges, travelling from different directions, had reached the same destination, thought Frances.

"But that doesn't matter," said Paul. "Unfortunately our job isn't to give him a character reference—we just have to breathe suspicion over him. I thought it might be enough if we did the exact opposite—Frances and I. But the stakes are too big for that, and if we don't provide the right answer they'll simply send down someone else who will."

Shapiro looked at Frances.

"Am I right, Princess?" asked Paul.

Shapiro continued to look at Frances.

"Princess?"

Frances looked at Shapiro. "When does David get back?"

"Not until midday tomorrow. He's got a meeting he can't break—Washington time," said Shapiro.

Washington time. Not enough time.

"I'll give you whatever help you need," said Shapiro.

Everyone was so helpful. There was altruism everywhere.

"I'm going to Blackburn," said Frances for the second time. But now she knew why she was going there.

XIII

FOR THE SECOND time in one morning Miss Marilyn Francis was in Thistlethwaite Avenue, at the entrance of the driveway to St. Luke's Home for Elderly Gentlefolk. But this time she was going inside.

Frances looked at her watch. It was 11.25, which ought to be just about right for visiting.

She turned to the woman beside her. "If you could wait here, Mrs Bates—just down the road, perhaps."

"Yes, luv." Mrs Bates gave her a motherly smile. Mrs Bates was a motherly person, almost grandmotherly. "Shall I have Brian bring your own car up, from behind the hotel?"

Mrs Bates was also a well-organised and well-organising person, who thought of everything, as befitted an Israeli intelligence cell commander.

Frances sorted Brian from Evan Owen and Mr Harcourt, who were taking it in turns to keep Colonel Butler in sight. Brian was the plump-faced young man on the motor-cycle, the junior partner in the team. Evan Owen drove the van, and Mr Harcourt was the commercial traveller in the nondescript Cortina.

She also wondered, for the umpteenth time, how Paul Mitchell had made out with Nannie on her return from night duty. The girls, mercifully, had accepted the unscheduled dawn departure of the potential Second Mrs Butler after she had reassured them that Paul was only a colleague, and that he would never be anything more than a colleague, and that he was too young for her anyway, and that she would be coming back to see them at the earliest opportunity; which reassurances—three truths and one lie (she would never come back to Brookside House, that was a near-certainty)—had been the least she could do for Paul, whom they would otherwise have either murdered or seduced during the night as an obstacle to their plans. But Nannie was a different problem—she would give Paul a hard time, supposing his charm didn't work; and she would also report on him to Colonel Butler at the earliest opportunity, after which the cat would very likely be out of the bag. But by then, very likely, it wouldn't matter much, he could think what he liked, it would be all over; and, anyway, it was all over for Paul, that part of it—Nannie's part—and by now he would be two hours up the motorway to Yorkshire.

(The same motorway that Colonel Butler had once travelled at another November dawn, nine years ago.)

She felt strangely fatalistic about it all.

"Thank you, Mrs Bates." As she stepped out of the car she saw Mrs Bates reach under the dashboard for the microphone which linked her to Brian and Evan Owen and Mr Harcourt in his Cortina.

A cobweb of rain brushed her face, fine as gossamer but nonetheless quickly soaking.

This was real northern rain—not so much rain as total wetness. When she had left Brookside House it had been raining—raining obviously, with real raindrops spattering on her. But somewhere along the drive northwards it had stopped raining and had become simply wet, the very air so saturated with moisture that a fish could have breathed it.

She put up Mrs Bates' big black umbrella, but the dampness ignored it. By the time she reached the porch she could feel it running down her face, spoiling Marilyn's make-up. If someone didn't come quickly to answer the bell Marilyn's blonde frizz, which had jumped so surprisingly from under the wig, would be reduced to unsightly rats'-tails.

The door opened.

"*Northern Daily Post-Gazette,*" said Frances quickly, hunching herself up against a trickle of rain which had infiltrated the top of her plastic mac. "I phoned up about an hour ago. To see Mr Sands, please."

"Mr Sands?" A blast of warm air reached Frances's face.

Rifleman Sands, *please*, begged Frances silently.

"Oh, yes—the young lady from the newspaper?" The green-uniformed nurse was as crisp and fresh as a young lettuce leaf. But she looked at Frances—at Marilyn—doubtfully for a moment, as though she had expected a better class of young lady, not something off the cheapest counter at the supermarket.

"That's right," said Frances desperately. Marilyn would just have to do, now. But the theory that as Colonel Butler and the North had never seen Marilyn, so that she might purchase a minute or two more of anonymity if the worst came to the worst . . . that theory of Paul's didn't seem so clever now.

She shivered uncontrollably, and the Florence Nightingale training of the lettuce leaf came to her rescue.

"Ee—but you're wet, dear—come inside!" The lettuce leaf opened the door wider. "Put your umbrella down there—in the stand—so it won't drip on the floor."

Frances collapsed the umbrella gratefully. The door closed at her back and the warmth swirled around her.

"And get your raincoat off—let me help you—there now—that's better! Oh . . . isn't it a right miserable day—that's better!"

That was better. And without the raincoat Marilyn was better too: she was only Marilyn from the neck up. From the neck down she was still Frances, in Mrs Fitzgibbon's best Jaeger suit.

"Thank you, nurse." Marilyn-Frances took in her surroundings. Everything that wasn't a cool, freshly-laundered, green-uniformed lettuce leaf was painted and polished in St. Luke's Home for Elderly Gentlefolk. And on the landing window-sill halfway up the staircase was a great spray of out-of-season flowers, too: one thing St. Luke's Home didn't need was a grant from the Ryle Foundation, it was doing very nicely thank-you on the fees from the Elderly Gentlefolk. Colonel Butler was certainly doing right by General Chesney's ex-gardener, ex-batman, in return for the old man's 50 per cent share in pulling the General off the barbed wire at wherever-it-was in France sixty years before.

"And you've got an appointment with Mr Sands." The lettuce leaf smiled at her this time, it was the influence of the Jaeger suit, no doubt. "He is having an exciting time!"

"Yes?"

"Oh yes—this way, if you please—" The lettuce leaf pointed up the stairs "—the Colonel this morning . . . with a big box of chocolates for us, and flowers for Matron . . . and the young man yesterday—" she glanced over her shoulder at Frances "—and he was from your paper too, wasn't he? What has Mr Sands been up to?"

She was moving at nurses' quick-step. "We're planning a series on veterans of the First World War," said Frances breathlessly.

"That's right," agreed the lettuce leaf. "The young man told me. There aren't many of them left, I suppose—didn't he get everything, the young man? Old Mr Sands talked to him for ages."

"I'm the woman's angle," said Frances.

"Ah . . . of course." Nod. "Well, when you do a series on the Second World War, you come to me—I wasn't born then, but my mum remembers it all, Dad was at El Alamein, and had his toe shot off in Italy, in a monastery there—would you believe it? Here we are."

She knocked at a gleaming door. "Mr Sands? Another visitor for you! You're really in luck today . . ." She filled the door for a moment. "All right, then? You don't want the bottle, or anything like that? You're ready to see your visitor?"

There came a sound from beyond her, a sort of croak.

God! Don't let him be senile, prayed Frances: he wasn't yesterday for Paul. Don't let him be below par for me. I have the right question for him, Paul didn't.

"That's good," said the lettuce leaf briskly. But she caught Frances's arm then. "Now, dear . . ." she murmured into Frances's ear confidentially ". . . he's a lovely old man, really—not like most of our old gentlemen, not exactly—but a dear old chap, all the same."

Most of their old gentlemen would be rich old gentlemen in their own right, that must be the difference.

"But you've got to watch him like a hawk. He pretends he can't see you properly—and it's him who's got eyes like a hawk. And he pretends he can't hear either, and he hears perfectly well when he wants to. He tells you he can't hear just to lure you close to him, that's all—he did it with the Mayor's daughter, I think it was, when they came to the Home last year, the old devil!"

"Did what?" whispered Frances.

"He put his *hand* up her *skirt*, dear—*right up*!" hissed the lettuce leaf urgently. "You should have heard her scream! I was down the passage—it frightened me out of my wits. . . . We're used to it, of course. But you—" she glanced quickly at Marilyn's hair "—you better just watch him, that's all." She straightened up abruptly, and poked her head round the door again. "Here you are, Mr Sands: it's the young lady from the newspaper. And you behave yourself, or I won't let you watch *The Sweeney*—I'll take your set away, and that's a promise!"

Which was *The Sweeney*? Marilyn had kept up with all the popular TV programmes, from *Coronation Street* upwards—

My God! *The Sweeney* was the violent one, where the cops and robbers were always putting in the boot.

She entered the room cautiously.

It was a beautiful room, high and peach-and-white, with bright-flowered curtains framing a window which gave a view of trees on a far hillside.

And a big colour TV set for *The Sweeney*.

And a little old man sitting up in bed, against a mound of pillows—

Like a little old wizened monkey, Paul had said. *Sans teeth, almost sans eyes, but not sans memory.*

Paul wasn't quite so clever though, again: more like a little bird of prey, with bright eyes fastening on her. (Or perhaps that wasn't quite fair to Paul, and she was being wise after the nurse's warning of his predatory habits once the prey was within reach.)

He didn't say anything, he just looked at her. There was a copy of the *Sun* under his hand, opened to page three's bare breasts. As she looked back at him he closed the page.

Well, she hadn't been so clever either. There was obviously nothing wrong with his eyes or his memory, but she'd forgotten to ask what was wrong with his legs . . . Though perhaps she should be grateful for their weakness, so it seemed.

"Mr Sands?"

"Yes?" He sank back into the pillows.

"I'm from the *Post-Gazette*, Mr Sands. A colleague of mine came to see you yesterday . . . About your war experiences."

"What?" He cupped his hand to his ear.

"About-your-war-experiences, Mr Sands."

"Speak up, Missy. I can't hear you."

Frances advanced towards the bed. "My colleague came to see you yesterday to ask you about your war experiences. When you were in the trenches with General Chesney."

"I still can't hear you. You'll have to speak up."

"You can hear me perfectly well," said Frances clearly.

"Don't shout. There's no call to shout," said Rifleman Sands. "I'm not deaf."

"I want to talk to you about *after* the war," said Frances.

"Ar? Well, you'll have to come closer," said Rifleman Sands, laying down the price by patting the bed. "You can come and sit on the edge here. Then I can hear you."

Then you can do more than hear me, thought Frances.

She looked down at the hand which had patted the bed, and which now lay resting itself on the coverlet. It was a working hand, one size bigger than the rest of Rifleman Sands, what she could see of him—a hand expanded by work, old and knotted now, the veins standing up from the parchment-thin skin, but very clean and manicured—a St. Luke's hand now. When she thought about it dispassionately, it didn't disgust her at all. It had been up a good many skirts in its time, that hand, without doubt. Now it was about to go up hers, but it wouldn't be the first—or the worst—to make that short journey. It had been cleaned by the earth of the old General's flowerbeds a thousand times over, and by that other earth of France and Flanders too, and it couldn't possibly do her any harm now. If her skirt was the last skirt, that was just the final bit of the unpaid debt.

The bed was high off the floor, her skirt rode up quite naturally as she hitched herself aboard it.

Rifleman Sands smiled at her happily, and she found herself smiling back at him in perfect accord, perfect innocence.

"Now, Missy. After the war? There was a big fireworks display on the top of Corporation Park, along Revidge . . . where there's now tennis courts—there was a bit of spare land there—where we used to go capertulling of a Sunday night—"

"Capertulling?"

The hand patted the coverlet. "A big fireworks display. We used to walk up Revidge—about this time of year, too—and on our front gate we used to have an arch of laurels, with candles in jam jars. . . . My elder brother used to say he was watching these people coming back, stopping to light their cigarettes on the candles in the jam jars. I didn't go, of course."

"Why not?"

"Fireworks reminded me of the trenches." He spoke as though it was a silly question, to which she ought to know the answer without asking. "We had enough fireworks . . . Though later on I did go up. You forget, see—in the end you forget."

It was after the *first* war, he was talking about—sixty years ago, nearly! She was going to have to watch her time-scale, thought Frances. He was dredging back into his memory, already prepared by Paul's question of the day before, telling her what he thought she wanted to know.

"Top of the Corporation Park, luv—you know it. Where the tennis courts are now." The hand fastened on her ankle, which dangled just over the edge of the bed beside him. "Top of the Corporation Park."

The Corporation Park.

Dripping, dripping, dripping wet. Under the umbrella, but everything dripping—the wet mist in her face.

She had walked alongside Brian. She had pushed the child's push-chair which he had provided, the mist fogging her glasses until she'd been forced to stop in a shop doorway and substitute her contact lenses for the glasses; and he'd made her take her green raincoat off and put on the beige-coloured one he'd produced from inside the push-chair; and also a head-scarf instead of the umbrella (not Mrs Bates' umbrella, but a smaller, useless feminine one, which he'd collapsed into an eight-inch cylinder and stuffed back into his pocket; Brian knew a thing or two about tailing a target, and was prepared to change their profile on the assumption that Colonel Butler knew a thing or two about being tailed).

"Yes, I know Corporation Park."

"Well, I remember that, then." He squeezed the ankle encouragingly. "And Blackburn Rovers won the Cup—in 1927 or 1928 . . . 1928, it was. And then, before the war—the other war, Hitler's War—Lancashire won the county championship three years in succession. That was under the captaincy of Leonard Green—Colonel Leonard Green, he was a friend of the General's, of course. . . . He lived at Worley, where we used to play an annual match. The Lancashire players in those days . . . there was Ted MacDonald, the most marvellous bowler of all time—and George Duckworth kept wicket—"

Frances closed her eyes. They were on to cricket now—cricket was Colonel Butler's game, so it wasn't surprising that it had also been Sands' game and the General's. But Rifleman Sands was also on to her calf and a different game now.

She had seen better with her contact lenses, blinking the rain out of her eyes, although she still couldn't see one hell of a lot of the Corporation Park.

But she could hear the ducks away to her left in the murk, enjoying the weather. The very sound of them frightened her.

Where was Colonel Butler going? He'd been to the shops, and

bought flowers and a large parcel from the confectioner's. But now he was walking in the rain, very straight and purposeful, as though he knew where he was going. Flowers and parcel had already been delivered to St. Luke's—Frances and Brian had huddled under the inadequate umbrella at the end of the road for twenty minutes; then Brian had taken the lead, but at the gate to the Park she had moved past him to keep the broad back, the deer-stalker (of all utterly ridiculous headgear, a deer-stalker!) and the multi-coloured golfing umbrella in view—if he'd set out to be obvious he couldn't have done better, so it wasn't difficult; but it was exceptionally wet and uncomfortable.

(All the same, she'd been glad about St. Luke's. That had been exactly, almost uncannily, what she'd been expecting, against hope.)

Perhaps he'd moved up from her ankle to her calf because her feet were still wet.

No way! He'd moved up because that was the way to her knee: *This is Number Three* (they'd sung at Robbie's battalion seven-a-side rugby contest, within earshot of the battalion ladies) *and my hand is on her knee!*

And Rifleman Sands had reached Number Three. But at least, if he was genuinely bed-ridden, he couldn't manage Number Four, Frances felt entitled to hope.

But just in case . . . and in any case, she had to keep his mind on her job.

She moved her leg warningly. He held on grimly.

"I saw Colonel Butler in the Park today, Mr Sands."

The hand relaxed—it didn't move away, but it relaxed.

"Oh ah? Been to see me today, has the Colonel—" He stared at her suddenly, as though she was not an ankle and a knee, but potentially something more, a human being. "There was a man came to see me not long ago."

"He's been to see you?" Frances pounced on what she wanted.

"From the newspaper, aye," Rifleman Sands nodded. "He was a good-looking lad, but a bit too pleased with hisself." He nodded again. "Mind you, he knew about the war, I'll give 'im that. Ypres, he knew Ypres—" he winked at Frances "—'Wipers' what we called, he knew that. And Bapaume and Albert, with the old Virgin . . ."

The old Virgin? That sounded like a contradiction in terms with young Rifleman Sands about.

"And Beaumont Hamel—he's been there. And he saw the Lone Tree!" Rifleman Sands shook his head in wonder. "He actually saw the Lone Tree! It's still there—I wouldn't have believed it, but he's seen it with his own eyes! After all this time! And it was dead when I knew it. But he's seen it!"

Frances winced at the sudden pressure on her leg, just above the knee.

"I've never been back. No point. . . . It's not pretty, like the Ribble Valley. Over the top, across the golf course over to Mellor—all that's open country . . . I mean over the top—not like we used to say 'over the top', that was different, that was . . . But over the top from the golf course, and you drop down to the Ribble—as youngsters we used to go that way, and wade the Ribble, and on to Ribchester. You don't want to go to Bapaume if you can do that, an' nobody shoot at you. Waste of time—waste of money! It used to cost Thruppence to get into Alexandra Meadows for the cricket—and you could see it for nothing from the Conservatory in the Park, 'the Scotsman's Pavilion' was our name for it. And when there wasn't any cricket—there was no telly then, but there was fifteen cinemas in the town, and a music hall . . . and the repertory—the Denville Repertory, I used to watch that. The beer was better too, not so gassy—Dutton's and Thwaites'—the next biggest brewing town to Burton we were, because of the good spring water, see. And of an evening we'd take a tram to Billinge End . . . eight-wheelers, they were. Four at the front and four at the back—Blackburn trams and Blackpool trams are best in country."

The past was getting mixed up with the present, but it would be a mistake to stop him too abruptly, decided Frances. She'd just have to judge her moment.

"—and then walk up Revidge for a bit of capertulling with the girls."

The present was also beginning to slip above her knee, and it would be a mistake to stop that too: he seemed to have judged *his* moment as right now, for a final bit of capertulling.

"—and back through the Park, past the lake. . . ." He looked at her, and she wasn't sure whether he was checking that she was still listening or to see if she intended to scream like the Mayor's daughter. "That lake's an old quarry, you know. That's why there's no boating on it, or skating in winter, it's that deep they don't rightly know how deep it is. And there's a stream runs down, right under the War Memorial—underground—and goes through the town, under a street that used to be called Snigg Brook—'snigg' being an eel—but the silly buggers have re-named it 'Denville Street', would you believe it! I suppose it was because the people from the Denville Rep. used to lodge thereabouts, and it didn't sound posh enough. They did the same with Sour Milk Hall Lane and Banana Street, silly buggers. It's not the same—" He stopped abruptly, pulling back his hand as though he'd been stung.

Frances couldn't bring herself to ask him what the matter was. He certainly hadn't encountered any resistance, quite the opposite. Could that be what had frightened him? Or was it her lack of encouragement? But that had never discouraged previous hands.

"Tights," said Rifleman Sands with disappointed scorn. "Tights."

Tights were death on capertulling, of course. It was just Rifleman Sands' bad luck that she was Frances below the waist, not Marilyn.

"But you're a good lass, all the same," Rifleman Sands patted her Jaeger-skirted thigh forgivingly, as though to reassure her that she wasn't a failure. "Not a catawauller, like some I could mention."

She smiled at him, and he smiled back. Nurse Lettuce Leaf was quite right: he was a lovely old man as well as a randy old devil.

And he was ready now.

"So Colonel Butler came to see you today, then, Mr Sands?"

"Aye, the Colonel." He nodded happily. "A good lad too, he is, young Jack. Happen you'd make a good pair, him and you."

"Does he come to see you often?"

"Oh, aye."

"This time of year?"

"One of the best," he nodded again. "The General—he'd be right proud of him. . . . Of course, he was proud of him already. When he won his medal, fighting those Chinamen, he was pleased as though it was his own boy—him that was killed by the Paythens. 'The M.C., Sands,' he says to me. 'That's a fighting man's medal, that is.' And he should know, seeing how he'd won it too—that was at Loos, up under Fosse Number Eight, where he was wounded the first time. And that was a terrible bad place, Fosse Number Eight, believe you me, lass. I was up there with the Rifles later on—a terrible bad place, that was."

He was rambling hopelessly now. *Damn tights*, thought Frances. He'd have been sharp enough with a suspender to twang.

"At this time of year?" she tried again.

He looked out of the window, up towards the high green ridge where he had once walked, on which he would never walk again.

"It's raining," he said. "It's not the same rain as it used to be, though."

Now he was into nostalgia, thought Frances despairingly.

"It used to be right dirty rain—mucky rain," said Rifleman Sands unnostalgically. "Woman couldn't put her whites out—couldn't put anything out—when it was raining. Bloody mill chimneys'd cover everything with bloody soot. It's a sight better now, thank God!"

Frances looked at her watch. She was losing him, and she was also running out of time. It had all been a dream, anyway—a four-out-of-ten guess which was going to end up in the losing six.

"Got to go, then?" He looked at her wistfully, memories of caper-tulling before the invention of tights in his eyes. "He had to go, of course. The Colonel."

He looked out of the window again.

"I remember in the old days, though . . . There'll be nobody out there now, not today. But in the old days there'd be the Regiment, with the red poppies in their caps. And the Territorials. And the nurses, and the Boy Scouts and the Girl Guides—and us, of course. The Old Contemptibles. And the Blackburn Prize Band. . . . We'd form up in the centre of the town, and we'd march up Preston New Road—with all our medals—the General, and young Jackie's father just behind him, that was his RSM—cor! you should have seen us then! The whole town was out. Didn't matter if it rained or shined—left, right, left, right—swing those arms! And the band playing the old tunes!

"And young Jack was there too, with the Scouts. And he used to stay behind with his dad afterwards . . . But now they do a bit of something on a Sunday, not worth going to—waste of time. But *then* it was right on the day—November the eleventh. Two minutes' silence at 11 o'clock: the eleventh hour of the eleventh day of the eleventh month—"

Frances had come past him, hiding her face behind the little umbrella heading towards the gates beyond the fountain.

Colonel Butler was standing in front of the ugly memorial obelisk which was topped by an even uglier representation of Peace—a female Peace presiding in bronze over the countless dead of the two World Wars (no room for the Korean dead, or the bad luck casualties of all the other little wars since, from Malaya to Ulster. No room for Blackburn's Robbie Fitzgibbons).

She hadn't watched him from the front, that would have been too risky. But from behind, from the cover—no shelter—of the gates she had observed that he was standing easily, his multi-coloured golfing umbrella over his head, as though reading the names.

And then a clock sounded, away somewhere behind her in the dripping town. As it did so, as though at a time-signal, a sheet of heavier rain—genuine rain—slashed down across the Park, blotting out the further landmarks she had passed a few moments before.

As the first strokes of the clock rang out, rain-muffled, Colonel Butler collapsed his umbrella and removed his ridiculous hat, and came to attention. Even after the sound of the last stroke had cut off—with the loud spattering of the rain and the noise of the traffic behind her it didn't die away, it ended abruptly—he still stood there, for what seemed like an age, bare-headed in the downpour.

Then, unhurriedly, for by then he was wet enough not to need to hurry, he replaced his hat and opened the umbrella again, just as Brian came trotting by him.

Not an age, but two minutes exactly, counted off in heartbeats.

"That's why he had to go, of course. He keeps the proper day, naturally. Never fails—leastways, not when he's in England, and not fighting somewhere. But always comes to see me first, even if only for five minutes—and I've been here ten years now, since me legs went, and he's not missed once."

He twisted awkwardly in the bed to feel under his pillows.

"He has to, see . . ." He turned back towards her. "He has to bring me my red poppy."

He displayed the evidence triumphantly.

XIV

ONCE UPON A time, concluded Frances, there had been a great mansion somewhere hereabouts; one of those huge northern granite palaces built out of coal or cotton, in a rolling parkland, with lodges at the gates—and a duck pond—and a dower house into which the first widow could retreat when her eldest son brought his young bride home from the honeymoon in Piranesi's Italy.

But now, amid the concrete high-rise towers and temples of North Yorkshire University, the Dower House (which was all that had survived of that splendid Once Upon a Time . . . except, of course, the duck pond) . . . the Dower House seemed more like a cottage out of the Grimms' fairy tales which had been magicked from its clearing in the forest into the open.

Not that it frightened her any more, as it might have done before—as the duck pond still did. She was no longer Gretel (was it Gretel?), if she ever had been; and she was no longer Miss Fitzgibbon, the fairy story blue-stocking; and, for all her bedraggled blondeness,she was no longer Marilyn—she no longer needed to be.

She was Mrs Frances Fitzgibbon returning to Paul Mitchell in triumph and victory.

Even the day wasn't so grey now, even the rain wasn't so wet. There was more fighting to be done—the Enemy had lost a battle, but not yet the war itself after the Pelennor Fields. But it was not a battle they had expected to lose, and she had won it.

So it was only reasonable to feel drained and a little light-headed.

It didn't matter, waiting in the rain outside the Dower House, as it had mattered outside St. Luke's home.

The door opened, and there was dear old Professor Crowe—brave old Colonel Crowe. It didn't even matter that he was looking at her with stranger's eyes, unrecognising her.

"Professor Crowe—you remember me?"

"*Miss Fitzgibbon*—I beg your pardon—*Mrs* Fitzgibbon! Well met, my dear, *very* well met!" He beamed at her more warmingly than the St. Luke's central heating. "But you're soaking—quite soaking—come in, my dear, come in! Come in, come in, come in!"

He bustled around her, half wizard, half Hobbit, all elderly bachelor. He fetched a towel. He thought about giving her coffee, but it was too late; he thought about making tea, but it was too early. He didn't mind that she covered his snowy towel with lipstick and mascara—'It'll look wicked, dear—it'll make my students think, and anything which makes them think cannot be bad.' And finally he presented her with a whisky even more outrageous than that which Isobel had given her once upon another time, which she wanted even less and needed not at all, a true Robbie-measure.

"Now—move up close to the fire—" It was a fire like Isobel's too, generous with well-selected pieces of coal "—take off that wet jacket, I'll put it in the airing cupboard—on a hanger, don't worry, so it won't lose its shape —it doesn't matter you've only a slip underneath: you won't lose *your* shape—hah!—and I'm practically old enough to be your grandfather, so if the incipient scandal doesn't worry you it won't worry me—there now, that's better! Drink your whisky, child . . . there's plenty more where that came from—see!"

Frances saw: it was a big new bottle of Glenfiddich from a tall cylindrical case, 86 per cent U.S. proof, out of the nearest duty-free air terminal or American base. It burned her throat as she sipped it.

At last he sank down into the chair opposite her, breathless from his exertions. So far as she could remember, she hadn't yet said a single coherent thing to him, least of all to ask where Paul Mitchell was—why the Dower House was Paul's new headquarters.

"Relief, my dear! The blessed relief of seeing you . . . And I know all about you now, too. *All* about you!"

That was a conversation stopper. Frances burned her throat again, speechless.

"I've been so worried about you. I haven't been so worried since the weather report they gave us before D-Day—'Shall we go or shall we stay?' I never admired Ike more than then, that was his moment. We'd discussed it, of course—every probability, every possibility. The state of the beaches, and so on. But I was to be one of his men on the spot, so I had to put my money where my mouth was, it was no problem for me—if I was wrong I wouldn't be there afterwards to worry about it. But he had to make the decision, and then sit around and wait to see how it turned out—I felt for him. But I really thought I'd guessed what that was like, but do you know I hadn't at all, not at all! Not until I started to worry about you, young lady."

In spite of the fire outside her and the malt inside her, Frances felt a chill shiver her.

"I'm sorry—" she croaked, the chill and the Glenfiddich interacting.

"And so you should be. You told the Death Story!"

"The Death Story?"

"Yes. And then you didn't die. Such effrontery! When we strolled over to the pond—and you were as cool and calm and collected as though you were about to feed those beastly birds with bread—I was much more frightened than on Sword Beach. I thought you were going to take me with you—absolutely petrified I was, I can tell you!"

"I'm—I'm sorry, Professor. You've quite lost me now," said Frances.

"I suppose I should still be worried, for it's still on the end of your finger—" He stopped suddenly. "Unless you've killed somebody already, of course. Have you killed anyone during the last twenty-four hours, by any chance? You don't look as if you have, but one can never tell these days . . ."

"Killed anyone?" The chill was an ice-block now.

"Or presided over a death, perhaps?" Crowe looked at her hopefully. "Or even *seen* a death? An accident would do, so long as you were nearby. Have you pointed at anyone? Or touched anyone deliberately?"

Frances thought of Rifleman Sands. He was old enough, and frail enough. But he had done all the touching. And she very carefully hadn't pointed at the young man in the petrol station—Paul's inexplicable advice had been loud in her brain then.

"No."

"Well, we'll have to leave it to Jack Butler. Perhaps that'll qualify." He blinked at her uneasily.

The Death Story.

"I—am sorry, Professor. But just what is the Death Story?"

"My dear . . ." She watched the scholar take over from the old man with his memories of Sword Beach and Eisenhower ". . . your so-called fairy story—the ugly princess and the blind prince—have you no idea what you really did?"

She knew exactly what she had done: she had told a fairy

story—Granny's creepy fairy story—to take the heat off herself in the Common Room of the new English Faculty Library. And although there had been a bomb just under her feet, no one had died after that—

Horrors, though: she had also told it to Robbie that last time, to get him searching for its origin among his books—to get his mind off going to bed with her.

Successfully, too.

And then Robbie had stepped off the pavement, and tripped over his big feet, three days later as the armoured pig was passing.

Was that success, too?

It wasn't possible. It was pure fancy—as accidental and coincidental as Sir Frederick's wild idea that she had some special wild skill in picking right answers. It was no more than some aberrant mathematical figuring by men who ought to know better.

All the same. "The Death Story?"

Crowe nodded. "Yes . . . I've been checking up on it, as a matter of fact. A lot of fairy stories can be explained in terms of very simple psychology. For example, little girls like fairy stories because of their oedipal problems—they can identify with beautiful princesses held captive by jealous step-mothers because that makes them unavailable to a male lover, which is their father. All of which is not something I like to go into, because it mixes up quite normal enjoyment of good stories with the most terrible pubertal situations. One ends up with Walt Disney's *Snow White* as a really frightful story of sexual jealousy . . . and, frankly my dear, I won't have that. Academics must be careful when they find they're playing with fire."

He gazed for a moment into the heart of the fire, and then came back to her. "But your story is different—with a different root. But it also seems to . . . play with fire, as it were."

"I don't see how." Frances took a firm grip on her imagination. Robbie's death was an accident. Accidents happened all the time. That was the beginning and the end of it. "It's just a fairy story. With a happy ending, too—a eucatastrophic ending, Professor."

"Hah!" For a moment he twinkled at her for being an attentive student, then he was serious again. "Your story is. My story isn't."

"Then tell me your story. I'm not superstitious."

"Bravely said! And the ritual challenge, too: where did you pick it up?"

234

Frances sighed. "As usual, Professor, I don't know what you're talking about."

"I don't think you have to know. You are your Grandmother's grand-daughter, I suspect!"

"You're doing it again."

"So I am! Forgive me. . . . Very well. But first I will demolish your story, my dear. Forget about the three princes. There is only one—the third, of course. The other two are medieval accretions. Or, more accurately, bowdlerisations of a sort."

"A dirty fairy story?"

He ignored her irreverence. "One prince, then. He comes upon a hideous old woman, but because he's blind that doesn't matter to him. He makes her young again by kissing her; she was a beautiful young thing all the time, just bewitched. And they live happily ever after. Presumably he was bewitched too, and the moment he gives the kiss he receives his sight in exchange?"

"That wasn't in my story."

"Good. Forget the bewitching too, anyway. But then what do we have."

"No story."

"We have a hideous old woman—a real woman. Once she was young and beautiful, like you. Now she is old, and nothing works properly any more—Candide's 'old woman' to the life: 'My eyes were not always sore and bloodshot, my nose did not always touch my chin. . . . My breast was once as white as a lily, and as firmly and elegantly moulded as the Venus de Medici's.'" He shook his head sadly. "It happens to all of us, except those the gods love, who die young, before they know the humiliation of missing a train because they are afraid to run that last fifty yards, as I am now." He smiled at her. "And I swear I clipped two seconds off the 220 record on Sword Beach that morning, running in boots on sand, armed *cap à pied*—I wasn't sure that the gods didn't love me, I suppose!"

It was Rifleman Sands all over again, thought Frances. It was one weakness that women didn't have, because they'd always missed battle and sudden death—this remembering with advantage their deeds of daring.

Crowe held up his finger. "Can she be delivered from all this? Of course she can! One kiss—and no more ugliness, no more aches and pains. No more remembrance of all that's been lost, and all that might have been but never was. One kiss—and either nothing, or youth and beauty again for ever and ever. Happy ever after!"

He nodded. "It's pre-Christian, of course. Or pre-medieval Christian—they were the ones who made the Prince himself ugly and frightening, before them he was a god, and a beautiful and merciful god in his own right. And a god who rewarded you if you played the game properly." Crowe pointed at the Glenfiddich bottle, and then at Frances herself. "Valhalla is good whisky and pretty women. No one who offers that can be ugly—it's against reason!"

He stared at her, for all the world as though imprinting her specification on his memory, with the Glenfiddich, for future reference.

"The trick, my dear, is to call the Prince up when you want him. If I'm right . . . your Grandmother—she knew it. Pass the story on, and die—that's the Neapolitan version of it. When you're tired of fighting, tell the story—and summon the Prince of Death!"

He frowned suddenly. "But the trick has a catch to it: once you've told the story you have to pay the score. Because if you don't, then someone else will have to. It's as though you've summoned *him*—it's actually called 'The Summoning Story' in one version—and *he's* not going to go away empty-handed. The Neapolitans say that the Grandmother has a choice—she can point at someone who is dear to her. Or she can let *him* choose at random, in which case *he'll* choose someone dear to her, so it amounts to the same thing. *He* likes the youngest and best, for choice."

It was totally insane. It was an old man's macabre game, nothing more than that. He had read his own book on superstition too often.

"Fortunately—very fortunately—you are not a grandmother yet, so it may not work for you like that. And also Colonel Butler may be able to provide you with a substitute, it now seems likely."

"What?"

"Haven't you been brought up to date?" He smote his forehead. "No—of course! You haven't seen your young man yet—the dashing Mitchell. But David Audley will be able to put you in the picture."

"David's here—now?" Frances sat up.

"Very much so. Though . . . I gather . . . unofficially." Crowe glanced at the clock on the mantlepiece above his fire. "He should be back here—I thought he was you, at the door. Except he doesn't knock, he always barges straight in. He hasn't changed one bit over the years. . . . Anyway, he went off to find young Mitchell, I think,

236

to ascertain from him the whereabouts of his friend Colonel Butler."

Frances frowned at him. "What did you mean— 'Colonel Butler may have a substitute'?"

"I think so. He's about to catch that fellow O'Leary—he thinks he's going to catch him alive, but David believes otherwise." He looked at her, eyes bright with excitement which he probably hadn't felt for years, thought Frances—maybe since he had sprinted across his Normandy beach. Teaching students English literature for half a lifetime would be no substitute for that drug, at a guess.

"You know a lot that's going on, Professor?"

"That I shouldn't, you mean?" He twinkled again happily. "Well, you started it, my dear . . . Or you started it again, I should say. I was half in your line of business after the war, but they were making such a fearful mess of it that I got out of it as soon as I decently could, before I was too old to do anything else. That would be about the time Jones did the same thing—R. V. Jones . . . though I wasn't in his class, of course. . . . Helping to win a war is one thing—it's rather stimulating, actually. But losing a peace can be intolerably frustrating." He regarded her mildly. "I've kept in touch to some extent, but I'm really no more than an interested spectator."

Frances counted up to ten, for the sake of good manners. "Colonel Butler is going to catch O'Leary?"

"That is my impression. You seem surprised?"

She didn't know how to answer that. For some reason she was surprised: the reason lay in the atmosphere of ants' nest disaster she had left behind her here only forty-eight hours earlier. Yet even then, Colonel Butler had been in the middle of the nest, but not part of its confusion, she remembered.

"He is a man with great drive and will-power, your Colonel Butler." The spectator's detachment was evident. "And, what is rarer with that conjunction, of some intellect, I fancy—though he is at pains to conceal it under a khaki manner." Crowe contemplated Colonel Butler's virtue for a moment. "So . . . we have had much excitement here, these last twenty-four hours. Already one of my staff in the Library has been detained. And one of our post-graduate students is . . . helping the police with their inquiries, as the saying goes."

Frances frowned with the effort of recollection. There had been Dixon and . . . and Collins. And Penrose and Brunton—Brunton the Great American Novel seeker, who had been unveiling his girlfriend when the Minister was scheduled to unveil the new Library. And if that, in retrospect, was too good an alibi to be true, she would have staked her reputation on both Collins and Dixon.

"Now you *are* surprised," said Crowe. "But you must accept, my dear, that life goes on, and great events occur, even when you are not there to observe them. Remember the Youth in Crane's *Red Badge*: his armageddon was only a skirmish, and the real battle was being lost and won on another part of the field. That is a very important lesson to learn—" He looked up, and past her, over her shoulder "—wouldn't you agree, David?"

Frances stiffened. As she swivelled in the direction of the Professor's look her bare shoulder reminded her of her relative state of undress, and of Marilyn's appalling hair, but there was nothing she could do about her appearance.

"The whole bloody battle can be irrelevant," said David Audley. "Battle of New Orleans—January, 1815. Peace Treaty of Ghent—December, 1814. Everything's a matter of communication. Or lack of communication, in this instance." He acknowledged Frances with an incurious blink, without a second glance. She might just as well have been stark naked, or dressed as a nun, for all he cared, the blink indicated. "Hullo, Frances."

Come to that, he looked decidedly rough himself, Frances noted. The good suit was creased and rumpled, the shirt was well into its second day, and the unspeakable Rugby Club tie—thin magenta and green stripes on yellow, ugh!—revealed his top shirt button, which was undone, even though the tie itself was savagely pulled into a tiny knot. He hadn't shaved either, and altogether he didn't look like a would-be emperor, even of a dying empire.

"They've both gone hunting with Jack Butler, Hugo. The whole damn place is crawling with Special Branch—it's like the Führer's bunker, the Science Block, there's no way I can get into it. I was able to talk to Jock Maitland for a moment or two, thank God—he can be trusted to hold his tongue if no one asks him any questions, but he didn't know much. How the hell Jack bamboozled the University into installing all that equipment, I'll never know."

"Money, dear boy. Your people stopped their mouths with gold, it never fails; Applied Science is king at the moment, and they've been offered all sorts of grants to turn a blind eye to it. Besides which your Jack can be very charming, you know."

"I don't know—not with me, he isn't!" said Audley feelingly.

238

"The long and short of it is . . . I don't know what the hell's going on out there, anyway, Hugo. Except that Jack's busy routing out an old KGB contact of his somewhere."

"They are about to ensnare O'Leary—I told you, dear boy," said Crowe.

"Not alive, they won't. The information they've got is false—he may be regular KGB, but he's not Russian either—he's Irish. And I had that from those Irish madmen in the CIA. He's a bloody kamikaze pilot, that's what he is."

"So you said," murmured Crowe mildly. "So they will kill him."

"That's not what I'm afraid of—" Audley caught himself up short and looked at Frances. "Bad manners. I'm sorry, Frances. I've got a headache. And part of a hangover . . . which has been dosed by a crazy pilot in the United States Air Force with an old Indian recipe of his, so the part of me that isn't hung-over now feels as if it's been bitten by a rattlesnake. . . . On top of which I've got jet-lag, and I don't know whether it's Monday or Christmas. It feels like Monday."

"It's Friday," said Frances. That was one thing she really did know. "Friday, the eleventh of November. In the afternoon. Hullo, David—good afternoon."

"And good afternoon to you, Frances. Although it isn't." He removed his rain-smeared spectacles, wiped them with a grubby handkerchief, put them back on, and stared at her out of eyes like blood-oranges. "Why, incidentally, are you partially unclothed?"

"She got wet, dear boy," said Crowe. "Like you."

"Eh?" Audley looked down at his jacket: "I see—yes. It's raining, isn't it!" He brushed ineffectually at his shoulders.

Frances felt herself smiling. The longer David was away from his wife, the more like a tramp he became. It was hard to imagine him as the source—or, rather, to imagine his abilities and his unpopularity—as the source of all their recent troubles.

He gave up brushing. The blood-oranges came back to her again.

Frances decided to get her information in first. "You know I'm responsible for calling you back?"

He nodded. "I've talked to Jake Shapiro. He was at the base waiting for me, the bastard."

But how was she going to say it? He was back, and now she didn't need him. He would roast her, and Sir Frederick would also roast her in due course. And then she would resign, and that would be that. But the inevitable outcome, which no longer worried her at all, did not solve the problem of how to break it to him now.

"No need to be scared, love." Audley misconstrued her silence. "You did the right thing."

"I did?" He wasn't making it any easier.

"Fred Clinton had you figured right, as my CIA buddies would say." Suddenly he was grim. "Fortunately."

She stared at him. "What?"

"You and Mitchell between you. A perfect recipe for disobedience. Or initiative, as Horatio Nelson applied it."

"Sir Frederick intended me to call you?"

"He surely did. He's determined to make me fight for Jack Butler, and so I will. Now he thinks I shall fight for you two as well—and so I will. But he'll never take 'no' for an answer—which is what I call a communications failure—and I won't have his job for all the tea in China. I have the same problem with that scheming bastard Jake Shapiro but at least that's understandable—Jake knows how I feel about Israel, from way back. But Clinton has let the thing become an obsession to such an extent that it's become dangerous. Now he's missing the things he should be seeing."

"What things?"

"Ever since I put Jack Butler up for poor old Tom Stocker's job they've been giving him tough assignments—putting him in the forefront of the battle like Uriah the Hittite. But that's fair enough—trial by ordeal will prove that God's on the Butler side as well as Audley."

"North Yorkshire University being one of the ordeals, presumably?" murmured Crowe.

"That's what I thought, when I heard about it," Audley nodded "A more diabolically stupid operation, that degree ceremony, I find it hard to imagine." He paused. "Too hard, in fact."

Frances could nod to that.

"You're not suggesting that Colonel Butler was to be discredited at the cost of other people's lives, David?" Crowe sat up angrily in his spectator's chair. "You're not serious!"

"I'm not sure what I'm suggesting any more, to be honest, Hugo. But I'm beginning to think I've been quite unusually stupid—almost as stupid as Sir Frederick Clinton. Stupid and arrogant and self-satisfied. And I'm only just in time to make amends—" he gave

Frances a little bow "—thanks to Mrs Fitzgibbon's commonsense disobedience."

Frances gritted her teeth. "David, I've got something to tell you. And you're not going to like it one bit."

He smiled at her tolerantly. "It's okay, love—I know. They wanted you to find a reason why Jack might have wanted to kill her, and of course you found one. But it doesn't matter, not now."

"But he didn't kill her, David."

"Of course he didn't! The idea's plainly ridiculous—you know it, I know it. She was a selfish, scheming, cold-hearted, unloving bitch, and if ever a woman needed murdering, she did. But he hasn't got murder in him. I could have told you that in two seconds flat. And Fred should have realised it too—when they fed him the dirt it should have put him on his guard. The moment I heard about it I realised how bloody stupid I'd been.

"I mean . . . it made me think about Jack himself for the first time, not about the great David Audley. Everything that's been happening to him, I thought it was because of me—because the department's full of faceless little bastards who hate my guts. So I rather enjoyed letting Jack rub their faces in the mud—I've always enjoyed letting them hate me."

"'*Oderint dum metuant*'", murmured Crowe. "Enmity is the most rewarding form of flattery."

"Yes." Now the smile was vengeful. "I've half a mind to take Fred's job and screw the lot of them, just for that, Hugo. Except that now I've put the whole thing together differently, and it fits much better this way."

"What way?" Frances heard the sharp note of fear in her voice.

"I turned Fred's job down flat—they were never serious about Tom Stocker's job, they knew I wouldn't take that. But then there were all these rumours about me wanting Fred's job—no matter how often I squashed them they kept coming up again—"

Crowe stirred. "You really don't want the top job?"

Audley scowled at him. "Christ, Hugo—not you too!"

"I only asked, dear boy. . . . Are you saying that these rumours were planted deliberately—by those who knew you wouldn't accept it?"

"That's exactly what I'm saying. And I was too stupid to consider the possibility—I'm saying that too."

"Ah—now I'm beginning to see! You thought that what was

happening to Colonel Butler was directed against you. But now you believe that the rumours about you were actually calculated to stimulate opposition to his appointment? A simple reversal of the obvious, in fact?"

"More than that, Hugo."

"More than that?" Professor Crowe gazed into space. "Yes . . . it would also account for what happened to Butler. A campaign directed against Butler would have made people suspicious—particularly you—because he is generally well-regarded. But a campaign against your acquisition of Sir Frederick's job wouldn't surprise anyone—least of all you. Is that it?"

Audley nodded.

"I see. So Butler has been the real target all along? And that effectively eliminates Sir Frederick—and your illegitimate Israeli friend—*and* all the faceless little love-children from your list of villains, dear boy." Crowe paused.

"Then it's just Butler." He started up again. "Someone must be very frightened indeed of his getting the job. Quite terrified, in fact, to go to such lengths. They've gone a long way beyond domestic politics and slander—they're into treason and murder, constructively."

"Yes," said Audley.

"Is the job that important?"

"It is and it isn't. It's basically a bloody thankless dogsbody job. But whoever gets it carries a lot of clout. And also gets to see a lot of things he's never seen before. From his own file upwards."

His own file, thought Frances. Even she had only seen an edited version of that. But he had never seen it at all and now he would be able to. In his promoted place that would be the first thing she'd look at: all her test analyses, all her fitness reports, all her successes and failures.

His file would be a lot bigger than hers, though. It would start before she was born, and it would follow him across the world and back. It would list General Chesney's last will and testament. It would miss the marital disaster, and the visits to Rifleman Sands, because those were private matters that he had never revealed to anyone, and in certain things Colonel Jack Butler was a very private man. . . . For a guess, it might also miss this investigation, if Sir Frederick decided to play that close to *his* chest now, after what she had done. But it would certainly include everything about the original disappearance of Madeleine Françoise, and—

Successes and failures—

"What's up, Frances?" said Audley.

Failures.

"What's the matter, Frances?" repeated Audley.

She looked at him. In fact she had already been looking at him, but not seeing him.

"Have you ever heard of Leslie Pearson Cole?"

"Leslie—?" He frowned at her. "Leslie Pearson Cole?"

"And Trevor Anthony Bond."

"Never heard of *him*. But Pearson Cole—what d'you know about Pearson Cole?"

"Very little. He committed suicide."

"That's right." Audley nodded. "I wasn't on the case, thank heavens. There was a botch-up of some kind. Pearson Cole was mixed up in a big security leak, but there was a delay in picking him up, so he took his leak with him. What—?"

"The delay was because a Major Butler was taken off the case, David. His wife had disappeared—he was delayed by that first. And then someone gave some conflicting evidence, for no reason. And nobody put two and two together."

They stared at each other.

"Yes . . ." Audley nodded slowly. "Yes, that would do very well—very well indeed. At least for a start."

"In what way, dear boy?" asked Crowe.

Audley turned to him. "Jack Butler's a good chap—he'll do a good job when he's promoted. He's very painstaking. Not a genius, but very, very painstaking. There's no general reason why anyone should go to such lengths to block his promotion—he isn't disliked. He isn't going to carry me up with him—so there has to be a *specific* reason. That's what I've been thinking ever since I came back: somebody doesn't want him to be able to put two and two together and make four. If he isn't promoted, then he never will—and two and two will never meet. And then somebody will go on being safe somewhere."

"You have a traitor in the camp, dear boy." Crowe sat back in spectator's comfort, hands at prayer. "It happens in the best regulated families from time to time."

"Yes." Audley gave Frances a grimly anticipatory nod. "Someone quite low down nine years ago, most likely. But quite high up by now. And someone who doesn't know that we know, by God!"

"Don't be too sure, dear boy. They'll be running scared now," Crowe admonished him. "That's when they'll become dangerous."

"They can't know. Because they don't know I'm back." Audley reached towards the Glenfiddich. "I think I'll have a celebratory slug of my duty-free USAF hooch. I'm going to enjoy this . . . And, above all, they won't be running scared because they'll be expecting Mrs Fitzgibbon here to come up any moment with a nice handful of sticky mud which will keep Jack Butler firmly and safely among the other ranks. A nice, neat bloodless solution. Nothing to stir nasty suspicions in nasty suspicious minds like mine. No need to put O'Leary at risk by using his special talents. . . . Cheers!" He swung towards Frances. "My manners! May I top you up—" he stopped.

"What—what d'you mean—O'Leary's special talents?" said Frances.

He relaxed. "It's all right, Frances. As long as Jack is under suspicion of murdering his eminently murderable wife then they'll strive to keep him healthy and unpromoted. You've actually saved him by giving him his motive, love—if you'd proved him innocent then O'Leary would have probably been given a new target by the name of Butler."

"*Oh my God!*" whispered Frances.

Crowe was looking at her. Crowe knew what Audley didn't know. She'd told the Death Story.

"I've already phoned Control," said Frances.

Once you've summoned *him, he* won't go away empty-handed.

XV

THIS YORKSHIRE RAIN wasn't like Lancashire rain, or even like Midland rain, thought Frances resentfully as the car thudded into another unavoidable puddle which had spread into the centre of the narrow road: in the Midlands it had been half-hearted drizzle, with the occasional well-bred little storm; in Lancashire it had been pervasive wetness; but here, on the shoulder of the high moors, it was an obliterating deluge which had to be fought every inch of the way.

The car juddered and skidded over a pot-hole hidden in the puddle and the spray rose up simultaneously ahead, to dash itself on the windscreen a fraction of a second later, and underneath, to strike the floor beneath them with a solid *thump*.

"You're going too fast," said Audley nervously. "If you kill us on the way we won't get there at all."

It was such a stupidly obvious thing to say that Frances felt a half-hysterical giggle beneath her irritation that he should have said it at all.

"If you can drive better, then you can drive," she snapped back at him out of her knowledge (which was common knowledge, for he had never concealed it) that the great David Audley was a bad driver who hated driving, and who would have still managed to put them at risk in this downpour, on this road, even at half her speed.

He lapsed into sullen silence beside her, and she instantly felt half-ashamed, and half-angry with herself for snapping him down. It was the sort of thing a shrewish wife might have said, all the worse for being true; and, worse still, she knew also that his fear for their safety was sharpened by a greater fear which she shared with him.

They were dropping down off the ridge, she could sense it rather than see it, between the low, half-ruined dry-stone walls with their occasional stunted bushes and trees in the featureless moorland landscape which the rain narrowed around them.

Somewhere ahead of them, down there ahead of them in the greyness, was the opening into the tree-shrouded valley of the Thor

Brook, still almost as secret and isolated as when the first monks and lay brothers trudged up it all those forgotten centuries ago.

"How much further?" asked Audley.

The child's eternal question—

"How much further, Mummy?"

"Not far, dear."

"But I don't *see* anything."

"You're not meant to see anything." Father always knew the answer. He always knew how much further and how long. He even knew, unfailingly, how the films on TV ended, whether they were sad or happy. He knew everything.

"Why not?"

"Because that's why they came here, the old monks. Because there was nobody here, and it was miles from anywhere. Remember Rievaulx, Frances—hidden there in its valley. Getting away from men to be closer to God, that was what being a Cistercian monk was all about."

"But why, Daddy?" She knew the answer now, he had told it to her before, but she wanted the comfort of hearing it again.

"Because it was a nasty, rough world, and they wanted to get away from it." Patient repetition.

"But Kirkstall Abbey's in the middle of a town." Unanswerable logic.

"It wasn't when they built it, sweetie. Things have changed a lot since the twelfth century, you know." Unarguable answer.

"It's still a nasty, rough world," said Mother dryly.

"And now you can't get away from it, either," said Daddy.

And so Frances Warren had come to Thornervaulx the first time.

"Thornervaulx?" The man presiding over the communications centre had not been overawed at first by Audley's appearance, for Audley's appearance had not been overawing. But the penny had dropped at last, with Jock Maitland banging the machine, and the man had accepted that the big dishevelled man with the little bedraggled blonde dolly-bird added up to something that was not what it seemed. "Yes, sir—Colonel Butler and Mr Cable have gone to Thornervaulx."

"And Paul Mitchell?" said Frances.

"Yes—" For the life of him, in spite of her warrant card, he couldn't bring himself to add 'madam' "—Mr Mitchell's gone there too."

"To see Trevor Bond?" It fitted too well to be wrong: O'Leary needed a safe house close to the University, and there, just across the high ridge of heather within sight of the top of the Science Block on a clear day, was someone Colonel Butler of all men would never have forgotten. It would be so close to the surface of his memory, the remembrance of that name and that place, that it was a certainty. And because it was a certainty it was more than that, was her fear: it was the bait on a hook for Colonel Butler if things went wrong.

Or was she imagining everything? And was David Audley imagining everything?

The man didn't answer her directly, and Audley started to growl something angry in his throat.

"Yes—" The man's answer pre-empted Audley's anger.

"We have to get a message to Colonel Butler—at once. About O'Leary," Audley converted the anger into a command.

"I'm afraid we can't do that, sir."

"Why the hell not?" Audley pointed to the banks of equipment. "You've got enough there to transmit to bloody Moscow!"

"The system is deactivated, sir." As the man's voice strengthened Frances's heart sank: he was no longer scared because he was sure of his ground. "I'm only here to watch over it—and to take any calls." He nodded towards the telephone on the table beside him.

Audley pounced on the phone. "Well—give me the line to Thornervaulx then, for God's sake. There has to be a line, damn it!"

"Yes, sir—but there isn't at the moment—"

"Why not?" Audley shook the receiver impotently.

"The line is out. Sergeant Ballard phoned me half an hour ago—not half an hour, sir. The Post Office says there's probably water in the cable somewhere. They've sent men out to look for the trouble, but . . . but we haven't been able to get through for an hour or more, Sergeant Ballard says. They're doing all they can—" He broke off abruptly, and Frances saw that he at last was beginning to become frightened too. Then he brightened. "Sergeant Ballard said he was sending men out to tell the Colonel, sir."

Audley looked at Frances, and the look confirmed her own fear—and Sergeant Ballard's too.

If the line was out, that might mean there was water in the

cable—it happened, and there was enough water to make it happen now. But she could remember Sergeant Ballard's cool competence, and she knew that even in the most torrential downpour he wouldn't accept water as the only answer to a breakdown in communications.

Well . . . there was a flicker of hope there, kindling against the bigger blaze of fear. Perhaps Colonel Butler's disdain of complicated modern electronics might warn him now, where a totally secure communications system wouldn't have hinted that someone was trying to isolate him. And even if it was a much fainter hope than the fear—not only because O'Leary was a kamikaze assassin, but also because he had no reason to believe that he was now O'Leary's target—then at least he would by now have Sergeant Ballard's reinforcements beside Cable and Mitchell to make the hit more difficult.

But it was still only a hope.

"Frances. We must go." Audley's tone betrayed the same inescapable conclusion. "You'd better drive."

"How much further?" repeated Audley.

"Not far now—" It was no longer a childish question. But childish memories, which she had never recognised as having registered at the time, came from nowhere to help her. "There's a bridge up ahead, over the stream—we go along beside the stream, and then we come to the bridge. It's a little narrow bridge—"

She knew what he was thinking, his thoughts burned her.

"Why did you phone Control?"

"Why?" Frances pressed her foot down to the floor. Why indeed!

"It was finished. I wanted to get it over and done with."

Not true. Or, not the whole truth, anyway. She had been very pleased with herself, very full of the pride before which every fall had to go, very pleased with her own cleverness, with her own unerring instinct.

She hadn't known how the instinct had come to her, but she'd been consciously saving that up for consideration at leisure, like a favourite sweet to be smuggled up to bed, past the tooth-cleaning ritual, to be sucked secretly and selfishly in the darkness after lights-out. Four out of ten had become ten out of ten.

And she had wanted the smug sod at the end of the telephone,

Extension 223, to squirm—she had wanted to hear him squirm as she gave him the answer he hadn't expected.

"He couldn't have done it. Not possibly."

Fact. He couldn't dispute fact.

"What?"

"He was in Blackburn at 10.30 that day—maybe earlier. Like he said in his report."

"What?"

"I have a cast-iron witness. He remembers the time exactly."

No answer. She would throw him a bone to gnaw at, then—out of sheer cruelty.

"He had a motive. But he'd never have done it then—or got anyone else to do it. Not on November 11th."

That had been sheer bravado, to go with the cruelty. She didn't even know how she would record that subjective evidence of character and temperament and upbringing and history, which was much stronger in the end—at least for her—even than Rifleman Sands' resolute evidence. She only knew that she could hardly write: *Of all the dates in the year, if he was going to murder his wife, or even wish her dead—which, being Colonel Butler, he would never do anyway, or even wish—that would be the very last, most impossible day. Because that was the day—*

It was the day that had thrown her, even when her instinct had told her it was important. Nowadays, when it didn't matter, when it was just a pious formality except for the older generation who knew which day was really which, Remembrance Day was always on a Sunday: that was the day they marched to the Cenotaph and to the thousands of war memorials up and down the country and planted their wreaths and poppies without really remembering anything at all, because they had nothing to remember, because yesterday's ghosts weren't worth mourning in a nasty, rough world. They would have mostly forgotten, as she had, that the Sunday was always only the closest day to that old real eleventh hour of the eleventh day of the eleventh month of that original year—it was almost an accident that she recalled her father telling her (he who knew everything) that in the old days everything in Britain had stopped for two minutes to remember something which had happened at 11 o'clock on November 11th in 1918.

But Colonel Butler had always remembered.

What exactly he remembered—he hadn't been alive when Rifleman Sands had first walked up Revidge for the big fireworks display, which had reminded him of the trenches, with the candles in jam jars at his front gate—what *he* remembered, she could only guess at: maybe his father, against whom he'd revolted, or his father's friends; or his own friends and comrades from Normandy and Germany; or his own men from those other trenches of Korea, Nannie's husband among them; or even the men he himself had killed so efficiently in his time. Or even the old General himself, who'd had a hand in it all from the beginning, father and son beginning.

That was something she intended to find out eventually—his girls could find it out for her simply by asking: they were probably the only human beings who could ask the question with a chance of receiving an answer; no one else (not even a second Mrs Butler) had the right to expect an answer—which she already knew in her heart, but which she would never write down, for it must always be his secret act of remembrance: *Because that is the day when he keeps faith with his dead, the day of love and honour and pity and pride and compassion and sacrifice, and he would never add a private ghost of his own to that list, on that day, not ever, not this man, not ever—*

A private ghost.

Yesterday's ghost—Frances could feel her heart thump—she had laid yesterday's ghost at the terrible cost of raising a new one for tomorrow—had she?

They were getting very close now. Through the rain-streaked side window she had been catching glimpses of the swollen Thor Brook between the fringe of trees which separated the road from the stream for the last half-mile before they met at the bridge of Thornervaulx.

The bridge was a colour-transparency in childhood's memory—high and hump-backed and narrow as the ordeal bridge of Al-Sirat between earth and heaven over hell—

A new ghost was waiting for her on the other side: there was still so much she didn't know, so much that was still guesswork, about that November 11th as well as this November 11th, but the new ghost was already an instinctive, stomach-churning certainty.

The enemy had revived the old Butler scandal into suspicion by dropping the right word into the right ear at the right moment—the classic disinformation stratagem.

And they had calculated its strength not only from the lying truth it contained, but also because all those who feared and disliked and mistrusted David Audley would work hard to make it true, blocking his advancement by blocking Butler's promotion—playing the enemy's game for reasons which probably ranged from pure selfishness and hatred and fear and prejudice to mistaken patriotism.

And also because, all the while, Sir Frederick himself had let them go ahead for his own reason, hoping that Audley would be forced in the end to take power simply for the sake of friendship and survival—

Was that how it had been?

If it was—

She caught a flash of grey through the trees, against the browns and yellows and greens of late autumn, rain-misted: ruined walls and pinnacles across the stream on the other side of the valley.

If it was, then she had made a ruin of it.

And if it was, then Colonel Butler might now die in that ruin, and maybe in those ruins: there must always have been a contingency plan for a last resort, and this was the ideal place for it, where it might just pass scrutiny as a natural hazard of duty.

Paul.

Frances clasped the name like a straw. Paul was Colonel Butler's last chance. Paul was always suspicious, Paul always had his eyes open. Paul, in the unseen presence of O'Leary, would have his hand on that gun of his, of which he was so proud, with which he was so born-to-the-manner good, as he was good at everything. Paul was the best.

She frowned.

Paul—?

"There's the bridge," said David Audley.

There was the bridge.

Childhood's memory had been wrong—

No. It wasn't so high, or so narrow as she had remembered, or as the ordeal bridge of Al-Sirat, between life and death. But as they had come up to it eighteen years ago there had been a big orange coach swinging on to it, and Mother had said *'Wait, Charles—it's too narrow—sit down, Frances!*' and they had waited while the coach-driver backed and manoeuvred.

Paul?
The youngest and best?

She twisted the wheel just in time, almost too late. Another second's hesitation would have carried them on up the valley, to somewhere she'd never been. A great splash of rain from the saturated branches of the trees above obscured the windscreen for a moment, then there was a bump as they crossed the bridge and the windscreen wipers swept the water away.

Hard left and hard right—her father's hands on the wheel, impossibly remembered, swung them on to the car park which the old Ministry of Public Buildings and Works had carved out of the monastic gardens, the wheels spinning and the gravel spurting.

Daddy had never driven that fast—Daddy had parked carefully under the trees on the right, between the wall and the ice-cream van from which he had bought her a choc-ice, and himself a choc-ice too—

But the path to the abbey ruins was at the top, on the left: she had walked across the gravel with him, licking the melting chocolate off her fingers—and he had been licking the chocolate off his fingers too, and grinning at her, while mother unloaded the picnic with Uncle John—it was at the top, the path.

She swung the wheel the other way, skidding round the vividly-striped police car—the day-glo orange and white flashed in front of her and was gone as though it had never existed.

"Christ!" said Audley.

She stood on the brakes, feeling the car slither under her.

Now she knew: Butler was a dream—the girls' dream which she had started to dream against all reason and all reality. Butler was already invulnerable—he had always been invulnerable, from the start, the stars in their million courses were running for him, as they had on his battlefields; his bad luck would always come from a different direction, from where it had always come.

It would be *Paul*—

Frances slammed out of the car, leaving her door swinging.

It would be Paul—

There was a man ahead of her. Audley shouted something, but the words were lost to her.

She could run. She had always been able to run. Some women couldn't run, their hips got in the way, their breasts went every whichway. But Frances Warren never saw anyone's back in the 100 and 220, no girl could touch her.

The man was gone, open mouthed. It was not James Cable, she saw only that—it was not James Cable, so James Cable was also up ahead somewhere, with Jack Butler and Trevor Anthony Bond—and with *Paul*—

Make it James Cable, prayed Frances. It won't be Trevor Anthony Bond, it can't be Butler—it'll never be Butler in this age of the world—*make it Cable, not Paul!*

There were steps up, between modern stone walls. She knew where she was going, it was past the lay brothers' dormitory, past the great kitchen and the wide quadrangle of the ruined cloister—

"Now sweetie: you're standing in the middle of the cloister—so you know where the Chapter House and the Parlour are . . . the Parlour where they were allowed to *parlez* to each other . . . and the Warming House where they lifted their cassocks and warmed their—"
"Charles!"

Not the Chapter House, not the Cloister, not the Parlour—the wall ended with the Galilee Porch.

There was a reason for *Galilee* Porch, and he had told her the reason; but she could never remember it then, and she couldn't think of it now. But that was where the wall ended, that was still the entrance to Thornervaulx Abbey.

The great quire of the abbey stretched ahead of her—quire and retroquire, monks' quire and presbytery, which had once been the glory and the wonder of the Thor Brook valley, and far beyond—and the High Altar, once gilded and jewelled, under which the miraculous bones of St. Biddulph had lain, which no virgin could look upon with safety, because they guaranteed pregnancy even to the most barren—

"Where, Daddy?" Virgin Frances had looked for the high altar.

Where, Daddy? thought Frances again, desperately.
But there was only the long sweep of broken pillars, like jagged

teeth, rising higher and higher out of the smooth turf, each with its swirl of dead leaves around it, until the towering walls of the roofless transepts reared up, and the perfect open circle of the rose window framing grey sky where once the Virgin and Child had been enthroned in glory—

Where?

Frances ran down into the wide empty quire of the lay brothers, between the dark woods of the hillside, almost leafless, on her left, and the labyrinth of abbey ruins on her right.

The emptiness mocked her and terrified her.

Paul—the rain ran down her face—*Paul!*

As though called by that soundless cry Paul Mitchell emerged from behind one of the slender columns of the opening into the south transept, beside the high altar's site.

Another movement caught her eye, away beyond the pillars in the labyrinth.

Colonel Butler walked out on to the green square of the cloister quadrangle, unmistakeable under his golfing umbrella.

Now they were both in the open: she could see them both. And now *he*, whom she had summoned, only had to make his choice—that was the story's ending.

She saw him rise out of the ruin of summer's growth on the hillside under the eaves of the trees, ten yards from her, his rifle lifting for the heart shot.

He hadn't seen her, she was half-masked by a broken pillar.

The choice was still hers: she could shout *Paul— there!*

But that would be too late for Colonel Butler.

Or she could shout *Down, Colonel Butler!*

And that would be just one second too late for Paul—

The choices were gone in the same instant of their imagining, as the rifle rose.

There had never been any choices, only the true ending.

Frances stepped into the open.

"O'Leary—" she pointed at him "—you're dead!"

That would give Paul and Butler the time they both—

XVI

Where she lay close to the stump of the third pillar in the ruined quire, it was quiet now.

For a moment it had been noisy—she had not truly heard the noises, but she was aware that there had been noises—but now there was only the steady *swish* of an infinite number of raindrops on stone and grass and leaves around her, where she lay.

Then she was aware that she had heard the noises at the exact moment when she had been punched such a terrible blow on the chest, so that the grey sky and the greyer stonework and the green grass had cartwheeled—no one had ever punched her so hard, it had quite knocked the breath out of her.

So now her eyes were full of tears, blurring green and grey into indistinguishable shapes of colour; but that was only natural, that she should cry after being hit so hard, to make her so breathless.

Daddy—I hurt—Daddy—

It wasn't tears, it was the rain on her face. But she couldn't close her eyes against the rain—

"Frances!"

That was the name she had wanted to remember.

That was the name in her handbag—

But there were other names in her handbag, and they wouldn't know which name was her name—

Where was her handbag? Without her handbag she had no name at all: they wouldn't know who she was.

"Mitchell. Are you all right?"

A different voice, far away but well-remembered.

"Yes." The first voice, much closer but far above her. "Over here, Colonel—Oh God! Frances!"

She had made a fascinating discovery: they were quite right when

255

they said *you never hear the one that hits you.* But they were also quite wrong, because she had heard it long before, and everything she had done had been only to make sure she was in the right place at the right time to meet it.

She wanted desperately to tell them that, but she couldn't, and that made her angry: it seemed to her that she had failed in everything she had set out to do in her life—

"Frances—Frances—"
The colours swirled and swam. She floated into them.
"Let her be, lad. Let her be."

"Frances!"

She no longer recognised the names, or the faraway voices. And yet the sound of them took away her anger and her despair at her failure.

Perhaps not everything, perhaps not everything—
And that was enough for the Act of Contrition, which must be the last feeling of all—

No, not the last.
The last feeling, as the greens and greys darkened, was the gentle kiss of the rain—of the Prince—on her lips.